CHROMA

BOOKS BY TIM FRANKOVICH

Heart of Fire
Until All Curses Are Lifted
Until All Bonds Are Broken
Until All the Gods Return
Until All the Stars Fall

Dragontek Lore
Viridia
Incarnadine
Auric
Onyx
Amaranth
Atramentous
Chroma

The Certainty of Blood
Wolf Chosen

CHROMA

DRAGONTEK LORE, BOOK 7

by Tim Frankovich

To the writers behind all the "boys" books I grew up on
(The Hardy Boys, Three Investigators, Tom Swift, Rick Brant)

Prologue

I set my pen down and look through the window. I'm getting near the end of this story, the story of Beryl and The Circle. Not much more to tell now. But I need to get it all down before... before I run out of time. My hand might not last long. Or my brain, for that matter. And it's what she wanted me to do. What they all wanted.

"His message said he'd arrive this morning," says a voice behind me.

"Hm? Yes. Sometime today."

A pause. "Do you want to go out to meet him?"

Ah, Chance. How can you continue to serve me? You've been more than I ever could have expected. "I think I'd like that, son." I call him "son," though he's not my own, not biologically. Technically, he's centuries older than me. But this is the relationship we have. And he's the son of my best friend. Can't overlook that.

"I'll help you in a moment," he answers. "How is the writing going?"

"You just told me your life story."

"Oh." A long pause. "Then you're almost done."

I nod. "It's still early. I'll get some more down, and then we can go outside."

I pick up the pen again.

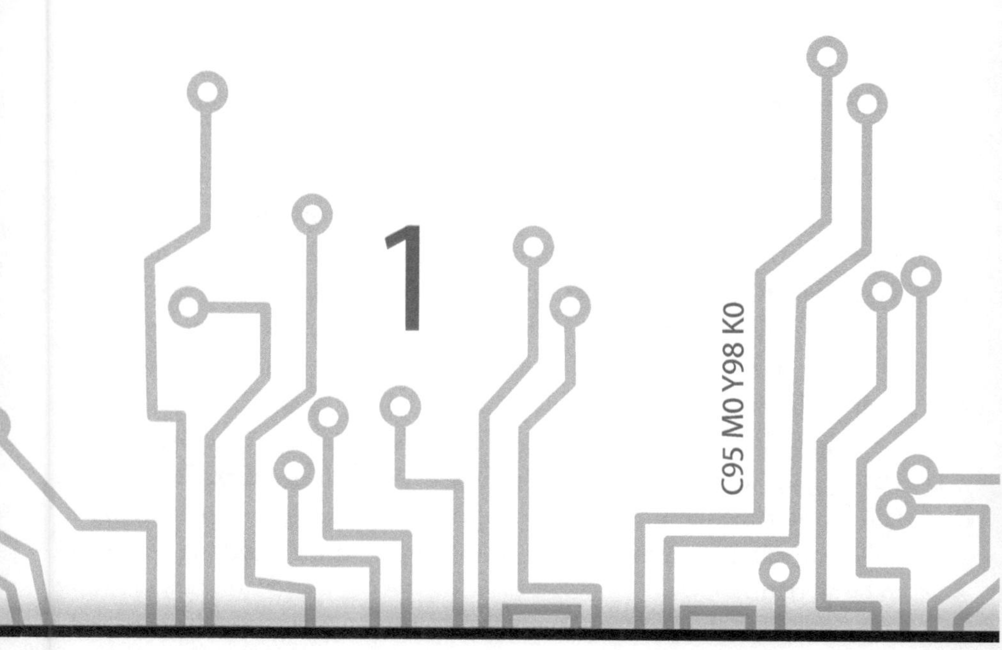

I wanted to run. After the disturbing conversation with Chance last night and the recorded message from Loden, my mind didn't want to process everything. I just wanted to run.

Ever since I learned to walk again with the cybernetic implant, I'd loved the feeling of power in my legs when I ran (even if it did leave me exhausted afterward). Problem is… my implant wasn't working so well right now. After banging my head against solid rock, I hadn't been able to boost myself much.

But I could run like a normal person. Or at least I hoped I could. When we'd returned, I'd been limping. But a couple night's sleep in an actual bed made me feel much better. I figured I could risk a little jog.

On my way up the stairs, I passed Turq and told him my intentions. He raised an eyebrow, but promised to inform anyone who asked. Climbing the stairs almost made me give up the whole idea. I still hurt in many places, especially my head. Hunter had given me medication, but I don't know if it helped much. Once outside, the fresh air convinced me to keep going.

Passing the trees hiding the entrance to our headquarters, I started walking down the hill. I could do that much. Once down, I could reevaluate myself.

After making it to the base of the hill without difficulty, I picked up my pace and headed north. I knew the terrain wasn't quite as varied in that direction. I tried sending a little boost to my legs. The pain in my head increased at the effort, but I'm sure I grew a little stronger. I broke into a jog... sort of. I guess it was more of an uneven canter. That's the right word, isn't it? Canter? Or does that word belong to animals?

At any rate, I kept going. It felt good to feel a breeze against my face, to be out in the open, away from cities and caves and all the people with their problems and dragons and...

I sprawled onto my face. I didn't remember falling. One moment, I was jogging, and the next, I was spitting grass. I felt the aftereffects of the fall, but not the fall itself. What happened? Did my legs stop working? I pulled myself up and tested them. I stood up slowly. Everything appeared to be all right.

I started walking again. After a few minutes, I picked up the pace and started jogging again. Whatever the fall had been, it didn't repeat itself.

I'd come out here to escape everything, but my brain wouldn't shut up. I kept thinking about Loden and Auric's connection. About Chance. About Chroma and the purple robes. About Lovat's injuries. About Amaranth, stuck in human form, still living with us. And about Lainey most of all. After the struggles in Viridia and the cave, especially the part with her father, would our relationship change permanently? She'd been pretty upset, but I thought she'd gotten over it. How would she react to what Loden said? Because if he'd told the truth about all of it...

A dark shadow passed over me.

Instinctively, I looked up toward the sun. My eyes adjusted at once. Whoa. Had I always been able to look at the sun this way? I'd never tried it before, because... why would I? Why would anyone look at the sun? It wasn't a smart thing to do.

But something had come between me and the sun. I turned and looked ahead.

Fewmets. It was him.

Onyx, the black dragon who had once been my best friend Rick, swooped low as he turned in a lazy arc. He would be back over me in moments. Had he seen me? Idiot. Of course he had. Why else would he be turning around? But did he recognize me from the air?

He didn't seem in any kind of hurry. And why would he be? Where could a human, even an enhanced one like me, run and hide from a dragon out here? My eyes darted around, searching for anything. I spotted a few bushes, little more than scrub, about fifty yards away. I hurried toward them as fast as I could, wincing from the pains that erupted from my effort.

I glanced skyward. The dragon completed his turn and came back toward me, dropping lower and lower. There was no doubt remaining: he'd seen me and was coming my way.

But he couldn't have recognized me from the sky, could he? I was just an ordinary human, out for a jog in the middle of nowhere… yeah, not suspicious at all. Even if he hadn't recognized me, his curiosity had been aroused.

I stumbled and almost fell again. At least that time I experienced it instead of blanking out.

The dragon dropped lower. Could I make it to the bushes before he reached me? Could I… no. I slowed down. Why bother running? Bushes weren't going to help now. It was too late. I took a deep breath and turned to face Onyx.

I don't think I've ever been able to communicate how terrifying and awesome it is to be in the presence of one of the dragons. Most people within The Circle think themselves fortunate if they see one flying overhead. Up close… they're so much larger than I always expect them to be. The size is… it's humbling, I guess. Being in the presence of something so huge—and powerful!—can't help but make you feel small. As Onyx landed in front of me, I experienced that smallness. He radiated power… heat… and smell. Dragons have a peculiar smell, all of them a little bit different from each other. I don't know exactly how to describe it. A muskiness? Burnt things, for sure. Onyx… I hated it, but he smelled familiar. Don't get me wrong: the size, the heat, the power were all terrifying. But the smell exuded a familiarity, like it would be all right in spite of everything else. It made no sense.

His front legs landed only a few feet from me. Massive scars ran from his clawed feet all the way up to his shoulders, evidence of the cyb implants he'd obtained to imitate mine. He'd wanted to become the most powerful dragon, and he'd accomplished that much (except maybe Chroma, I suppose). He was also the only dragon left in dragon form. Amaranth remained trapped in human form unless I let her out. And Viridia… I didn't want to think about it.

The gigantic dragon head bent down toward me. His teeth spread in an enormous grin before the mouth opened and said, "Hello, Beryl."

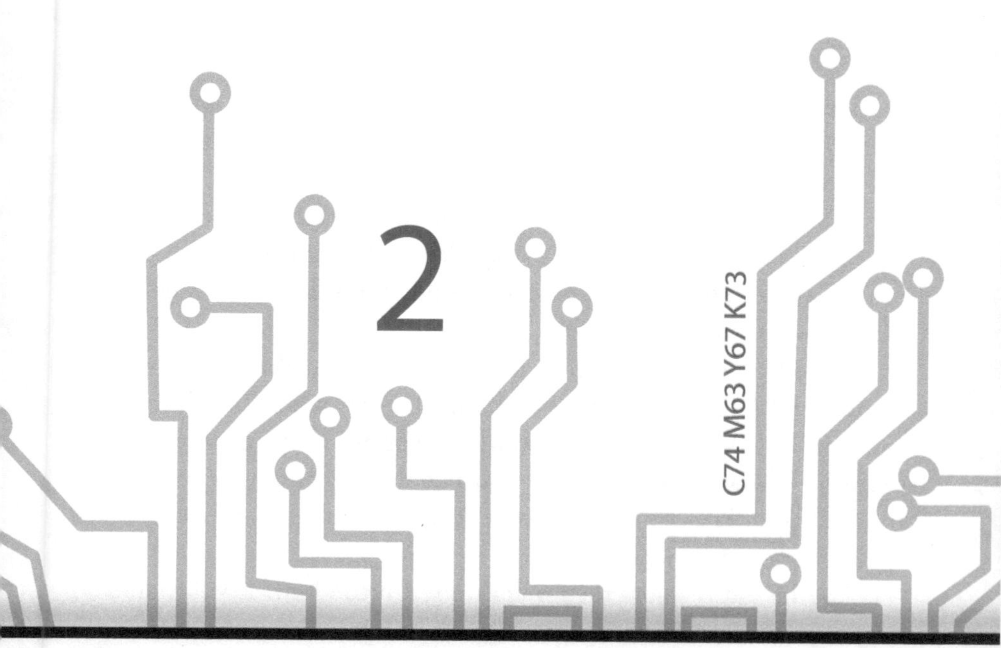

The dragons are not gods. I think I said that somewhere back at the beginning of all of this process. But standing completely human and weak in front of one can easily make you think it's a distinct possibility.

"What do you want, Onyx?" I asked. My voice sounded a lot less firm than I'd wanted.

The dragon's head pulled back. "I'm making you uncomfortable. Let's change that so we can communicate better."

I'd seen Rick's first transformation into Onyx, but not the other way around. He lowered his head and closed his eyes. His massive wings folded in against his body. Together with his tail, they fused into the rest of the body which shrank at a rapid pace. In a few moments, he'd lost over half his size and kept shrinking. At that point, his black scales started fading away. The snout pulled in, the horns vanished, the claws shrank into fingers and toes.

And then Rick stood before me. Human. Still with the horrible scars and the cybernetic hand. And also completely naked. He flexed the cyb hand and then his human one. "It gets harder to do this each time, once I've gotten used to being a dragon again. I don't know how Auric and Amaranth changed so often. It's… annoying."

I looked the other direction. "This isn't much more comfortable, you know."

I could almost hear his eyes rolling. "You're still such an innocent, Beryl. Even after all this. Have you even slept with that new girlfriend of yours yet?"

"That has nothing to do with being around a naked man."

"Ha!" He moved a few steps away. "There. Is that better?"

I checked. He'd stepped behind a handy bush that hid... well, it hid the important stuff. I shrugged.

Something was wrong, though. Why hadn't he stayed in dragon form so he could kill me with ease? His human form was vulnerable. When we'd fought before, I'd put my sword through his chest. Unfortunately, I didn't have a sword with me now. But I could beat him without weapons if I needed to. His cyb implants weren't as powerful as mine. I could take him... if mine were working.

And he didn't know they weren't. He'd made himself vulnerable on purpose. Or he was just arrogant.

"You're trying to figure out why you're still alive," Onyx said.

"The thought had crossed my mind. You must want something."

"Or I could simply want to see you with human eyes one more time before I kill you."

"Sure. There's that."

Onyx scratched at the scar on his left arm. "I would very much like to know why you don't have scars, of course."

I didn't say anything. I wasn't going to tell him about Hunter.

He sighed. "Has it occurred to you, Beryl, that we've won? We did what we set out to do. We killed the dragons."

"Except you."

"I wasn't in the original goals."

"Only because I didn't know about you."

"Whatever. Caesious, Viridia, Incarnadine, Atramentous, Auric, Amaranth — they're all gone. We did it."

"Oh? Did you kill Amaranth when I wasn't looking?" I couldn't help taunting him at least a little.

He shrugged. "She's gone, isn't she? Probably hiding out somewhere in human form in her city. We'll find her eventually. The point is: we won!"

"Except the humans aren't free yet. That was the whole point. You've just traded six dragons for one."

"Two."

I wrinkled my brow. "You mean Viridia?"

"Gods, Beryl." He threw up his scarred arms. I looked away. The bush wasn't covering enough any more. "No, I don't mean that abomination in the green city. I'm talking about Chroma!"

"Your mom." For some reason, I took great satisfaction in saying that.

"Yes, her. I know you've had some experience with her agents. And yet you're still alive. That's impressive."

"I've fought dragons," I pointed out.

"Yes, but those guys…" He shook his head. "You're very fortunate to be alive."

"Which brings us back to why." I definitely wasn't going to tell him what Loden said about my enhancements being specifically designed to fight the purple robed agents of Chroma. I still wasn't sure what to think of that myself.

"You're alive right now because I will it."

"You're not back on the god thing, are you?"

He chuckled. "Compared to humans, I am a god. But it's all right. We can let that one slide. My point should be obvious: I could kill you at any moment."

"You could try. Seems like you didn't do so well last time."

He spread his arms. "No swords here. We would have to fight bare-handed. And out of the two of us, I'd give myself the edge in killing someone with bare hands. And that's even without transforming into my other body."

"But while you waste time transforming, I'd run. And you'd never catch me."

"So your base is near here, is it?"

"I never said anything about a base. You destroyed my last one."

"And then you lived in mine for a while. Yes, yes." He paused. "Did I tell you I found all of them? The power sources? I can live wherever I want now, go from city to city. I get power everywhere."

"I'm so happy for you."

He snorted, and a puff of smoke emerged from his nose. "We're wasting time here. I wanted to make a proposal."

"Not again. I'm done being your errand boy."

"Hey, that last time worked out, didn't it?"

I squeezed my fists and tried again to get some boosts going. Nothing happened. "None of my friends are here for you to threaten this time," I said.

"I'm not here to threaten anyone. I want to make a deal." He paused. "You want the humans free from dragon rule? Fine. I'll give you half of The Circle—three cities—to rule however you want. Be a king. Let them choose their own rulers. Whatever. It'll be your choice."

"And you keep the rest?"

"Of course. I have to have something for my trouble."

This was so weird. "I'll never agree to you ruling anything. But even if I did, why offer me all this? You have it all right now."

"No, I don't. And you know it."

"Chroma," I said. "She's causing you problems, isn't she?"

"She wants it all," he snarled. "She wants to control everything."

"I thought you were working with her... agents."

"I was. It was an alliance of convenience. I'd like to end it now. But I can't do it alone." He smiled. "Come on, Beryl. Let's work together again. We take Chroma down, and then we're free of her interference." He snorted. "For that matter, we'd be setting the humans free outside The Circle too. Who knows how many live there. And you could free them too."

"While letting you keep control of hundreds of thousands here. No deal." I gave a short laugh. "You know, Amaranth once offered me almost the same thing if I helped her defeat you."

Rick growled, and a wisp of smoke emerged from his nostrils. "You don't want to fight me too, Beryl. Look, I'll take Viridia, Atramentous and Caesious. That gives you the red cities and Auric. Isn't that enough?"

And if Amaranth returned, I would have to deal with her, and he wouldn't. I didn't miss that. Over the past couple of years, I'd started to understand how his mind worked. "You're the one I want to fight most," I said. "And I will take you down. Eventually."

"Then wait until this is done," he answered. "We can work together until Chroma is taken care of. Then you can go back to scheming against me. And you'll have three cities full of people to help you, instead of the handful you have out here in the hills."

"Why?" I asked. "Why are you willing to give me all this? What is--" I broke off. "Oh. You're scared, aren't you? You're scared of Chroma."

"Maybe I am. You don't know her power, Beryl. You thought the dragons of The Circle were bad? Wait until you learn more about her."

"And yet you think I could help, somehow. Why?"

Onyx gestured wildly. "Because they're all dead! You did it! You killed the other dragons! I killed Viridia, of course, but I wouldn't have been able to if not for you. I don't know whether it's all luck or a combination of fortunate circumstances or what. But you've done more than anyone would have ever dreamed possible. And now? I think you can do even more." He shrugged again. "Worst case scenario for me: you fail and die. It doesn't change my situation at all."

"Unless I tell Chroma I was working for you," I countered.

"Try it. She'll either laugh or roll her eyes before she kills you."

An odd thought occurred to me. "When was the last time you saw her?"

He blinked. "I don't—why do you ask?"

"Just curious. What color is she? Is she the same size as you, or much bigger? I just wanted an idea of what we're up against here."

"That's irrelevant. She's purple. Look, think about my offer. I'll give you a couple of days."

"And then what?"

He shrugged. As he did, black scales erupted from his shoulders. I took an involuntary step backward.

"I suppose…" he began, smoke puffing from his mouth. "I suppose I shall have to track you down and finish off your entire team."

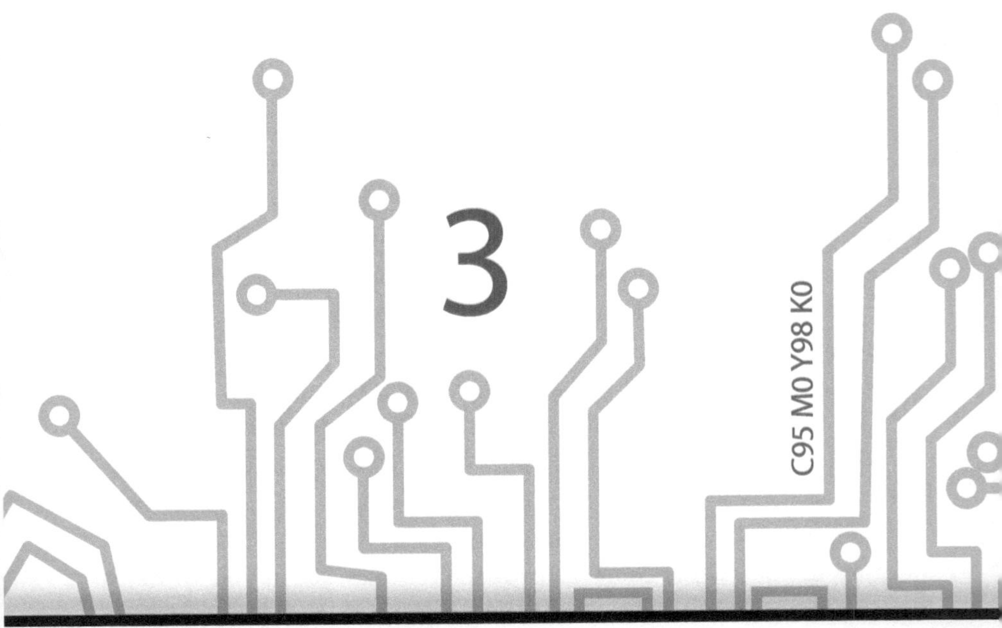

3

I wanted to make some kind of sarcastic remark about how he hadn't been able to track us down yet, but... I might have been a bit freaked out from watching my former friend turn back into a dragon. I'd seen it before, of course, but it was still highly disturbing. In a few moments—it seemed faster than the last time—the full-size black dragon stood before me again. He gave me a bit of a smirk before taking to the air.

I waited until he disappeared from view. The last thing I wanted to do was lead him back to our base. I might have waited even longer, but the sound of a four-wheeler drew my attention.

Caedan rode up near me, coming to an abrupt stop and lifting the back two tires a bit. One of these days, he might flip that thing. He coughed from the dust he'd kicked up and grinned at me. "I was sent to find you."

"You found me. I could use a ride." I limped to the four-wheeler. When did I start limping?

Caedan lost the grin. "You don't look so good."

I climbed on board. "I just had a talk with Onyx."

His eyes widened and jerked up to the sky. "He was here?"

"Yeah. Get me back, would you?"

The ride back to our headquarters took only a few moments. Onyx had been so close to finding all of us. Remembering what he'd done to our last base, I shuddered. Too close.

"We need to talk," I said as we got off the vehicle. "Get Bice and Lainey and Kelly. Meet in my room."

"No one else?"

"Not yet. Just the core." I frowned. "And tell Kelly to come alone. I don't want Chance there this time."

Caedan raised an eyebrow, but hurried off to gather the others. I made my way down the stairs, said hello to Fern and Hunter in passing, and took refuge in my bedroom. Lovat usually shared the room with me, but since his injuries, he'd moved to a different room where Hunter could monitor him. With no one else around, I collapsed on my bed. Exhaustion, mental and physical, overwhelmed me. I hadn't even done much. I shouldn't be this tired.

I might have dozed off for a few seconds before the door opened to admit the four I'd requested. I jerked up, wincing as my injuries complained.

"Why are we meeting in here?" Kelly asked. "And why keep Chance out?"

I waved for them to find a seat on the other bunks. "We can have a larger meeting later. I just wanted to talk to you four first." I rubbed my head. "And we're in here because I might collapse, and I'd rather collapse on my bed than a chair or table."

"You shouldn't have gone for that walk," Lainey said, sitting next to me.

"I know, I know. But I met someone out there." I told them about my encounter with Onyx. Once we got past their exclamations of shock and anger, I moved on: "But that's actually the least interesting conversation I've had, er, heard in the past twenty-four hours."

"You talked with Chance," Kelly said.

I nodded and pointed to the recording device. "And I heard from Loden."

"I'm sorry. Could you repeat that?" Bice asked.

"It's a recording of Loden." I picked it up and pushed the button to show him. Loden's voice came across, saying, "…and that's why I did what I did with your hand." I cut it off.

"Wh-what all did he say? Was he talking to you?"

"Yeah." I hesitated before continuing. "And get this: his mysterious patron? It was Auric."

Expressions of disbelief followed. After a pause, Caedan added, "Makes sense, really." He was smarter than I gave him credit for.

I looked down at the floor before continuing. "Auric saw Loden's brilliance when Viridia didn't. After some time, he started telling him everything." I looked up at Lainey. "He told him about Chroma and the zealots. And that's when they started working on tech solutions to counter Chroma's, uh, cyb stuff. The robes and everything." I flexed my hand.

"And he incorporated it into you," Bice said softly.

I nodded.

"Your hand came later, though," Kelly pointed out.

"Oh, right. Loden said he wanted to give me the cyb hand at first, but Hunter talked him into the other option. That's why this one was in his workshop waiting for me."

Caedan whistled and sat back. "Not built to fight dragons, but built to fight those guys."

"We talked about this," Lainey whispered.

I looked into her eyes. "I know. And it's real. Sort of." I took a deep breath and looked at the others. "I wasn't 'built,' though I know you didn't mean anything by it, Caedan. I was rescued. Loden saved my life. But while he was at it, he gave me the power to fight back. Not just against our oppressors, the dragons, but against the oppressors outside The Circle: Chroma and her zealots."

We sat in silence for a few moments. I flexed my hand again. The fact that it worked at all meant my implant couldn't be damaged too bad, right? And my eyes. They worked. Hmm.

"All right," Kelly said at last. "And what did Chance tell you?"

"He didn't tell you?" That surprised me.

"No. He said he had to talk to you alone."

"Huh." I shrugged. "It wasn't… I mean, I don't think it was anything I can't tell the rest of you. He filled me in a little more on how everything started here, things he learned from his father, Onyx, during his first, uh, life."

"So weird," Caeden muttered.

"The way he told it, the dragons came here, not as an act of rebellion like we joked about, but kind of as a test. Chroma knew she wouldn't live forever and wanted her children to have time to learn how to lead on their own. So she sent them here to basically practice. Each of them brought a bunch of humans with them, as the first inhabitants of The Circle."

"But what about the power sources?" Bice asked. "Surely it couldn't be a coincidence that they just happened to find seven power sources here."

"No, they knew about them before they came. That's why this place was chosen. Or at least Chance thinks so."

"What is Chroma's power source like then?" Caedan wondered.

"That's a good question." I looked at Lainey. "Got any ideas about that?"

"No." She shook her head. "I told you I've never seen Chroma. Neither has anyone else I know. Only the priests, the zealots, are allowed to see her."

"I assume she lives in some grand temple or something?" Bice asked.

Lainey shrugged. "I mean, we're told she lives at the temple. It's actually not far from the mountains. But no one gets in there except…"

"The zealots," I finished.

"So is Chance, um…" Caedan looked at Kelly and rubbed his face. "I mean, I hate to even ask. But now that he's got his memories back, is he even on our side?"

"Yes," Kelly said without hesitation.

"And it's all because of her," I added. Kelly gave a brief smile and looked down. "Seriously," I went on, "when his memories came rushing back, they were confronted by the past few months of growing up as her child. He'd never had a mother before."

"Because they all died," Bice said.

"Right. And infant draconics are raised by whoever the dragon assigns. There's no room for love, not a mother's love, anyway."

Lainey put an arm around Kelly and squeezed her. "Pretty cool, huh? Your decision to love that kid overrode centuries of dragon beliefs."

I shook my head in wonder at Lainey's statement (though I still wasn't used to her use of the word "cool").

Bice cleared his throat. "What other information did he have for us out of these centuries?"

"I didn't ask for more yet," I answered. "But he's willing to talk about it. He said his memories are still a bit jumbled up, but they're starting to settle, if that makes any sense."

Bice chuckled. "How would we know if it does? It's beyond any of our experiences."

"Yeah. So I think you should talk with him when possible." I glanced at Kelly. "Do you think that's all right?"

"Now that he's talked with you like he wanted, I think he'll be more open," she said.

"I don't even know why it had to be me first," I said. "He could have told all of us or any of us."

Kelly pretended to smack my head. "You're the leader, you idiot. And the closest thing he's had to a father since he was born."

"Told you," Lainey added. "Daddy."

"This is a lot," Caedan said. "So what do we do now?"

"Isn't it obvious?" I looked around the room at them. "We need to go find Chroma's temple."

4

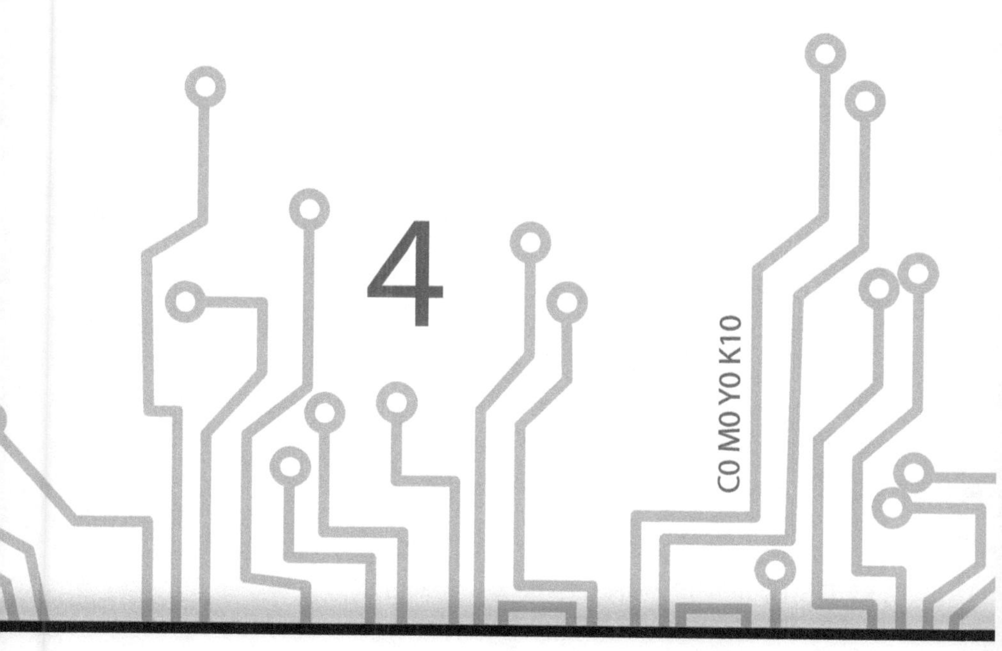

"You're not going anywhere!" Lainey burst out.

"We have to," I argued. "It's our main threat right now."

"Is it?" Kelly asked. "We still have Onyx here. I think he should be our focus."

"Yeah." Caedan inched forward on the edge of the bunk. "We set out to get rid of the dragons. There's one left. And Amy, of course. But she's stuck here with us."

"I don't see any way to get to Onyx right now. He's moving from city to city. He knows our tactics. He's not vulnerable." I paused. "But we'll get him. Eventually."

"Then we make things harder for him," Caedan said. "Maybe we go back to hunting draconics. That was fun."

"What good would that do if they're all replaced by Chroma's zealots?" I threw my hands in the air. "They're going to be running everything before long. Onyx is letting them, even if he doesn't like it. We have to stop them at the source."

"You may be right," Bice said. "But—"

"You're not listening!" Lainey jumped to her feet and pointed at me. "I mean you! You, Beryl. You can't go anywhere. You're in no shape to do anything right now. You're supposed to be resting and healing. Instead, you tried to go on a run and met the one remaining dragon! And now you're talking about walking into more danger!"

"Lainey, I—"

"Your implant isn't working! You have nothing right now. No powers. No enhancements. You can barely stay on your feet! If you try to do anything else, you're going to be dead. Dead, do you hear me?"

I opened my mouth, but didn't say anything.

"I am not going to be a part of you killing yourself!" With that, she stormed out of the room, slamming the door behind her.

I closed my mouth, maybe the wisest thing I'd done yet. I probably should have done that much sooner.

"She's right, you know," Bice said.

"I've been hurt before."

"Not like this," Kelly put in. "You really need to take a break, Beryl. And didn't you tell Lovat you'd be here for him?"

I hesitated. I had said that. "But we're so close. We've done so much. And, and, we can win everything. I know it."

"We can." Bice stood and took my hand. "And we will. But sometimes, we have to wait for things. Hunter has told you to rest, hasn't he?"

I shrugged. He had, but I wasn't going to admit it. He always said that.

"Then rest. Make plans, have a big meeting with everyone, but rest."

I knew they were all right, but...

Bice pulled on my hand, forcing me to stand up. He looked into my eyes. "And Lovat needs you," he said.

"He needs you. And Don."

"And you. You know what he's going through."

He had to hit me with that one. I couldn't argue any more.

"All right. Fine. Chromatic hells. I'll rest."

"After you go find Lainey," Kelly added.

Yeah. I needed to do that. I pulled myself up from the bed. "Tell the others we'll have a general meeting tomorrow morning."

"You got it," Caedan said.

I stepped out into the hall and walked a few doors down to Lainey's room. Only Glacier shared it. No one else wanted to sleep in the same room as a huge saber-toothed cat. I knocked and heard only a growl from inside. I hoped it came from Glacier.

"Lainey, it's me," I called. "You were right."

I waited. A moment later, the door opened. Lainey looked at me with red eyes. Had she been crying? Her cheeks were kind of puffy too.

"I'm sorry. I was wrong. I'll rest."

"For how long?" she demanded.

"I mean, um… until I'm healed enough? I don't know."

She crossed her arms. "Who decides when you're healed?"

Royal came down the hall. I waited until he passed before answering: "Um, I feel like there isn't a correct answer to that question."

"Yes, there is. We have a doctor here."

"Hunter? You want me to let him decide?"

"He's the most qualified to determine your health. And your implant's functions."

I scratched my head. "I guess?"

"So you'll let him determine it?"

Another growl came from Glacier inside the room.

I didn't want to say it, but… "Yes. I'll listen to Hunter."

Lainey leaned out and checked down the hall. She grabbed my shirt and pulled. "Come here."

A moment later, we were inside her room with the door closed. Glacier, lying next to the far wall, lifted her head in curiosity.

"Lainey, um…"

"Shut up and listen. You think you know what it's like outside The Circle, but you don't."

I didn't answer. I'd already said the wrong thing enough times today.

She gestured at her room. "Let's say this is the building where you live out there. Everything is fine in here. And then…" She opened the door and pulled me back out into the hall. "Imagine this is the street outside."

"All right…"

"Once you're out here, it's not fine any more. Now you're being watched."

"Chroma has spies?"

"Some, yes. But it's more than that. Remember the screens in Onyx's tower?"

"Yeah. We could watch the cities. It was pretty hue."

"Cameras. Up in the sky somewhere. That's how it works. In the city where I live, cameras are everywhere." She pointed at the corners of the ceiling. "Mounted on other buildings, watching the streets. Watching inside a lot of buildings too. Everywhere."

I rubbed at my chromark. "You're saying Chroma is watching every-one?"

"No." She shook her head. "I keep telling you. No one sees the dragon. It's not her. Or if it is, there's no evidence that she's the one doing it. It's the purple robes. The zealots. They control everything. And they come and go, like you've seen. You never know when one's watching, or might turn up."

She walked back into her room. I followed, not sure if the conversation would continue. Glacier watched us enter.

"So… in some ways, you have more freedom than us, and in others, you have less," I observed.

She sat down on the bed. "That's what I've been trying to tell you. And I'm terrified of you stepping outside these mountains." She rubbed the back of her hand in her lap, watching it instead of me. "Because of your mark, you'll be recognized instantly. They'll see you on the cameras. And they'll come down on you. All of them."

Glacier put her head down and closed her eyes.

"Lainey, we've disguised our chromarks before. We can—"

"I don't want to lose you too!" She looked up, tears glistening in the corners of her eyes. "You can talk all you want about how, how you were 'made' for this fight or whatever, and you've done well against some of them. But you can't fight all of them. There are too many!"

"How many are there?" I wasn't sure I wanted to know the answer.

"No one knows for sure. But hundreds. At least." She inched forward. "And if they see you as a threat, Beryl, they will come after you. All of them."

"But then they couldn't keep your people under control, could they? They can't all come," I argued.

"They've done it before."

I paused for a moment. "What?"

She looked down again. "When we first met, you told me the stories your people believed about the destroyed city. We have stories like that… but not just one."

I didn't answer. I didn't know how to answer.

"People. Families. Communities. Even whole towns that displeased the zealots. They died. They all died."

"Because they stopped being useful to Chroma," I realized. "Like the zealots said to me. All of the dragons that have died here died because she wanted them to. That's what they claimed, and it made no sense." I took a few steps across the room. Glacier opened an eye to watch me. "But they said anyone who stops being useful to Chroma or stops serving her or whatever will die."

Lainey nodded, but I shook my head and kept going: "Don't you see? It doesn't matter whether we go or not." I looked into her eyes. "Because of what I've done, we're already marked for death."

She didn't answer. I hadn't forgotten how she told me recently that I gave her hope against the zealots. But I didn't bring that up. Maybe I'd gotten a little wiser over time about what to say when people are emotional.

"Look, I'm not going out there for a while now. I gave you my word. For now…" I shrugged. "I guess we rest."

Lainey took a deep breath and nodded. "We rest."

I hated rest.

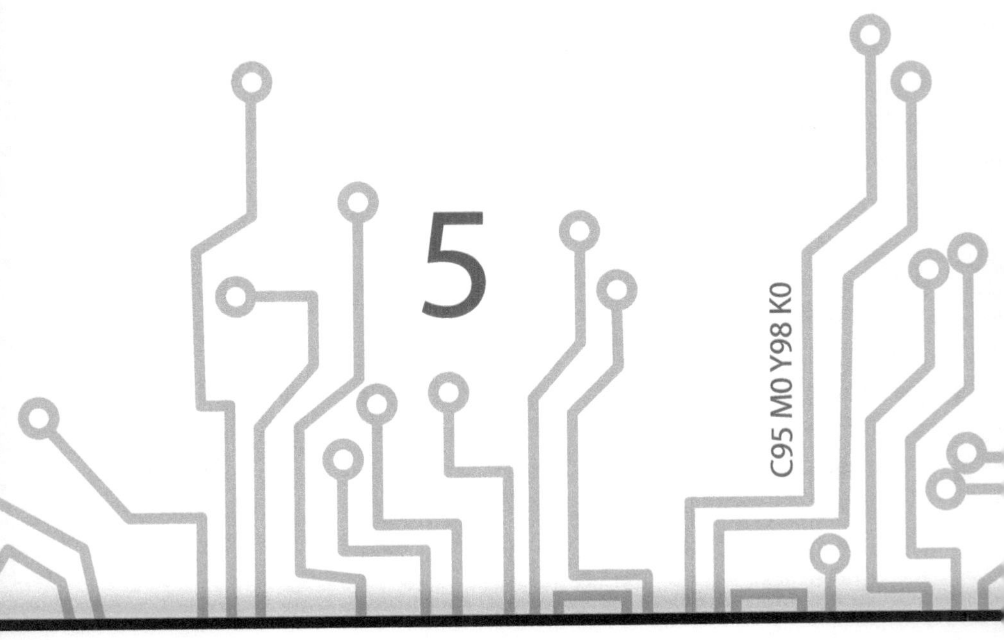

5

We held a big meeting the next day. Everyone came. Even Amaranth ventured out of her secret room to sit in the far corner and sulk while she listened to us talk.

I told them some of what the four of us had discussed the day before. Chance spoke little, but corroborated what he could. Hearing such mature language come from the small draconic continued to be a bizarre experience.

Stacy and Jaden wanted to know when it would be safe for them to return to Viridia. I couldn't promise anything. Troilus Green still ruled, though supposedly under the command of Onyx and the zealots. He didn't like it either. In some ways, it made us allies, but I couldn't accept that.

Caiden dispatched Turq, Saxe, Royal, and Cobalt on information-gathering missions. At least some of us could do something.

Don, as usual, didn't speak at all. But it was different from before. His silence held anger behind it now; he hadn't forgiven me for what happened to Lovat.

After the meeting, I joined Hunter, Fern, and Lainey in the medical room. I explained to Hunter my agreement with Lainey.

He looked at her with what could only be respect. "I am impressed. How did you talk him into this?"

Fern slapped his shoulder. "She's a woman, and he loves her.

That should be enough."

"Perhaps, perhaps."

"So what do you think?" I asked. "How long?"

He sighed. "I told you already that I am not a cyberneticist. There is room for hope, however, since you are still able to walk. It must be functioning to some degree."

"But I can't boost."

"Does it hurt when you try?"

I closed my eyes and made the attempt. "Yes. Some." I opened my eyes. "I mean, it's hard to tell, since my head has been hurting pretty much since it got hit."

Hunter nodded. "I also told you that you had a serious concussion. For such a thing, you must rest. Not go running across the hills. Let me see the back of your head again."

I dutifully turned and allowed him to examine my head.

"I cannot tell much, of course. The swelling has gone down. I do not think you are bleeding inside." He stepped back. "It may be that your ability to use the boosts will return once the concussion is healed."

"And it may not?"

"I have told you this also. You may never regain them."

I did not want to hear that. I could not believe it. Without the boosts, without my special abilities, how could we ever succeed? No one else could do anything like me. No one but Onyx, that is. Maybe an alliance with him would…

No! What was I thinking? Onyx was evil. He'd betrayed me. Betrayed all of us. He'd killed Protogonus Blue. He'd manipulated Kelly and gotten her pregnant with a draconic child meant to kill her on birth. And he had a host of other crimes throughout history. Sometimes, I forgot that part.

I thanked Hunter and told Lainey I needed to be alone. I slipped off to my room to think.

If I couldn't use boosts, there would be no more secret missions. No defeating Onyx. Certainly no defeating the zealots. We might have a chance against Troilus Green, but even so…

I considered talking with Bice. He'd probably tell me my ego was out of control. "It's not all about you, Beryl," I said to myself in his voice. I knew that. I did. But there were thousands of people here in The Circle, and none of them had come anywhere close to what I'd done so far. And apparently thousands more outside The Circle… and what had they done? Who had done more than me?

Loden.

I wouldn't even be here if it weren't for him. But that was my point: he'd given me the tools to fight our oppressors, and now those tools were breaking. I needed them fixed. Besides, Loden had been a once-in-a-million-years genius. We weren't likely to find anyone else like him.

No one else had… ouch. It hit me. Hard.

Peri.

He'd saved his entire city, by himself, with no special powers, no cybernetic implants, or anything. And it cost him his life.

I took a deep breath. Everything wasn't over. We could still make a difference. Ordinary people could make a difference. It would be much better if my abilities came back, of course. But we'd be all right. Maybe.

I spent most of the rest of the day with Lovat. Don hung around too, distrustful. I couldn't blame him. Bice joined us for a while. It would still be some time before Lovat's casts were removed. There wasn't much I could do except talk, so I did that.

"How does it feel?" he asked.

"How does what feel?"

"When you do the boosts thing." He awkwardly pointed to the back of his head.

"I just kind of think it. Um." I paused, trying to figure out how to describe it. I formed my hand into a fist. "You know how you do this and then…" I squeezed the fist tighter with a sudden flinch. "You squeeze it? Like that? Really fast?"

Lovat wrinkled his brow. "Yeah?"

"It's like that, but with your brain. You're flexing the muscle real fast." I watched his face. "This isn't really helping, is it?"

"Nah."

I laughed. "We'll work on it. We've got time." I know he hated to hear it, but I repeated the story of how long it took me to learn to walk. "But you'll do better than I did. You've got me. And Bice." I glanced over to where the other man watched. "And Don."

Lainey showed up a few minutes later. She smiled and waited until our conversation ended, then pulled me away. We ended the day lying on top of the hill, watching the stars.

"Are the stars the same outside The Circle?" I asked.

She chuckled. "Why wouldn't they be? Stars are"—she waved at the sky—"way up there. Our little divisions don't mean anything to them. Not even mountains. Or dragons."

I didn't answer. I found myself wondering if there were other places where the stars shone down, places where they didn't have dragons.

"The mountains do make a difference, though," Lainey said. "They block our view of some of the stars. And they make the sun set sooner. And rise later. You have longer nights in here."

I rolled over to look at her. "Is that a bad thing?"

She rolled onto her side to look back at me. "Not necessarily. We have more time to look at the stars, you know."

I chuckled. She wasn't wrong.

The next several days passed in a similar fashion. I slept in late to "get my rest." I spent a lot of time with Lovat. I checked around the base, seeing if I could help anyone with anything. I drove people crazy with my annoying presence (they'd didn't complain, but I could tell). And I spent the evenings with Lainey on the top of the hill.

Everything seemed to be going smoothly, though my healing took way too long for my liking.

Until one evening, Caedan interrupted our star gazing. "I think you'd better come see this," he said. "I, uh, think Amaranth is drunk."

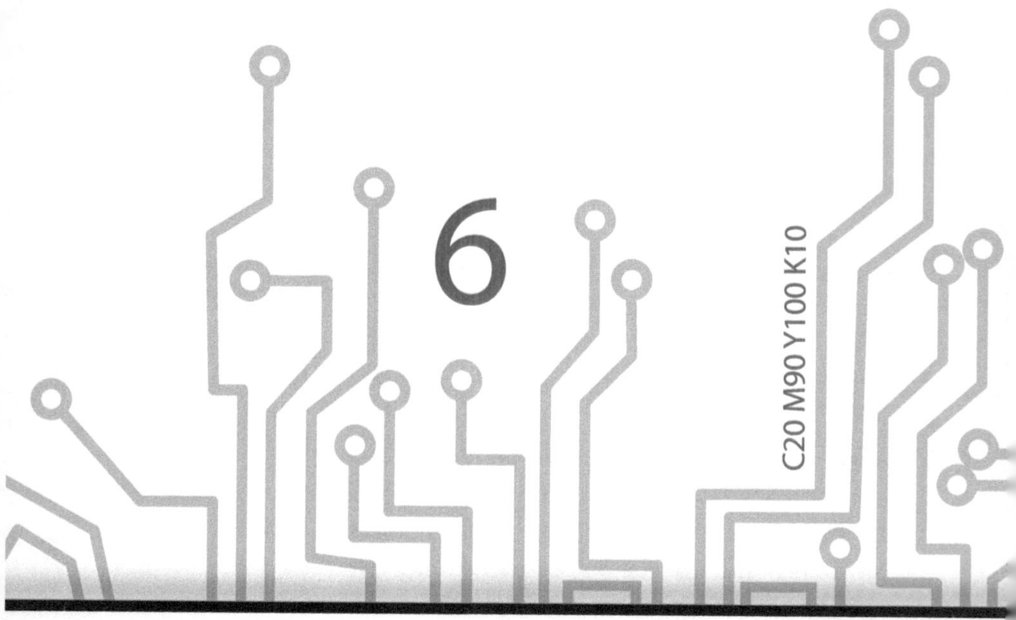

6

I found our resident dragon-in-human-form in the meeting room. "Hi there," I greeted her. "What's going on?"

She didn't answer at first. I took a few steps closer. She sat at the nearest table, a drinking glass beside her. There wasn't much liquid in it, but what I could see didn't look like anything familiar. At last, she looked up at me. My eyes widened. Her hair was disheveled, and her eyes were red. Even her fine clothes looked askew somehow. For a dragon lady who'd always, always valued her appearance, this was way out of character. I looked back at Caedan, who raised his eyebrows.

"I'm just having a drink before I tell you things," she answered with a giggle.

I recoiled as the odor struck my nostrils. "What are you drinking? It smells vile."

Amaranth chuckled and waved the glass in the air. "Onyx and I found this valley. Did he ever tell you that?"

I glanced around before taking a seat across from her. I could endure the smell for the sake of new information. "No, he didn't."

Her eyes fixed on Caedan standing behind me. "Why are you here?" For that question, her voice sounded hard and normal again.

He took a step back. "Uh... I can leave."

I nodded and waved him back. He rolled his eyes and left the room.

"It started as a dare." Amaranth eyed her drink before setting it with exaggerated care on the table in front of her. "We were trying to see who could fly the highest." She waved toward the ceiling. "And there were these mountains. Sooo high."

"Very high," I agreed. I'd never seen her like this. She wasn't… normal. Her words slurred, and she looked around like she could see things I couldn't. I'd seen drunk people before, but this was on a different level. Dragon drunk?

"We kept flying to higher points. Higher and higher." She waved again. "Onyx said I couldn't make it to the peak." She laughed. "That's a funny word, isn't it? Peak. Peak, peak, peak."

"And did you make it? To the… top?"

"Onyx said I couldn't do it. He didn't think I could. But I did." She looked at me, but her eyes didn't focus. "All the way. I did it."

When she didn't continue, I prompted, "Did Onyx make it to the top?"

"I made it first! But then he came too. He was second. And don't let him tell you otherwise." She stared off past my shoulder so intently, I almost turned to look. "And then I saw it." She stood up, almost fell over, and steadied herself against the table. She spread both arms out wide. "I saw the land. Empty and green. Like my brother Viridia." She snorted. "He's green. And empty. In the head." She thought that was incredibly funny and fell back in her chair, laughing.

I waited until the spasms of laughter subsided. "You saw the land from the mountain."

Amaranth looked down at her drink again. She eyed it for a few moments, then took a quick swallow. "It was beautiful, you know. Before we came. Before the cities. Before humans." Her eyes narrowed as she looked at me. "Like you. Human." A snort turned into a laugh. Her eyes lost focus again. "Like me. I'm human now."

I didn't know what else to say, so I waited.

"Onyx saw it too. He didn't even wait for me. Dove right down over the mountain." She looked at me with a serious face and nodded. "He could feel it, you know. The power. So much power. This valley was full of it." She buried her face in her hands. "So full."

Was she crying? "Um, maybe you can tell me the rest later," I suggested. "Right now, you can—"

Her head jerked up, and she glared at me. "I told you I would tell you this stuff, remember?" She patted the back of her neck. "And you said you'd take this off."

Uh-oh. This complicated things. When I'd made that promise to her, we were short on information. It had seemed like a good idea at the time. But if I released her now…

"We found two of the strongest spots, Onyx and me. We… feasted. It was wonderful." She paused for a long time. "When we left, we talked about keeping it a secret. But he wanted to tell Auric. Auric would understand the power more than we could. He's smart like that, you know."

I nodded. That made sense.

"We told him. And then later, the others." She snickered. "We almost didn't tell Viridia. Empty-head Viridia."

"When did you tell Chroma?" I asked.

Her eyes widened. "We didn't. Not for a long time. Not until we'd worked out the plans. Big plans." She put a finger to her lips. "Secret plans."

"Secret?"

"Yes. Secret. Can't tell you." She leaned forward. "We decided to start our own place. Here. The Circle place. The Circle. Here. Our place. Not Chroma's."

"Oh, that secret—"

"But we didn't tell her everything!" Amaranth leaned back again, shaking her head. "We didn't tell her about the power. Not the sources."

Wait. Something wasn't right. "What do you mean, Amaranth?"

"She never knew." She giggled. "We never told her about the power. She didn't get it. We did." She waved her arms. "Made us stronger. Made us live soooo long." She looked at her glass and frowned at it for being almost empty. "Too long, maybe," she added in a whisper.

My mind whirled. Was I hearing right? I leaned across the table. "Amaranth, this is very important."

"So many colors." She reached a hand toward my chromark. "Everyone else only has one."

"Yes, yes." I tried not to flinch. "But you just said you never told Chroma about the power sources here in The Circle. But the dragons depend on the power sources, don't they? Didn't you have power sources outside The Circle?"

Her finger traced part of my chromark. "I like the red part. Red is best."

"Did you have power sources outside The Circle?"

Her eyebrows twisted in frustration. "I already said we found them here. Weren't you listening?"

I swallowed. "What about Chroma? Did she have her own power source?"

"My mother." Amaranth pulled away and leaned back in her chair. "My mother had everything. And she never shared with us. That's why we left."

"But did she have a power source?"

She pushed the chair back and stood up. She swayed a moment before grabbing her empty glass from the table. "This is empty. Like Viridia's head." She snorted. "I think I'm going to bed."

I stood up too. "But—"

"I told you everything." She sashayed away, patting the back of her neck. "And tomorrow, you can take this off."

Great. Now what should I do?

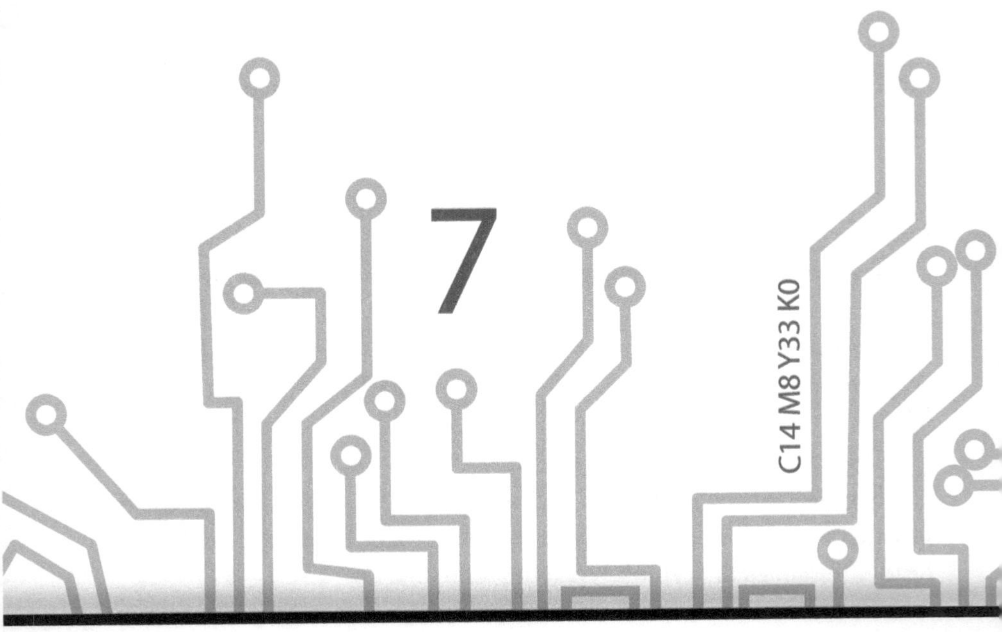

7

I swiftly gathered Bice, Kelly, Lainey, and Caedan. In the meeting room, I poured out Amaranth's story and her final comment about removing the device from her neck. "What should I do?" I concluded.

"There's no way we can let her free!" Caedan smacked the table with his palm. "We've sacrificed everything to get rid of the dragons. We can't put one back!"

"If we let her turn back into a dragon, what will she do?" Kelly asked. "What can she do?"

"The second she transforms, she'll turn around and burn this whole place down with us in it!" Caedan insisted. "She'll want revenge for us keeping her trapped for so long."

"I don't know." Kelly shook her head. "She has no love for us, sure. But she's not on good terms with Onyx or the purple guys and Chroma, either."

"Would she go to them and try to make amends?" Lainey asked.

"She was pretty upset at Onyx when she came with us," I said. "But she's been pretty upset with me too. It's hard to know who she hates more."

"She's a hateful person," Caedan agreed.

"She's also a thousand-year-old dragon who has funded her own opposition for generations, just to keep them under her control," Bice said. "Don't underestimate her, or think she'll act on pure emotion. She's smarter than you think."

"So you think she's got a specific plan in mind?" I asked.

"I don't think it matters to your decision." Bice gave me one of those pleasant smiles of his that could be comforting or outright annoying. "Who Amaranth is doesn't matter. What matters is who you are."

I frowned. "What do you mean?"

Bice glanced around the room and then back at me. "You've been the leader of this rebellion for some time now, Beryl. And it's not only because you're the one who believes the strongest in our cause."

"He believed enough to sway me," Caedan pointed out.

"Yes." Bice nodded. "At first, certainly. And we have had a great cause to fight for. But Beryl has more than that. He has a code he lives by." He pointed at me. "In the beginning of all this, you had conflicts with Rick and even Loden a time or two, all because you disagreed with their way of doing things. Rick believed it didn't matter what we did as long as we accomplished our goal. You didn't."

"I guess…"

"All along, you've told our team to avoid killing humans, even the Viridian Guard. Why?"

"It, uh, it wouldn't have been good for our cause."

"Nonsense. The cause had nothing to do with it. It was because you thought killing humans was wrong. When you were forced to kill that one guard to rescue me, it tormented you for weeks."

The guard. I could still see his face in my memory. I hadn't dreamed about him in months, but…

"You see? It's about you, not your enemies. Or even your allies."

"This isn't the same thing," Caedan protested. "If we let her go, she could kill dozens, even hundreds of humans! How would that fit with this code idea?"

"Caedan, when Beryl first took you hostage, what persuaded you to stick around?" Bice raised an eyebrow. "What about Beryl himself made you stay?"

"He kept his word to me."

"Exactly."

"Wait," Kelly protested. "You just established a difference in killing humans and dragons. But now you're equating making a promise to both of them?"

"It's not about the recipient of the promise." Bice looked back at me. "It's about the one who made the promise."

I didn't like the comparison at all. Yes, I'd made a promise to Caedan and kept it. Did that mean I had to keep it to Amaranth? Were they the same?

"Beryl, it may not be written down anywhere, but you have a code you live by, all the same," Bice went on. "Whatever the others may think, I say it's the key to your leadership, more than your implant or your sword or anything else."

"Bice... it's not that simple."

"Why not? I know you try to do the right thing." He cast a quick glance at Lainey. "I know that back in her city, Amaranth tried to seduce you. But you resisted. Why?"

I didn't know he knew that, and wasn't sure I appreciated him bringing it up. "I have a girlfriend."

"So you were faithful to her, right?"

"Yes."

"This is who you are. You are faithful to those around you. Your decision now is: should I be faithful to an enemy too?"

"That's why I asked you in here! Because I don't know!"

Bice sat back with a small shake of his head. "I think you do."

Part of me wanted to smack him. The other part knew he was right. I sighed. "Then I suppose... we're going to have to make some preparations."

The next morning, I met Amaranth outside her room. She narrowed her eyes at seeing me. "Are you keeping your word?" she demanded.

"I always do. But I have some stipulations."

She folded her arms. "So now you're going to try to weasel out of it."

"No, nothing at all like that." I pointed toward the stairs. "We just have to be outside when we do it."

I headed up without waiting for an answer. I could feel her eyes boring into the back of my head. The walk up the stairs had never seemed longer. Upon exiting, I led the way outside the trees that hid our headquarters' entrance.

"Why did we have to come all the way out here?" the dragon demanded.

"I thought that would be obvious. You can't change back into a dragon inside." I rolled my eyes, fighting the urge to look toward the trees where Caedan hid.

She snorted and turned her back to me. She pulled her crimson hair away from the back of her neck, exposing the circular device. "Let's do it then."

I took a deep breath. I'd given my word. She'd done what we asked. Caedan waited nearby, but everyone else hid in the rooms furthest from the entrance. I hoped that even if she attacked, she'd be unable to get to them.

Auric hadn't been altogether clear about how to remove the devices. The person who put it in place could remove it; that's all I could remember. I reached to the back of her neck and grasped the edges of the device. To my shock, the circular piece of metal fell off in my hand.

Amaranth gasped and put her hand to the spot. "That… that's it?"

I took several steps back. "Looks like it."

She flexed her shoulders. A puff of smoke emerged from her nostrils. She looked back at me with a sly grin. Red scales rippled across her face, but faded as quickly as they'd appeared. "Thank you."

"Uh, you aren't turning back?"

She shrugged. "Where would I go if I did? I can't stand against Onyx with his new abilities, and he has an alliance with Chroma. For now, this is the safest place for me."

"Oh." I had to admit: I'd expected her to at least fly away somewhere else. She couldn't possibly enjoy this place.

"I do have a request, however." She reached inside a pocket and produced a pair of envelopes. "I know you are sending your people into the cities. Could you have one of them mail these letters for me?"

I took the envelopes with a wrinkled brow. "Um, I guess."

She waved as she turned away. "I fully expect you to open and read them first. I won't object. You'll see that I'm expressing concern for my children and inquiring as to the state of the city. Just see that they are sent. It's the least you can do."

"I guess?" Ugh. Saying the same thing twice. Stupid, stupid.

Amaranth sauntered back to our base and descended the stairs. When she was out of sight, Caedan emerged from his hiding place, holding the weapons we'd been able to scrounge up. I hadn't expected any of them to be of use against Amaranth's dragon form, but he'd insisted we had to try. "That was not what I was expecting," he said, looking toward the stairs.

"You and me both." I opened one of the envelopes and started reading. "It looks like just what she said. Huh."

"I don't trust her." Caedan handed my sword to me.

I took it and looked back at the letters. "Neither do I. I'll show these to Bice before we send them."

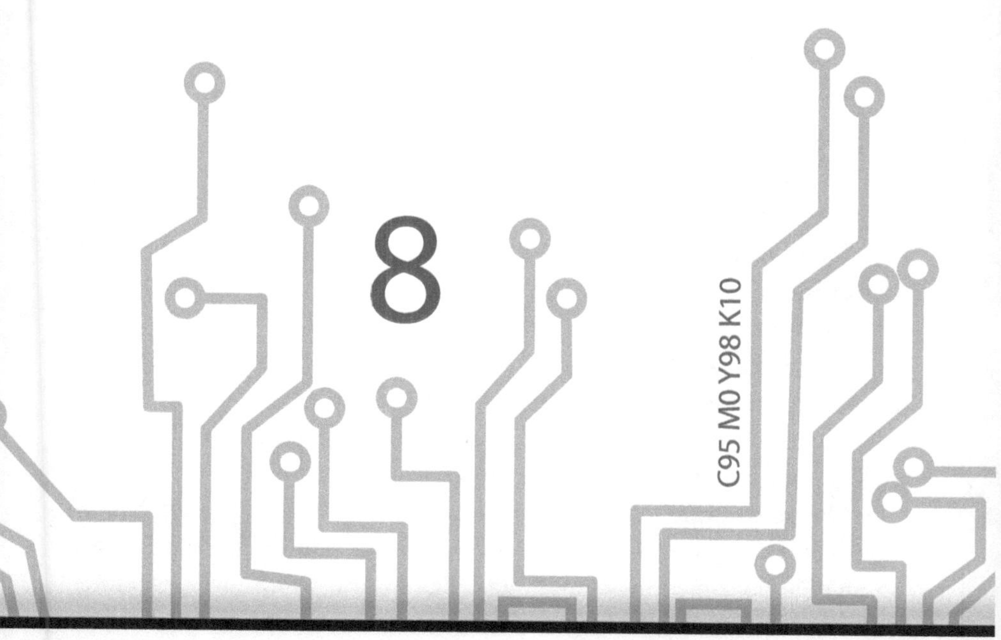

8

Bice couldn't find anything suspicious about the letters, but I couldn't accept it. He'd been right when he said not to underestimate her. At my insistence, he hand-copied the letters onto new paper, changing some of the words and spacing, just to tamper with any hidden messages. We put them into new envelopes and gave them to Turq, who would be scouting the city of Amaranth next.

And with that, I went back to resting. I hated it.

Every day, I attempted to get my boosts working. My head ached each time, but nothing improved. Every once in a while, I thought I felt a tiny flow, but not enough to make me certain. My frustration grew with each failure.

Hunter confirmed that I continued to heal in every other aspect. If not for the implant's problems and my promise to Lovat, I could have set out on a new mission. As it stood, I was stuck. Stuck, stuck, stuck. I hated it so much.

Apparently, my attitude showed as much. Lainey informed me that the others were tired of being around me. "I've been begged to take you on a walk," she said. "Are you feeling up to it?"

"Yes, please! I've been stuck here for weeks!"

"Hardly. It's been…" She thought for a moment. "Maybe two weeks. Since that run you took."

"That's more than one, isn't it? Like I said: weeks."

She rolled her eyes. "Let's just go, shall we?"

To no one's surprise, Glacier joined us as we walked down the hill. "Which direction shall we go?" Lainey asked.

"Southeast," I answered at once. "Maybe we can get a glimpse of the city of Auric."

She frowned. "That's a long way. Are you sure you're up to it?"

"We don't have to go too far if we go higher into the foothills," I pointed out. "I don't want to get near the city; I just want to see it."

She shrugged. "All right. We have water. We should be fine." She pulled out a compass, examined it, and pointed.

Maybe we were getting too relaxed. We'd been walking for half an hour before I noticed Lainey hadn't brought her rifle along. And I'd been so eager to do something—anything—that I didn't bring a weapon either. Still… things were different now. When the dragons had been at war, we had to be careful because of wandering patrols and small armies. When the war ended, but other dragons knew about us, we still had to be careful not to be seen by any of them flying around. Now… no patrols. Only one dragon to watch out for, and he didn't seem as interested in coming after us any more. Chroma's zealots had been showing up within The Circle, but nowhere near this area. Maybe we could be relaxed after all.

We hiked along, aiming toward the foothills of the mountains. Glacier, as always, couldn't decide whether to walk along with Lainey or to explore ahead, behind, or to the side somewhere. We'd long since learned to let her choose her own way; she'd come back.

When we reached the beginnings of the foothills, my muscles complained. I hadn't used them for anything strenuous for a while. It's amazing how swiftly the body adapts to inactivity. "I need to do more of this," I said. "You know, to stay in shape."

"Your body needs time to recover," she said, repeating the line I'd grown so tired of hearing. "You put it through some amazing stuff. Let it rest."

As if trying to confirm her words, I stumbled. I fell forward and caught myself on my palms. Since we were on an incline, I didn't fall far. I shook my head and pushed myself back up. I looked down, but didn't see anything that might have tripped me up.

"Oh." Lainey's exclamation came from several feet above, where she stared out to the south. She hadn't noticed my stumble. "I don't think we're going to see a city today."

I looked in the same direction. A dense fog floated at our eye level, not far away. The sky had grown grayer as we walked, but I hadn't thought much about it. Even so, this seemed to have come out of nowhere.

"Oof. I guess we'd better turn back."

"Yeah, walking in the fog is not my idea of fun. Exercise can wait."

We turned and hurried back down. By the time we reached the bottom of the foothills, the fog almost caught us. In another ten minutes, it enveloped us completely. Our visibility dropped to around a dozen feet.

"I've never seen it this bad out here," I said. "This is crazy."

"When my father and I were camped in the mountain cave, we saw fog from time to time." Lainey shook her head. "But not since I came down here with you. Not like this."

I stopped walking. "The zealots have a little mist around them when they do their disappearing trick. Do you think this is related?"

"I don't see how. They don't control the weather."

We resumed our walk, guided by Lainey's compass. I couldn't help feelings of paranoia. If the zealots made mist when they moved around, what if Chroma did the same on a much larger scale? My imagination concocted the outline of a massive dragon moving through the fog. I swear I saw purple everywhere I looked.

Lainey took my hand. "It's getting harder to see. Better stay connected."

I couldn't argue with that. The warmth of her hand made me smile in spite of everything else.

Maybe that's why I didn't notice anything wrong when we approached the base. Maybe the fog had freaked me out too much. Maybe... ugh. Who knew? My guard was down.

So it caught me completely by surprise when four soldiers of the Scarlet Brigade materialized out of the fog, crossbows aimed at us.

"Move them inside quickly." The voice belonged to a rust-red draconic who emerged from the mist behind them. "And keep an eye out for that cat creature."

"Beryl?" Lainey whispered.

"Do as they say," I answered. My mind raced. Amaranth had betrayed us after all. Despite our best efforts with the letters, she'd somehow gotten a message through to her people. But what had happened to the others? Were they all prisoners already?

The Brigade moved forward, motioning with their weapons. Still holding hands, Lainey and I descended the stairs into the base. Our home suddenly seemed darker and more menacing, especially when the draconic closed the doors behind us. Glacier wouldn't be coming to the rescue this time, unless she learned how to open doors.

Amaranth waited for us at the bottom of the stairs, arms crossed and dressed in her finest Lady Rust dress. Behind her stood two men in white clothes and red chromarks. I caught a glimpse of more Scarlet Brigade members down the hall, but no sign of any of my people.

"How swiftly things change," the dragon gloated.

I shook my head. "You hid some secret message in those letters somehow. I don't know how you did it."

She laughed. "I did no such thing. The letters were exactly what they seemed. Except they also served to make you more paranoid." She unfolded her arms. "That was fun in itself."

I wrinkled my brow. Then how did she communicate… oh. It hit me. She'd done it with me, after all. "Dreams."

She leaned forward and tapped my forehead. "Sometimes you can think. I even told you I could do that. I've been in communication with my children this entire time. I merely waited until the right moment."

"Once I removed the disk."

She nodded. "And it helps that you're powerless." She gestured at the men behind her. "It will make things much easier for them."

"What do you mean?" Lainey asked.

"Every one of us have wanted the same thing since this all began." Amaranth stepped forward and looped her arm through mine. I pulled away, only to have one of the Brigade poke me in the back with his weapon. "Even Auric, though he wouldn't admit it. Onyx has it now, and my only chance to fight him is to gain it for myself."

"My implant," I said.

The dragon smiled. "Exactly. But I'm not going to waste time trying to analyze and duplicate it. The one you have now will do just fine. These are the finest cyberneticists in my employ. They're going to strip all of your cybernetics from your body… and give them to me."

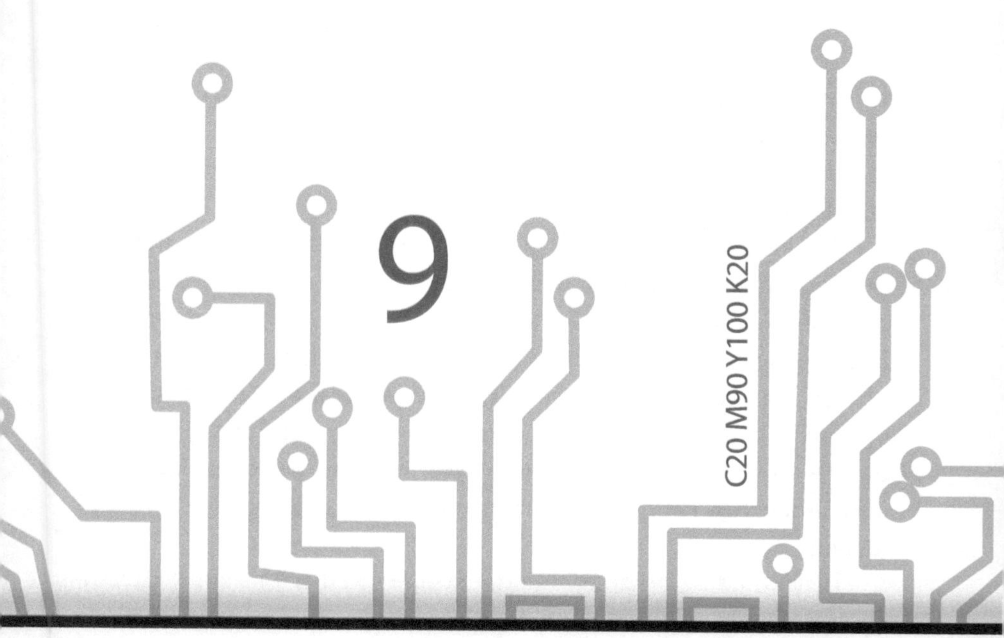

9

"You can't!" Lainey exclaimed. She tried to push forward, but a soldier seized her from behind.

I lunged at him, but another of the Brigade knocked me over the head, sending me sprawling to the floor.

Amaranth patted Lainey on the cheek. "You, my dear, are exactly why I can. You and the others being held in the bunk room over there." She looked down at me. "Beryl will cooperate with my scientists… or else I will burn the skin from your body in front of him, then let Ammuna Red dissect you until you scream yourself to death."

I pushed myself up from the floor. I needed my power more than ever. I strained until the skin on my skull ached from the effort. No boosts flooded my limbs. I was an ordinary, weak human with no way to save my friends.

"You win," I said.

Amaranth nodded. "I thought you'd see it my way. You will obey whatever these men tell you to do."

"I will."

She waved to the Brigade. "Put her with the others."

"No!" Lainey shrieked as they pulled her away. "Beryl! No! You can't!"

I turned to face my fate. What else could I do? Lainey's protests continued, burning my ears even as they grew fainter. I followed the two scientists into the medical room. They'd already made some changes, I saw. The examination bed had been modified for face-down usage. They'd even added more lighting. Tools I didn't recognize lay on several trays positioned throughout the room.

"You know what I want," Amaranth instructed. "Find his implant. Figure out what's wrong with it and remove it."

"If the notes we've received are accurate," one of the scientists said, "then there are cybernetic veins extending throughout his body as well."

"Rip it all out. I'll need every bit of this power if I'm to contend with Onyx." She gestured toward the door. "The doctor here is the one who helped with the original installation. We'll need his assistance later." She smiled and patted her face. "I don't intend to have scars marring my beautiful body."

"That would be a shame," I said, not sure whether I meant it sarcastically or not.

"Take off your shirt," the older scientist ordered. I complied and tossed it to the side. I shivered at the sudden chill.

"On the bed, please." The younger of the two scientists pointed before pulling a mask across the lower part of his face.

I took my time climbing into place. I could think of no options. Amaranth controlled everything. I'd always known I'd probably die in pursuit of this cause, but not like this… not lying on a bed while someone cut me apart.

"Strap him down," the older scientist instructed.

They stretched my arms out onto two wings jutting out from the main bed and tied them down with heavy straps. They put another one across my back and two more on my ankles. I stared down at the floor as some kind of clamps were placed on the sides of my head to hold it in place.

"I'll use a local anesthetic for now," the older one said right as I felt a needle pierce the back of my head. "We may need to ask some questions during the process."

Amaranth bent down and peered up at my face from beneath. "I suppose I should say I'm sorry it had to end this way, Beryl." She paused for a moment. "But I'm not sorry. Ever since you put that thing on my neck, your fate was sealed. It was only a matter of time. Now before that… well, I thought you had potential." She put her hand on my cheek. "Such a shame."

I don't know why it came into my head, but I asked anyway: "Was the story about you and Onyx finding this valley the truth?"

She chuckled. "Yes, as far as it goes. You wanted to know, and now you do. Not that it will do you much good." She straightened up. "Goodbye, Beryl. I'll be sure to take good care of your friends."

"You'd better. I'm only submitting to this for them."

This time, she laughed loud. "As if you had any choice! You have no power. None. And once you're dead, I'll do whatever I want with your friends. My relationship with Viridia will no doubt be improved if I return some of his people to him. As for the others… I'm sure I can think of something creative to do."

I strained at my bonds to no avail. I wanted to say something biting, something angry and defiant… but nothing came to mind.

Still laughing, Amaranth left the room. "I'll make the incision now," the scientist said. "Stand by with some pads."

I felt a pressure on the back of my head. He was cutting me open. Think, Beryl. There must be something. Something you can say to stop this.

"We've been killing the dragons, one by one. Why do you serve her? She's going to die like the others." I tried to keep my voice calm.

"Shut up," the younger one muttered.

I shut my mouth. And then wondered why I did. I closed my eyes with sudden realization. Amaranth's power of suggestion. Of course. I'd made her promise not to use it while she was with us, and so we'd all forgotten about it. But she was using it now, obviously. She'd told me to obey the scientists. I'd defeated it before. I could do it again. But I probably need working boosts.

I continued to feel pressure and some tickles from the work being done on the back of my head. So strange. The scientists continued to discuss their progress.

"There. See that?"

"I can't. Let me get some more of the blood out of the way… Oh. Is that metal?"

"Yes, it's a metal plate. It would have to be. To implant in the brain, you have to cut through the skull. And then you can't just leave a hole there."

"So we'll need to remove the plate?"

"Yes, and… Huh. Look at that. It's dented."

"Whoa. What could have done that?"

I forced my lips apart. "A big rock."

"That would do it. Must have hit you in just the right spot." The older scientist grunted as he did something else back there.

"Would that be the source of the problems, then?" the younger asked.

"Probably. Let's take it off and see what's going on underneath."

I heard the whirring of some kind of electrical tool. The pressure on the back of my head grew and grew… and then stopped with an abruptness that made me gasp.

"Careful with that. We'll need to either repair it or duplicate it for the goddess when we replicate this procedure."

"Whoa. Look at it. It's… beautiful."

"I've never seen anything like it. Whoever did this was an absolute genius."

"More than you'll know," I said.

"We'll understand it once we take it out and examine it," the older scientist said confidently.

"It'll never work," I mumbled. "Nerves."

"What?"

"Autonomic nerves. Pain receptors. Have you considered that?" In truth, I didn't fully understand what I was trying to say myself. I remembered some of it from Hunter's explanations. I only brought it up now for one reason: to stall them.

Because when they removed the metal plate, I felt something else: boost energy.

At first, a trickle of warmth spread through my head and neck. I couldn't even be sure it was one of my boosts and not some side-effect of whatever they were doing to me. I closed my eyes and focused. "Please, please, please," I whispered to the god Bice still believed existed somewhere. On my thought command, energy flowed into my arms. I smiled.

"I mean, there's no question the proposed surgical operations would require a constant level of anesthesia and create significant scarring."

"Yes, but would that—"

I sent stronger boost to both arms and ripped them free of the straps.

"Whoa! How did he do that?"

"The implant is working again!" The scientist tried to grab one of my arms. "What are you doing? Remember what she said she'd do to your friends!"

"I am." I pulled the clamps away from the sides of my head. I rolled over, sending boosts into my legs to pull them free as well. "Oh, this feels good. I've missed this."

The scientists backed away. "You can't do this!" the older one sputtered. "Amaranth gave you orders!"

"I've got news for you boys." I got to my feet and swayed a little. "I've been breaking her orders since I met her."

The younger scientist moved toward the door. "I'll get the Brigade!"

I grabbed a bowl of something from the tray next to the bed and launched it at him. It smacked him on the side of the head and sent him to the floor. I turned to the other one. "Now. You're going to tell me everything I need to know." Blood tickled the back of my neck as it ran down. "And maybe patch this hole in my head."

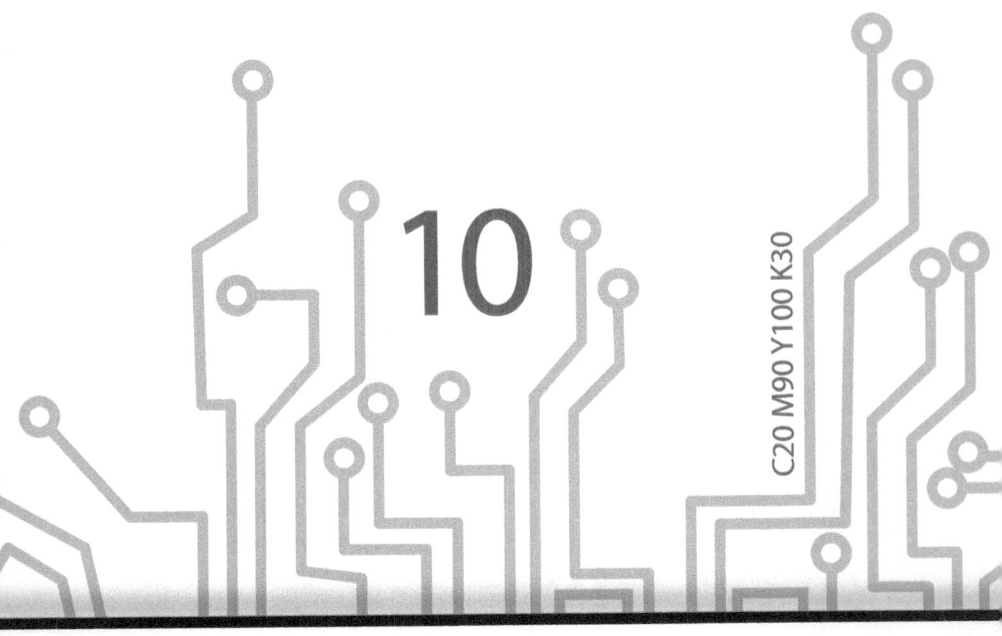

Twelve Scarlet Brigade soldiers. Two draconics. And Amaranth herself. Those were my odds, according to the scientist. Did she really need to bring two draconics? I suppose I should have taken it as a compliment that she felt she needed so much power against us.

I made the scientist bandage the back of my head before I knocked him out. I'd have to get Hunter to replace the metal plate later; couldn't run around with a hole in my head too long, I suppose. And I'm sure Stacy would get great delight out of making jokes about it.

My shirt was another matter. In my struggle to escape, I'd upended the tray of pads they'd used to soak up my blood. Naturally, it had landed on the shirt. I sighed. I didn't have many clothes left at this point. Something I'd need to take care of next time we made it to a city.

I picked up a scalpel. Not much of a weapon, but all I could find at the moment. I would need to get to our armory. Or should I break the others out first? I'd feel more comfortable with Caedan beside me, but… No. Weapons first. I didn't know where the draconics (or Amaranth) were right now, and if I ran into one of them, I'd need more than a scalpel. And then I'd be able to equip Caedan and the others right away.

Easing the door open, I took a quick look into the hall. When Auric finally showed us the armory's location, I'd laughed. A hidden closet in the meeting room? Really? We'd been right in front of it the whole time. To get there, I would need to move down the hall in plain sight for at least a dozen yards and duck into the meeting room. And a single Crimson Brigade soldier stood just inside that doorway—or at least, that's as much as I could see with my quick look.

I closed my eyes and took a moment to steady myself. The boosts still worked; I could feel the flow through my limbs at a single thought. In addition, I felt a return of part of the glow I'd received from Auric at his death. Hard to believe I still possessed any of that after all this time.

I tossed the scalpel aside. I would get a better weapon from the Brigade. I eased the door open again, sent hard boosts to my legs, and charged down the hall.

The guard started to turn a moment before I arrived, maybe hearing my footsteps. It did him no good. I slammed into him, forcing him into the meeting room. He staggered several steps from the impact and momentum. In that time, I boosted my arms, grabbed one of the nearby chairs, and smashed it over his head. He fell without a sound. Except the chair smashing, of course. And the pieces falling on the floor. And his electrical prod weapon bouncing and rolling away before I could grab it.

And Amaranth clapping.

She pushed away from the wall where she'd been leaning, next to the hidden armory door. "You're so predictable, Beryl. But I'm happy to see they got the implant working. That will make things much easier."

"You can't threaten my friends from here," I pointed out. "It's just you and me." My eyes darted to the side. Where had that weapon rolled to?

"I don't see how that's a problem." Her voice changed slightly as she added, "Stand still!"

This time, I knew what she was doing with the command thing. I could fight it. A good thing, since she followed up her command with a burst of flame from her mouth. A boosted dash to the side saved me. Should I charge her? Or...?

A second flame breath came at me, forcing me to dodge again. Fire rolled across our primary meeting table. Ugh. I liked that table.

For the third burst of fire, I dove over another table. Even so, the heat of the blast warmed my feet. One inch closer, and it would have melted my shoes. I rolled back to my feet, bracing for the next breath. Though the meeting room was the largest in the complex, I still had limited options for dodging around. Eventually, she would catch me. I had to change the dynamic.

I grabbed another chair and threw it at her right as she shot another burst of flame. The chair erupted and fell apart in the air, but it dissipated the fire, giving me a moment to catch my breath. Amaranth was using her powers at a furious rate, between the voice commands and the fire. Since she hadn't been in contact with her source in a long time, she wouldn't be able to keep this up for long. At least, that had been our theory…

"This is pointless!" I shouted. "We can still—"

My legs stopped working.

One moment, I stood poised to run or dive to either side. The next, I collapsed onto the floor. All feeling in my legs vanished. I boosted my arms and struggled to pull myself back up.

"What's this?" Amaranth took a few steps toward me. "It appears not everything is working right, after all." She chuckled and cocked her head. "More work for the men, I suppose. But maybe it'll be easier for them once I burn the flesh from your bones."

"You might… damage it." Yes, it was a lame thing to say, but it was all I could think of in the moment. I could not feel anything in my legs. When I tried to boost them, nothing happened.

I looked up. Red scales rippled across Amaranth's face as she inhaled. In another moment, flames would erupt from her mouth and consume me. I lifted my cyb hand to shield myself. Maybe it could block enough to help me survive long enough to get my legs moving again.

The door to the armory slammed open.

A blast resounded through the room.

Amaranth fell on top of me.

Warmth flooded back through my legs along with boost energy. I shoved Amaranth's body off me even as her blood poured out of the hole in her chest. I climbed to my feet and stared.

Caedan stood in the armory doorway, covered in dirt and grime from head to foot and holding Lainey's smoking rifle. Behind him, Stacy looked about the same, holding a sword at ready.

Caedan lowered the rifle. "So… has your day been as crazy as ours?"

11

I looked down at Amaranth's body, then back at Caedan. "You killed her."

"Is she dead?" Caedan took a step closer.

I took another look. "Yeah. Pretty sure. I mean, I don't think we've seen what happens when you kill a dragon in human form, but... looks like you did it."

"Yeah, I guess I did. Hope you didn't need her for anything else."

"No, no. It's just..." I grinned. "You're a dragonslayer, Caedan."

His eyes widened for a moment before he grinned back. "I guess I am."

Stacy pushed past him. "Yeah, yeah. Whatever." She glared at me. "You told me this place was safe!"

I put my hands on my knees, thought better of it, and leaned against a table instead. "It was. Hand me that sword, and we'll go free the others and make it safe again."

She snorted. "Get your own sword. Or have you forgotten who trained you?"

"I'll get you one," Caedan offered, turning back to the armory closet.

"How... how did you end up in there, anyway?" I asked.

"Do we have to go into this now?" Stacy stalked across the room and peered down the hall. "Why hasn't that enormous noise brought others?"

A good question. Maybe they were used to Amaranth making lots of noise on her own. I glanced down at the body. She would never do that again. I felt a twinge of sadness. We could have continued to work together if her ego hadn't been so strong. She couldn't handle working with humans, I guess, even when it was in her best interest.

"We were on the surface when the fog rolled in," Caedan said, handing me a sword. It was one of the curved blades used by Auric's forces, not the straight blade I favored, but I didn't mind at this point. "We saw some of the red soldiers, but managed to avoid being seen ourselves." He ran a hand through his hair. "A few weeks ago, I persuaded Lovat to show me the air vents he'd been crawling through. Some of them are big enough for me, turns out."

"Barely," Stacy added.

Caedan also took a look down the hall. "I knew where to find the access vent outside. We pried it open and crawled our way down into the armory. I mean, it was a lot worse than that, but it doesn't matter now. The rest you know."

"I had to push him a few times," Stacy said. "And those things are filthy!"

"What were the two of you doing outside?" I wondered.

Stacy and Caedan glanced at each other. "Uh, a story for another time," he said. "But once we free the others, what do we do? I don't think we'll find another base like this one."

"Who says we need a new base?"

Caedan pointed at the guard I'd knocked out. "Unless you intend to kill all of these guys, however many there are, they'll go back and tell everyone where we are. Onyx will find out. And maybe the purple gang too."

"We're not killing them."

Stacy rolled her eyes. "Do you two always talk this much in the middle of a crisis? We need to move here!"

I nodded and took the lead. "There are eleven more Scarlet Brigade and two draconics," I told them. "I think one of them is outside, but I don't know where the other is."

"Auric's hidden apartment," Caedan suggested.

"Good thought. But let's get the others first." I led the way into the hall. We faced a much longer stretch past the medical room, the kitchen, and the stairs to the bunk rooms on the other side. I assumed they'd herded all of our friends into one room to guard them more easily.

Three guards waited on the stairs. They lifted their crossbows when they saw me, but I held up my hand. "Amaranth is dead," I announced. "We don't want to kill you too."

Stacy grabbed my arm and yanked me back just in time. A crossbow bolt ricocheted off the wall where I'd been standing. "Are you trying to get yourself killed?" she hissed.

"I have to give them the chance!"

"Hey!" Caedan yelled past me. "Your dragon lady might not be completely dead. She's bleeding on the floor back here with a hole in her. Maybe you can save her."

"You lie!" came the response.

"Can you take that risk?" I called. "You know where I'm supposed to be right now, and I'm not there. So what do you think happened?"

I heard some mumbling between the three guards. "What proof do you offer?" one challenged.

"We don't have time for this," Caedan muttered. He stepped out into the open, rifle leveled at the guards. "Look, do we want to shoot each other full of holes, or do we want to resolve this like real men?"

I stepped out too, holding my sword pointed at the three confused guards. "Let's go our separate ways, shall we?"

"This is why I don't stay with you people," Stacy said just loud enough for me to hear. "You're all insane."

"Interesting," boomed a deeper voice. From the shadows higher up the stairs, a large figure moved into view. One of the draconics. This complicated things.

The monster looked from Caedan to me. I'm sure I looked impressive with Amaranth's (and my own) blood all over my bare chest. Well, maybe "impressive" is not the right word.

"We have three crossbows aimed at you," the draconic observed. "Assuming that cylindrical device is some kind of projectile weapon, what makes you think that... and your sword"—the word dripped with disdain—"will win the day?"

Caedan pointed at me. "Him. You, at least, should know what he can do. Sure, one of you might take me down while I do the same. But in that moment, he'll shoot forward, dodge whatever comes at him, and take down at least two others. Then it's just you and him, and I, for one, would give Beryl the edge."

"Thanks," I said.

"He's bluffing. He doesn't mean it," Stacy whispered. I shot a glare at her. There was a time and place for that kind of talk. This wasn't it.

"I am Ammuna Red, son of the almighty Amaranth," the draconic said. "You do not intimidate me in the slightest."

"We should," I answered. "I'm Beryl the dragonslayer, and this is Caedan the dragonslayer. Between us, we've killed Incarnadine, Atramentous, and Amaranth."

"And we helped with Caesious," he added.

"We've also killed draconics of all varieties: green, red, black..."

"No gold, though," Caedan said.

"Fair enough." I paused. "Did we kill any blue? I mean, there was the time I crashed Incarnadine into the peace summit. I think some of them died there."

"Enough prattle!" the draconic boomed. It pointed at me. "You will surrender and return to the operating table."

"Hmmm." I twisted my face as if considering it. "No, I think I'd rather prattle some more."

"You're good at prattle," Caedan said.

"Gods," Stacy muttered.

"How about this?" I said before the draconic could say anything else. "Why don't you and I, together, check this room over here. Then you can see whether we're telling the truth about Amaranth."

"And step into whatever trap you've arranged?"

"Do we look like we've had time to arrange a trap?" Caedan asked.

Stacy let out a sigh I was sure could be heard all the way up the stairs. Then she hurried back into the meeting room.

The draconic snorted. "Very well." It pointed at Caedan. "You and my Brigade will remain here."

"Fair enough."

I took a cautious step backward. Ammuna Red descended the stairs and followed me. I led the way back into the room filled with broken and burnt furniture... and one dead dragon lady. I didn't see any way she could still be alive. The pool of blood beneath her body spanned several feet now. But where had Stacy gone?

The draconic knelt beside Amaranth and put a hand over her head. "One by one, they fall," he murmured. "Alas that I lived to see such days.

Mother, you will ever be in our thoughts and hearts."

"All right," I said as the draconic stood. "Now you know. There's no reason for you and your soldiers to stay here any longer."

"Yes. There is."

Despite all of my enhanced abilities, the draconic's backhand caught me completely by surprise.

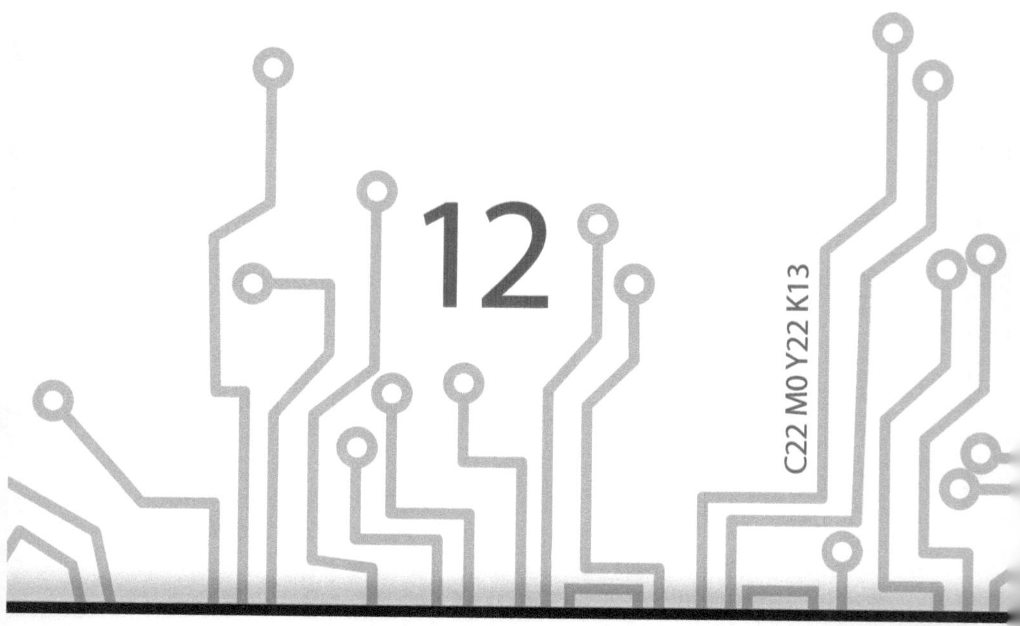

12

The local anesthetic they'd used on the back of my head must have still been in effect or the blow might have ended my consciousness. Even so, the pain of the impact shot through my entire body before I slammed onto the table, slid across, and crashed onto the floor, breaking yet another chair in the process. I struggled to remain conscious, feeling every bruise as they formed all over my body. I'd lost my sword.

"I will tear you limb from limb!" Ammuna Red bellowed. He grabbed the end of the table with one hand and flipped it across the room.

I wanted to respond with something reasonable, something that might give the monster pause for at least a moment. At the very least, I wanted to suggest we talk about this. But my head was still spinning; I couldn't put two syllables together. In fact, my jaw hurt so bad, I wondered if I could speak.

Ammuna Red took a step forward and reached toward me. I back-pedaled on the floor, scrambling for anything I could use as a weapon. I grabbed a chair leg and broke it over the draconic's outstretched hand. It didn't even flinch.

I stared up into its furious reptilian face. My vision blurred, but the focus snapped into place as a sword blade emerged through the draconic's left eye. It made a strangled grunt before falling forward. I managed to roll out of the way in time to keep from being crushed. Stacy rode the beast to the floor, still holding tight to the sword hilt with both hands.

Staggering a few steps, I gasped and leaned against the wall.

"Are you all right?" Stacy got up and stared at me. "That blow would have taken anyone else's head off!"

I opened my mouth and managed to say something like, "I-ar-ow."

She snorted a laugh. "I think he finally shut you up. We'll have to get the doctor to look at your jaw."

I pointed at the fallen draconic with Stacy's sword still through its head. I gave her a thumbs up and clapped.

She glanced at it. "Always wanted to do something like that. Except in my imagination, it was green, not red."

"Hey, what's going on?" Caedan called.

I put my hand to my jaw. Everything still hurt, but it most of all. I gestured for Stacy to lead the way. She blew a heavy breath out. "Right. Guess I have to do the talking now. Well, at least it'll be more intelligent."

I would have frowned at her if it hadn't hurt so much.

"We're coming," she yelled to Caedan as she stepped back next to the body. She yanked the sword free before leading the way into the hall. I gathered enough strength to follow her.

"So." She stepped out into the open beside Caedan, facing the three Scarlet Brigade. "It turns out your draconic was stupid enough to attack Beryl. So now he's dead too." She held up the bloody sword. "We don't mind killing dragons and draconics, but we'd really rather not kill humans. You guys can leave."

I stepped out beside her, trying to look like I was still strong enough to charge them like Caedan had threatened earlier. In reality, I might collapse if I took another step.

One soldier lowered his crossbow. "Then Amaranth is truly dead?"

"Don't believe them!" one of his companions snapped. "The goddess cannot die!"

"You mean like Incarnadine?" Caedan asked. "Or Viridia? Caesious?"

"Amaranth is not like them!" he insisted. "They were weak gods. She—"

"Blah, blah, blah," Stacy interrupted. "Do you know how many times I've heard that kind of religious nonsense? It's old, man. Old and wrong. The dragons aren't gods. And they're dying. One by one." She lifted the sword, and blood dripped from it. "You can join them, or head for home and live. Your choice."

"What about Telipinus Red?" the first one said to the others. "What will he do?"

Right. There was another draconic. All at once, concern for Lainey and the others washed over me. We'd been so busy dealing with these guys, we hadn't gotten to them yet. And according to the scientists, there were twelve Scarlet Brigade. Minus the one I'd knocked out and these three, that left eight still unaccounted for. Oof.

"I am way too tired of this." Caedan lifted the rifle, aimed above their heads, and pulled the trigger. The resulting explosion of sound made everyone jump. One of the Brigade fired his crossbow (probably by accident) but didn't aim it. The bolt skipped off the wall near Caedan and ricocheted down the hall.

"We're not playing games any more!" Caedan shouted. "Now get out of our house!"

The three soldiers turned as one and scrambled up the stairs. They opened the door and then screamed as an enormous white-and-spotted cat burst through. She cornered them and growled menacingly.

"Down here, Glacier," Stacy called. I stepped up and waved to the cat, since I couldn't seem to speak.

Glacier turned and bounced down the stairs to us. The soldiers rushed outside. Glacier came to a stop in front of me. I scratched behind her ear and pointed down the hall toward the bunk rooms.

"Lainey's that way," Stacy translated for me.

Glacier started in that direction, but I grabbed at her fur. "Wai—" I croaked. Ow, that hurt. I almost doubled over from the pain.

"Let me go first," Caedan suggested. He moved past the big cat with a smile. Glacier narrowed her eyes at him, but let him pass.

We found five soldiers guarding the bunk rooms. With the added intimidation factor of the giant saber-toothed cat, they surrendered and left to join their comrades. Stacy made sure they retrieved the unconscious scientists and guard. They also took Amaranth's body, I discovered later.

Where had the second draconic and three remaining Scarlet Brigade gone? Caedan suggested they might be outside, waiting with the vehicle they'd arrived in. I wasn't sure. But we had no time to investigate further or even think about it: the rest of our people were free.

Lainey smashed into me with unusual ferocity. I whimpered from the pain of impact.

"Uh, you might want to avoid his head just now," Caedan pointed out.

"I thought you were dead!" She reached for my face but stopped herself.

Kelly smiled nearby. "I told you not to give up. He has a habit of doing this."

"Also a habit of giving me lots of work," Hunter said. He stepped around to look at the back of my head and made a clicking sound with his teeth. "Lots of work to do right now, it appears. We should take care of that right away."

I couldn't argue. I mean that literally: I couldn't open my mouth to argue without great pain. But before he led me away, I looked at Caedan and made a circle with my finger. He nodded. "We'll make sure they're all gone," he assured me. "Go let him take care of you."

I accepted that and followed Hunter. Fern and Lainey came with us.

Hunter expressed his displeasure at what Amaranth's scientists had done to his medical room and equipment. He immediately assigned the others to straightening things up and bringing him what he needed. As for me, I found myself lying face down on the bed again.

"You will need more than local anesthetic," Hunter observed. "For this, I must put you to sleep. Are you going to complain about this?"

Was he trying to be funny? I couldn't complain, even if I wanted to. In this case, I welcomed the sleep. Too much had happened in the last few hours. I didn't even want to think about it all. And, thanks to the good doctor's drugs, I didn't have to for long.

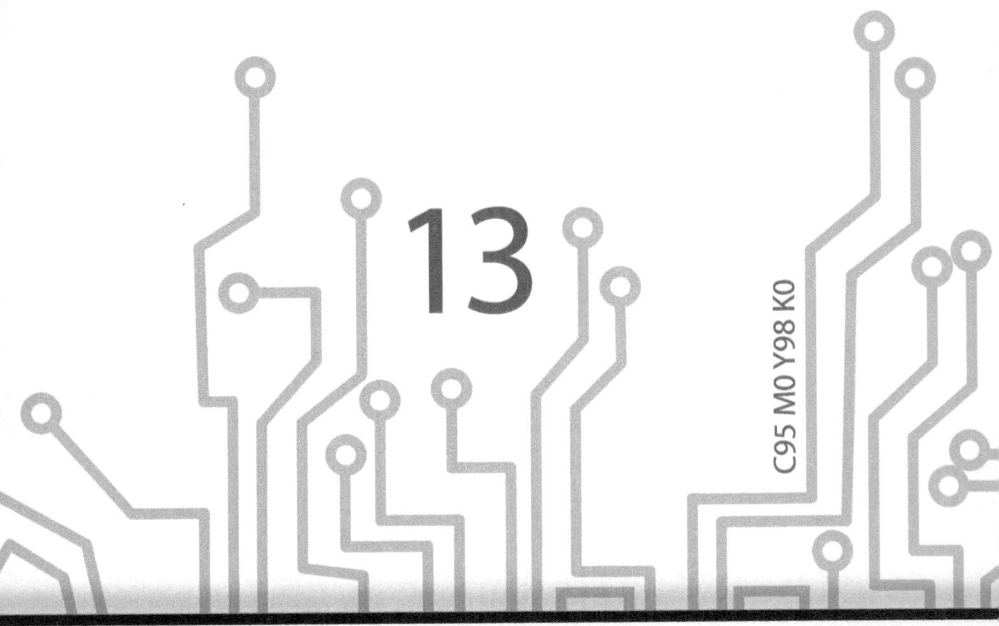

"…not safe…"

"Royal's back, and…"

"Who says that?"

"…Viridians in Caesious?"

"I said it."

"Look, we don't know…"

As my consciousness drifted toward awareness, I heard bits and pieces of multiple conversations. They may have taken place at different times, or all at once. I didn't know. Some things I heard made me want to jump up and take action, but I couldn't even wake up all the way. Stupid anesthetic. Stupid Hunter. Why did he always want me to sleep so much?

To make matters worse, I had trouble breathing right. My mouth wouldn't open as far as I wanted it to, and my nose felt half-clogged. So what sleep I could get wasn't very restful.

I finally clawed my way to full awareness to discover myself still in the medical room. Hunter bustled around, busy with something, while Lainey sat in a chair beside the bed. She smiled when she saw my open eyes. "He's awake," she called.

Instinctively, I reached for my face. Everything about it felt stiff and painful. Hunter caught my hand. "No, no. Do not touch it." He looked over my face. "And do not try to talk, if you can help it. You broke your jaw in two places. I have set it and wired it in position."

"He says you'll have a liquid diet for a couple of weeks," Lainey added, still smiling. Was she happy about my injuries? No, idiot. She's happy I'm alive. I told myself to stop being so negative.

Hunter brought a drink into view and directed a straw into my mouth. I took a sip of cool water. I closed my eyes and let it fill my mouth with its pure wetness. So good. I snorted as I swallowed. I tried to frown and pointed at my nose.

"Ah, yes. The congestion. Your nose was not broken, but a lot of blood came through your nasal passages due to the other injuries. It takes time for it all to clean itself out." Hunter spoke, as always, like this was the most obvious and natural thing in the world.

"I'm sure it won't be easy. The not talking, I mean," Lainey said. "I'll have to be your translator."

I tried to smile back at her, but like the attempted frown, I couldn't be sure what my face looked like. Suddenly anxious that I not be misunderstood, I said, "I'm smiling." Except all that came out was something like, "eh iling." Even my tongue didn't feel right.

"Caedan and Stacy told us what all happened to you yesterday," Lainey went on, ignoring my attempt at speech, either because she didn't hear it or because she was being polite. "I've thanked them so many times for saving you."

That was nice. Seriously. Caedan and Stacy were the heroes this time, not me.

"It is only because of your enhancements that you are not dead," Hunter said. "The draconic should have broken your neck along with your jaw. As it is, you have another concussion. You know what the prescription is for that."

I did. Rest. Ugh. Just when I was getting better. At least my boosts were working again.

"I also repaired the back of your head." Hunter helped pull me into sitting up. My vision swam for a moment. Lainey grabbed my other hand. I blinked a few times and the room stabilized.

Hunter walked behind me to examine his own work. "First, I had to straighten out the metal plate that covers the hole in your skull." He chuckled to himself, probably thinking of some kind of joke involving me having a hole in my head. "It should not cause you problems now, I would think.

Everything is stitched back up but will also take time to heal. All told, your head probably does not feel very good."

No, it didn't. Between the concussion, the jaw, and the two surgeries on the back, my head hurt all over. Probably didn't look very good, either. I thought about trying to ask for a mirror but decided it wasn't worth the effort.

In fact, sitting up no longer seemed worth the effort. I motioned to Lainey to let me lie back down. She helped me and took a step back. "I guess you need to sleep again?" I gave a slight nod, the best I could do.

"That is a good plan," Hunter said. He patted Lainey on the shoulder. "You should go get some rest yourself."

"I'll be back," she promised. I barely heard her as I drifted off again.

And so my enforced rest effectively started all over again. I hated it, but at least this time I had no worries about my implant. At least it worked. Except for when it cut out in the middle of the fight and I lost my legs. I assumed the damage from the bent plate caused the leg problems. Once repaired, that symptom would go away too. Or at least I hoped so.

Hunter kept me in the medical bed for another full day before letting me return to my own room. A day later, we gathered in the meeting room for an overdue discussion. Thanks to the damage from the battle, we didn't have enough chairs. Don repaired one of the broken ones, but the rest were no better than kindling. People sat on the floor or the table itself, in the case of Lovat. He'd learned enough now to be able to walk somewhat awkwardly. I took comfort in that.

Unfortunately, with my jaw wired shut, I had to let others take the lead in the discussion. It wasn't easy. I kept a notepad and pen close to write things I absolutely had to communicate.

"It may not be safe to stay here," Caedan insisted. "The Scarlet Brigade and the rest of Amaranth's draconics now know we're here. They're probably planning to return in force."

"Are they?" Stacy asked. "Are we really worth it?"

Caedan scowled at her, as if her disagreement were personal. What was going on between those two?

"Never underestimate the drive for revenge," Bice said. "The question is whether the draconics can put together enough of a force; that is, whether they have enough humans still loyal to them."

"Draconics rule by fear," Chance said. "We rarely inspire loyalty of any kind beyond that. Without Amaranth to back them up, they may find it difficult."

"But it's not about them, is it?" Kelly asked. "All they have to do is tell Onyx. Or Chroma."

"Would they?" I wanted to ask. Figuring out the connections between our remaining foes gave me a headache.

"They might tell someone else," Royal spoke up. "I saw Viridian Guard in Caesious, and Saxe saw them in Incarnadine too. They're showing up everywhere. We haven't been able to figure out what they're doing."

I tried to frown, but that hurt too. What could Troilus Green be up to now? He might be able to get a larger force together as he could still claim to be Viridia returned or whatever. But his city was the furthest away from us.

"I did tell you I wasn't sleeping outside," Stacy said.

I wrote a note down for Lainey, and let her read it to the others: "I don't think we need to evacuate just yet. Let's set up a way to keep an eye out for approaching armies. It shouldn't be too hard. Stacy, would you coordinate with Caedan and the guys for that? Maybe get some of your contacts in on it?"

"If it means I get to keep my bed, I'm for it."

"And when we do see one, what then?" Caedan asked. "Where will we go?"

I wrote again, and Lainey read: "Auric. It's not far, and we have friends—wait, he crossed that out and wrote… is that acquaintances?" I rolled my eyes and nodded. "Taizong Gold and Captain Tawn. They can help us find a temporary shelter."

Caedan gave me a skeptical look. "They didn't leave here very happy with us."

"But their boss was our friend," Bice said. "They have to respect what he did."

"He saved me," Lovat piped up.

I struggled to write the correct words. I wasn't much good at this. "It's a—what's that word? Oh—contingency plan," Lainey read. "Let's hope we never have to use it, but we have that option."

Bice stood and looked around the room. "Does anyone else think we should leave right now?"

Jaden raised his hand slowly, saw no one else had theirs up, and lowered it again.

"All right," Caedan conceded. "Let's get these things set up, and keep trying to watch what's going on with the cities."

As everyone started to file out, I wrote a note to Lainey. "Start planning a trip over the mountains."

"You need to rest!" she exclaimed.

"I am resting," I wrote, and underlined "am." "But as soon as I'm well enough, I want to make that trip. We need to know what's happening out there."

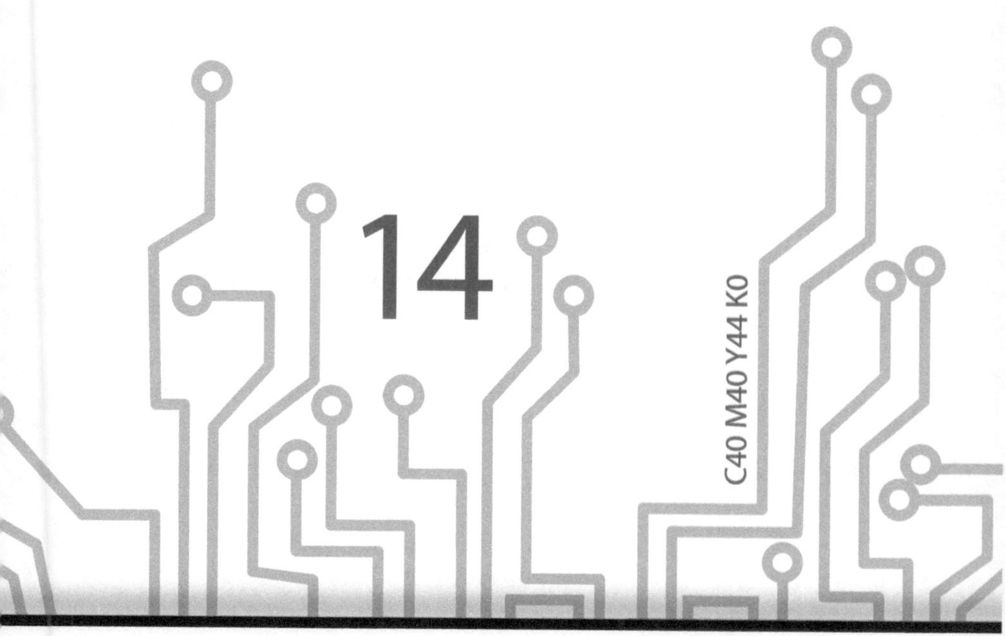

14

Resting. Have I mentioned how much I hate it? I knew I had no choice in the matter. The pain in my head reminded me on a constant basis. Hunter's pain-killers dulled it, but it didn't go away. I tried to add it to all of my other pains that wouldn't go away.

I didn't talk about it much with anyone, but in spite of all the medical help I'd received over the past couple of years, I still dealt with pain from many of the injuries I'd suffered. Every so often, a cough would show up, and I'd taste some of Viridia's poison again. My right shoulder always felt a bit off from the dislocations. Both wrists ached from time to time. I had scars on my head, my chest, and my side. Most painful of all were the burns. They'd all healed by now, but the pain lingered, especially from Onyx's acid burn on my face.

Two weeks passed.

Turq reported seeing work resumed at the tunnel beneath the mountains. The zealots weren't even hiding it any more. I wondered what they did about the enormous dragon carcass blocking the tunnel. For that matter, whatever happened to the other dragon carcasses we'd left behind? I'm glad we didn't have to figure that part out.

I pulled Cobalt into the laboratory one day. "I need your help with something," I told him, setting one of Loden's electric batons and a shock-spear on the table. I could talk a little, but it wasn't pleasant.

"Um… all right. What do you need?"

I'd written this part down: "You're the closest thing we have to a tech guy right now." I pointed to the two devices. "These are our best weapons against the purple robes. The electrical charge disrupts their cybernetic abilities."

"That makes sense. Do you need me to make more of them?" He picked up the baton and turned it over in his hands, examining it from every angle.

"No." I flexed my cyb hand in front of him. "I want to be able to do that without one of those."

Cobalt's eyes widened. "I think… let's see what we can do!"

Lovat's walking improved day by day. "I can't run yet," he complained as I helped him up the stairs one day.

"That will come," I promised. "You'll outrun me before long." With him, I had to talk, regardless of the pain.

He brightened. "You think so? I can't even outwalk anyone now."

"You will. You'll run everywhere."

We reached the last step, and Lovat turned to look at me. "I can run to every city in The Circle!"

"Why stop there? Someday, you'll run outside The Circle!"

He looked out through our open door toward the mountains. "Outside…"

I nodded. Who knew what waited for us on the other side of those mountains? I'd be finding out sometime soon. And if I could do it, Lovat could.

The day for our departure finally arrived. Caedan drove Lainey and I across the Circle to the location between Incarnadine and Atramentous, the same place where we'd once descended from the mountains. As we unloaded our gear from the four-wheeler, Glacier caught up. The cat bounded up beside us, paused to see what we were doing, then continued on her way as if she were the one deciding our path.

"Are you sure about this?" Caedan asked for at least the fifth or sixth time.

"Yes," I said. I looked to Lainey, who rolled her eyes and added, "He's sure we need the information."

"But you're not."

"I'm just not happy about going back there," she answered with a shrug. "But he's right. We need to do it."

"We could still try that tunnel they're building," he suggested.

I made a disgusted noise. He knew how heavily guarded that place would be now.

"We barely got out of there the last time," Lainey said.

"Yeah, yeah." Caedan paused and scratched something on his ear. "Well… we'll keep things going."

"I trust you," I said and smiled at him.

He snorted. "If you survive this, and we're still there when you get back, then maybe you're right." He screwed up his face and looked up at the mountains. "Did that even make sense?"

Lainey and I both laughed. "Not entirely," Lainey said, "but that's all right." She gave him a quick hug. "We'll see you in a couple of weeks."

She estimated our climb over and back would take that long, including a few days on the other side. I thought she might be exaggerating, but I also didn't have the experience of climbing that she did.

I gave Caedan a nod. He hopped back on the four-wheeler and drove away with a wave. I wish I'd said more, but… it hurt.

Lainey and I shouldered our heavy backpacks and started walking. I remembered from our previous descent that the first part of our journey wouldn't be too difficult as we ascended the slopes. It would take longer going up, of course, but we shouldn't run into anything hard until tomorrow, I guessed.

I soon felt the burn in my calves from walking continuously upward, but I'd take that over the blistered toes I'd gotten on the descent any day.

Glacier, when she came within sight, bounced around as if the incline didn't affect her at all. It probably didn't; this was her environment. She'd been born up here. Before we left, I'd asked Lainey if she worried the cat would leave her in the mountains.

"Glacier is her own animal," she said. "I can't control her, but I love her. And she loves me too. She'll probably wander off a lot, but I think she'll always come back." She paused. "And if she doesn't… maybe it's because she found someone, and decided to go have babies of her own. That would be nice for her."

She acted like it wouldn't bother her, but I knew better. Early in our relationship, I'd believed nothing much bothered Lainey. She seemed to adapt to all the insanity in my life with ease. But it wasn't that things didn't bother her; she was just good at hiding it… until she really, really cared.

After only a few hours, Lainey stopped. "We should make a camp here for the night."

I looked around. "Why so soon?" I asked.

She pointed up. "We started too late in the day. I should have thought of that. From this spot up, it should take us around a full day to reach the cave, which will be the next best place to stop for the night."

I nodded. It made sense. I still hated to waste a couple of hours of daylight. But… sleeping up on the rocks would be less fun.

"And you probably need the rest, anyway," she added. I scowled at her and was rewarded with a giggle.

We started up again the next morning before the sun's light even reached us. We picked our way up the rocks with extra care until the light and warmth arrived. Afterwards, we made good time in our ascent, stopping when necessary. While I'd been annoyed at Lainey's suggestion that I needed rest more than she did, I did find myself using a boost every once in a while to keep my legs moving. I guess all of my enforced rest hadn't helped with my own stamina.

Right as the sun began to disappear for the night, we reached the cave. Nothing about the area looked familiar to me, but Lainey recognized everything. She led the way along a narrow path and ducked into an entrance I never would have seen without her help.

"Here we are," she announced in an almost giddy tone. "Back again!"

"Back where we met," I said.

She shrugged. "Technically, we met down that way"—she waved back the way we'd come—"where you crashed into the mountain."

Right. I missed that flying machine. It would certainly have come in handy for getting over these mountains.

Lainey grabbed my hand. "But this is where you woke up and met me."

I smiled back at her. "Good times."

She let go of my hand and pulled out a flashlight. "I think we left some fuel in here. We can make a fire."

She wasn't wrong. Before long, we had a decent fire near enough to the entrance for the smoke to escape. We huddled up next to each other for warmth and whispered about our memories here and how things had changed since then. It might have been the nicest evening I'd had in months.

The next morning, we started the real climbing.

15

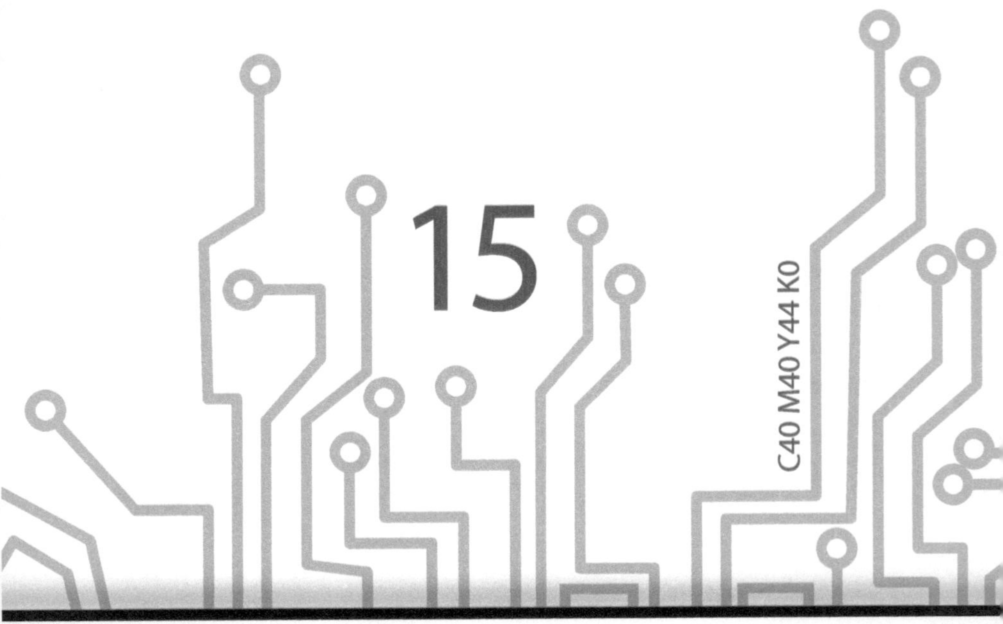

I did not know it was possible to get so cold. Lainey and I had bundled up, of course, wearing thick and heavy clothing over our regular clothes, not to mention the heavy backpacks on top of everything else. And yet the cold air penetrated all the way through. My fingers—the real ones, anyway—and toes felt like they'd never be warm again.

Boost energy could give me a tiny bit of warmth, but it didn't seem right to use it. Lainey didn't have that advantage. Plus, I might need it later.

If that weren't bad enough, the higher we climbed, the harder it became to breathe. Lainey warned me about this confusing phenomenon, but I thought she had been exaggerating. How could air be thinner? It didn't make sense to me. And yet she'd been right. I found myself inhaling deeply and not getting nearly as much air as I usually did.

We'd gone way beyond inclined trails that made the calves burn. We'd gone beyond pulling ourselves up steep inclines. The way up now consisted of literal climbing up and up over a wide variety of rock shapes and sizes. Each new hand- or foothold had to be tested for safety before committing your weight to it. Lainey tied a rope around my waist and tied the other end around her own. If one of us fell, the other would be their anchor. I hoped we never had to use it.

This was so far outside my realms of expertise or knowledge. The climb to Onyx's tower had been a casual hike compared to this. I might as well be blind, following Lainey through absolute darkness. Everything depended on her remembering how all this worked. I never would have been able to do this alone. Fortunately, trusting Lainey was a place where I felt comfortable.

Above me, she pulled herself up onto an much flatter area than we'd seen for hours. She reached back her hand to help me the last bit. I accepted it, though I didn't really need it. We stood up, side-by-side, and caught our breath as best we could.

"Look." Lainey gestured down.

I hadn't wanted to look down in quite a while, but I let my eyes drop at her suggestion. I would have gasped if I could spare the breath.

The mountain we'd climbed took up about half of my view going down, but the rest of it… wow. The Circle spread out below us, a shining glimmer of green surrounded by gray darkness. I thought I could make out at least three of the cities, but they appeared only as darker areas amidst the green.

Even as I stared, a whiteness came across my view, obscuring the green below. I blinked, confused, until I realized: the whiteness was a cloud. We were above the clouds! I looked up and saw clouds higher still, so… not above all of them. Even so… what a strange thing.

Lainey leaned in close to my ear so I could hear her. "Looks so different from up here, doesn't it?" She pointed up. "Not too much further, and then you can look down on the other side."

Now that was something I wanted to see.

Hours later, we crossed over. I had been so intent on the labor of climbing, I didn't even realize when it happened. All of a sudden, I noticed we were moving down instead of up. Lainey had shifted to below me instead of above. I did remember we'd sort of walked through a gap in the rock a while back. A simple move, but momentous in its way.

Annoyance at missing the moment fell away to relief that we'd made it. Then it hit me: we'd left The Circle. I was outside the world I'd known, crossed over into the unknown. It seemed momentous. I wavered for a moment, gripping the rock with my cyb hand to steady myself.

"Are you all right?" Lainey called up.

I looked down at her and nodded. I would have liked to explain, but between the cold and my sore jaw, I didn't want to speak. She nodded back and resumed her descent.

About an hour later (by my best guess), Lainey led us to another somewhat flat area where we could rest and catch our breath. She reached up to my head and pulled her own close to it. "The sun is setting." With those words, she turned my head away from the mountain and pointed to the west.

I almost fell over. I stared at a sunset like I'd never seen before. About two-thirds of the sun remained visible, but it was slipping below... below... flat land. Not mountains.

Seriously, I don't know how to describe how utterly strange this was to me. For my entire life, sunset meant the sun descended behind the mountains. Out here, to the west, there were no mountains, only a flat horizon line so far away it seemed impossible. How could the world be like this?

I sat down hard. My eyes, though cybernetic, watered from staring at the setting sun too much, but I couldn't stop. No barriers. That's what it meant. No mountains meant no barriers. Someone could travel for... how far could you travel out here? How big was the world itself? I had no idea.

Lainey sat down beside me. "I'd almost forgotten how it looked without your mountains," she said, leaning close.

"I never... never imagined," I responded.

"Huh." She nodded, as if she'd just realized how I felt. We sat in silence together for a while, watching the shining ball of fire go down behind that flat, flat line of the world.

"We should find shelter," she said at last. "If I remember right, there's a place not too much further down from here."

She remembered right. We found the place before the darkness overtook us completely. It wasn't much, but we could huddle in together inside an indentation in the rock, almost a miniature cave. Our comfort increased dramatically when Glacier showed up. She curled up in the entrance of the indentation, pressing against us and blocking out everything else. We welcomed her warmth.

I don't know how long we slept there. The sunrise came much later than usual, since it came over the mountain behind us. Glacier left sometime in the early morning, letting the frigid air back in. I never thought I'd miss the cat's presence that much.

Getting to my feet, I stepped outside and looked down. The night before, I'd been preoccupied by the sunset. Now, I looked out over the unfamiliar land outside The Circle. I saw green land like I'd seen inside, but so much more. Some darker green parts puzzled me at first until I realized they were trees… lots of trees. There must have been hundreds and hundreds of them in one enormous cluster. And I saw more than one cluster! I also saw what I took to be cities, small and large, scattered about as far as I could see. One very large one lay almost directly below us.

Lainey appeared beside me and wrapped herself around my arm. "You left, and I got cold," she murmured.

I pointed toward the city below. "Is that where you lived?"

She nodded. "Jennestown. I grew up here, looking up at these mountains and wondering about the other side."

Huh. Imagine that. We'd been looking up at the same mountains from opposite sides.

"It's also where Chroma lives," Lainey added. "When we get lower, I can point out the temple."

I hadn't expected that. Chroma herself lived in a city right next to the mountains? Why hadn't she ever flown over to check on her children? If they'd been able to make the flight over, why hadn't she? We were still missing some key information somewhere; I knew it.

Lainey shivered. "I think we should make some progress getting further down before we eat anything. By then, the sun will make things warmer."

I agreed. Moving would warm us up faster, anyway.

We shouldered our packs and began a new descent, drawing closer, moment by moment, to the home of Chroma, mother of dragons.

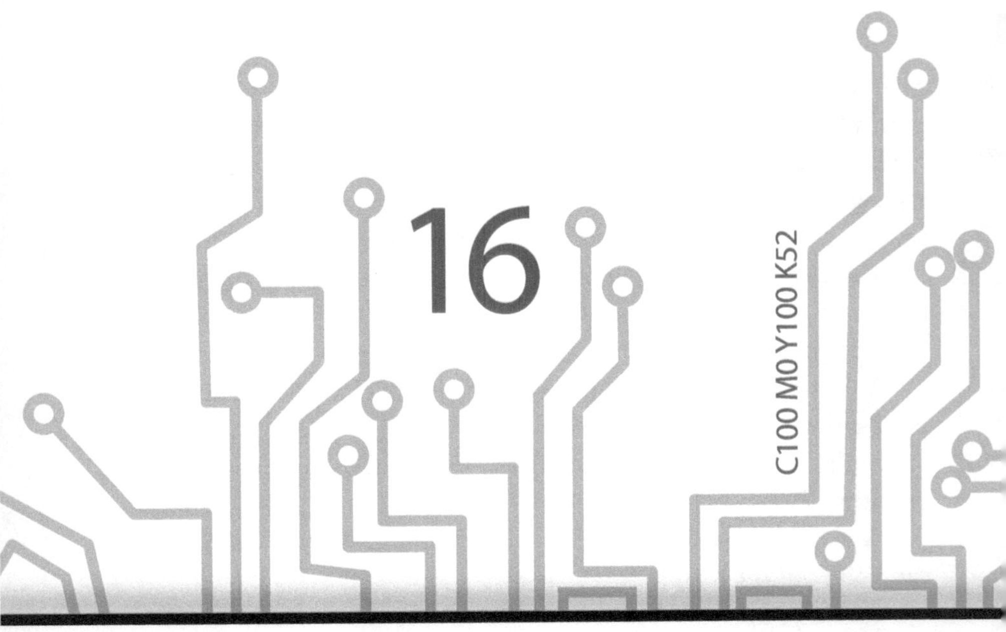

I don't remember much about the descent into the outer world. To be honest, the entire passage over the mountains might have taken far longer than I recall. The endless climbing, the endless cold — it all blended together. I don't even remember how many times we slept along the way.

But one late afternoon, we reached the base of the mountains and removed the outer layers of our clothing. I stared around me at a new world.

In most ways, it didn't look any different from the world I knew. I saw rocks, trees, grass, hills, and in the distance, a city. But everything felt wider, wilder even. Unsafe. I still couldn't get over the long-distance view with no mountains framing the horizon.

"We'll go to my place," Lainey said. "After that, I can show you what you need to see."

Lainey's "place." Her home. Somehow, I had completely put that out of my head. I mean, of course I remembered she came from out here. Her bare facial skin reminded me every time I looked at her. But I'd never thought much about where, exactly, she might live.

"I don't know if I could live here," I said aloud. My jaw still ached when I used it, but I was determined to get back to normal.

Lainey paused stuffing her warmer clothes into her backpack and looked at me with raised eyebrows. "What do you mean?"

I gestured broadly. "All of this… no mountains. No barriers." I screwed up my face, trying to think of how to explain it. "With nothing to stop me, I'd either start traveling and never stop, or… I don't know. Go insane."

Lainey chuckled. "There are barriers, silly. Water. Fences. Even more mountains. The world's a big place, but you can't just go where you want." She frowned. "Especially if you live under Chroma."

"Your travel is restricted." I think she'd told me this.

She nodded and resumed packing. "I have a cousin who lives in Hartland. That's a city about fifty miles to the north." She pointed, but I don't think she quite got north right. "If I want to go visit her, I have to file a travel report and get it approved. It's weird, though. She can come visit us without filing one. It all depends on the direction of the travel, the miles traveled, and so on. Nobody really understands it all." She stood and pulled her backpack on. "You ready?"

I finished up with my own pack. "But your father had special permission to go over the mountains."

"It was an assignment." She started walking, and I followed. "The zealots wanted him to scout things and report back. Apparently, they've done this before, throughout the years, but of course they've never told the rest of us about it."

I looked back up the mountain, thinking about Amaranth's story of the first time she crossed it. I still had trouble accepting that the dragons had entered The Circle, and then never left for a thousand years. Maybe they didn't see time the way we did. My parents always used to say that time went by faster the older you grew. How did that apply to the dragons? Did they turn around and realize they'd lost a hundred years here and there? I smiled at the thought, which hurt my jaw. Ouch.

Lainey led me through some rough terrain until she found what appeared to be a well-traveled path. We followed it downhill, trees multiplying alongside us as we went. So many trees in one place—and so random! Large groups of trees within The Circle were groves, carefully organized and tended for their fruit and lumber production. Sure, we had other trees here and there, wild growths, but nothing like this. And even this paled in comparison to the vast forests I'd seen from the heights. How easy it would be to get lost among such trees!

Many hours later, the path led to the outskirts of the city we'd seen from a distance, Jennestown. Lainey left the path and skirted around the outside, much like we'd often done when scouting one of the cities of The

Circle. I found it amusing that in this society, I would be the one out of place because of the marks on my face. Lainey said some people did get marks on their skin out of their own choice, but rarely on the face. People would stare and wonder at my multi-colored chromark. And it might get back to the zealots sooner than we'd like. I had no illusions we'd be able to hide from them forever, but I hoped to avoid conflict as long as possible.

Glacier joined us at various stages along the trip. Lainey gave her strict orders not to go into the city and to wait for us. I have no idea if the cat understood her, or if she would obey. I never knew what to expect with that animal.

We waited until twilight and then entered the city. In design and layout, it reminded me most of the red cities, Incarnadine and Amaranth, though without the perpetual red coloration, of course. Every color appeared in the decor here, though purple seemed to be a favorite choice. I wondered if it were by choice or coercion.

Lainey took me to an apartment building. It was taller than most I'd seen, at least ten stories, but otherwise I felt almost at home as we entered. We walked through a kind of lobby to a set of elevators. Once we boarded, Lainey pushed the button for level seven. She shifted her weight from one foot to the other several times as we ascended. She fumbled through a pocket in her backpack and withdrew a key.

"Excited?" I asked.

She shrugged. "Nice to see home again."

The elevator doors opened, and we stepped into a well-lit hallway with a patterned brown-and-tan carpet. Lainey turned left and led me to a door numbered 713. She inserted the key, unlocked the door, and we entered her home.

Lainey dropped her pack by the door and rushed into the living area. I found the light switch and flipped it on. The living area was nicer than I'd ever owned, but nothing spectacular. A couple of couches faced each other. A bookshelf stood against the left wall. And one of those strange screens hung on the far wall, like the ones we'd used in Onyx's tower. A small kitchen and dining area lay to the right. Lainey spun around the room and hurried past the kitchen to push through another door. I looked around a few moments more before following her.

This room was dark, though a trickle of light came around the edges of blinds over the single window. A very large bed filled most of the room.

A single night table stood beside it. Another door led to a bathroom on the left. At first, I thought this might be Lainey's bedroom, but then realized: it was her father's.

Lainey knelt beside the bed, arms thrown over it. Sobs shook her. A little confused, I got down on a knee beside her and put my hand on her shoulder.

"I didn't… I knew it couldn't be true, but…" She struggled to control herself. "I still hoped we might find him here."

Oh. Of course. "Um, you know, maybe they're holding him at this temple you talked about. We can try to find him there."

Lainey turned a teary but angry face toward me. "Can you stop trying to find answers and just comfort me?"

I wrinkled my brow, not sure I understood. But I pulled her to me, anyway, deciding maybe I shouldn't say anything else at all. I held her close for a while, letting her get through all the emotions. I guess I didn't have to understand it.

A little later, Lainey showed me the rest of the apartment, which consisted mainly of her own modest bedroom. She also pointed out the pantry adjoining the kitchen: a walk-in closet for food storage and the laundry machines. Everywhere I looked, I saw the familiar with a few oddities. The screen on the living area wall was the biggest such oddity. I asked her about it.

Lainey giggled. "I don't think I'll introduce you to television just yet. You'll never want to leave the room again."

I had no idea what she meant but let it go for now. This was her world.

"What about that device hanging on the wall?" I pointed to a spot next to the kitchen. A rectangular box hung there, with a springy-looking wire hanging down, connected to it in two places. It looked like one of the connections was another rectangular box, smaller and slimmer, attached to the first.

Lainey laughed this time. "That's a telephone. It's like your talkers, but… better, I guess."

"Why does all of your tech start with 'tele'?"

She cocked her head. "Huh. I've never thought about that."

With the dry food stores in the kitchen cabinets, we were able to eat something other than the scant supplies we'd brought in our packs. Though mostly bland, I welcomed a change in our diet. Once satisfied, I looked out the window at the lights of the city below us. So strange to see vehicles moving around on the streets from time to time. Trucks, of course, like I knew, but also smaller vehicles used for transporting people alone. And some people even owned their own vehicles. How insane was that?

Lainey stepped up beside me and leaned on my shoulder. I wanted to ask her many things. After all, it was just the two of us here. We could do whatever we wanted for a while, couldn't we? The rest of the world could wait. I put my arm around her and pulled her a little closer.

But no. I sighed. Bice was right about me: I did have a code I lived by. Some things had to come first.

"Ready to tell me about that temple?"

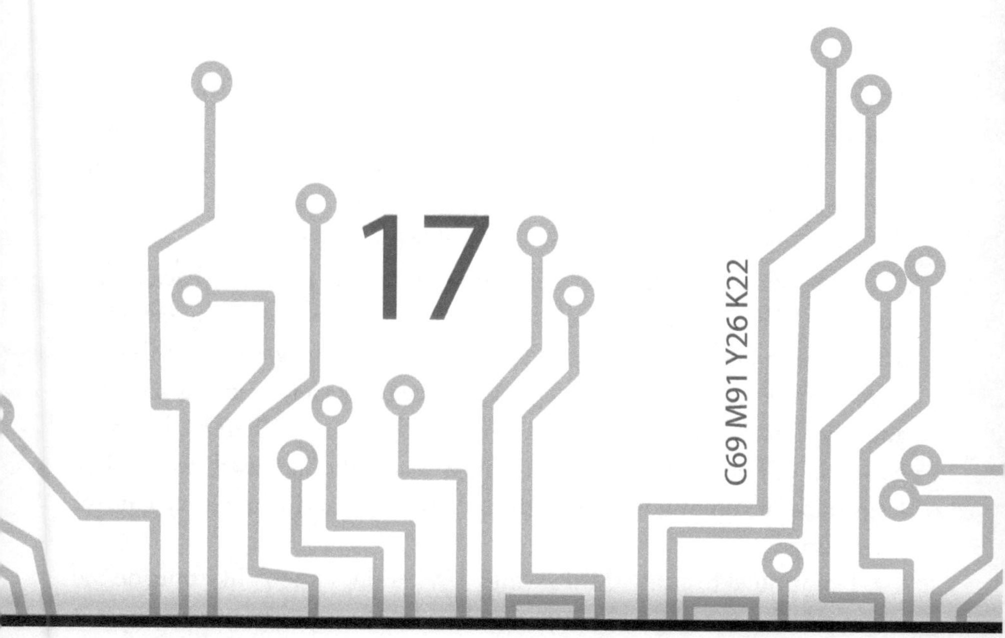

Lainey pulled a large hardback book from the shelf. "This is the easiest way to begin." She brought it to the table and flipped it open. She flipped through several pages until she found what she wanted and turned the book toward me. "Here it is."

I looked down at a large diagram labeled "Chroma's temple complex." "They put this in books for everyone?" I couldn't believe it.

"It's meant to show the glory of it all." Lainey pointed to large blank areas. "But they obviously don't show the important parts."

I looked closer. Sure enough, very little of the complex was actually labeled and explained.

"This first area is the outer court." Lainey leaned over the table and traced the areas as she discussed them. "Anyone and everyone can enter this part. Maybe even you. But it's intended for people interested in giving homage or worship to Chroma. You can meet with a priest—which is one of the zealots, of course—and either give an offering, or accept some kind of assignment to prove your piety, I guess. I never understood that part.

"Now this next section is where the worship of Chroma actually takes place. I've seen photos of this. You've got a huge altar and other religious stuff going on here."

"It's got a roof?"

"A glass one, made of lots of big windows, I guess. Usually only the zealots are allowed in here, but there are some holy days throughout the year where a few ordinary people—mostly rich and powerful—are allowed inside. There's an enormous window behind the altar where Chroma herself sometimes appears to look on her followers, or so they say."

I pointed at the next large area. "So this is where Chroma lives?"

She nodded, and her hair fell into her face. She pushed it back in annoyance. "That's what we're told. Like I said, I've never met anyone who's actually seen her, not even through that window." She gestured at the rest of the temple complex. "But you can also see there's a lot more space here, and my father said there are more levels underground. There's a lot more going on in here with the zealots. This is where they're based, where they keep track of things going on with the rest of us, and where they control everything."

I continued to study the drawings. "What does it look like outside the complex? This is outside the city, right? So are there lots of trees?"

"There's some open space, but then sure, you've got forest further out." She sat back and frowned. "I know you've gotten into the dragon's homes in your world, Beryl, but I don't see how you can do that here. It's too much."

"I don't see how. It's just… bigger."

"The technology here is more dangerous." Lainey paused. "You remember how we could see all the cities in Onyx's tower?"

"Sure. On screens like the one over there." I pointed.

"The zealots… they do more than watch from above. They watch up close too. They have cameras to watch all around their temple. No one can get close without being seen."

It was my turn to frown. I didn't know how all of that worked, but I could grasp enough. "You're saying I can't sneak up to a wall and knock a hole through it or jump over it."

"No." Lainey sighed. "It's late, and I'm tired. We can try to figure something out tomorrow." She stood up. "I'm going to sleep in my own bed for the first time in months." She paused for a very long time before continuing: "You can sleep in my dad's bed. I don't think he'd mind."

I glanced back in the living area. "One of those couches will be fine. A blanket would be nice, though."

Without answering, she went back to the bedrooms, but returned a moment later with a light blue comforter. She handed it to me, and we stood there for another long moment, looking at each other. At last, she broke off and returned to her bedroom.

This whole situation reminded me of the night we spent in Auric, when we met the gold dragon for the first time. She took the bed, and I took the couch then too. Weird how circumstances tended to repeat themselves. I put a pillow on one end of the couch, stretched out, and pulled the comforter over me. After sleeping on the mountains, this was absolute luxury. I fell asleep almost immediately.

I woke once in the middle of the night. I jerked upright, certain I had heard movement. Lainey stood in the kitchen. "It's all right," she whispered. "Go back to sleep." I put my head back on the pillow but kept my eyes open. My night vision kicked in, letting me see her. She stood behind the counter, dressed in some loose-fitting sleeping clothes. She finished a drink of water but didn't leave. She stood there, watching me as I watched her. I smiled a little and closed my eyes.

When I woke again the next morning, Lainey was already up, dressed, and making some breakfast. I stretched and got up to join her.

"Any brilliant ideas come to mind in your sleep?" she asked, pouring me some water.

"Nope. I don't think a single thought crossed my mind." Well, that wasn't true. I'd had thoughts about her, but I wasn't going to say that.

"We can walk around that area later, so you can see it firsthand. But I doubt it'll do any good." Lainey stepped inside the pantry. "I think I'll wash our mountain clothes this morning."

I frowned. I couldn't blame her for being happy about her own home, but she acted as though we weren't under any kind of pressure here. I opened my mouth to say something about it but changed my mind. I could give her a day, I suppose.

Lainey stumbled, trying to get something off a shelf, and almost fell back out through the pantry door. She laughed at herself and shook her head.

I watched her move around. What had that little stumble reminded me of? Oh, right. When Caedan burst out of the armory and shot Amaranth. He looked as though he'd almost fallen out too. But he and Stacy had come…

"That's it." I slapped the counter. "I know how to get in."

Lainey leaned out from the pantry. "What? Are you serious?"

"Your dad said there were underground levels to the temple. We've been living in an underground base ourselves, and we've learned a little bit about how that works."

"And?" She stepped out and joined me at the counter.

"To keep air flowing underground, you have to have openings. That's why our headquarters has such huge vents that Lovat is always climbing in." I pointed up. "And at least one of those vents leads outside. That's how Caedan and Stacy got back inside when Amaranth took over."

Lainey wrinkled her brow. "So you think there's a way to get into the underground levels of the temple with air vents or something? How does that help us?"

"We have to find where the vent draws air in," I explained. "Then we can get in that way."

"What makes you think it'll be outside the temple complex? Why wouldn't they have it inside their own buildings?"

I hesitated. She had a point. But the idea wouldn't leave. "No. I think it's outside. Or at the very least, right at the wall. They need a source of fresh air, not the recycled atmosphere of their own buildings." I snorted. "Especially if there's a dragon in there. I've been in dragon's lairs. You need fresh air. A lot of it."

She still looked skeptical but nodded. "All right. Let me finish up here, and we can get ready. It'll be a lot of walking if we're going to search all around the outside of the temple. Might want to bring some food with us."

"You're so practical."

"One of us has to be, and I've always known you weren't."

I feigned shock. "I'm the very model of practicality."

"I met you after you crashed a flying machine into the side of the mountain!"

"Not by choice!"

Lainey smirked. "You know what they say about first impressions."

"Not really."

She laughed then. At least I could be funny, even if I hadn't been meaning to. I stood up. "Right. Let's get packing."

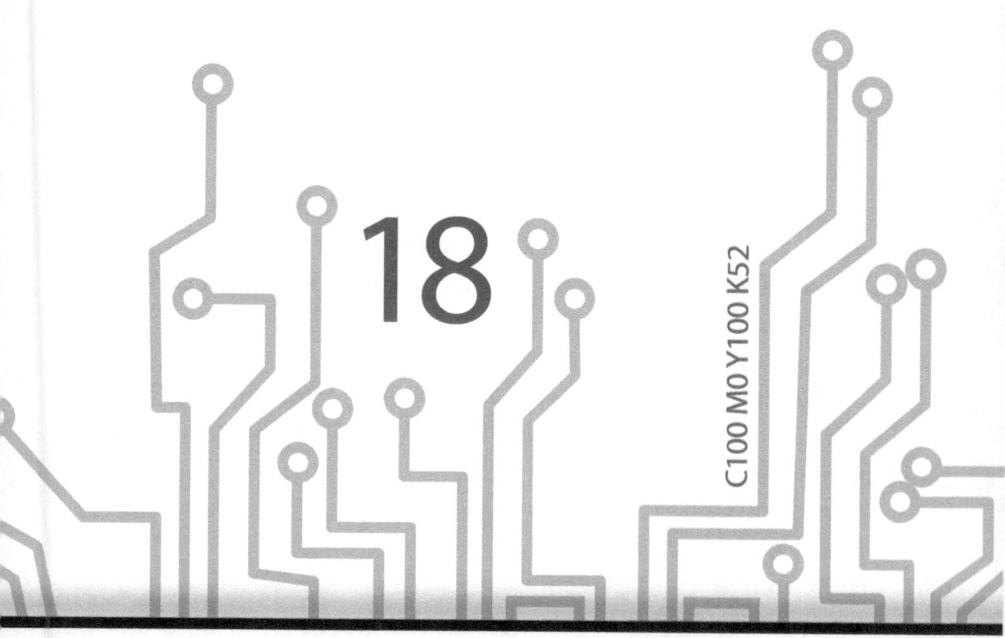

Glacier met us outside the city, even though we came out a different way. I do not understand how that cat figures these things out. Lainey greeted her with joy and rubbed her fur behind her ears. I watched for a moment. Maybe they had some kind of mental connection? Glacier could sense Lainey's thoughts? I don't know. It seemed crazy, but what in our lives wasn't crazy?

Lainey led us down a small incline to another well-used path that led through trees, rocks, and scrub. "This will take us near the temple," she explained, heading down it without hesitation.

"Who uses these paths?" I wanted to know. "Why are they here?"

Lainey grinned. "Kids. I grew up on these trails." She pointed back at the city. "Some people like cities, I guess. They like the streets and the people and places. Not me." She shrugged. "Some of us were thrilled when we found out we could take a short walk and be completely outside the city. It's not like that in other places. But here?" She spread her arms. "We're practically in the wilderness here!"

A loud siren erupted from the city. I froze, but it stopped as quickly as it started.

Lainey laughed. "Except, of course, we're not. We still have the sounds of the city with us." She pointed at a pile of trash next to the trail. "And some people bring the city with them."

"Outside of Viridia, it's farmland," I said. "None of us ever saw any reason to leave the city."

"Not even to go toward the mountains?"

"Nah, there were mines over there. People working. Boring stuff." I picked up a stick from beside the trail and swung it in the air. "But now? I don't ever want to live in a city again." I struck the stick against a tree with a satisfying thwack.

"Where would you want to live?"

"Where we live now. Except not underground. I love the hills." I tossed the stick end-over-end between the trees. "But I probably won't live long enough to do that."

"Don't say that!"

"Why not? It's true."

"No! Stop it!"

I stopped walking. "Since I suggested this trip, you've been telling me how impossible it is. If I believe you, then I have to accept that I'm going to die sooner or later." I knew my words were a little cruel, but I had grown tired of the negativity.

"That's why I didn't want you to do it, you idiot! I want you to live!" She glared at me. "After… after what happened with Amaranth…"

"Yeah." That might be the closest I'd come to dying, multiple times. I took a step closer to her. "Look, I don't plan on dying, but it's been a very real possibility—honestly a probability—since I started this whole thing. I can't even count the number of times I've almost died now."

Lainey looked away but didn't say anything. Glacier looked back and forth between us and cocked her head.

"But I have to keep going, don't you see? I have this reason, this cause, that I'm fighting for. It's so much bigger than me." I touched her arm. "Even bigger than you and me together."

She sniffed. "That's hard."

I took a deep breath and let it out. "Yeah. Life is hard. But it's better than the alternative."

Lainey stifled a laugh. "Idiot."

"You keep calling me that."

She finally turned back to me with a smile. "Only because you deserve it."

"Can we get back to the job now? All this talking is kind of painful."

She gasped. "Oh. Right. Stop talking. Let's get moving."

We set out again. As we followed the trail, I started to notice occasional bicycle tracks. So the kids out here used bikes too and liked using them on dirt, not streets. Interesting. I remembered working in the bike shop—it seemed so long ago now—and one guy who did the same. He worked in the mines, so he was outside the city more than most. He rode his bike on rough terrain all the time, which also meant he came in for repairs more often than anyone else. I told Mr. Brunswick that he needed wider tires. "Wider tires are for children," he told me. I paused at the next set of tracks and bent down for a closer look.

"Wider tires. I knew it."

"What?" Lainey asked.

"Never mind." I got up, and we kept moving.

After a couple of miles, the trail climbed up a rocky slope. At the summit, we stopped and looked down at the temple complex. "You can see almost all of it from here," Lainey said the obvious.

It was even bigger than I'd expected based on the drawings. The book also hadn't shown the outer wall separated from the main buildings and courts. It created an open space of around a dozen yards all the way around.

"I'm going to look closer," I told Lainey and triggered the zoom function of my bionic eyes. I took a brief look at the outer court. A few people milled about, including at least three of the zealots. I moved on, scanning the open space inside the wall. I searched all the way around, as much as I could see from this angle.

"No sign of an outer vent," I reported, returning my vision to normal. "Not within the walls, anyway."

Lainey sighed. "Then I guess we have to search everywhere else."

"Under the trees. It's got to be there."

Lainey looked like she wanted to argue but kept her mouth shut. She led the way down the hill, clambering over a tree fallen across the path. They had so many trees here, some were falling over. Crazy.

For the next few hours, we searched. We skirted around the complex, staying inside the tree line. Lainey stayed closest to the edge, while I moved parallel to her about a dozen yards further outside. We made a slow circuit of the entire place, with no luck.

"I think we need a new plan," Lainey suggested while we took a lunch break.

"We just need to go wider." I downed some water and sprinkled some drops onto my face. With the sun reaching its apex, it got quite warm under the tree cover. No breeze reached in here. It almost made me wish for the cold of the mountain.

Lainey closed her eyes. She wanted to argue; I could tell. But she nodded instead. "All right. We'll swing all the way around in a wider pattern." She looked up at me. "But if we don't find anything, we go back home and come up with a new plan."

"Agreed."

After lunch and a decent rest, we set out again. The scrub brush grew denser further away from the complex, making our passage more difficult. But also, I told myself, providing great camouflage for the thing we were looking for.

Every time I found a more open area, my eyes drifted west toward the mountains. What was happening back over there in The Circle? Was everyone still all right? Would this trip affect things inside or not?

"I hate when you're right!" Lainey called.

I broke from my reverie and turned in her direction. "What?"

"Over here!"

I pushed my way through some bushes and found her and Glacier. She gestured to a concrete cylindrical object protruding from the forest floor. I stepped up beside it and pulled a leafy vine out of the way. At the top rested a metal grate. Warm air blew upwards, and I could hear the sound of machinery somewhere far below.

I climbed on top of the cylinder and tried to look down through the grate. I couldn't tell how deep it dropped.

"We don't have any rope," Lainey said. "Do we need to find some and come back?"

I glanced at the sky. We were at mid-afternoon at the earliest. I didn't want to try to find this place in the dark. "No. I can manage without it."

I took hold of the grate and pulled. It appeared firmly anchored, but with a solid boost to my arms, I managed to tear it free. I tossed it in the grass, where Glacier sniffed at it. A broken shard of concrete crumbled loose and ricocheted its way down the hole. An audible series of clanks echoed back up to us, ending with a rapid series of them, as if it were striking a lot of surfaces very quickly.

"That sounds weird," Lainey observed.

"Yeah." But there was only one way to find out what it meant. I lowered myself down and braced my back against one side of the shaft. With boosts enhancing my limbs, I should be able to descend without falling.

Lainey reached over and took my good hand. "Be careful. I'll wait right here."

"If I'm not back by nightfall…" I looked around. "I don't know. Don't come after me, whatever happens."

I released her hand and began my descent into the darkness.

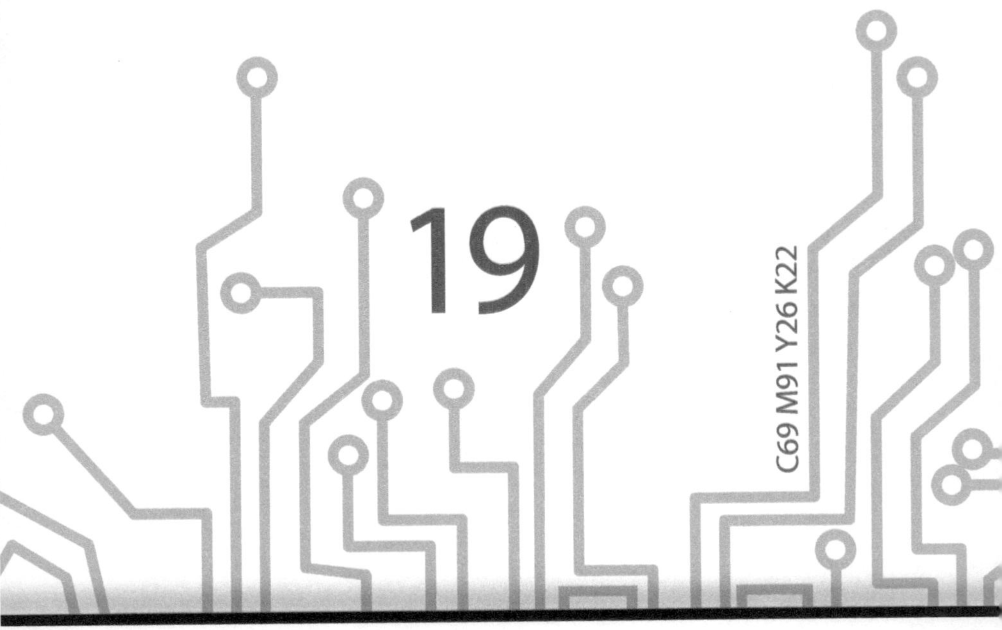

19

I made slow but steady progress downward. Lainey's face looked down at me for as long as we could see each other. Even with the boosts, my muscles soon grew strained. Maybe if we hadn't done all that walking already, this would be easier.

The warm air flowing around me didn't help. I thought it had been warm outside in the sun, but this was much worse. Sweat dripped from my face, tickling my nose.

The sound of machinery grew louder. After a few more minutes of descent, I realized why. My night vision came on as I looked down between my legs. A large metal fan spun directly below me, blowing the air upward and also blocking my descent. That's what had made the rapid noises when the rock fell.

For a brief moment, I considered climbing back up. Maybe we could find another way in. But I was committed now. I twisted myself around as best as I could in the narrow space and reached down with my cyb hand. I closed my eyes and stuck it into the spinning blades.

The impact almost jerked me loose. Frantic boosts kept me from falling. The fan made a horrible screeching sound as I tore through one of the blades and seized hold of the next. Once it came to a stop, I yanked upward and ripped the entire thing apart. A few more yanks tore the rest of it out, leaving room for me to get through. The broken pieces fell a few feet and thumped hard against a flat surface.

I grasped the walls and lowered my feet down to the surface. I tested it with my weight until I could be certain it would hold me, then I dropped down among the debris.

"Are you all right?" Lainey's voice drifted down to me.

"I'm good," I called. The air duct stretched off in one direction, presumably toward the temple. I crouched down and pushed in. It wasn't large enough for me to crawl in a normal position, but I could work my way through it, albeit slowly.

So slowly. After way too long, I wanted to stop and rest, but… without the fan blowing behind me, the air wasn't moving. Combined with the heat, I didn't think it would be wise to stop. I might pass out.

A puff of cool air struck my face. I pushed on a little faster and spotted light ahead. As I got closer, my night vision faded away. Soon enough, I looked down through a vent into an empty room. Literally. I saw a plain white room with no furniture or anything. A single closed door marked the only exit.

I didn't know what to think, other than the room simply wasn't in use. Maybe it would make more sense to keep going and find another room, but I didn't think I could handle much longer crammed up in the duct. It might be all well and good for Lovat, who was half my size, but I couldn't keep this up. I pushed the vent open and dropped down into the room.

I leaned against the wall and slid down to the floor. Wow. That whole process took a lot out of me. A few moments of rest would not be a problem, would it? I sucked in the cool air. Man's ability to make things cold inside a structure had to be the greatest invention in the world. Forget cybernetics.

The door opened. Before I could jump to my feet, a man slipped inside and closed the door behind him.

"I have to admit: this was not what I expected from you," said Carl Roberts.

I slid back to the floor, mouth agape. This was the last thing I expected as well.

Lainey's father looked thinner than the last time I'd seen him, but otherwise healthy. He held a clipboard in one hand and a cloth bag in the other. He chuckled and tossed the bag on the floor.

"There are listening devices in my apartment," he said. "I've known your every move since you and Lainey arrived. Thanks for sleeping on the couch, by the way."

"You're… you're working with them?" It was the best I could manage to say.

He frowned. "Don't be ridiculous. I told you from the beginning that they hired me for the trip to your valley."

"But—"

"But I turned on them. Yes, yes. And they took me back. But they know my value." He tapped the clipboard, and it lit up. Was it some kind of portable screen? "I know too much about their operations to let me go, but at the same time, they need me here to help run things. As it turns out, brain power decays over long-term cloning."

I blinked. "What?"

He scratched his head. "I don't know if I can explain all of it to you in ways you'd understand."

I pushed against the wall and stood up. "Are we safe in here? Do the zealots know I'm here? Do they know about Lainey?"

"No, no. As soon as I discovered they had planted devices in my home, I re-routed the reception so only I received it. They don't know anything about the two of you. Yet."

I didn't understand that part either, but it didn't matter. "You listened to our discussions, but you didn't expect me to show up here?"

"Oh, no. I expected you to show up. I just didn't think you'd have the patience to find the vent and make it all the way through the ducts." He pointed at the opening in the ceiling. "I thought you'd give up and try a more direct approach."

"Would that have worked?"

"Of course not. They would have swarmed you right away, and you'd be a prisoner now, if not dead."

Yeah, probably true. I wiped sweat from my face with the tail of my shirt. "So, where are we in the complex? Can I get further in?"

"We're in the lower levels, of course. Restricted to the zealots and their forced employees, like me. And no, you can't get further. You should climb back up that vent and leave."

I raised my eyebrows. "I didn't come this far just to turn around."

"No, I don't expect you would." He sighed. "But I had to try. Here."

He kicked the cloth bag over to me. "If you're going to move around here at all, you need to look the part."

I picked up the bag and reached inside. "Seriously?" I pulled out a purple robe.

"I'm a bit surprised you didn't bring one with you," Carl said. "Didn't you get one or two from that fight outside the tunnel?"

"We had one, but I didn't think of bringing it." I pulled the robe on over my clothes. "Does this mean I'll be able to turn invisible like they do?"

"No." Carl pushed something on his little board, and a brief rush of cold air surged around me. The edges of the robe began to move about on their own.

"You can control this thing?"

"All of the robes—indeed, all of the zealots' powers—are controlled from here." He waved his board. "Not with this, of course. I can only do some things with the one you're wearing. Pull it further to hide your face. That's it. The good news is: you're close in size to the clones, so you won't arouse immediate suspicion. But if anyone gets even a partial look at your face, it's all over."

I adjusted it a little further. "I can barely see," I complained. "How do they do that?"

"Eh. Who knows?" Carl reached out and adjusted the flow of the robe over my shoulder. "I think they look at the ground far too much. Now. As we go, do not walk behind me. You're one of the elite here, one of the chosen ones. Walk beside me at the least, and ahead of me if it's obvious where we're going."

"Where are we going?"

He took a deep breath. "This may be insane, but… I think I've discovered the biggest secret of all. The full truth about Chroma."

"Then let's get moving. Lainey is waiting for me."

"Yes, she is." He nodded. "All right. Try not to speak out loud. I'll do all the talking, which is fine. It will look as though I'm explaining some things to you, which is what I do around here a lot. Ready?"

I nodded.

Carl opened the door, and we stepped out into the temple complex.

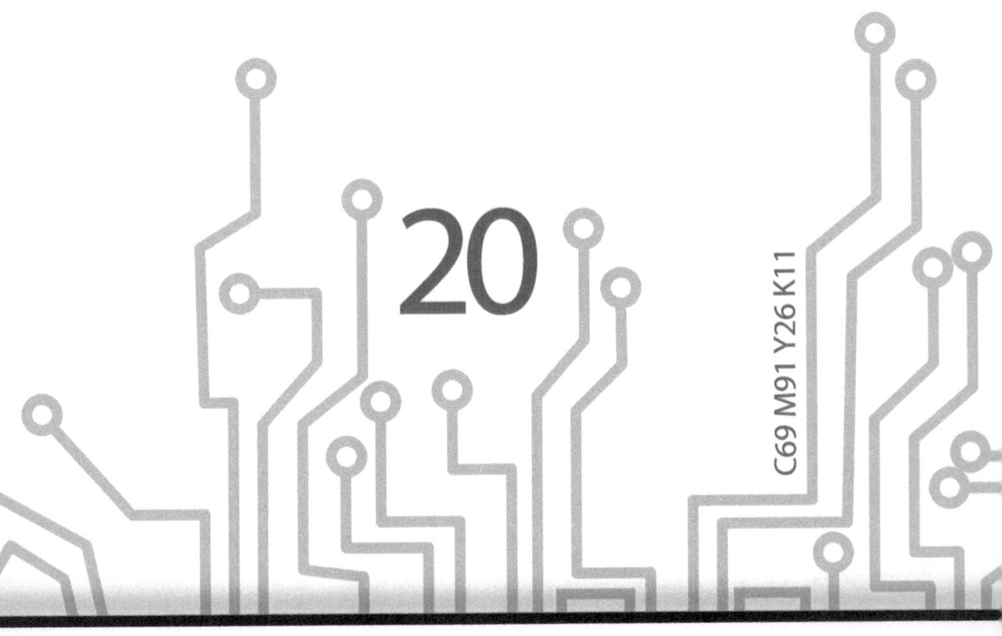

20

A hallway. Somehow, I'd half-expected something else, something bizarre and unusual. But no, it was a hallway, like all the hallways in all the buildings. But I mean… what else could it be? I suppose you could design a building without hallways, in which every room connected to another room, but…

"To the right," Carl said in a quiet voice.

I abandoned my ridiculous no-hallway thoughts and followed this one to the right. I stayed just ahead of Carl and tried to look like I knew where I was going.

"These lower levels are devoted to keeping the zealot program running," Carl explained, continuing the quiet voice. "Most of the rooms in this immediate area are just storage, but there are a few labs too."

"How did I happen to find an empty one?" I whispered.

"Once I understood your plan, I checked the schematics, figured out where you were likely to come in, and cleared the room myself. Take a left at this intersection." We turned and kept going. "I thought an empty room might be enough to get you to stop there, rather than keep searching for something interesting."

I would have stopped even if it hadn't been an empty room, but I wasn't going to admit how much of a struggle I'd had inside the duct.

"Now down here is the interesting part. See those double doors ahead on the right? Let's go in there."

I turned and pushed open one of the doors. Carl did the same beside me. Together, we entered an enormous chamber. We stood on a balcony overlooking… a lot. Stairs led down on either side of us to a chamber filled with what looked like large glass canisters along both side walls. Each of the canisters held a human being: a man, hairless and floating in some kind of liquid. Purple-robed zealots moved about or worked at more of the screens set into desks.

"This is where new zealots are born," Carl said. "Or grown, more precisely."

"This is insane," I murmured. "You can't grow people like this."

Carl pointed to the far end of the room. A single canister stood upright there. The figure inside this one was harder to make out, though I assumed he was the same as the others. A darker and thicker liquid filled this canister. A number of tubes ran into the canister. Some appeared to be fastened to his body.

"That's the original, the first zealot, the prime servant of Chroma. From what I can tell, he's been in there for hundreds of years. They couldn't accept losing him when he grew old, so they put him in here and began experimenting until they perfected the cloning process." He snorted. "Perfected is probably too strong a word. It still has a lot of problems."

"Why did they want copies of him? What made him so special?"

"Total devotion to Chroma and unprecedented physical capabilities. He was her prime servant, as I said. They didn't want to lose him."

Something clicked in my head. "You keep saying 'they,' not 'she.' Was this all Chroma's idea or someone else's?"

"Yeah… that's where we get into the big secret. I'm—" He broke off. "Don't look now, but two of them are coming this way. Quick. Pretend you're angry with me and storm out. Go right in the hallway, and take the first door on the left. Wait for me there."

I threw up my arms and then pointed at Carl, shaking my head. I turned and slammed the door open. Even as the other two approached Carl, I hurried down the hall and did as he suggested. The door he specified led to a maintenance room full of cleaning supplies. I waited anxiously for at least five or six minutes.

Finally, Carl opened the door and joined me. "Whew. I had to come up with a really good story for why you were so angry. I think they believed me."

"Do I want to know the story?"

"Not unless you want me to explain what DNA sequencing is."

"That depends. Will it help us kill the last dragons and free everyone?"

Carl laughed. "Nice to see your hard-core focus hasn't changed. But no. It wouldn't help that particular mission, unless you don't mind it taking a few generations."

"I'd kind of like to be done a little sooner than that." I frowned and pushed the hood off my face. "Look, you're the one who first filled my head with wanting to free everyone. You told me about a fight for freedom out here, about how what I did back in The Circle could help with things here… although at the time, you left out everything about the mother of all dragons being in charge."

"I know, I know." Carl sighed. "You were about to give up, after what happened with the black dragon. I had to give you new motivation." He gestured toward the door. "There is no fight for freedom out here. Not an organized one, at any rate. The zealots rule all. No one can stop them."

"Then why are you even showing me all of this?"

He shrugged. "Maybe I'm getting stupid in my old age. Or maybe it's because my daughter likes you. But I'm willing to give anything a shot now."

"You and Lainey keep saying they rule everything. How far? How many cities are under their control? Could there be even more cities out past theirs, where Chroma doesn't rule?"

He looked at me with one lowered eyebrow and shook his head. "Sometimes I forget your total ignorance of world geography."

"What does that mean?"

He made a vague sphere-shape with his hands. "Look, if the entire world is like this, your valley, The Circle, it's…" He held his thumb and forefinger as close together as he could without them touching. "It's about this size. There's so much more out here."

I still had a hard time grasping it.

"Chroma and the zealots rule all of this continent. That's a land mass, surrounded by oceans. Water, that is."

I stared at him. "So… are there other land masses?"

"Yes. And other people. But they keep to their side of the world, and we keep to ours."

"Are they ruled by dragons too?"

"No." He screwed up his face. "At least, I don't think so. Not that we've ever heard, anyway." He glanced at the door. "We should move on. Pull your hood back up."

"This thing is hot," I complained, but obeyed him. Carl smiled and pushed a button on his little screen thing. Another burst of cold air hit me all over, within the robe. That was handy.

"I showed you this part first for a reason," he explained as we left the maintenance closet. "This part of the complex is down here, underground, for a reason. If, for some insane reason, anything happens up top, they can still make more zealots and keep things going."

So to stop them, we'd have to take out this underground area too. Or… "What if we just got rid of the prime servant?"

"That would slow them down, for sure. But I suspect they could keep going, at least for a while. The new clones might not be as… stable as the current ones, but they could probably keep it up. There are stairs at the end of this hall. Go up."

We passed by a large mirror on the wall. I paused and had to admit my cyb robe looked pretty hue with the way it moved around on its own. "So you said you're controlling this robe. Do all of the robes have a controller like that?"

"Let's keep moving. I've programmed the one you're wearing, but the rest have a central control mechanism."

"Now that sounds like something I want to see."

He snorted and started up the stairs behind me. "That's where we're going next."

The stairs continued up two levels. "I'm assuming we're going to be in one of the areas the public isn't allowed within?"

"The stairs lead to the primary temple, where some people are allowed from time to time."

I stopped at the top before I opened the door. "Isn't that where they have the giant window into Chroma's domain?"

"Yeah. You might just be about to see Chroma herself." He reached past me and pushed open the door.

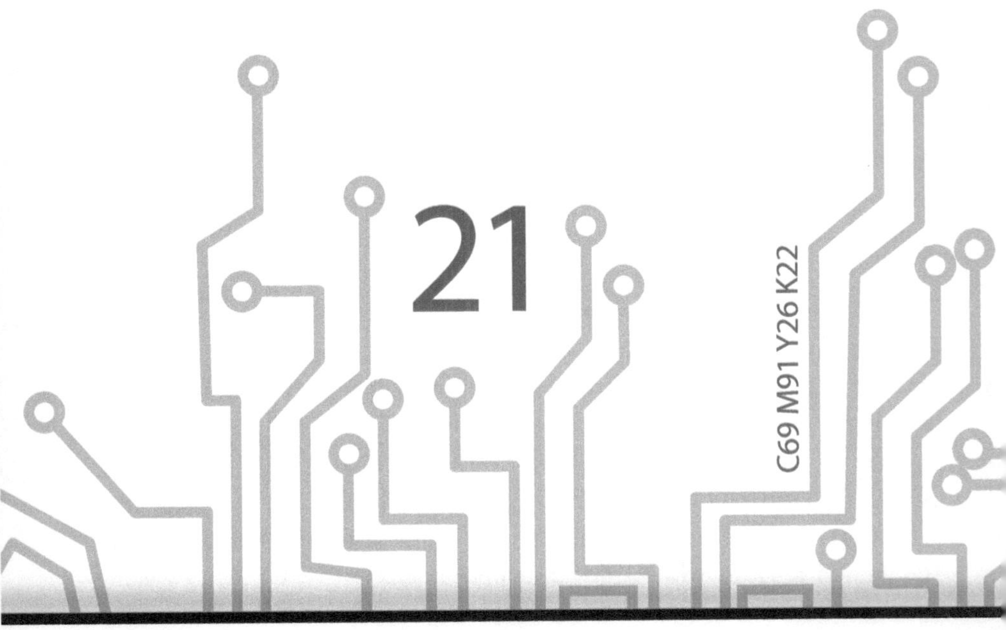

21

The setting sun cast an orange glow into the purple-bedecked temple in front of us. The light came through that vast, arched ceiling of windows Lainey and I had seen on the diagram. To the right, I saw a series of enormous, ornate doors, leading back into the outer court. To the left, I saw the altar, and beyond it... the window.

Calling it a window wasn't accurate, though I could see why people would. In reality, it was an entire wall of windows, maybe three dozen or more. Through them, I could see a purplish haze, consisting of mists of black, gray, and various shades of purple. It reminded me of the green haze I'd experienced in Viridia's lair. As I watched, something else moved within the mists. Something enormous.

"Did you see it?" Carl asked.

"Something is there. Is that the best view people get of her?"

"Your bionic eyes have a zoom function, don't they? Take a closer look at the window."

I lifted the hood enough to get an unobstructed view, then zoomed in. I wasn't sure what Carl wanted me to see. The various panes of the windows were rectangular with black trim between them. The light from the setting sun reflected off some of them, making my job more difficult. I squinted and scanned back and forth. I didn't see...

Wait. One panel on the top left drew my attention. It flickered, as if...

My vision snapped back to normal. "They're not windows, are they?"

"No. They're screens. Pull your hood back in place." Carl pointed as if he were explaining something to me. "It would take a whole bank of cameras to create that montage, or maybe not. Maybe it's not cameras. Maybe it's fake."

"What are you saying?" I still struggled with the basic concepts of screens anyway.

Carl kept pointing, but turned to look at me. "I'm saying that's not a view of what's inside Chroma's lair. Or if it is, it's a view from a long time ago. I don't think she's in there at all."

I took that in for a moment. "Where would she have gone? Is there another temple, maybe, in one of the other cities?"

He shook his head and lowered his hand. "No. This is Chroma's dwelling. This is her temple. This is the central hub of the zealots for the entire continent. If she's not in there… maybe she never has been." He shrugged. "I wondered that, at first. But then I saw your dragons, and they must have come from somewhere. So maybe she's real, but she left long ago. Maybe she found her own valley somewhere and started over."

"Or maybe she's dead," I said. I'd been wondering that for some time now. Lainey said no one had seen the mother dragon in years. Amaranth's drunken story seemed to imply she didn't have the same kind of power source as existed within The Circle. Without one, how could she have survived for a thousand years? I explained my thoughts to Carl.

He rubbed his chin. "I don't know. Your dragons have also been using cybernetics to keep themselves alive, and our tech is better than yours in that regard. And then there's the whole cloning possibility."

"You think they may have… made copies of Chroma?"

"I'm sure they've tried. Whether they've succeeded or not, I can't say." He looked around. "Come this way now."

We walked across the open space beneath the glass roof. "See that door ahead on the right? Lead us there, and brush one of the tendrils of the robe against the panel beside the handle." Two other zealots came in our direction. Carl pointed at his screen and launched into a discussion about electro-magnetism, I think. I couldn't follow it. He stopped as soon as they'd moved past hearing range.

I followed his instructions at the door. When I waved the tendril against the indicated spot, I heard a loud click. The door swung open, leading to a small room with nothing more than another door opposite this one. Curious.

"I've only been in here a couple of times," he said in an even lower voice than usual. "And only with a zealot escort."

"But you know where to go?"

"I've looked at the schematics, I told you. Not the ones they put in books for the common people. The actual schematics they use for themselves. Let's go to that second door up ahead. Open it the same way."

I repeated the tendril maneuver and opened the second door. We stepped into a large room that stretched off to the left, while we stood at the right wall. If the "window" were true, Chroma's lair was behind that wall. But I wasn't thinking about the lair as I looked at this new room.

Technology like I'd never seen covered every bit of the room, leaving narrow pathways between which walked zealots and a couple of other men in white lab coats. "What is all this?" I breathed.

"This is where they control all the robes," Carl said. "All of them are linked to this room. In simplest terms, the robes themselves are way too small to contain all the tech needed for what they do. When a zealot activates his robe to attack someone or 'turn invisible,' as you call it, the robe sends a signal here. And all of this here"—he gestured at everything—"enables it."

"And those signals are strong enough to reach through the mountains?"

He paused. "They didn't used to be, which is one of the reasons I was sent over there. But they've planted boosting towers along the way, and with the tunnel now complete—"

"The tunnel is done?" I interrupted.

"They finished making the final connections last week. It's not completed enough yet for full train movement, but it will be in a few days."

Fewmets. I clenched my fists. "We'll have to do something about that now. We can't allow them to have that much access to The Circle."

"Are you serious?" Carl looked around before escorting me back outside to the room between the two doors. "After all you've seen? Do you honestly believe your little band has a chance against all this?"

"Maybe. I'm getting new ideas the more you show me. We could start by finding and taking out those boosting towers you mentioned. Without their robes, they—"

"They'll just send in regular military. The zealots are only the forerunners to all the rest." He shook his head. "You can't fight an entire continent, boy."

"I don't have to." I pointed back at the tech room. "You said it yourself. They control everything from here. We just have to take this place out."

"And how would you do that? Charge around here with your cybernetics and tear stuff apart?" He waved his hand around. "You're good, Beryl, but even you can't fight everyone here. And once they stop you, they'll repair the damage you did."

"I'll figure out a way." I knew I sounded stubborn, but I couldn't think of anything else at the moment.

Carl rolled his eyes. "You can't—"

The door opened behind us and two zealots entered. Carl shifted into a different topic at the first sound of the lock: "The drives on bank three are starting to degrade with age. We need to shut down that entire bank and replace them."

One of the zealots paused. "That sounds serious," he said in that weird voice they all possessed. "Will it compromise any of our agents at long range?"

I folded my arms and tried to look serious myself.

"It won't be a problem if we take care of it soon," Carl answered. He gestured to me. "I was just seeking the proper permission to initiate the project."

The zealot glanced at me then inclined his head. "Carry on." He and his partner moved on into the tech room.

"What if they'd asked me a question?" I whispered.

"Then we'd be in trouble. But it's not likely. They generally don't like conversation if they can help it." He watched the other two to make sure they kept moving. "All right. We should move on from here to avoid any more attention."

"Then there's only one more thing I need to see."

Carl turned to look at me with eyes narrowed. "What do you mean?"

"I need to see Chroma's lair."

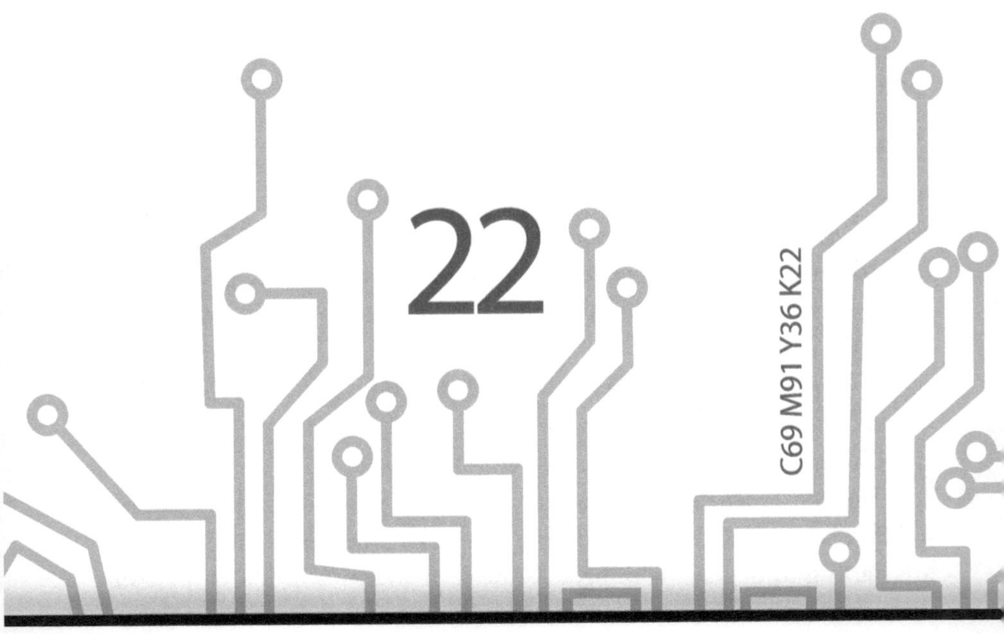

"I can't get you in there," Carl protested. "No one goes in there."

"Someone does. The highest-ranking zealots, maybe?" I opened the door back into the tech room. The two zealots who'd passed us continued off to the left side. How did they tell rank apart, anyway? They all looked alike and dressed alike!

"No one," Carl repeated. "I've never even heard of someone getting in there. Come on. We should leave this room."

I pointed across the room. "Where does the door go on the far side?"

"I don't know. I've never been through it."

"Guess I'll find out on my own." I took a few steps into the room.

Carl reached out to grab me, but stopped himself. That would look awkward. "If your robe doesn't have access, you can't even open it!" he hissed.

"Then I'll break the lock. I didn't come over those mountains and through that stupid vent to turn around now."

Carl hurried to keep up with me as I strode between the tech stuff. "This! This is insane! Why do you always behave this way? You're going to get us both killed!"

I stopped and pointed back toward the door. "Then you should go back and wait for me. I'll join you back out there around the altar when I'm done."

"You're not going to be able to get in." His shoulders slumped. "At least you won't get me or Lainey killed with you. Fine. Go ahead."

"I'm getting you out of here too."

"No. No, you're not. Farewell, Beryl."

"Wait for me," I repeated. "I'll be back."

Carl and I went in opposite directions. I strode confidently to the other side of the room without pause or looking back. I brushed a robe tendril over the door panel, just as I'd done on the previous ones. I'll admit being surprised when the door opened for me. I stepped through and found another hall that took an immediate turn to the left. I wanted to go right. Maybe Carl was right, or maybe the entrance to the lair was actually in the underground level.

But that made no sense. Carl and the other humans worked in the lower levels. They weren't allowed in this area; therefore, the lair entrance had to be here somewhere.

I followed the hall. It turned right after a few yards and stretched straight ahead for a long way. To my frustration, I saw doors only to the left. At the very far end, I could see a right turn, so I hurried on that way. I passed another zealot who didn't even take a second look at me. In some ways, the robe made this far too easy. Then again, without Carl and his ability to turn the robe on, I would never have been able to do this.

I made it to the end, which probably came close to the back corner of the complex, and turned right… only to see another long hall stretching ahead. Except this time, I saw one door to the right, only a few feet away. I hurried to it and tried the panel and handle. This time, the robe failed me. Nothing happened with the tendril. I tried a couple more times with no luck. I checked around to make sure no one else was near, and then I jerked the handle with a boost to my cyb hand. It broke open much easier than I anticipated. I braced myself for some kind of alarm but heard nothing. I stepped inside and pulled the door shut behind me.

I don't know what I expected to find, but a fully-furnished apartment was not on the list. I walked through a living room/kitchen combo. Everywhere I looked, I saw evidence of occupation: dirty dishes in the sink, a well-worn spot on the recliner's seat cushion, etc. It looked like… two people? I caught a glimpse of a bedroom through a partially-open door. I peeked through and saw two single beds. Interesting. One heavy door remained in the living room, looking out of place with the rest of the decor.

I pulled it open and found stairs going down. The stairs weren't lit up, but a purplish light spilled in from an open door one flight below. That seemed promising.

As I descended, I heard voices, two of them. I paused and listened.

"…I'm just saying."

"And you're saying wrong. A beach is superior to a mountain in every way. You can get a tan at a beach. What are you going to get on a mountain? Frostbite?"

"Climbing a mountain is an adventure. The only adventure on a beach depends on whether you can swim."

"It's not like you or I will ever see either of them up close, anyway." That voice definitely sounded grumpier.

"Don't be like that. How else are we supposed to waste our time here?"

Who were these guys? With no other obvious course of action, I decided to walk right in.

Two middle-aged men sat with their backs to me. They faced two screens like the television in Lainey's apartment. One of the screens appeared filled with text like a book, but the other one showed the same kind of swirling haze as the "window" in the temple.

My appearance must have also cast a reflection on the screens, because both men spun out of their chairs and stared at me.

"It… it isn't time for an inspection," the one on the right said.

I stared at them through the folds of my hood. Neither man looked like a soldier of any kind. Both seemed a little pudgy, in fact.

"Everything is normal," the other man added. "We haven't had any mishaps or, or problems in weeks."

"One of the monitors has a little flicker to it," the first hastened to say, "but it isn't noticeable unless you're looking for it."

They stopped talking and stared at me. My continued silence confused them. I considered for a moment and let out an exasperated sigh. I ripped the hood back, exposing my face.

Their eyes widened. "Wh-who are you?" one asked. The second stepped back within reach of his screen and the devices attached to it.

"I'm here to learn the truth," I told them. "You have nothing to fear from me."

"Why is your face painted?" The same man kept asking questions. The other watched nervously. "Why are you wearing one of their robes? And how are you doing that?" His eyes swept over the robe. "It's operational. That shouldn't be possible if you're not one of… them."

"I'll answer your questions if you answer mine," I challenged. "What are you doing in here?"

"We keep the window running," he answered, as his companion exclaimed, "Don't talk to him! He's an intruder!"

"So everything on the window is fake. I thought so." I stared past them at the haze on the screen.

"You have to answer my question now! Who are you?"

I looked back at the men. "My name is Beryl. I'm from the other side of the mountains."

Both men laughed. "There's nothing on the other side of the mountains!"

"We thought the same about this side," I told them. "Why do you fake the window? Why can't people watch Chroma's lair?"

"See for yourself." The man gestured to a door to my left. I hadn't noticed it at first.

"He can't open it," the other man said. "No one goes through that door. They use the other one."

"Well, this is the one I've got now," I said. I stepped toward the door and paused. "You guys live here. Why?"

"We're… not allowed to leave. Anyone this close to the lair is here for the rest of their lives."

That struck me as incredibly sad. I pulled the hood back over my face and tried the door. It was locked.

"Told you," the man by the screens muttered.

I used a boost and my cyb hand to break this lock too.

"What the…?"

I opened the door to a blast of frigid air and stepped out into the lair of Chroma, mother of dragons.

Before me stretched an enormous room, lit by dim lighting and devoid of anything except… a massive skeleton.

Chroma, mother of dragons, was dead. And had been dead for a very, very long time.

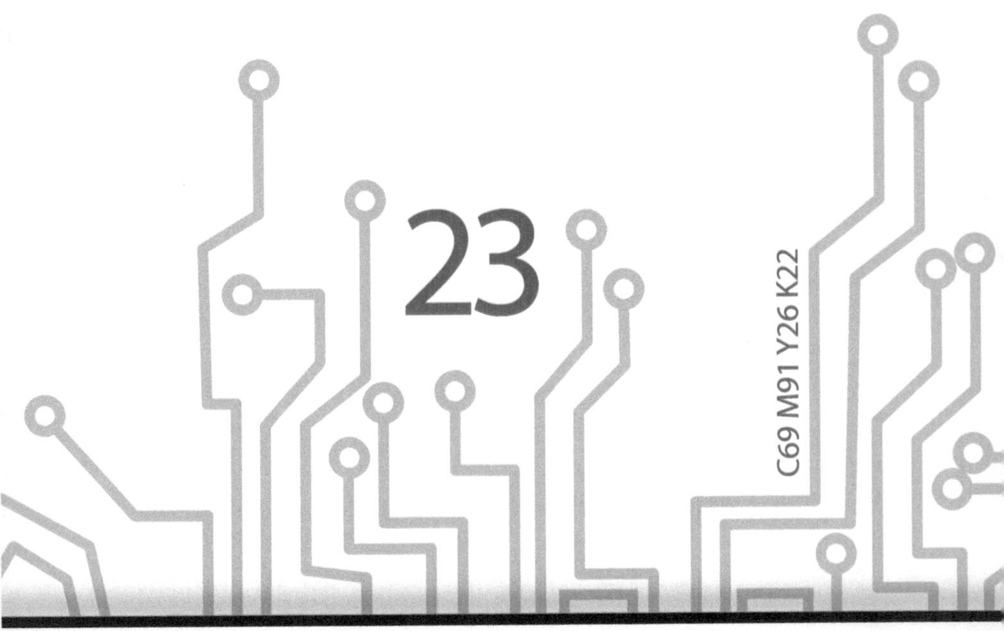

I'd been expecting this, based on everything we'd learned so far, but still… I stood in shock for a few moments. The truth of the revelation washed over me, triggering so many thoughts and questions.

The zealots had kept things going for decades, maybe centuries, without a dragon. They'd deceived the people with images of smoke and vague movements behind a false window and maintained control with their tech and fear. In some ways, this was worse than a dragon ruling everything. I don't know who had it worse: my people in The Circle or the people out here.

Did any of the other dragons know about this? When Auric, Amaranth, and Onyx talked about Chroma, it sounded like they assumed she still lived and wanted to regain control over them. How would Onyx react if I told him about this? How could I use it against him?

I took a few more steps into the chamber. Did they keep the temperature so low to help preserve the bones? Why even bother? Was it for religious reasons, or… were they trying to keep something for the whole cloning thing Carl talked about? And clean! This whole place was spotless, from the unremarkable floor to the bones themselves. Many years ago, someone had done an impressive job cleaning this place up. I wondered if Viridia's people had made progress in doing the same in his lair. Come to think of it, Auric's lair had been pretty clean too, at least what I saw of it.

How could I reveal this to the common people? If they knew the dragon didn't exist, would they rise up against the zealots? Would it matter? Lainey and Carl both believed the zealots' tech advantage was too high.

No. This whole place needed to be brought down. I had no idea how we could do it, but I couldn't think of any alternatives.

"What are you doing?" The voice of a zealot intruded on my thoughts. I turned and saw three of them near the dragon's tail, moving rapidly toward me.

I gave them what I thought was a gentle nod, then turned and walked calmly toward the door. "Wait right there!" one of them shouted.

Seriously, though. How could they possibly know I wasn't supposed to be there? They all looked alike! I gritted my teeth and kept going.

Somehow, they moved with far greater speed than I'd expected. Right as I reached the door, someone grabbed my arm from behind. I spun around with my head down to keep my face hidden, but in what I hoped was a stern pose. The three other zealots stood right in front of me.

"You are well aware that only level fives are allowed in here. Explain yourself!"

Level fives? They had levels? And how could they tell I wasn't one? Did they count tendrils on the robes? Regardless, the minute I opened my mouth, they would know I wasn't one of them. I could either pretend I couldn't talk, which would be ludicrous, or...

I grabbed the nearest one's robe with my cyb hand. In the instant he looked down and realized it wasn't human flesh, I activated the modification Cobalt and I had installed. An electric shock shot through the robe. Its cybernetics failed, and it collapsed like normal cloth. Releasing him, I did the same to the one still holding my arm. With a boost to my other hand, I punched him in the face.

"Intruder!" the third zealot cried. He backed away faster than I could grab at him.

"I knew it!" shouted one of the other men in the room behind me. I heard both of them rushing to the door. That was a problem. I could still turn and push my way back through them, through their little apartment, and around and down all those long hallways, back through the tech room, running into who knows how many enemies by then. Or I could take a more direct route to the main temple.

I broke free of the zealot trio and boosted my legs. I raced across the massive room, skirting past parts of Chroma's skeleton and ducking under other parts. Running in the robe proved easier than I'd anticipated. Whether due to its cybernetic properties or its drape, it moved effortlessly with my pounding legs.

Another zealot warped into view directly in front of me. I barreled right through him, destroying his robe's tech with another jolt as I did. Cobalt, you're brilliant.

Around me, I caught glimpses of others appearing. I guess level fives weren't so rare, after all. By the time I passed Chroma's giant shoulder blades, I'd seen at least two dozen zealots. Most were now behind me, but a few tried to anticipate my movements and raced to cut me off. It wouldn't do them any good unless I let a group catch me all at once. As long as I could keep moving and keep them from swarming me, I could get out of here.

Up ahead, I saw what I hoped to see: The back side of the multi-screen "window." A huge wooden frame held all of the screens, connected to each other by what looked like miles of wiring. A metal scaffolding offered a way for Chroma's faithful to repair and maintain the illusion's mechanisms.

I wondered if there had ever been a real window, back when Chroma still lived. Did they shut it down the moment she started aging? Or did they replace it with the screens long before that, at her request?

Somehow, I needed to get through that mess. I could try to tear out a couple of the screens, but that would take time and they'd catch up to me. I couldn't slow down. I needed something larger than my fist to smash my way through.

Fortunately, Chroma herself provided me with exactly what I wanted. I ducked to the left to dodge a zealot who tried to grab me from one side, then threw an even stronger boost into my legs and arms. I ran right up to the enormous skull lying clean and empty on the vast floor, mouth agape as if she were about to eat. I selected one of the teeth almost as big as myself. Seizing it with my boosted hands, I ripped it free from the lower jawbone.

In that brief pause, two of the zealots caught up to me. I swung the tooth in a circle, even as a cacophony of identical voices cried out in horror about sacrilege and desecration. Sure. I guess you could call it that. The tooth proved itself solid enough to knock the two zealots off their feet. I used the momentum of my swing to redirect myself back toward the wall of screens.

My pursuers were much closer now. I could feel bursts of cold air as their robe tendrils grabbed at me from both sides. They shouted imprecations against me, even as others demanded to know who I was and how I got in. Yeah, I would definitely have to take Carl out with me. They would discover his role in this and punish him. It might be enough for them to decide his usefulness wasn't enough any more.

I chose my spot on the first level of the scaffolding. I aimed my course, waited until the right moment, and leaped up. Even as I soared through the air, two zealots warped into place on that level, waiting for me. I landed right between them; their hands and tendrils reached for me.

I grabbed at the nearest one with my cyb hand, sending a jolt as soon as I made contact. But doing so almost made me drop the tooth. I seized it with both hands as it started to slide loose, then spun all the way around.

Chroma's tooth smacked into the remaining zealot and propelled him through two of the screens. I launched myself with the tooth after him.

With a burst of sparks and shouts, the zealot, Chroma's tooth, and I exploded into the main temple in front of a crowd of worshippers.

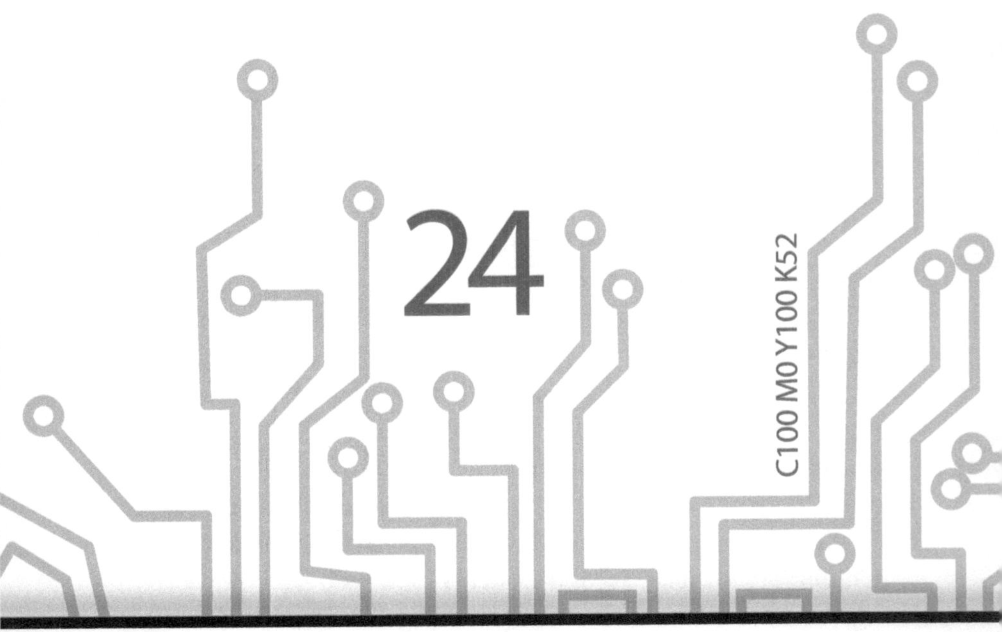

In retrospect, maybe running the halls would have been safer. On the other hand, bursting through the screens exposed the lie of their existence to all those gathered before the altar. That's assuming they bothered to look after the zealot and I crashed through and tumbled together thirty feet to the ground.

I tried to roll with the dragon tooth, positioning it below me as I fell. Even so, I hit hard, rolled and lay dazed for a few crucial moments. I used to be able to handle things like that much easier. Shaking my head, I scrambled to my feet and took a few steps. I scanned the room as fast as my cybernetic eyes could move.

The worshippers scattered in all directions. I spotted Carl in a group heading toward what appeared to be the main exit leading to the outer court. I could have imagined it, but I think he was shaking his head. I could practically hear his eyes rolling. I couldn't blame him. He'd predicted I would do something rash, and… here we were.

Three zealots who'd been leading things at the altar raced toward me. Others began appearing, warping in from pursuing me in the dragon's lair. If I stood still any longer, they'd be on me.

I boosted my legs again and ran toward the exiting crowd. Fortunately, I timed it so that most of them made it through the doors before I arrived. I shoved my way past the few remaining. In the process, I grabbed Carl's arm and pulled him with me a few steps.

"You said the tunnel's open," I said in a rush. "What's the fastest way to get to it?"

"Get back to Lainey," he answered. "I'll try to get a vehicle and meet you. Tell her: the old treehouse."

I shoved him away from me, as if he'd just been another obstacle in my path. I turned to my right, but ran almost directly into two more zealots. These rushed in and seized me faster than I could anticipate. Tendrils from their robes wrapped around my arms and legs, hands grasped at my shoulders, and cold enveloped me. I came to a stop and bent over, pulling them in closer. A third and fourth zealot joined the pile.

Cobalt and I had discussed a contingency for a situation exactly like this. Hunter called my boosts something like thermoelectricity, which meant there was at least some electric element to them. And we knew my cyb hand and these robes were both excellent conductors of electricity. I'd used it through my hand so far, but this time, I grabbed my own robe and concentrated. The electricity arced through my robe, rendering it useless, but also all four of the other robes entwined with it. Cries of dismay surrounded me.

My cyb hand also worked great for ripping the purple robes. I tore my own off and broke free from my captives, stumbling in a circle before getting my bearings. In that moment, they saw my face. "Apostate Beryl!" one of them cried.

In one sense, I felt a little bit of pride in being instantly recognized. But... now they would all know who I was and why I was here, as opposed to thinking I might be a local rebel or something. There would be no easy throwing them off my trail now. Also, I liked it better when they called me "Godslayer." Even though I disagreed with the premise behind the title, it sounded more impressive than "apostate."

The outer court did not have a roof. The walls were high, but not high enough to stop me. I'd been jumping that high before I knew my implant could affect more than my legs. I leaped to the top, wobbled for a few seconds, then dropped down to the ground outside. Right as I fell, I heard what sounded like Lainey's rifle. Had she seen me and fired at pursuers? Or did someone else have a rifle? I'd never even thought about that.

I raced across the outer open area and amongst the trees. Ugh. I had a long way to go to reach Lainey and the vent opening. But maybe leading the zealots in that direction would confuse them. It confused me enough. As I tore through the brush, I focused on remembering exactly where I needed to go. Zealots appeared from time to time in my peripheral vision, but none of them tried to stop me. I didn't know whether to see that as a good thing or not.

Fortunately, Lainey heard all the commotion and met me long before I reached the vent. She took a shot at the first zealot who showed himself. The others faded back from view, avoiding her gun, not to mention Glacier, who bounded up next to me as well.

"I should have known," she greeted me. "What did you do this time?"

"Your dad said to meet him at the old treehouse." I bent over and gasped for air. "I suggest we go as fast as we can."

Another gunshot resounded somewhere nearby, and a bullet tore through the branches near my head. "They have rifles!" I exclaimed.

Lainey was already running the other direction. "Did you think I had the only one in the world? Of course they do!"

I raced after her. "I just never thought about it!"

Out here, keeping pace with Lainey and Glacier, I didn't need to rely on my boosts as much. But without them, I stumbled a few times and even fell face-first into the dirt when I vaulted over a fallen tree. Lainey helped pull me up. "What's wrong with you? Are you hurt?"

"No, keep moving. Just my own clumsiness."

She narrowed her eyebrows at me but turned and ran on. This time, as I followed, I kept a steady but light boost going to both legs. Stupid things had not been working right since Atramentous.

No more bullets followed us through the trees. Maybe we'd lost the pursuit, at least for now. A few minutes later, we stumbled out onto a dirt road.

"There it is!"

I looked where Lainey pointed, and at first, I saw nothing. I blinked and then realized she was pointing at one large tree. About fifteen feet up, someone had nailed a handful of small boards between a couple of branches. It didn't look at all like a house; in fact, it didn't look very safe.

"That's the old treehouse?"

"Some kids built it years ago." Lainey paused at the base of the tree, looking up. "It, uh, used to be bigger."

I bent over while we caught our breath. "I don't understand. Why is it called a house?"

"Kids never built a treehouse in The Circle?"

"Not that I know of… we live in cities, remember? The only trees I knew for years were inside the dragon shrines."

Lainey shook her head. "So sad. If we ever have a kid, he needs a treehouse, so both of you can enjoy it."

I opened my mouth to respond, but the implications of her statement hit me. A kid? Us? That would be… I didn't know what to think. I'd never even imagined myself as a father. Did I want to be a father? Could I become a father? After all that had been done to me medically, was it even possible? I needed to ask Hunter sometime. I knew one thing now: if I ever became a father, I would want Lainey to be the mother. Should I tell her that, or was it assumed by the nature of her statement? Why did I over-think things so much?

The sound of an approaching vehicle cut off any further thought or discussion. We hid behind the treehouse tree and watched a truck race into view. It looked smaller than the trucks I knew from Viridia. If it had been built for hauling things, it couldn't haul a whole lot.

It came to a halt in a cloud of dust right in front of us. Carl Roberts leaned out of the window. "Get in!" he shouted.

Lainey squealed and rushed around to the passenger side. She scrambled in and threw herself onto her father. I jumped in the back. "Come on, Glacier." The cat stared at me before turning her head to lick one of her paws.

Lainey stuck her head back out. "Glacier! Get in!" The cat obeyed at once, jumping in beside me. We barely had room for the two of us in this little truck.

Multiple gunshots rang out. I ducked and tried to pull Glacier down with me. The back window of the truck's cab shattered. The truck's wheels kicked up dust and rocks as Carl took off.

The chase was on. But where could we run?

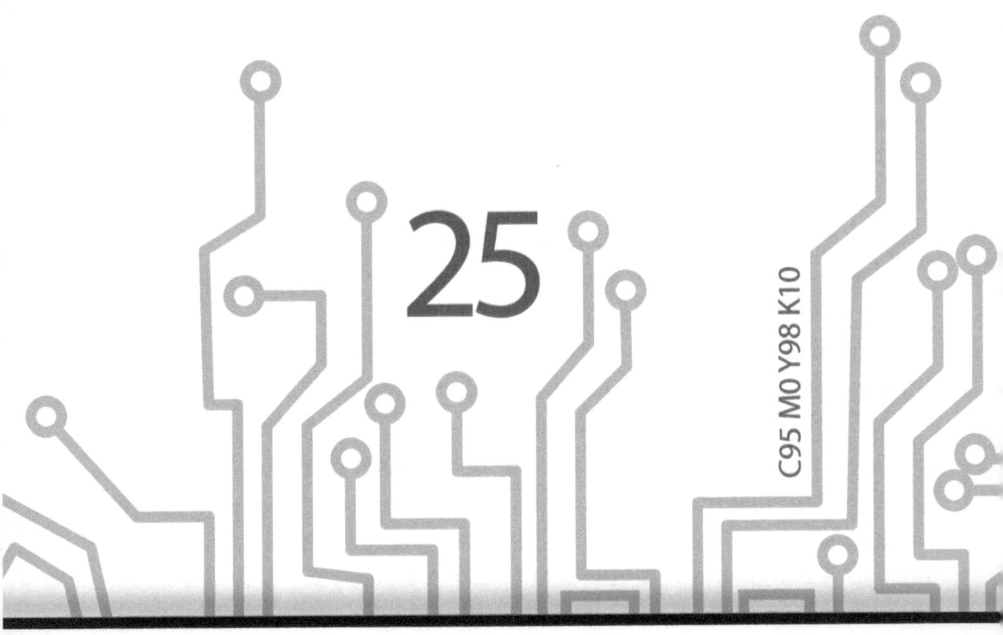

More gunshots followed us, some of them so rapid it didn't make sense. I leaned up near the broken back window. "Their guns shoot faster than yours!"

"I keep telling you about our tech, but you don't listen!" Lainey shot back.

"Are you starting to see what you're up against?" her father added. "It's not just the zealots!"

Maybe he did have a point. I was in way over my head. Admittedly, that had been true since Rick and I first started our little rebellion in Viridia, but this... this was a whole new level.

The truck roared down the winding dirt road, leaving a cloud in our path. I could hear vehicles in pursuit, but I hadn't seen them yet. We still had something of a lead. And the twisting path through the trees kept them from having clear shots at us with their guns, at least for now.

"Where are we going?" Lainey asked, loud enough to be heard over the engine and the wind whipping around us.

"Your boyfriend has the crazy idea that we can get through the tunnel under the mountains!" Carl shouted.

Lainey shot a look back at me. "Is it possible?"

"We can't get all the way through in the truck, but..." Carl shrugged. "I don't have any better ideas. Anywhere we go, they're going to follow."

Another good point. If we made it through the tunnel, then what? The zealots weren't worried about invading The Circle. They'd been there in numbers already. But would they bring these soldiers and their guns inside? Were they ready to go that far? If they did, our best chance might be to lead them to one of the cities, Caesious or Incarnadine. The resident security forces would not take kindly to such an invasion.

But we might never get anywhere close to that situation. First, we had to get to the tunnel alive.

The truck careened off the dirt and onto a concrete road. On the better surface going almost completely straight, Carl accelerated. We flew down the road. Behind us, two more trucks emerged and chased after us. I watched them anxiously for a few moments, but they didn't appear to be gaining on us.

"We're keeping ahead of them! I think we can do it! They can't catch us!"

"They aren't the only ones we have to worry about!" Carl responded. "Keep an eye on the sky!"

The sky? But the skies belong to the dragons. Or at least they had, until I violated that law with Loden's Sky Claimer. Wouldn't Chroma have the same law?

A few moments later, I had my answer. The sound of another engine, louder than the truck's, drew my attention. And then I saw it: a flying machine coming up fast above and behind us. In some ways, it resembled my lost Sky Claimer, being about the same size. But the pilot was in a kind of chair beneath the wings instead of strapped to them like I had been. And it was painted purple, of course.

In a few seconds, it caught up to us and flew straight over. Impressive, but...

"What can it do to us?" I asked.

"Hopefully not much by itself," Carl answered. "But it guarantees we can't outrun or elude them. They'll always be able to see where we are and by now, they've probably guessed where we're going. He'll call it in, and they'll have people waiting for us at the tunnel."

My mind raced, trying to think of a way out of this. The flying machine buzzed over us again. "If only I had something to throw," I muttered. My eyes darted around. The back of the truck held nothing but myself and a giant cat. But maybe there was another possibility. I pushed past Glacier to look over the back end, then returned to the broken window.

"Take a turn in a different direction!" I told Carl. "Let's try to make them think we're going somewhere else."

He grumbled something about not seeing how that would help, but he yanked the wheel to the left. The truck literally tilted as we took a sharp turn. One of the wheels might have left the ground. We raced down a new road, one with a few more turns.

"I'm going to get rid of the flyer in a few minutes," I said into the window. "Can you get us turned back around toward the tunnel after I do that?"

"How are you going to do that?" Lainey demanded.

"I... I think so," Carl answered. "It may take a few extra turns, but... yeah."

"Great." I stepped over Glacier's leg to move toward the back end of the truck. We hit a bump, and I lost my balance. I fell back next to the window. Hm. That might be a problem. Lainey and I hadn't brought any rope with us, but... "Any rope up there?"

"I had enough trouble stealing this truck!" Carl shouted. "You didn't ask for rope too!"

"What are you going to do?" Lainey repeated.

"Hold on." I clambered over Glacier again and reached the tail end of the truck. I knew the gate here opened up. I took a quick look down the road behind us. The other trucks were out of range of their guns for the moment, thanks to the road's twists. The flying machine circled back toward us from a distance.

I unhooked the truck's gate, but held on to it to keep it from falling all the way open. I looked at Glacier. "Catch me if I start to fall off," I told the cat. In response, I got a blank look. Why could it follow complicated instructions from Lainey but not me?

I channeled strong boosts into my arms and locked my cyb hand into the gate. Then I pulled with all my strength. Metal groaned and bent. I pulled harder. It popped free with a sudden jolt, and I fell back toward Glacier. But the weight of the gate pulled me back forward. I would have tumbled off the truck entirely if a huge mouth had not closed around my upper right arm. Glacier held me firmly but gently. Even so, her teeth scored into my skin. Wow. Maybe the cat had listened.

Scrambling back, I returned behind the cab. "Lainey, I need you to keep me anchored."

She turned around and leaned out through the window. "Tell me what you're going to do."

I pointed at the truck's gate and pointed up. Her eyes registered understanding, and she wrapped both arms around one of my legs. That should work. Maybe.

The flying machine roared toward us. I had to time this right, or it would all be pointless. I hefted the gate into position and waited. Closer... closer... closer...

With the most powerful boosts I could muster, I hurled the truck gate into the air in the path of the flying machine. I almost pulled myself completely out of Lainey's grip; almost, but not quite. The pilot turned as hard and fast as he could, but it wasn't enough. The gate crunched into the right wing a few feet from the end. Debris rained down onto the road, causing problems for our other pursuers - bonus! The flying machine wavered and wobbled while the pilot fought for control. I couldn't see exactly what he was doing, but something else must have gone wrong. The machine pitched over to the left, started spinning in circles, and disappeared behind the trees. A few moments later, we heard the impact.

"That was awesome!" Lainey shouted behind me. She gave my leg a final squeeze and let go. I slumped down next to Glacier, feeling the strain of my muscles. It would be nice not to use my boosts. I hadn't exerted myself this much in a while.

"Hang on back there," Carl warned, two seconds before turning sharply to the right. I slammed my cyb hand down and seized the side of the truck bed to keep from flying off. Glacier complained with a loud rowr.

"How much further?" I asked.

"I'd guess about twenty minutes."

Right. If we didn't have too many more of those wild turns, maybe I could rest up a bit. In twenty minutes, I might have to deal with the people chasing us. And then we'd see what awaited us in the tunnel.

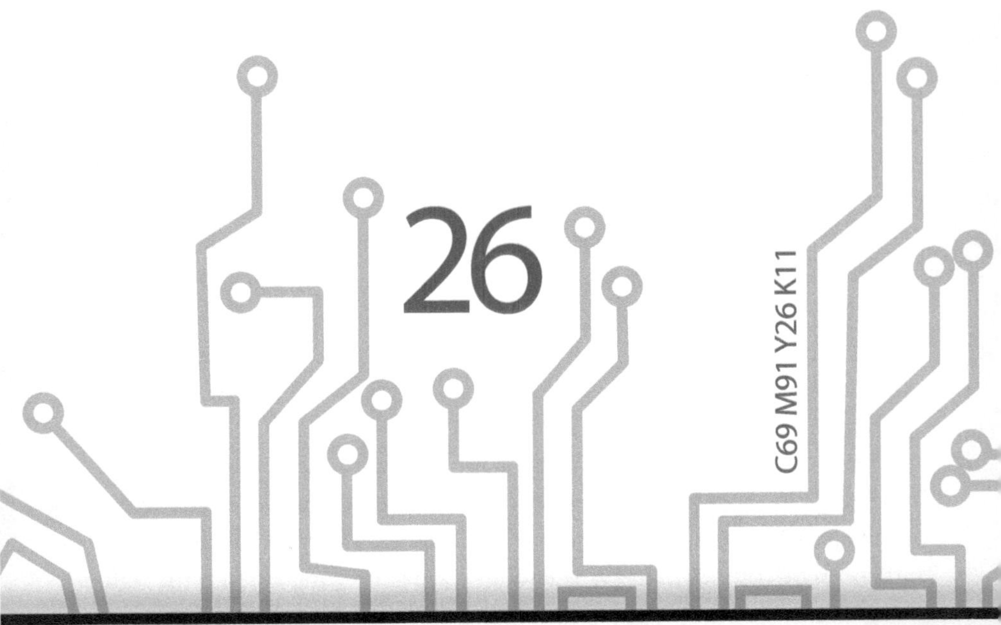

We dumped the truck in a ditch once we reached the foothills. At my suggestion, the four of us hid behind the nearest pile of rocks and waited.

The two pursuing trucks arrived a few moments later. Two zealots and five other men carrying guns exited the vehicles and started a search around our abandoned truck.

"Can you shoot from here?" I whispered to Lainey.

She hesitated. "I don't like shooting people…"

"Hand me the rifle," Carl said. "I'll do it."

I understood Lainey's reluctance. I'd much rather fight draconics any day. I could handle the zealots, but I didn't know what to do about the men with guns.

"Five riflemen," Carl said, sighting along the rifle. "As soon as I shoot one of them, the other four will locate us and start shooting. Any ideas?"

I considered the distance. "I could maybe get to one of them before he fires, but that leaves three. Glacier might take one… but then the other two would shoot us. And that doesn't even include the zealots."

"We need a better plan," Lainey stated the obvious.

"I'm thinking!"

"Think faster."

"You could contribute here too, you know."

"Maybe you should throw something else."

"That—" Huh. That wasn't a horrible idea. I examined the ground and found a rock about the size of my head. It could take someone down, assuming my aim was good enough.

"Don't throw it at them," Carl said. He pointed off to the left. "Throw it over there and draw their attention."

I hefted the rock, using boosts, and threw it as far as I could. It smashed into the ground and rolled. Seven heads spun in that direction. Carl fired and one of them dropped. "That will only work once," he observed as he reloaded.

"At least it narrowed the odds."

The other four ducked, looking this way and that. The zealots, arrogant in their robes, floated around without concern. One of the gunmen took a few steps in the direction I'd thrown the rock. Another one stopped him and pointed in the opposite direction. An argument ensued.

Glacier growled and crouched down as if ready to pounce. Lainey patted her and whispered in her ear.

"I need a plan. I need a plan," I muttered.

"I'll surrender," Carl said. "Then while they're dealing with me, you two can sneak away."

"No!" Lainey exclaimed at the same time I said, "Not a chance."

"Then what?" Carl looked at me with exasperation. "What did you think would happen, Beryl? There are just too many. This isn't the Viridian Guard here. We're outmatched and outnumbered."

I studied the terrain between us and them. "How bad does it hurt to get shot?"

"You're not going out there either!" Lainey insisted.

"If I keep down, moving fast, and change directions a lot…"

"The instant you're spotted, one of the zealots will tel— reappear right next to you, or worse, right next to us," Carl said. "Remember what they can do."

I paused. "If they know where we are, you think one of them will come here?"

"Almost certainly. And yes, I know you could defeat him, but then the gunmen would come after us, and…" He trailed off at seeing my grin. "What?"

"Trust me. I have an idea." I stuck my head out over the rocks. "Hey there! We're over here! You've got us!" I ducked back.

"Are you insane?" Carl hissed. "That's—"

With a rush of cold air, one of the purple robes warped in behind us. "Beryl Go—"

Before he could complete the word, I seized the robe with my cyb hand and yanked him to me. "I need your help," I told him. I leaped up out of the rocks, taking the zealot with me. I propelled him forward, keeping him between me and the gunmen and boosting everything at once.

"You can't do this!" he sputtered. He tried enveloping me with his robe's tendrils, but I kept moving with a firm hold.

Carl caught on and started firing.

After a few moments' hesitation, letting me close half the distance, two of the gunmen fired at me. Their bullets did no harm to the purple robe, as I expected. "If you start to disappear, I'll turn off your robe," I warned him.

"Nonsense." With that, the familiar blast of cold air hit me, indicating the use of his power. I released the electrical charge. The robe collapsed. The next bullet struck him in the shoulder, and he screamed.

"I warned you."

Another bullet struck him before I reached the others. I threw him into one of the gunmen and lunged at another, trusting Carl to do his part. One hard punch laid out the one I attacked; I ripped his rifle free as he fell. I spun around to find Glacier leaping on to the last gunman. He screamed like a girl before his head bounced off the rocks. Glacier stood over him and looked around for any more enemies.

Only the one I'd knocked down with the fallen zealot remained conscious and unharmed. He threw his gun aside and lifted his hands. "I surrender!"

"There's no need for that," said an all-too-familiar voice. In that moment, purple tendrils wrapped around my left arm from the elbow to the shoulder. I'd forgotten the final zealot, and he'd neutralized my cyb hand.

"Without this hand, you can't touch me," he observed. Glacier pounced at him, but found herself unable to seize hold of the flowing cybernetic cloth. She snarled in frustration.

I pulled against his grip. Only my cyb hand had ever been able to even make contact with the robes, let alone harm them.

Carl and Lainey approached, rifle at ready. "You can put that down," the zealot intoned. "This momentary insurrection is now over."

"I don't think so." I pulled, moving him toward me, then let him pull my arm back. With a heavy rush of all the boost energy I could muster into my left arm, I yanked forward again. This time, it threw him off balance enough that he stumbled. Glacier pounced again and landed on him this time. In order to slip away from the cat's weight, the zealot was forced to release some of the material wrapped around my arm. One strand of it drifted near my hand. That was all I needed.

I seized the tendril of cloth and released my electrical burst. The purple robe collapsed. Carl stepped up and slammed the butt of the rifle into the zealot's face. "That's all of them," I said, bending over to catch my breath.

Lainey pointed to the last gunman, who still held his hands in the air. "What do we do with him?"

I straightened and stepped over to the man. He literally trembled in front of me. "How about if you take a little nap?" I suggested. "Lay down right here, and don't get up for… oh, let's say an hour." He lowered himself down, keeping his hands elevated as long as he could, then kind of curled up on the dirt and closed his eyes.

I blinked. I didn't expect him to obey me quite like that. Well, whatever works.

Carl took a deep breath and pointed. "The tunnel is that way."

"Lead the way." I bent over and took a few of those breaths myself.

"Do you need to rest?" Lainey asked.

"We don't have time." I nodded to Carl who set out across the foothills. Ignoring the concern in Lainey's eyes, I followed him. I could rest when we got home. I could do this. I had to.

About half an hour later, far longer than I'd hoped, Carl motioned for us to duck down as we approached the crest of a ridge. We peered over it and looked down at the opening to Chroma's tunnel, blasted and dug out of the mountain. A railroad led into it, but I didn't think they'd started running trains through yet. The opening didn't appear large and stable enough yet. A handful of men were hard at work on that process as we watched.

"How long did we decide this thing would be?" Lainey asked. "Wasn't it six miles?"

"We would need to get past these men," Carl added. "And after that, I don't know that we could walk six miles without anyone catching up to us."

A grin spread over my face as I spotted something. "We aren't going to walk."

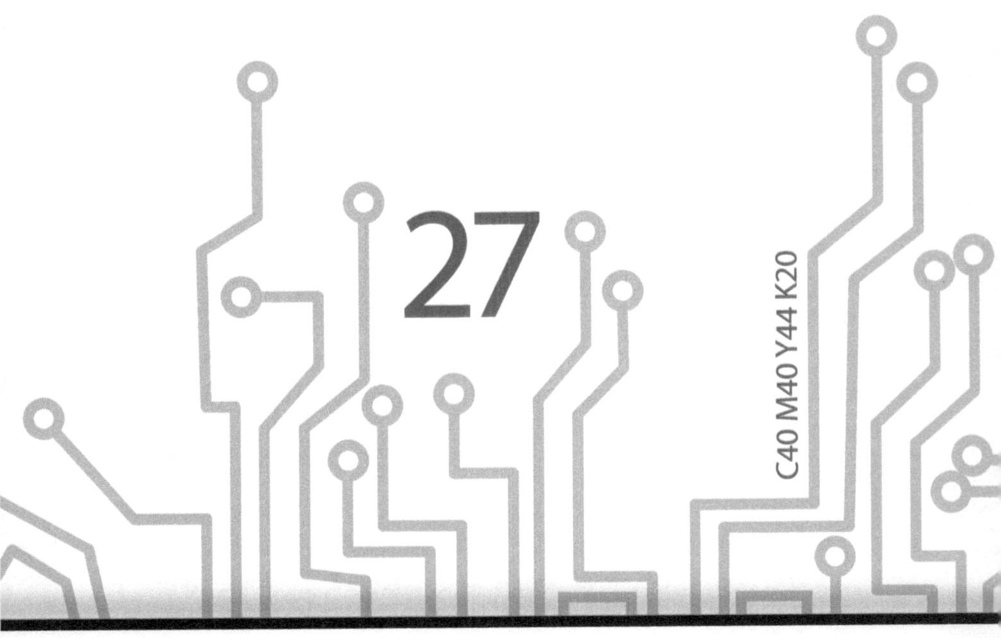

27

"What are we going to do? Fly?" Carl asked drily.

I pointed near the entrance to the tunnel. "They have a rail rider!"

"A what?"

"A rail rider. I rode one once before. It's like a miniature train… thing."

Carl and Lainey looked where I pointed. "Looks like it might be crowded," Lainey said. "For all four of us, that is."

Right. Glacier took up a lot of room. "We'll make it work. Even if we have to go slow, it'll still be better than walking." I continued to scan the area. "Do you see any soldiers or zealots anywhere?"

"No, but they can't be far. Our misdirection wouldn't prevent them from at least sending a token force here." Carl sighted with the rifle scope again. "If we move now, we might get going before they show up."

"Then let's do it." I stood up and descended the ridge, kicking up dust and loose rocks. One of the workers spotted me almost at once. He watched our descent a few moments before alerting the others. The work around the tunnel's entrance came to a halt as, one-by-one, everyone turned to watch us. Maybe we'd have been less conspicuous without the giant saber-toothed cat.

When we reached the bottom, we were approached by three men carrying pickaxes. I assumed the leader was the foreman; he wore a shirt with a collar. They stopped about ten yards away.

"I don't know who you people are, but we've placed a call to the nearest priest for assistance," the foreman announced. "You should probably clear out."

I pointed at the rail rider. "We'll be taking that and be out of your way in no time."

He shook his head. "I can't let you do that. It's Chroma's property."

"Really?" I laughed. "My friend here has a rifle, I have cybernetic parts,"—I flexed my hand in front of me—"and then there's the cat." Glacier growled on cue. "Do you really think you can stop us?"

"I can't be held accountable for what will happen."

"We're not asking you to," Carl said. "Just get out of the way."

The three workers stepped back to let us pass, eyeing us—and especially Glacier—nervously. I paused in front of them. "One more thing: how far do the rails go now? Have you completed the tracks?"

"Almost," he grunted.

Between the three of us, we got the rail rider into position facing the tunnel. Lainey climbed into the driver's seat, and convinced Glacier to climb on behind her. The cat barely fit and looked clearly uncomfortable. Carl and I would have to cling to the sides. I wouldn't have much trouble, but I worried that Carl could hang on the entire way.

"I don't suppose it's got lights all the way through," Carl said.

"If not, we'll depend on my night vision." I showed Lainey the controls. She flipped the switch to start the engine and released the brake.

A commotion erupted somewhere behind us. "Go, go, go!" I shouted. Lainey moved the speed lever. With an abrupt jerk, the rail rider started forward.

"Might want to go faster," Carl said.

"I'm trying!" Lainey snapped. The rail rider picked up its pace a little. We rolled into the tunnel itself. Behind us, I spotted a zealot floating down next to the foreman.

"Trouble," I said.

"Fine." Lainey slammed the speed lever forward. With another jerk, we launched forward into the dimly-lit tunnel. If the zealot wanted to catch us now, he'd need his own transportation.

The floor and the tracks looked mostly complete to me. The sides and ceiling remained rough and broken in many places. Carl and I often had to lean in close to avoid getting knocked off by uneven rocks protruding from the walls. A series of low-voltage lights hung loosely from the roof. Combined with the rider's built-in light, they provided just enough illumination to see far enough ahead that we wouldn't be caught off-guard by any sudden turns.

But none came. For the most part, the tunnel stayed straight, though the elevation varied many times. A few broad turns required slowing the rider down to keep from coming off the rails.

"This is much smoother than I thought it would be," Lainey said a couple minutes in.

"I know! This is the way to travel," I agreed. "I'd like to do it one day in actual daylight, though."

"At our top speed, we're going maybe thirty," Carl said, mostly to himself. "If the tunnel is six miles long, we should get through in somewhere over twelve minutes."

"Twelve minutes? I thought we'd be in here for hours!" Lainey's face brightened. "That's incredible."

"Twelve minutes at our current speed," he cautioned. "It will probably be longer."

The air grew steadily cooler as we continued. Within a few minutes, I shivered. We'd left our warm clothing back in the apartment, along with our climbing gear. I hoped we hadn't left anything important there, now that I thought about it.

"We'll have to slow down when we get closer to the other end," I pointed out. "We might run into trouble there. The zealots had a shrine or something in the largest cavern."

"No might about it." Carl pointed at the ceiling. "Do you see that extra wire running alongside the lights? Telephone wire. They'll be calling ahead to alert them."

"Would it help to tear it down? If we stop, I could jump up there and…"

Carl shook his head. "It's far too late. We should have thought of it right away."

About six minutes in, halfway by Carl's reckoning, Glacier had enough. She jumped off the back of the rider. Lainey slowed down with a cry, but the cat shook herself and trotted along behind us.

"I wonder how fast she can run." Carl patted Lainey's shoulder. "Speed us back up. I'll bet she can keep up."

Lainey obeyed, taking the rider back up to the speed we'd been traveling. Glacier dropped back a few feet, but maintained a steady pace with us. She didn't seem to be straining too hard either, but I wondered how long she could sustain it. Lainey insisted one of us keep an eye on her, so we could slow down if needed.

Eight minutes in, the lights flickered and went out. Lainey slowed the rider almost to a crawl. The rider's own light showed only about a dozen feet ahead. When I'd ridden one alone, that had been enough… but the night darkness of The Circle didn't compare to the total darkness of this cave.

"I'm surprised it took them this long," Carl muttered. "They're definitely planning some kind of greeting for us now."

"Turn off the light," I told Lainey. "We'll go by my night vision, and our light won't let them know we're coming."

"They can hear the engine," she pointed out, but she flipped the light off.

"Sound isn't as easy to pinpoint as light, not in this darkness," I said. "My vision's good. Start us up again. Take it slow at first."

She did so. I kept a whispered commentary going to her about upcoming changes in the tracks. In this way, we continued for another five or six minutes at least. We had to be nearing the parts of the tunnel we'd explored on foot, back on the day I killed Atramentous.

Thinking about that probably distracted me an extra second or two. I didn't see the huge figure on the tracks until it was too late. "Look out!" I shouted right as a clawed hand extended toward us and guttural words erupted from a draconic throat.

I had no time to make any kind of decision. By sheer instinct, I sent boosts everywhere, including my heart.

The wave of resomancy struck us. Lainey might have hit the brake a half-second before. Either way, the rider came to an abrupt halt. We would have all flown forward, but the wall of power kept coming. Lainey and Carl were thrown backwards as I launched forward. I landed with a stumble and fell to my hands and knees only a couple of feet from the draconic. Behind me, Glacier yowled in shock and pain.

A low chuckle came from the draconic. The sickly-sweet odor flooded around me. Troilus Green? No. I blinked and clambered to my feet to face a black draconic.

"Welcome back to The Circle, Beryl," it growled as several members of the Sable Legion moved into position behind it. "Welcome to your death."

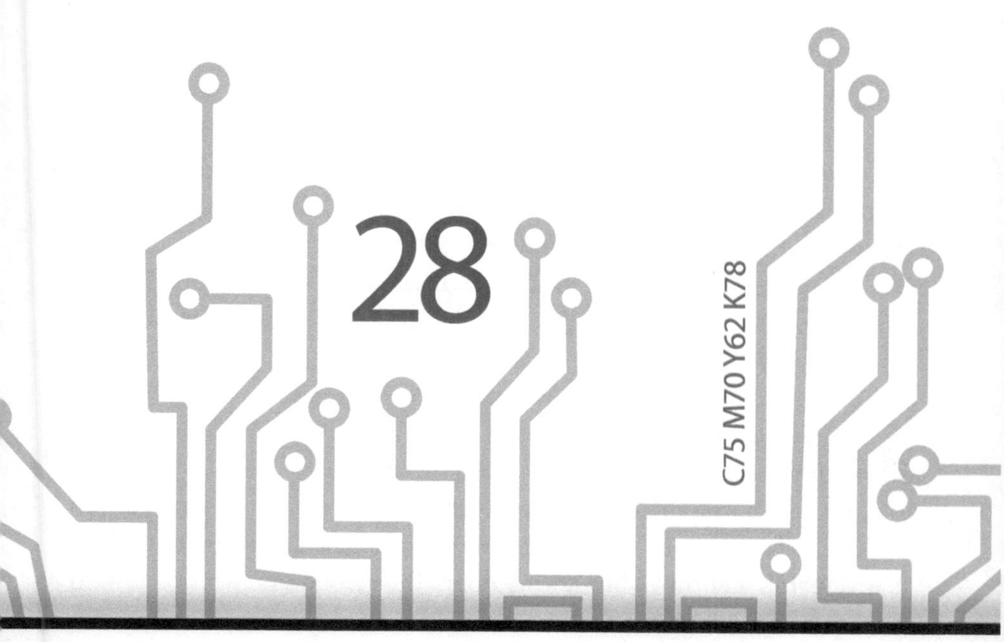

28

The overhead lights came back on with an odd thump. I risked a quick look behind me. Lainey and Carl weren't moving. Glacier lay further back but lifted her head.

"The others speak of you in such hushed tones," the draconic said, "I expected so much more."

My eyes darted back and forth, trying to analyze the situation. The black draconic stood a few feet in front of me, dominating the railroad tracks. Two Sable Legionnaires moved forward on either side of him with their weird staff weapons leveled toward me. Three more waited behind. The soldiers didn't concern me too much; I could take one down and steal his weapon to use against the others. But… without a blade of some kind, I didn't have a way to even harm the draconic. The staves would only shatter on his scaled skin.

More importantly, what about Lainey? Was she all right? Was she even alive? And her dad? The stress of not knowing kept pushing into my tactical thoughts.

"Which one are you?" I asked, buying time as I took a step backward. "I don't think we've met."

"I am Rimush Black. Ordinarily, I would be deep beneath the city of Atramentous, engaged in my studies. But strange events brought me to the surface."

"You mean like when I killed your god?" I took another step back.

"You are trying to goad me." The draconic scratched the back of one hand with the claws of the other. "It won't work. I have heard everything humans have had to say for hundreds of years… as I discovered how much pain their fragile bodies could endure."

The rifle. Carl had been holding it. It would be on the ground somewhere behind me. But even if I could find it fast… I'd never learned how to use it. Ugh.

"Legion, take him." Rimush Black gestured at me.

I crouched and boosted arms and legs in preparation for a struggle. The two black-armored soldiers stepped toward me.

An ear-splitting roar came from behind me. Before I could even spin to look, Glacier leaped through the air past me. She landed on one of the Legionnaires and drove him to the floor. The second one whirled toward her with his staff, giving me an opening. I lunged forward, seized it with my cyb hand, and wrenched it free of his grasp.

Glacier made sure the fallen soldier wouldn't be getting up, crouched again, and glared straight at Rimush Black. "Glacier, no!" My shout meant nothing. The cat sprang at the draconic.

This was not what I wanted. Glacier had grown into a terrifying creature in her own right, but she stood no chance against a full-grown draconic, especially not after that crash. Furious over Lainey's injury—I hoped only injury—Glacier would not be stopped by me. And Rimush Black would kill her without my help.

I smacked the remaining soldier with his own staff. Fueled by my boosts, the impact threw him against the cave wall. I leaped forward to join the attack on the draconic.

Rimush Black and Glacier rolled back and forth over the railroad tracks, tearing at each other with claws and fangs. The other three Sable Legionnaires watched cautiously. One extended his staff, trying to clamp on to one of Glacier's limbs, but their movements were too fast and erratic. Only with more boosts could my eyes even keep up with them.

Glacier's rage helped her do more than I'd expected. She actually held her own for a brief minute. But then the draconic got a hand on her neck. He seized one of her front legs with the other hand. With incredible strength, he stood up, lifting the giant cat off the ground. Glacier snarled and tore at him with her other paws. Rimush Black heaved and threw her over the heads of the three soldiers. "Deal with that," he told them, before turning to face me again.

As he turned, I lunged forward with the staff. I didn't know how to use the clamp device on the end, but I shoved it at his face. He grabbed one end of it and twisted. We struggled back and forth for a moment, pitting his strength against my boosts. His strength won. He tossed the staff aside.

We faced each other. The draconic bled from dozens of scratches all over his body, but none of them looked debilitating. As for me, I'd been boosting too often and too long. What I could do was already less effective than even a few minutes earlier.

"I give you the opportunity to surrender now," the draconic said.

"Funny. I was about to say the same thing to you." I congratulated myself on actually thinking of a good line and saying it, in the moment. How about that?

Rimush Black shook his head. "They told me you were arrogant and reckless. You have certainly shown that to be true." His eyes glanced past me. "They did not tell me you possessed a callous disregard for your compatriots, though."

"I care about them more than you can understand." I fought against a rising rage of my own. If I gave in to it, I'd attack just like Glacier had done. "I will take care of them as soon as I deal with you."

"You possess impressive abilities for a human, but you are unarmed. You can do nothing here."

I couldn't possibly match him in strength, but with the right combination of boosts, I could move much faster. Fast enough to do... what? I still had only my bare hands. And one of them was cybernetic.

I backed up a few feet, then charged forward at my highest possible speed. The draconic swiped at me, but he moved in slow motion from my point of view. I ducked under his swipe and jumped. I kicked off the side wall to push myself back at him. With my cyb hand, I seized the draconic's lower jaw. And then I yanked it around as I kept moving behind him. I heard and felt the snap of his jaw breaking.

"Now you get to experience that," I muttered.

Rimush Black flailed at me, making furious noises I couldn't understand. I found a laceration on his back, left by Glacier's claws. I jammed my metallic fingers into it, dug as deep as I could, then tore free. Black blood gushed out.

I staggered back a few steps. I couldn't do this much longer. But I hoped my enemy couldn't either, especially with the damage he'd taken now. Behind me, I could still hear yells from the three soldiers and Glacier's continued anger. She was still fighting! Good for her.

Rimush Black reached up and adjusted his broken jaw. "You prolong the evitable," he managed to say. At least, I think that's what he said. All right, he probably meant "inevitable." I thought it was funny.

I wanted to say something clever in response, but having flipped our positions, I now could see Lainey still lying on the ground. She hadn't moved. My worry escalated.

Near my feet lay one of the Sable staves. It might be the same one I'd already tried to use, or another one might have dropped. I kicked it up with my toe and caught it. Huh. I'd never done that move before. And no one saw it.

The draconic rushed at me, claws extended. I used the staff to push off against him and dodge around again. If I could keep the boosts going, I could elude him indefinitely this way. Big "if." As he passed, I caught a glimpse of the bleeding wound on his back. It might be a vulnerable spot, if I could do something else to it.

I jammed one end of the staff under the railroad track. Channeling as much strength into my arms as I could, I yanked it up. The end snapped. A piece about five inches long hung loose from a much sharper point now. I tore the hanging piece off. Now I had a makeshift spear.

"You aren't giving up already, are you?" I taunted. I needed him to keep attacking. The arrogance of the draconics was their biggest weakness.

His actions seemed even slower now, even though I hadn't increased my boosts. I took that as a good sign. I maneuvered past him, spun around, and stabbed my broken staff into his open wound. The bellow of pain and anger came through despite the broken jaw.

He spun himself, yanking the spear out of my hands. I stepped back to avoid his awkward punch. Rimush Black took a stumbling step toward me, staggered, then fell forward onto his face.

The draconic lay as still as the woman I loved. I rushed to Lainey's side.

I think Glacier still fought against the remaining soldiers. I didn't know or care at the moment. I also had no idea what to do. Was Lainey even alive? What if she wasn't? A million other questions ran through my head. In that moment, I desperately wished for Bice's faith: that somehow, some way, there was a god or gods above who cared about us.

"Don't let her be dead," I whispered, not knowing to whom I spoke.

I leaned in close. She was still breathing! My chest shook, and my breath came in short gasps. Alive, but... I had no way of knowing how badly hurt. A nasty bruise was growing on the left side of her brow. I scrambled over to check on her father. Carl Roberts also still breathed. One of his injuries was obvious: his left leg twisted in the wrong direction.

I stood up and looked down the tracks. Glacier had downed one of the soldiers. The other two were backed up against a wall, keeping her at bay with their staves.

"Hey!" I ran up near them. "If I call off the cat, will you help me?"

One of them took his eyes off Glacier long enough to give me an open-mouthed stare. "You can't be serious!"

"I am." I pointed back. "I've got two badly injured people here. If I call off Glacier here, will you help me get them to a doctor?"

"No chance!" the other one snapped.

"Fine. Your draconic is dead." I stepped closer and flexed my cybernetic hand. "I'll just take your little toys away and let the cat finish you off. How's that?"

Glacier added a brutal snarl to my words.

"If-if that thing will listen to you, then I'll do whatever you want," said the first soldier.

"No! Don't do it!" his companion insisted.

"You want to end up like Ash over there?"

The second soldier hesitated. "I… all right. Fine. But if anyone asks, we fought until we were knocked out."

"I can knock you out later, if that helps," I offered.

"Call off the beast." He hesitated again, then added: "Please."

"Glacier." I stepped toward the cat. "Lainey is going to be all right, Glacier. Come on. Let these two go. They'll help us." I kept my voice as soothing as I could. I kept repeating the same things over and over. At first, Glacier didn't change. She held a tight pose, muscles clenched and ready to spring as soon as the opportunity presented itself. A low growl echoed out of her throat at a constant level.

I continued my soothing words and reached out to touch her fur. I placed my hand on one of the few spots I could see that wasn't coated in dirt or blood. The draconic's claws had torn her up so much, it was a wonder she still stood. I petted her and kept telling her it would be all right. I pointed back to Lainey over and over. At last, her muscles relaxed. She turned her head and licked my face. Yuck.

"Yeah, yeah. It's good. You're good. I'm good. Can you go wait beside Lainey now?" I pointed and the cat took a tentative step that direction. "That's it. Go stay with her. Keep her safe. I'll be with you in a few minutes."

As Glacier finally followed my instructions, I turned to the two soldiers. "All right, drop the sticks. Let's get busy. What's your names?"

The more compliant soldier dropped his staff at once. "I'm Slate, and this is Crow."

"Crow? Really? Who would—never mind. Crow, drop the staff already. Don't make me take it."

Crow scowled and obeyed.

"Great." Exhaustion ate at me. I sent a small boost into my brain to help me stay cognitive. It worked sometimes. "I need some new transportation. What do you have that we can use to get my friends to the doctor?"

They looked at each other. "Uh, we have a sort of truck that runs on the rails," Slate said.

"Perfect! You go get it. Crow, you stay here and help me prepare."

Slate took a step, then stopped. "You're trusting me to go by myself?"

"I can't monitor your every move, and I don't want to. We made a deal. I'm sticking to my end. I hope you'll do your part." I shrugged. "If you don't, if you come back with more of your Legion or whatever, then Glacier eats Crow here, and we both come after you in particular. Makes sense?"

"Right." Slate took off.

I looked Crow over. "Take off the armor."

"What?"

"Take off the armor. We can use it with two of your sticks to make a stretcher."

When Slate returned with the truck, we'd constructed a stretcher. I moved Lainey onto it by myself, then together, we lifted her into the back of the vehicle. We repeated the process for Carl. I straightened his leg a little, so it wouldn't dangle over the side. He moaned in response. At my urging, Glacier jumped up in the back of the truck as well.

"All right. You two, up front. Get us out of here."

"Where should we go outside the tunnel?" Slate asked.

I hesitated, considering. "Caesious," I decided. In the choice between the blue city and Incarnadine, I thought we might be a bit safer with blue. And I knew at least one person there I could try to contact.

The truck started up, much smoother than the rail rider. Instead of normal tires, it had metal rims which fit directly onto the track, like train wheels. In a few minutes, we were moving at a rapid clip. We passed through the parts of the cave I recognized from our previous visit. All of the rock formations I'd admired back then were gone now, destroyed to make room for the tracks. They'd also removed the body of Atramentous; I wondered again how they'd taken care of that.

The light grew ahead of us. I'd completely forgotten the time of day. When we'd entered the tunnel, it had been late afternoon. Our trip through, the fight with the draconic, getting the truck: all of it had taken less than an hour. We burst out of the tunnel into early evening sunshine. Here, the work of the laborers truly impressed me. When we'd found the tunnel before, the entrance had been well below the exterior foothills, hidden by other rock formations. They'd altered everything. The track emerged be-tween two high embankments before coming out and descending toward the lower parts of The Circle.

When we reached the main track, my drivers obeyed and turned right toward Caesious. I worried about what might happen if we met a train along the way, but I soon noticed diversions along the rails every so often to make room for passing vehicles.

In time, we crossed the river and entered the city of Caesious. The blue spotlights weren't as impressive at twilight, but they still cast a fascinating glow over many of the buildings. We passed between a number of them before entering the train station. The truck stopped in front of the massive mural of the blue dragon, near where I'd met Caedan for the first time. Unlike then, piles of flowers lay in front of the mural, honoring the dead. Many of them were withered and dry, but some fresh bunches showed some still grieved here… or at least, my cynical mind said, some of the officials and priests wanted others to believe the grief continued.

Slate jumped out and called to a nearby controller, "We have two bad-ly injured people here! We need to get them to the hospital!"

"Wait here. I'll get the paramedics."

A few moments later, medical personnel hurried to the truck. I climbed down, and Glacier joined me. I put one hand on the cat to calm her, while I stared at the medics. I'll give them this: despite my unusual appearance and the giant cat, they hurried to do their jobs. In short order, they trans-ferred Lainey and Carl to real stretchers and started taking them away.

Before following, I looked at the two Sable Legionnaires. "You did your part. You're free to go."

Crow leaped back into the truck. Slate gave me a long look before join-ing his companion. The truck accelerated quickly and disappeared down the tracks, no doubt heading for Atramentous. I wondered how fast their story would get back to the zealots… or Onyx. Regardless, I had other worries now. I hurried after Lainey and Carl.

30

I did not have good experiences with actual hospitals. There had been those medical facilities in the Emerald Ascendancy where Troilus Green's people saved Lovat's life. But before that... I could only remember my own hospital experience after the accident and all that Loden did to me. Learning to walk again had been difficult, far more difficult than Lovat's recovery so far. My cybernetics were also far more complex than his.

At the emergency entrance, the guard on duty balked at Glacier. "Are you going to tell her she can't come in?" I asked. After that, we didn't have any trouble.

Seeing the condition of Lainey and Carl, the medics rushed them right in for examination. A nervous clerk tried to ask me a few questions. I explained there had been an accident in the new tunnel and left it at that. He took their names, stared at Glacier and at my chromark, and hurried back behind his desk.

While I waited, I found a notepad and wrote a short letter. I found an attendant who could take it to a delivery service and explained where I needed it to go. I only hoped she would get it before anything dangerous happened here.

With that taken care of, I finally let myself collapse in a chair. Glacier curled up at my feet and put her head on her paws. I examined the cat's injuries from above. Some of them looked bad, but what could I do about it?

The hospital probably wasn't equipped to deal with giant saber-toothed cats.

My breath came out in shudders. Now that I'd allowed myself to relax a bit, exhaustion took over. My hands shook. I slumped in the chair and closed my eyes. Maybe I could rest until a doctor came out with news. Just a minute or two…

I jerked awake with a gasp. Glacier lifted her head and growled. I wanted to growl myself. Six members of the Cerulean Corps stood in front of me. Four of them aimed their electric projectile weapons at my chest. I sighed. I was in no condition for another fight. Glacier wasn't either, as she didn't even get up.

"Are you Beryl, the rebel?" one of them demanded.

"Yes, I'm Beryl. Beryl the dragonslayer. Beryl the exhausted. What can I do for you gentlemen?" I closed my eyes and let my head rest on the back of the chair again.

"Our… boss wants to see you." Odd. He acted like he didn't want to say the word "boss."

"Then your boss will have to come see me here. I'm not moving until I find out what's going on with my friends." I opened my eyes and gestured toward the examination rooms.

"She's coming now," one of the others said.

Another figure approached from the outer doors. "Put those weapons down," a female voice snapped. "I told you he was our guest."

A small woman in a Cerulean Corps uniform came to a stop and put her hands behind her back, looking down at me. "You've looked better, Beryl."

Recognition finally hit me. "Sapphire. You got my note." I hadn't seen her in… months? Had it been over a year by now? My brain didn't want to calculate numbers. She'd been one of Caedan's first recruits, but had returned to the city instead of staying with us.

"Yes." She pointed to the others. "Spread out. Form a perimeter around this place. If they're not bleeding, don't let anyone in." They moved to obey.

I wrinkled my brow. "I don't remember you being a part of the Corps."

"A lot has happened since we first met." She looked toward the examination rooms. "Who's in there?"

"Lainey. You met her, I think." I pointed at Glacier. "This was her kitten back then. The other one's her father. They were both hurt bad." I hesitated. "In the tunnel to the outside."

Sapphire nodded as if she'd expected that. "How bad is it?"

"I don't know. They haven't told me anything since I got here."

"I'll find out." She strode confidently to the doors and walked right in.

I couldn't get over the change in her. When Sapphire joined us back at our first base, the Achromatic Asylum, she'd been eager to help, young and respectful—she called me "Mr. Beryl," even though I couldn't be more than two or three years older. But confident and commanding? Not back then. She'd followed Caedan's lead without question. I struggled to remember what else I knew about her. Then I remembered the most important thing: she was Peri's sister. Peri, the ex-priest who'd sacrificed himself to save this city. She'd joined Caedan because of him.

Sapphire re-emerged through the doors, escorting a slightly overweight doctor with her. "Tell him," she ordered.

The doctor wiped sweat from his brow and eyed the enormous cat at my feet. "Yes, well, the two patients are... Ah, the older male is stabilized. His left leg, of course, was severely broken, along with three ribs, two fingers, and his collarbone. He has a concussion and multiple other contusions across his body. We're still in the process of setting everything, but there do not appear to be any serious internal injuries. The next twelve hours should tell if we've missed anything."

"And the girl?" I half-rose from my seat.

The doctor glanced at Sapphire. "Uh, she is... in more serious condition. While she has fewer broken bones, her head injury is much worse. She suffered some kind of traumatic brain injury beyond a concussion. She also sustained a dislocated kneecap on her right knee, numerous contusions like the other patient, and—"

"What do you mean by brain injury?" I stood up. Glacier lifted her head from the floor and looked at me.

"It's impossible to say right now," he answered, wiping his forehead again. "When the brain is suddenly jolted by an impact, which I assume happened in this case, brain cells are damaged. Concussion is the most common form this takes, but as I said, her damage is more severe. She has not regained consciousness, and... I cannot say when she will."

I trembled and clenched my fists.

The doctor hurried on: "Both probably also have some soft tissue injuries: sprains and muscle damage of various kinds, but—"

I spun and slammed my cybernetic fist through the wall. Glacier jumped to her feet. The doctor backpedaled. One of the other Corps troops ran across the room toward us.

Sapphire put a hand on my shoulder. "Beryl. We're on thin ice here." Her eyes darted around the room, and she waved off the soldier. "You need to control yourself. It may not be as bad as you're thinking." She looked to the doctor. "Is it?"

"I-I have no guarantees," he stammered. "She may come out of this coma, or she may not. We just don't know enough yet. It's too early to say."

"Can I see her?"

The doctor glanced at Sapphire again. "I, uh… for a few moments only. We are still treating her injuries and searching for any we may have missed."

I took a step. The doctor turned and led the way. I followed him; Glacier stayed at my side. Sapphire came as well, staying several feet behind.

Lainey lay still, her skin barely creating a contrast with the white bed. Bandages wrapped around the top of her head, hiding the bruise I'd seen growing there. Her right leg was elevated in a kind of sling. The knee area looked swollen and discolored. A nurse held her left hand, gently exploring each finger.

Glacier started forward. I knelt and caught her around the neck. "Stay here, girl. She'll be all right," I whispered. Glacier gently strained against my hold. I'd been told once that animals could detect emotions in people. If so, Glacier knew I didn't believe what I'd said.

She might die. I might never see her sparkling eyes again. Never hold her in my arms. Never— I buried my face in Glacier's fur and fought against the sobs that wanted to explode.

"Beryl…" Sapphire stepped closer. "Beryl, I'm so sorry. But we need to talk about this."

I swallowed hard and took a deep breath. Lainey would… she would want me to…

It didn't matter. A sob escaped anyway. I choked against it and stood up, wiping my face. I turned, expecting Sapphire to guide me out of this room of pain.

Instead, she put out her arms and held me. "I understand," she whispered.

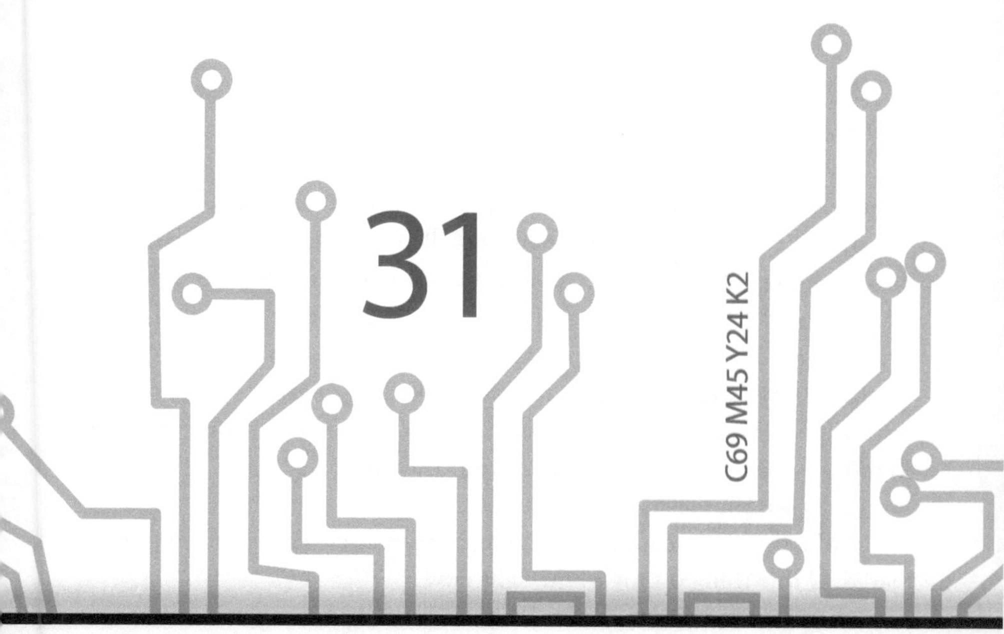

Of course she understood. Out of anyone I knew, she understood. I let the tears fall, dampening her stiff and shiny Cerulean Corps uniform. She let me have a minute or so before breaking the hug. She gestured to the doctor to join us back in the hall. I did notice her wiping something from one of her own eyes as we left.

While I composed myself, she exchanged a few words with the doctor. As soon as I could speak without choking, I asked, "Are they the best?"

The doctor looked at me with a furrowed brow. "I'm sorry?"

I pointed back at Lainey's room. "You and the doctors working on her. Are they the best?"

The doctor sighed. "I hear that question too often from worried family members. Look, this is the finest hospital in Caesious. Everyone here has taken great pride in their medical education. I would trust my life to any one of them."

"I need Hunter," I muttered.

"What?"

I turned to Sapphire. "Can you keep them safe?"

Sapphire looked at the doctor and nodded back toward the patients. The doctor hurried away, probably grateful to get away from me. "Safe from who, exactly?" Sapphire asked. "No offense, but I need to know what I'm dealing with here."

"Onyx. Troilus Green. Chroma's zealots. Anyone else that would want to hurt her. Or me." I guess I did have a long list of enemies.

She folded her arms. "I will do everything I can. You have to understand this city… it's been messed up since you killed Caesious. At first, Incarnadine took over things. Then you killed him too, and the black dragons took over. The constant void at the top made things pretty chaotic." She gestured to her uniform. "There are currently four separate factions within the Cerulean Corps. After I came back here, I made it my goal to push my way to the top. Right now, I almost control most of one of those factions." She gave a significant look at each of the other Corps members stationed around the room. "But as you could probably tell, I have dissension even within these ranks."

"What does that mean for Lainey?" Her story was interesting, but I had only one thing on my mind right now.

"I will do everything I can, Beryl." She looked straight into my eyes. "But I cannot promise you. None of us are truly safe. None of us have ever been truly safe since you started all of this."

That was fair. I nodded.

"But I have people I can trust," she went on. "We will watch both of them for you. We'll do everything we can to protect them. But they'll be much safer if you and your cat get out of here. You attract too much attention."

I took a deep breath and nodded again. "I know. You're right. I know a doctor I'd like to check on them. I'll send him with Caedan or one of the other guys."

"Sure. I'll make sure they let him in." She paused. "You should also know that Viridia is up to something."

"I've heard something about that."

"His people have been here a lot. I think they found Caesious's source. That's all I know for now."

The blue dragon's source? That couldn't be good.

Sapphire looked toward the door and frowned. "Now how are you going to get back to wherever you live now?"

I considered it for a minute. "If not for the rush, I'd be happy to walk back, honestly. But if you can get me a train ticket to Auric, that'll be a lot faster."

"You can't take a train in your condition." She gestured at me with a bemused smile, and then at Glacier. "Or with her."

I guess. We'd done it before, but we'd taken an entire car. That might not be within Sapphire's capabilities. I wanted to hear more about the Corps factions and everything, but… not now.

"Fortunately," Sapphire went on, "I have a better idea. Come with me."

After giving orders to the others, she led us out through the back of the hospital. Only then did I notice Glacier limping hard, favoring her back left paw. I hoped this walk wouldn't be far. From the hospital, we traveled several blocks away to a kind of warehouse. In the early evening glow from the ever-present blue lights, we saw only one or two other people. They appeared in too much of a hurry to even notice our strange appearance.

Sapphire pulled open an overhead door and flipped the lights on. "How about this?"

I stepped inside and stared. "A four-wheeler?"

"Please." Sapphire grinned and walked past me and patted the vehicle on the hood. "This is much more than those little carts you and Caedan drive around the hills."

She was right. This vehicle was significantly larger than our four-wheelers, but smaller than a truck. It had a cover, but no doors or windows. Most important for right now: Glacier could fit in the back seats without any trouble. I walked in a circle around it.

"It's beautiful."

"I wouldn't go that far." Sapphire checked the fuel. "You should be good to go. There are two extra fuel cans on the back here."

"Caedan will be jealous." I helped Glacier climb in.

"He can drive it back. This is a loan," Sapphire warned as she gave me a boost into the driver's seat. "I want it back."

"Not a problem," I answered. "He'll be coming back with Hunter. Our doctor."

Sapphire looked me over. "Don't try to drive too far. Get outside the city and find a place to sleep."

I nodded. "Yeah." I started the engine. "Thanks, Sapphire. For everything."

"We'll take care of them, Beryl. Be safe." She waved me off.

I gunned the engine and drove out into the street. This vehicle responded a little faster than the four-wheelers. It took me a few minutes to get used to the differences. We crossed the bridge and left Caesious behind. After about twenty minutes, I found a dell between two hills and parked the vehicle.

Glacier was already sound asleep on the back seats. I found a way to lay across the two front seats myself and joined her. I was out in seconds.

The pesky sun woke me earlier than I would have liked. I groaned, feeling the ache all over my body. Glacier made a similar noise. I laughed. "We're both not ready for another day, are we?"

But Lainey needed us. A few minutes—and a few more groans—later, I started up the vehicle and headed back toward home.

On the long drive, I had plenty of time to think. I couldn't get the sight of Lainey in the hospital bed out of my mind. When Onyx had taken Kelly, I'd felt somewhat like I did now. Despair threatened to overwhelm me. After all we had done, all the fights we'd won, was this it? Would I lose Lainey now? Six dragons were dead, yet victory seemed further away than ever.

But now, as then, I replaced the despair with something else: something I'd spent years nourishing, the foundation for my first rebellion.

Rage.

I brought the vehicle to a stop and closed my eyes. Behind me, I heard Glacier shift, curious about the halt. I'd started all this because of the hate and anger I held toward Viridia, because his priests killed my baby sister. The rage I felt now was no different. Fine. If that's what it took, that's what I would do. That's who I would be.

I opened my eyes and started driving again. Chroma's zealots would pay for this. They were the real enemy now. Onyx had proposed working together? Fine. That's what we would do. Whatever it took, I was going to take them down.

And I already had an idea of how we could.

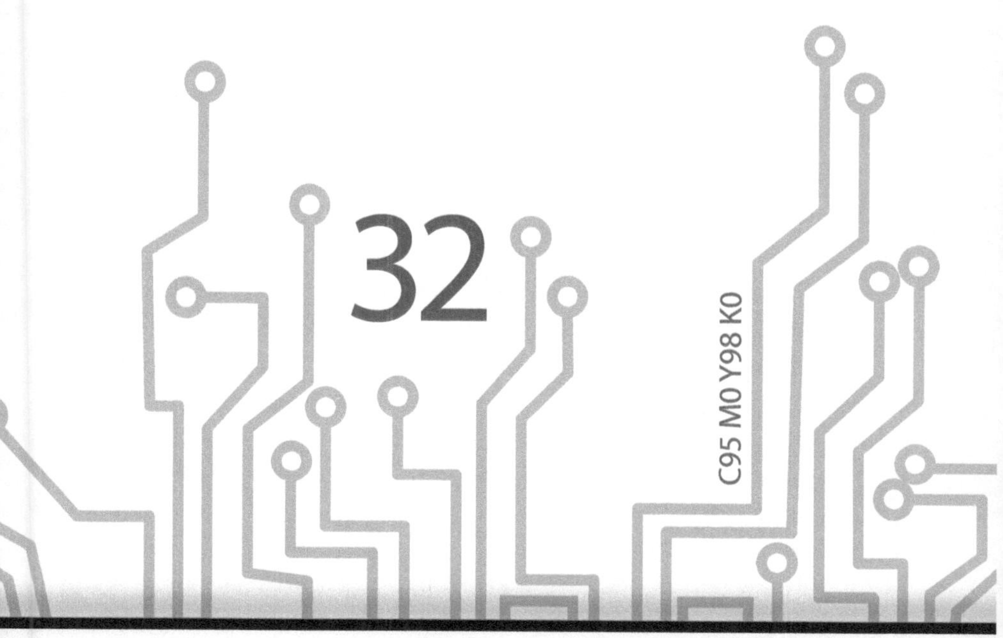

32

The new vehicle didn't save much time in the trip across The Circle, but it was certainly a nicer ride. My poor bruised body needed that.

When at last I arrived at the hill, Saxe met me with wide-eyed admiration of the four-wheeler. I jumped out and issued orders before he could say anything: "Get Hunter out here right away! Tell the others I need to meet with them as soon as possible."

"Uh… which others?"

"Everyone!" I pointed toward the doors, and he took off. He'd barely disappeared before Lovat ran out to meet me. It took a moment for that to register: he ran. I met him with a hug and congratulations.

Together, we checked on Glacier. The cat had barely moved since we left Caesious. She lifted her head at my touch. Poor thing.

"What happened?" Lovat asked, stroking the cat's back.

"A lot. Let me tell everyone at once."

Hunter emerged from the base a few moments later, followed by Caedan. The former hurried to look at me, while the latter admired the vehicle.

"Are you badly hurt?" Hunter asked.

"Not me." I pointed to Glacier. "Her."

Hunter took a step back. "I am not an animal doctor."

"It can't be that different. We'll get her down to one of the rooms, and you can treat her there. I know her paw is injured, besides all the obvious." I gestured at the scabbed lacerations.

Hunter still didn't look convinced. "Will she let me help her? She is... most formidable."

"Can't you put her to sleep while you do it?"

"I do not know the proper anesthesia for such a beast. I—"

"I don't care!" I interrupted. "Do whatever you have to. Recruit whoever you have to. Just do it. And then get ready for a trip. You're going to Caesious."

Caedan stepped closer. "What happened, Beryl? Where's Lainey?"

"I'll explain everything down below. Then you get ready too. You're driving Hunter."

Caedan brightened. "In this?"

I couldn't help smiling. I patted the hood of the vehicle. "Yeah. Sapphire wants it back."

Glacier followed my instructions for some reason. Maybe without Lainey around, she defaulted to me as the boss? I definitely didn't understand it, but I appreciated it. Especially since no one else seemed inclined to follow my instructions. Almost everyone came outside instead of gathering in the meeting room.

With plenty of help, we managed to get Glacier into one of the unused rooms. Hunter recruited Fern and Royal to help him anesthetize the big cat. I summoned everyone else back to the meeting room. Inside, I saw Don had been repairing some of the furniture destroyed in the fight with Amaranth.

Thus far, I'd refused to answer anyone's questions. Gathered together, I could ignore them no longer. I narrated everything that had taken place in our journey outside The Circle. The revelation about Chroma's lack of existence created quite a stir. But of course, Lainey and Carl's condition trumped everything else.

"Can we trust the doctors?" Kelly asked. "How can they possibly keep it a secret that they have two patients from outside The Circle?"

"I trust Sapphire," Caedan said. "She'll keep them in line."

"Even so, it won't be easy," Stacy put in. "I'll come with you to help out on that front."

"You can't come," Caedan protested. "You're not—"

"Blue?" Stacy interrupted. "Who taught you people how to use make-up, my boy?"

My boy? What was going on here? And then it hit me. Oh. That's why they'd been outside together the base when Amaranth's people attacked. They were a couple. I can be dense, but sometimes—eventually—I catch on.

"Maybe we should all go," Cobalt put in. "Those of us from there, I mean."

"I don't know. Caedan, what do you think?"

He scowled at Stacy, who folded her arms across her chest. I knew who would win that argument. I don't think I'd ever seen Stacy lose one. "That new four-wheeler carries four comfortably, from what I saw. With Hunter and me, we have room for two. I don't think—"

"We knew that much," Stacy mumbled loud enough to be heard.

"Good," I cut in. "That's settled. Let's move on to making plans for Chroma."

"Beryl…" Bice had been quiet up until now. "Are you sure we should focus on that right now? You've just been through several horrible days. Maybe we should come back to this tomorrow."

"I've had the entire trip back here to recover and think about this. Another day isn't going to change how I feel." Now it was my turn to glare.

Bice sighed and sat back. "I would prefer to talk with you privately first."

"Maybe later." I looked at the others. "Everything related to those zealots is connected to the one temple. If we could destroy that, we would destroy every advantage they have. The people outside and inside The Circle would be free of them."

"What about Onyx?" Don asked.

"We can deal with Onyx later. In fact, for now, we're on the same side." I heard several exclamations of negativity, but I didn't care. "I've got a plan," I pushed on. "And we may need Onyx to help with it. We need to go talk with Taizong Gold first."

"What is this plan?" Caedan asked.

"I don't want to say just yet. I need to know if it's even possible." I knew I was being stubborn, but I didn't care. "And for that, I need Taizong Gold."

"I'll go with you to Auric," Lovat spoke up. "I haven't been there yet."

"It's nothing special," Don muttered.

"Look," I said. "We started all of this with one goal: to free humans from the dragons. Since then, we discovered we had another enemy: the zealots of Chroma. We have to destroy all of them to be free. All of them."

"Killing dragons is one thing," Bice said. "But killing other humans—"

"Have you been listening?" I exclaimed. "The zealots aren't really human! They're, they're copies. Carl called them clones. They're not like you and me."

"Are you sure about that?"

"As sure as I can be. And I don't remember you complaining when we blew up The Flame building."

"We were forced into that, and we did our best to get everyone out."

"Fine. You can try to get people out, if you can find a way there." I glanced around the rest of the room. "I'm going to Auric tomorrow. Whoever wants to come is welcome."

Lovat pumped his fist.

"But what about Viridia?" Jaden asked. "He's up to something."

"Yeah," Royal said. "We're seeing Viridian Guard everywhere."

I frowned. I did not want to deal with that problem right now, but…

"They're right," Kelly said. "Something is going on."

"I know." I sighed. "Sapphire said she thought they had found Caesious's source." Seeing a couple of confused looks, I reminded myself that not everyone had been a part of all our conversations and discoveries. "Each one of the dragons had a special place called a source. It's where all the magic power, the resomancy, comes from. And it's part of what kept them alive for so very long."

Caedan looked thoughtful. "Viridia finding them can't be good."

"Maybe that's what they're looking for in the other cities," Royal said. "We've seen them in Incarnadine and Amaranth."

"Is Troilus Green looking for a way to power himself?" Bice wondered. "Does it work when he's not actually a dragon?"

"You know more about the power than any of us," I pointed out. "You've even used it."

Bice frowned. "I didn't know what I was doing back then. But this troubles me. A lot."

It troubled me too. I couldn't see any reason for it, but… I wasn't a thousand-year-old dragon either. After all this time, I still forgot how much more they'd seen and known than I did.

"All right. Caedan, see what else Sapphire knows about this. Get as many specifics as you can. I'll also ask around in Auric about it. And we may need to send someone to Viridia." Ugh. Who could we send there? Troilus Green knew all of us who came from there, and the others didn't know much about the city. I looked down at the table and mentally went through all the possibilities.

"If I might say something…"

I looked up to see who'd spoken. "Chance?"

"Indeed." The young draconic stood up next to Kelly. "It seems you are going to need to contact Onyx. I can provide a way to do that."

"Chance, are you sure?" Kelly asked.

He nodded. "Whenever you are ready, Beryl, I will mentally connect with my father and let you speak with him."

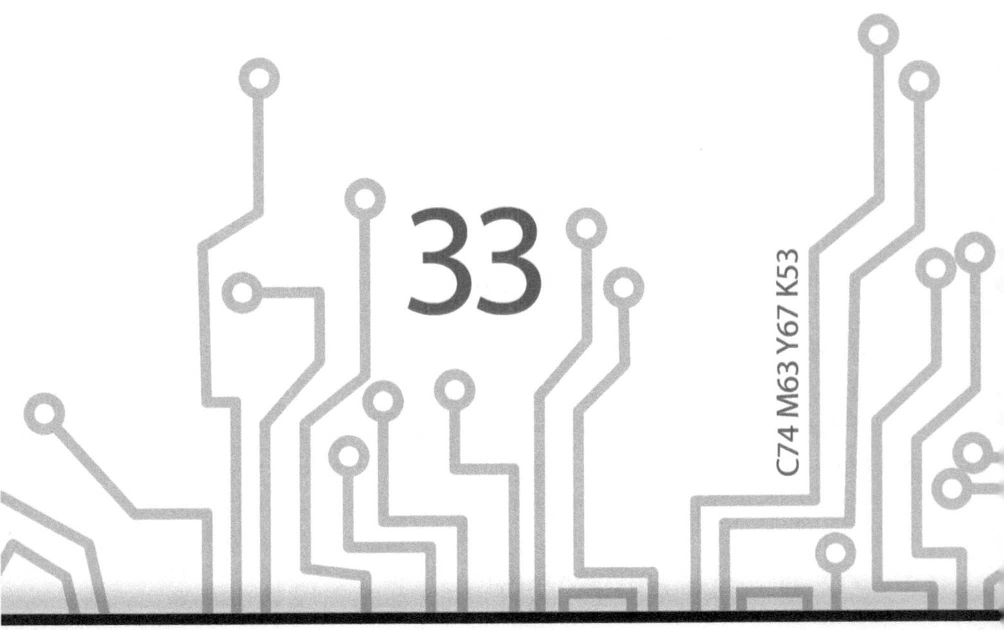

It sounded like an incredibly dangerous thing to do, but Chance insisted he could do it. After I dismissed the meeting, he and Kelly stayed behind to discuss the idea. Bice also lingered. I tried not to notice.

"I told you a few weeks ago," Chance explained, "that when my memories returned, so did my connection to my father. He knew me in that moment, and he spoke to me."

"You didn't tell me this part," Kelly said.

"I didn't want to worry you, Mother."

I remembered Chance's words to me, but I couldn't remember all of the details. The multiple concussions I received not long afterwards might have affected my thoughts of that conversation. And maybe others. I should listen to the recording of Loden again.

"He couldn't tell where you were, though," I recalled. "And couldn't take control of you."

"No. He can… know where I am in a general sense. For example, if I left The Circle, I believe he would know it. But he can't pinpoint this exact location."

That probably explained how he had found me when I went out jogging. It didn't make me feel much more secure.

Chance pulled himself back into a chair. His legs dangled, not quite touching the floor. "He has tried to communicate with me twice more since then. I have not responded."

"But you responded the first time, right?"

"I spoke with him, yes." Chance looked away. "He was not happy when I did not immediately guide him here."

I could imagine. Onyx possessed very little in the way of patience.

"And he couldn't control you or find you, right?" Kelly said.

"I have said that."

"I know. I want you to assure me again."

"He could not control me or find me, Mother."

"How long did you talk with him?" Bice broke in.

Chance looked to him. "Only a few minutes. I made my choice before he spoke. I am staying here. With my mother and Beryl."

Staying with his mother: I could understand. Staying with me? I didn't get that part. Who was I to this… being? He possessed memories dating back several hundred years, at least. He'd helped rule the lost city of Onyx before the other dragons destroyed it. Why in the world did he think I was significant?

Bice sat down across from Chance. "I would suggest limiting the conversation to as short as possible, then. It may be that with enough time, Onyx could reassert some degree of… connection. Didn't you have such a thing in your previous life?"

Chance hesitated. "Yes," he admitted. "We had a much stronger connection then. But I will not allow it to happen again."

"You don't want it to, of course," Bice said gently. "But in spite of all these memories, your body is still young. You may not be able to resist as much as you think you can."

"If he wants to do it, let him do it, Bice," I said.

Bice looked at me with his eyes narrowed. "If you want to throw your life away after all this time, son, that's up to you. But I will not sit here and let you do it to anyone else. We all have to make our own choices, based on all the possible information. You're not a king, Beryl."

I wanted to explode at him. It felt like the other times he'd lectured me, back when we first started all this. Back then, he made me so angry, even though he'd been trying to calm my anger. He… he'd been right some of the time. Most of the time. Maybe all of the time. And I hated that right now.

"Chance… I'd like to try it, but we'll keep it short." I looked to Bice and Kelly. "Is that all right with everyone?"

After their hesitant agreement, I turned back to the draconic. "So how does this work?"

"Give me a moment." He closed his eyes. Nothing happened for at least an entire minute. Kelly, Bice, and I exchanged looks but didn't say anything. I didn't want to interrupt the process, whatever it was.

"He's here," Chance announced without opening his eyes. "He's annoyed but willing to listen."

"How do we do this?" I asked. "Is he going to speak directly through you?"

"No. That would give him control."

Bice's eyebrows went up. I knew what he was thinking: Chance had said Onyx couldn't control him at all, but he'd just contradicted that.

"You speak, and I will relay your words back and forth," Chance added.

"All right. Um. Tell Onyx I've been to Chroma's temple, and now I'm reconsidering his suggestion of an alliance."

"It's not an alliance," Kelly said. "Not even close."

"Shh. We'll deal with that later." I waited for Chance to communicate with the dragon.

"Onyx is pleased you agree with him," he related. "What do you have in mind?"

"Tell him to remember Peri." I could have spelled it out, but I knew Onyx would get it. Plus, I wanted to remind him how I still held him responsible for Peri's death. I might be willing to work with him, but I would never forget what he'd done.

"He understands. Auric took back the other large explosives. Do you know where they are?"

"I'm going to find out. If I do, does he think he can get one to the temple?"

Both Kelly and Bice had sudden intakes of breath at that.

After a long pause, Chance said, "He says he'll fly the bleaking thing over the mountains himself if he has to."

Wouldn't that be something? And exactly what I'd been thinking. "That was my idea," I told him. "Tell him we'll be in touch when we know more. Oh. And tell him to pull all of his people out of the three cities we agreed on."

A muscle spasmed on Chance's face. "He… he says…"

Oh no. I grabbed Chance and shook him. "Break the connection, Chance! Come back!"

"Chance!" Kelly shouted.

His eyes opened and rolled back in his head. He wavered as if about to pass out. Kelly scrambled over and grabbed his hand. His head snapped into position, and his eyes returned to normal. He blinked three times and shook his head. "I am myself and unharmed," he said.

We all sat back in relief.

"Are you sure?" Kelly asked.

Chance nodded. "Onyx attempted to assert some measure of control over my mind, forcing his way in so that he could see all of you. I resisted. When you both touched me, I was able to cast him out. The connection is broken."

He said all this in such a matter-of-fact way, he might have been describing how he retrieved a snack from the refrigerator.

"I'm sorry, Chance," I told him. "I won't ask you to do that again." I paused. "Not for a conversation, anyway. Maybe just to send him a message…"

"Beryl!" Bice snapped.

"Right, right. Sorry."

"Both of us," Kelly mused. She looked at me. "Why do you suppose that is?"

I shrugged. I didn't want to think about it too hard.

"You really don't know?" Bice asked. "It's obvious."

Kelly turned to him. "What do you mean? I'm his mother, but what about Beryl?"

"Beryl is the reason Chance is alive," Bice said. "In almost every sense that matters, he is Chance's father."

"The lifegiver," Chance added without looking at me.

I looked from one to the other in the room and shook my head. "I can't deal with this right now."

"Why do you resist this?" Bice asked. "You're a father figure to Lovat too, or at the very least, an older brother. You're the leader of this band, and that means you have relationships with all of us, like it or not. And a lot of those put you in the lead position of the relationship."

"I didn't ask for that."

He stood up. "Yes, you did. When you started gathering people around you to fight the dragons, you assumed a position of leadership. You can't be a leader without this kind of thing happening." Bice took a step toward me, his eyes locked on mine. "Father. Brother. Leader. Hero. That's who you are. So you have to decide: how do you live up to those titles?"

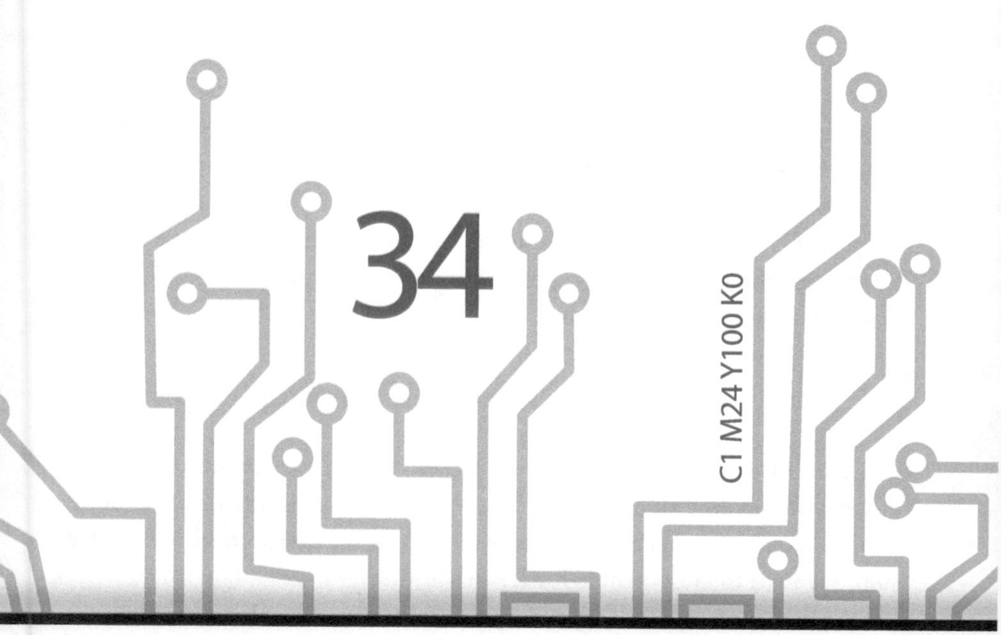

I made sure Hunter had everything he needed. "Keep an eye on the cat," he told me. "I treated the wounds I could find. I do not know if it was enough. She should sleep for a long time."

He, Caedan, and Stacy left a few minutes later. I watched Sapphire's four-wheeler until it vanished from view. Hunter was the best. If anyone could help Lainey through this, he could. I still wished I were going back with them, but… I had other things to do.

I wanted to head out now, but my own fatigue convinced me to wait at least one night. I avoided any more conversations with Bice, or anyone else, for that matter. I found my own bed and spent a restless night. I thought my exhaustion would make me sleep hard, but I was wrong. I'd slept better in the four-wheeler than I did now.

My brain would not shut up. Over and over and over, I saw Lainey lying there unmoving. I saw Rick transforming into Onyx. I saw the explosion that killed Peri. I saw Loden dying in my arms. I saw my baby sister.

It was too much. I sat on the edge of the bed and put my head in my hands. Where did it all end? Immediately, I answered myself: it ends with the death of all the dragons and Chroma's zealots. I'd come this far. They were all dead now, except for Onyx and… Viridia. Troilus Green. Whatever. We'd accomplished so much. But was it worth it?

If I'd never run into Rick, where would I be now? Still working at the bicycle shop? Would I have ever gained the courage to pursue a real relationship with Kelly, or would we still just be co-workers? Loden would be alive. Peri would be alive. And Lainey… I would never have met her.

I took a few deep breaths. I didn't know what time it was, but I couldn't sleep, and I couldn't just sit here thinking about everything. I got up and headed for the kitchen. I'd get something to eat and wait for the others to wake up. I had work to be done.

Don insisted on coming with us to Auric. I suspect he didn't trust me alone with Lovat. Not any more. But he wouldn't say it. He trudged along behind us, his usual silent self, but I could feel his disapproval with every step. He held me responsible for Lovat's injuries.

As for Lovat, he ran back and forth, chattering about how much better he was getting at using the boosts to his legs. He demonstrated his new prowess with frequent long jumps and bursts of speed. We discussed the weird feeling that boosts gave us. I cautioned him against overdoing it, remembering how fatigued I used to get when I boosted my legs all the time.

In one sense, I enjoyed having a conversation about cyb implants with someone who understood. I never could explain how it felt to anyone else, but Lovat experienced it. And it excited him. His antics brought a smile to my face multiple times during our walk to the golden city. As long as I didn't look back at Don's face, I could enjoy the moments.

We could have taken a four-wheeler, but that would have kept Lovat from demonstrating his abilities. And the walk would do us all good. I needed a way to burn energy before I talked with Auric's representatives.

Four members of the Aurelian Sentinels met us at the edge of the city. As always, they looked very impressive in their golden armor. I motioned for Don and Lovat to wait while I stepped forward to speak with them.

"You know who I am," I declared. "I am here to speak with either Taizong Gold or Captain Tawn."

"We have instructions concerning you," the leader said. "You are to come with us." He glanced at Don and Lovat. "Alone."

I nodded and walked back to them. "You two wait for me on that hill over there. If I'm not back in… four hours, head back to the base."

"It's a trap," Don said.

"It might be. You're right. But at this point, I'm very tired of sneaking around and trying to figure things out." I clenched both fists. "If it's a trap, I'm going to spring it and fight my way out of it. If it's not... then maybe I'll find what I need here."

Don unslung his tall backpack. "You need any weapons or anything?"

"He is the weapon," Lovat said.

I snorted. "I doubt they'll let me carry anything obvious." Curiosity made me ask: "What do you have in there?"

"Everything."

"Good. Keep yourself and Lovat safe. If I need you... I'll let you know somehow."

Don nodded. "Let's go," he told Lovat.

The boy hesitated longer. "I wanted to see the city," he complained.

"You will," I promised. "Later. For now, let's do what they want."

With that settled, I returned to the Sentinels. "Take me where I need to be."

The leader nodded and turned. I followed him while the other three moved into position to surround me. It was cute how they thought they could control me.

We took a short walk through the streets of Auric. Once again, I admired the architecture: the pointed roofs with rounded corners, wraparound decks and balconies, so different from any of the other cities. Auric allowed his people to develop their own culture, I suppose, rather than enforcing things on them like Viridia. Our visits here always challenged my long-held beliefs about the dragons.

We entered a large glass-covered building that looked vaguely familiar. I noticed a few panes replaced with temporary pieces of plywood, remnants of the black dragons' rampage. The Sentinels took me to a descending staircase. At its bottom, we stepped on to one of the moving sidewalks and waited while it took us deeper into and under the city.

I expected to be taken to the dragon's former home, but we stopped at a different spot between two of the moving sidewalks. The Sentinels took me to a door which led into something like a cross between a fancy office and a meeting room. Captain Tawn sat at a sprawling desk at the far end of the room, talking with a Sentinel officer and two civilians. If he swiveled his chair around, he would be at the head of a long table surrounded by other chairs. I noted the nearest chairs, at the other end of the table, were designed for draconics.

Tawn glanced up as I entered but continued his conversation. He handed some papers to the civilians and dismissed them. The officer looked at me before stepping back and standing at attention behind him. The civilians avoided the door behind Tawn and left through the one I'd entered, but not without some odd looks at me. I lifted my cyb hand in a short wave to confuse them further.

"Beryl," Captain Tawn said after the door closed. "To what do we owe the… honor of your visit this time? Quite frankly, I did not expect to see you again, at least not so soon."

"Good to see you too," I answered. "I see you're busy cleaning up from the black dragons. Is it going well?"

"That particular job was well in hand before I returned to the city." Tawn picked up a cup of hot liquid and took a sip. "You haven't answered my question. Why are you here?"

"Is Taizong Gold around?" I craned my head as if searching the room. "I wanted to speak with him about his, uh, grandmother."

Tawn's eyes narrowed. He made some kind of gesture I didn't recognize, and the other Sentinels left the room. He set his cup back on the desk and stood. "We're alone now. What news do you have of… Chroma?"

I considered my options and decided on being straightforward. "She's dead. Her zealots keep things running and pretend she's still around."

Tawn showed no reaction. He placed his hands behind his back. "And how do you know this?"

"I visited her temple. I saw her skeleton."

"And they let you live?"

"They tried to stop me."

Tawn regarded me impassively. "Were any other man in The Circle to bring such a report to me, I would dismiss it as a ridiculous fabrication." He turned his head to look toward the wall. "But you… you have a peculiar proclivity for wandering into dangerous situations and somehow emerging. I cannot immediately disregard your story." He turned back. "But neither can I accept it at face value. Do you have any proof of what you say?"

I blinked. "No, of course not. How could I gain proof of that? I couldn't exactly steal one of her bones." I chuckled at the memory. "But I did use one of her teeth in my escape."

Tawn said nothing for a few moments, then sighed and returned to his chair. "Let us assume, for the moment, that I believe you. I'll report your findings to Taizong and the other draconics, of course. But why did you come here? What is your purpose in bringing us this news?"

"Because Chroma's zealots are enemies of us all." I took a step around the table toward him. "We can fight together against them."

"The zealots are immune to our weaponry, if we even wanted to fight them."

I held up my hand. "They're not immune to me. And I know how we can take all of them out at once."

He leaned back and steepled his fingers together. "And how is that?"

"I need one of the giant explosive devices you brought to the Hub and used to threaten the other cities."

He laughed in my face.

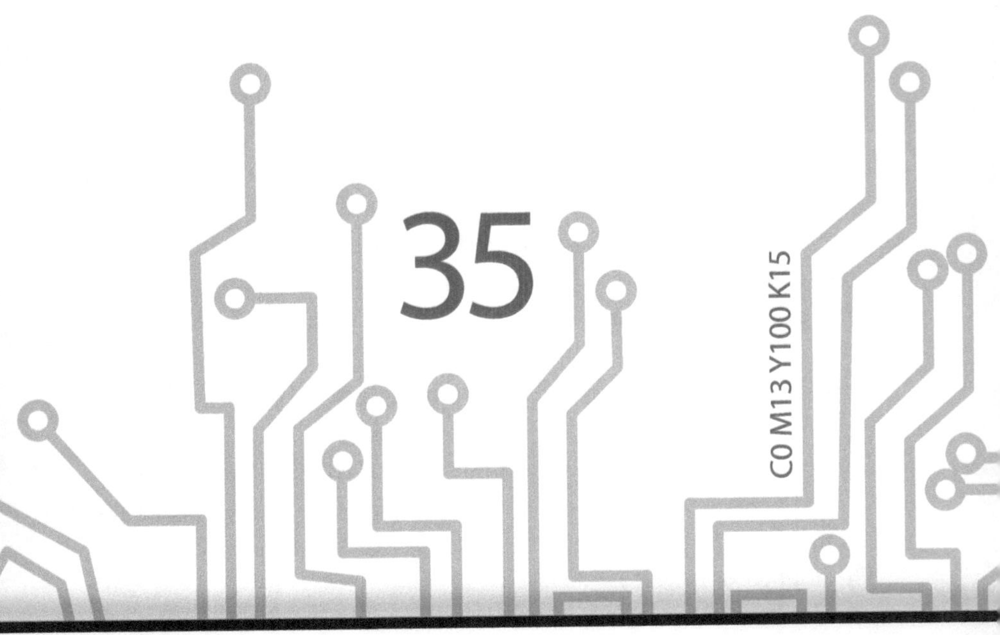

"I'm serious," I insisted. "If we destroy their temple, it will destroy all of their special abilities. We can be free of their influence all at once."

"Even if—" Tawn broke off and shook his head. "Even if I believed you, and even if we still possessed one of those devices, how in the almighty name of Auric do you think you could deliver such a thing outside The Circle?"

"That part is my secret."

He snorted. "I will concede that with your enhancements, you are significantly stronger than an average human. But you've seen the size of these things. You can't carry one. The only ways to the outside are by climbing the mountains or through Chroma's new tunnel. You can't do either with one of those devices."

"I have a way."

"You stubborn claims notwithstanding, the idea is preposterous and impossible." He turned his chair back toward the desk. "You may leave now."

"If you don't have any of the devices left, what happened to them?" I persisted. "Where can I get one?"

"You can't. Their creation is a closely-guarded secret."

I folded my arms. "I want to speak with Taizong Gold."

"That will not happen." He waved dismissively. "Go back to your little hole in the ground and leave the governing of this world to your betters."

"You pathetic man." I'd had enough of this.

His head turned sharply. "Excuse me?"

I stepped closer and caught hold of the edge of the table with my cyb hand. I ground my fingers into the wood's surface. "I came to you with a plan to rescue all the humans, both inside and outside The Circle. This is your chance to be a part of something huge. And this is how you treat me? Pathetic."

Tawn stiffened. "If you wish me to call the Sentinels and have you physically removed from our city, I will be happy to oblige."

"Oh, stop it. Stop with the fancy talking and the, the—" I gestured at his posture. "Whatever this is. The dragons are dead. All of them except Onyx, and we'll get to him. This is our chance to be our own people, to govern ourselves however we decide. To be free! Doesn't that mean anything to you?"

"Do you think—" The captain stopped himself and took a deep breath. "Everything you have said today has been ridiculous. I have no reason to believe you."

"The woman I love was almost killed getting this information." My cybernetic fingers punched through the table's surface.

The door behind Captain Tawn opened and Taizong Gold stood in its frame. "Now that is a reason to listen, Captain. Let's hear what the boy has to say."

I bristled at being called a "boy," but I controlled myself. "Have you been listening this entire time?"

"That is inconsequential." The draconic ducked its head and entered. A wave of heat and sickly-sweet odor filled the room. "Tell me of your visit outside, Beryl Godslayer. I enjoy a good tale, especially one with dire consequences."

I let go of the table and frowned at them both. I couldn't tell if Taizong Gold was being serious or mocking me. "We climbed the mountains," I said. "And visited Chroma's temple."

The draconic moved around the table and found one of the larger chairs. It gestured for me to continue as it sat. I told a little more about my adventures in the temple, leaving out Carl's name and any details about Lainey. "And then we escaped through the tunnel," I concluded. "It's almost complete. That makes the necessity of dealing with these zealots a top priority."

"And when, exactly, did your paramour almost die?" the draconic asked.

"My what?"

"Your woman."

"Oh. In the tunnel. We were attacked by one of the black draconics."

"Of Atramentous or Onyx?"

"Onyx doesn't have any draconics."

"We both know that isn't true."

I glared at him. "Atramentous. Called itself Remus or something like that."

"Rimush Black. Curious. He rarely leaves his city."

"Yeah, that's what he said. Are you going to help with this problem or not?"

The draconic rested its enormous cybernetic forearm on the table. "Think about what you are requesting here, young Beryl. You are asking for us to deliver to you a weapon capable of destroying an entire city. Why do you think we would entrust you with such a thing?"

"Because Auric would have done it."

Taizong Gold froze for a brief moment. I almost didn't catch it. "I do not believe that to be true," he said. "And you would do well to remember to whom you are speaking when you claim knowledge about the almighty Auric."

"Yes, I get it. You're his son. But did either of you listen to the audio recording you gave to me?" I wished I had brought it with me. Idiot. "Auric funded Loden, the genius who created my cybernetics. And they did it so I could fight the zealots."

Captain Tawn and the draconic exchanged glances. "That is still not reason enough to give you such power," Taizong Gold said. "Even if it were possible."

"What do you mean?"

"After we removed the devices from the Hub, Auric ordered their dismantling," Tawn said. "All of them."

"But you know how to rebuild them, right?"

"That is an even more preposterous request," the captain answered. "As if we would build such a thing for you."

"I'm trying to save all of us. It's in your best interests."

Taizong Gold stood up. "This conversation is going in circles now.

Your request is denied, Beryl. If you have nothing more to say—"

"You're making a mistake," I interrupted. When neither responded, I bowed my head and sighed. "Fine. I'll go somewhere else."

"Where else—" Tawn stopped when the draconic lifted his hand.

I turned to leave, but remembered the other news. "Oh, that's right. You need to know that Viridia is up to something."

"What would that be?" Taizong Gold asked.

Captain Tawn looked uncertain for the first time since I'd entered. "We have had some reports of Viridian agents within the city recently," he said.

"They're everywhere," I said. "In all the cities. And they're doing something with the dragons' sources."

"How do you know this?" Tawn demanded.

"We are not the only ones keeping an eye on the other cities." Taizong Gold waved at the captain. "It would be well to check on this."

Captain Tawn got up and went to the door. He spoke with another Sentinel and sent him away.

"You may as well sit," the draconic told me, doing the same himself. "This will take a few minutes."

While we waited, Taizong Gold questioned me further on the visit to Chroma's temple. I kept trying to emphasize the urgency of dealing with the zealots, but he showed no further interest. Finally, the Sentinel returned. After hearing his report, Captain Tawn turned to us with an odd look on his face. "The Viridians are at Auric's source now."

Taizong Gold leaped to his feet. "Let's go find out what they're doing for ourselves."

I took his words to include me, and no one stopped me from following them out of the room. We returned to the huge tunnel with the moving sidewalks. Upon entering one, neither of my two hosts were inclined to stand and wait. They kept moving, walking down the sidewalks faster than the moving devices could carry us. At one point, we had to leave the moving sidewalks and detour around a collapsed area of the tunnel. Another relic of the black dragons' attack.

Another Sentinel met us along the way with a further report. "The Viridians have been taken into custody," Tawn told us, "but they have erected some kind of device."

"Outrageous," Taizong Gold muttered. "How did they even find the source?"

"I don't know," Tawn said. "I didn't even know its location until a few weeks ago."

"It was a secret known only to Auric and three of his children," the draconic grumbled. "And it would have remained that way if he were still with us." He shot a look at me.

Did he blame me for Auric's death? I could understand that, I suppose.

We made our way down further tunnels and through some heavily locked doors. At last, we emerged into another enormous cavern. I saw nothing unusual about it, save that the floor appeared smooth and a little shiny, probably from centuries of a dragon's belly rubbing against it.

I caught a glimpse of some kind of mechanical device toward the center of the cavern, but my attention was drawn to a group of six Viridians being held by Aurelian Sentinels. I took a step toward them, but I was distracted by a Sentinel reporting to Tawn. "They claim to be scientists working on an experiment on behalf of Viridia," he said.

A low chuckle came from the prisoners "He said I might run into you here," said a vaguely-familiar voice.

I turned back, my eyes darting from face to face until they settled on a rough one with skin like leather.

Basil.

"Do you know this individual?" Taizong Gold asked.

"Yes." I fought to contain my anger. "He's a criminal and a traitor. He serves Viridia. Now."

"Hm. Another tale I would be interested in hearing at some point. But for now…" He looked over Basil and the other Viridians. "What are you doing here?"

"We told your men already," one of the others said. "We're scientists. With the death of the other dragons, Viridia is interested in knowing what is occurring with their sources."

The draconic folded his arms. "Until recently, humans were not even aware of the existence of dragon sources."

"Yes, I understand. It's a fascinating area of study that has just opened up to us."

Throughout the conversation, I kept my eyes fixed on Basil. I hadn't forgotten how he'd been responsible for what happened to Stacy, or even how his presence affected the female members of our group throughout his time with us. He hadn't changed since then, other than improving his wardrobe.

Taizong Gold pointed to the device. "And what is the purpose of this apparatus?"

"It's a monitoring device," the scientist answered. "We're trying to learn all we can here about the true nature of the gods—"

"It is a sacrilege. We will remove it at once, and you will be leaving."

"I wouldn't do that if I were you," Basil said.

Taizong Gold looked down at him. "You have something to add, little man?"

"Only that if you tamper with our device, it will detonate. Who knows what will happen to this place if that happens?" Basil hadn't had this kind of arrogance before. Every word he spoke dripped with disrespect.

The draconic beckoned to a Sentinel. "Have the techs examine it without touching it for now. Bring me their assessment as soon as possible."

I followed the tech experts over to the device, not because I thought I could help, but simply to get a better look at the thing. I estimated it at about eight feet tall at its peak and three or four feet wide at the base. The peak came to an actual point in the middle of multiple circles. All of this had been constructed out of polished metal of some kind. It didn't look cybernetic, necessarily, but I thought I could see some similarities between the design and some of Loden's work.

"Multiple incursions into the ground," muttered one of the techs. I stepped closer and looked at the base. Amidst more of the circles, I saw several bars and wires descending into the dirt.

"Explosives?" I asked.

"Oh yes." One of the techs started pointing. "Here, here, and here." Then he apparently realized he didn't need to answer me, and gathered closer with the two others. They whispered together for several minutes before returning to Taizong Gold. I followed along.

"What is it?" the draconic demanded.

"We… are not sure. It may be a monitoring device, as they said," the tech reported. "But it may be something else entirely. The explosives attached to it are quite sophisticated."

"Can you remove it safely?"

The tech hesitated before answering: "I would not want to bet my life upon it, your excellency."

"Very well." Taizong Gold turned back to the Viridians. "We will bet their lives. You installed this device. I demand that you remove it."

"We can't do that," the Viridian scientist said. "The design comes from holy Viridia himself. We don't know how it works. Once activated, only he can remove it."

Captain Tawn rolled his eyes. "You're telling us that this is nothing more than a monitoring device, but it was built by Viridia, and you don't even understand it. This is laughable."

"The captain is correct," Taizong Gold said, folding his arms over his chest. "You are contradicting yourself. You will remove the device, or you will die."

Die? "I don't think—" I started to say.

"I am not requesting your input," the draconic cut me off. "This is my city and my responsibility."

"We, we can't," the Viridian scientist stammered. "We literally can't."

Taizong Gold stepped forward, seized one of the other Viridians with his cybernetic hand, and snapped his neck as if it were nothing. He dropped the body on the ground. "There are five of you left. I have no qualms about summarily executing each and every one of you here and now. So. Who will do as I have commanded?"

My eyes met Basil's. The arrogance he'd shown a few minutes before was no longer there. I could almost see the thought filling his head: "I'm about to die."

He was a horrible human being. And these scientists worked for Viridia. They might have been responsible for some of the terrible things I'd experienced in that city. But… they were humans.

"Very well," Taizong Gold said. He reached out again.

And my cyb hand met his. "Stop."

The draconic's eyes narrowed. "You will remove yourself, Beryl. You are no longer welcome here."

"I'm not welcome in a lot of places. But standing up for humans and life is the main reason for that, and I'm not backing down on it now." Too bad Bice wasn't here; he would have been proud of that line.

"You are alone. You have no weapons. What makes you think you can stop me here?"

"As your father and my… friend liked to say: I am a weapon." To illustrate, I gave my hand an extra boost and pushed his back a few inches.

Taizong Gold shook his head. "I fail to understand your defiance. Even if you were able to defeat me in single combat again, you are surrounded by my soldiers in the most secure place in the city."

"We got in," Basil muttered.

"Are you truly going to try to fight your way out of this entire city?"

The draconic pushed back. I let him move my hand this time.

"If that's what I have to do to keep these men alive, then that's what I'll do."

"Wait." Captain Tawn stepped forward, lifting a hand to hold off Taizong Gold and the other Sentinels. "I'm curious. You have a clearly-defined mission you've been pursuing for years now, if I understand correctly. You've wanted to overthrow all of the dragons and even those who come from outside The Circle." He paused, his brow furrowed. "And you would throw any chance of completing that mission away... for the sake of these men?"

I hesitated, but I knew what I should say. "If I abandon the code I live by, then what's the point?"

Taizong Gold released my hand and stepped back. "And yet... you came here seeking a weapon that could destroy hundreds of lives at once. How does that fit within your code?"

"They... the zealots aren't human. They—" I broke off. I hated this. Hated it so much. But... "You're right. I'm wrong. I just can't think of another way to defeat them."

Captain Tawn stared at me with an expression I couldn't identify. At last he nodded. "I have never agreed with your goals, Beryl. I thought my lord's involvement with you was a whim of his, an amusement. And when he died helping you..." He closed his eyes and took a deep breath. "But. But a man who will stand on his principles and even admit when he is wrong... that is a rarity indeed. You have my respect." He turned to the Sentinels. "Lock the Viridians up. We will decide their fate at a later time."

"When I'm gone?" I challenged.

He looked back at me. "I assure you they will not be tortured or killed. We will attempt to remove their device, and if we are unable... then we will wait and see what happens. That will determine their end."

"Captain, I object," Taizong Gold said.

"Security is my domain, Lord Taizong. I will not relinquish this to you."

"Well." The draconic snorted and stepped back. He folded his arms and watched the Viridians be led away.

Basil met my eyes once more and nodded. Was that gratitude? I didn't know and didn't much care. If I never saw him again, I'd be all right with that. I had much bigger things to worry about.

"I have no idea what to do now," I muttered.

"You fixated on one idea and pursued it without any thought of alternatives," Tawn said. "We are all guilty of doing something similar."

"That's not much help, but thank you. I guess."

He chuckled. "You're so blind sometimes. Auric himself gave you the solution. Don't you remember?"

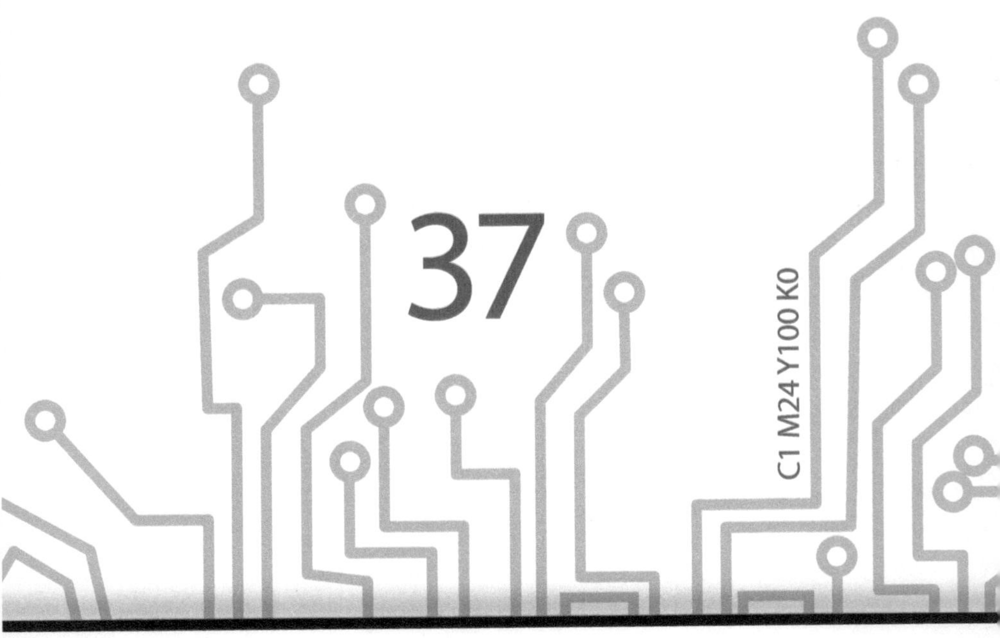

37

"What?" I stared at the captain with no clue what he meant.

He chuckled again. "Let's return to my office. We can discuss more freely there."

I glanced once more at the strange device left by the Viridians. I had to assume they were planting similar devices in the other cities. What did it mean?

The return trip to Tawn's office took longer than the trip to the source. I suppose none of us were in much of a hurry now. Taizong Gold didn't say a word the whole time. He seemed grumpy, if a draconic can be grumpy. Did his annoyance come from not being allowed to kill anyone else? I also couldn't quite understand the chain of command here. I'd gotten the idea that the draconic ruled over everything without Auric. But it appeared to be more complicated.

Back in the office, Captain Tawn pulled his chair over to the table and motioned for me to sit. As I did, Taizong Gold moved to the back door and stood there, arms folded.

"It's honestly somewhat amusing that you don't remember," Tawn said. "But though you have your… code, as you said, you've never struck me as particularly bright."

I scowled. "Did we come back here just so you could insult me some more?"

"No, no. I want to remind you. Do you recall your last conversation with Auric? Before you left for Viridia?"

"Yeah, we went to rescue Stacy."

"He gave you something."

"He—oh." I remembered now. I might be slow, but my brain eventually catches on and fits all the pieces together. "The device I used against Atramentous."

Tawn smiled and nodded. "The electromagnetic pulse. Yes."

"If I had one of those, big enough to affect all of Chroma's temple…" I jumped to my feet and walked around the room, much to Tawn's further amusement. "That would work. But would it be permanent enough? How long would it take them to rebuild?"

"When all of their cybernetics fail, how will they enforce their rule? How would they do anything at all?"

I put my hands together in front of my mouth. "I can see that. Yeah. Yeah. And no one would have to die."

"Not at first, anyway. But there will be deaths when the people out there rise up against their former masters. You can't stop that."

"I'm not worried about that. It'll be up to them. I just want to make sure they can't affect us here." I paced some more. "Then once we've got things under control and organized here, we can maybe help them out there. Or they can help us. Yeah, this could be great."

I stopped pacing and looked at him. "Do you have one of those? That you're willing to give me?"

"How would you deliver it to the temple?"

"If it's the size of the last one, it wouldn't be difficult at all." I'd carried that one in my bag.

"It would have to be larger, for the size of the temple you describe."

"Would I still be able to carry it?"

He looked off to the side, presumably calculating in his head. "With your strength, yes. It would not be easy, however."

"Then I'll climb the mountain with it on my back if I have to." I liked this plan. I told the others I would work with Onyx, but if I could leave him out of it, so much the better.

Captain Tawn exchanged looks with Taizong Gold before continuing: "This is a request we are willing to fulfill, so long as we have your word that the device will be used only against this temple."

"Where else would I use it?"

"I don't know." His face grew harder. "You have been given tech for specific uses before and chosen to use it in other ways."

That was fair. "You have my word. I will use it against Chroma's temple."

I saw one big catch with this plan. If I were anywhere near this electro-device, it would shut down all of my cybernetics and almost certainly kill me. When I thought to use it against Atramentous, I'd considered whether it was worth it. In this case, my life in exchange for shutting down all of Chroma's forces sounded like a fair trade. I would try to come up with a better plan, of course, but... I could see that.

Tawn moved back to his desk and wrote something down. "You may return in two weeks' time. The device should be ready for you by then."

Two weeks. On the one hand, it was impressive they could have it ready so soon. On the other hand, what would I do with myself until then?

"Thank you," I said. "And, I, uh, apologize for, um, being so upset earlier."

"Yes... you would do well to control your emotions better." Tawn stood. "You will be escorted back to the outskirts of the city."

A thought occurred to me. "Could I have a brief word with the Viridian prisoners? I might be able to get some more information from them."

Taizong Gold stepped forward. "I'll escort you to them myself. You can question them in my presence."

Not exactly what I had in mind, but I didn't want to press the issue now. The draconic already seemed quite irritated with the turn of events. I agreed to his terms.

After another short trip walking through tunnels and riding the sidewalks, we made our way to Auric's jail. The only jail I'd seen before had been the place Incarnadine's people held Rick. And Viridia's horrible pit. This place was altogether different. If not for the bars on the windows, I would think these people were guests, not prisoners. They had furniture at least the equal of my old apartment.

"Basil," I called through the barred window. The scientists looked from me to the draconic, wondering what we wanted now. They might even be wondering if Taizong Gold had convinced me to his side of things, in which case they were in mortal peril.

The one familiar face among them stepped into view from the side of the door. "What do you want now?"

"I'm curious. You're not a scientist. Why are you here?"

He shrugged. "I'm their guard."

"Great job," one of the scientists muttered. Basil glared at him.

"So you betrayed us to Troilus Green, and he makes you a guard." I absently tapped the bar with a cyb finger, making a "ting" sound.

"I didn't betray you."

"You told him about Stacy."

He shrugged again. "That was her fault."

"What?"

"She said no."

I stared at him for a moment then closed my eyes. No wonder he'd made the girls uncomfortable. I wanted to rip the door open and punch his face. Instead, I took a deep breath and leaned a little closer. "What is Viridia planning? Tell me, and maybe I can get you all out of here."

He laughed. "You may have kept that one from killing us, but that doesn't mean I'm going to tell you anything."

"Why not? Viridia threw you in the Virescent Pit! Why give him any loyalty?"

"He gives me what I want. You don't."

I tried not to think about what that meant. "So you're willing to give up freedom for all humanity for… whatever he offers?"

Basil laughed again. "Freedom? You haven't set a single human free, even with all the crazy stuff you've done."

"We're closer than we've ever been!" I protested. "There's only one dragon left."

"Two," he corrected me.

"Viridia isn't much of a dragon now."

"Viridia is far more than a dragon. Viridia is a god."

I slapped my forehead. "Not this again. Come on, Basil. You know better than that."

This time, he leaned closer to the bars. "You haven't seen what I've seen."

"I've seen everything. I've been all over the Emerald Ascendancy. I've been in his lair. Now I've even been outside The Circle." Exasperated, I shook my head. "There's not a human alive who's seen what I've seen."

"You only think you've seen it all. Viridia has secrets inside secrets."

He chuckled. "You don't even know what he did to your little friend."

My blood ran cold. "What?"

"You think he helped you out, saved that kid, don't ya? You don't have a clue."

My cyb hand gripped one of the bars and started to bend it. Taizong Gold made a sound behind me. Could draconics clear their throats?

My eyes bored into Basil. "You're going to rot in here until this draconic gets tired of your smell." I turned and stalked away.

38

I returned to the outskirts of the city, where Don and Lovat waited. The sun had already begun to dip beyond the mountains. How long had I been in there? Surely more than four hours, but they hadn't left. Huh.

"I made a deal," I told them. "It went well. We should head back home."

Lovat kicked a rock. "This is it? All I got to do was sit here all day?"

"Not every mission is exciting. All I did in there was talk." I winked at him. "Talk about boring. Want to race?"

"Ha! All the way back?"

I feigned shock. "And leave Don here? Rude!" I pointed to an outcrop in the distance. "We run to that spot and back to Don. Ready? Go!"

I boosted my legs and took off. Lovat ran right beside me. He'd gotten more proficient with his boosts. If I let him, he'd be able to keep up with me. But my legs were still longer than his, at least for now. If he kept growing the way he'd been, he'd be faster than me pretty soon. I waited until we turned back from the outcrop and then stopped holding back. I pulled several yards ahead of Lovat. I glanced over my shoulder to grin at him.

And my legs quit.

I plowed into the ground at full speed with almost no time to get my hands out in front of me. I barely kept my face from bouncing off the dirt.

Lovat reached Don, gave him some sort of hand slap, and ran back to me, laughing. "You looked back and tripped!"

I laughed with him as I pushed myself back up. "That'll teach me!" Except I hadn't tripped, and I couldn't feel my legs at all. I brushed dirt off my arms and concentrated. A trickle of energy went down each leg. They twitched. A stronger boost finally made its way through, and feeling returned. I got to my feet slowly.

Don eyed me. "You all right?"

"I will be."

How many times had that happened now? I should probably mention it to Hunter. But if I did, he'd want me to stay home, and Lainey would gripe at me, and… No, she wouldn't. Lainey wasn't here. Neither was Hunter, for that matter. I clenched my fists.

Lovat jogged on ahead, while Don and I resumed walking. "You didn't trip," he said a moment later.

"No, I didn't."

He grunted. I didn't say anything else. We walked on.

"Is your implant quitting?" Don asked a few minutes later.

"I don't know. Something is going wrong."

He pointed ahead at Lovat. "Will that happen to him?"

"It shouldn't. He won't abuse it the way I have, for one thing." But Basil's insinuations filled my head. What if the Viridian scientists had done something to Lovat's implant?

My thoughts wrestled with this as I watched him make games out of the rest of our trip home. His enthusiasm for his new abilities was infectious. I joined in on a few more, like seeing how far or high we could each jump. But Basil's suggestion and my own struggles colored every moment.

We arrived long after the sun had gone down. I promised to tell the others about our trip early the next morning and went to bed. The long walk helped push me into sleep right away, curing me of the insomnia of the night before.

The next morning after breakfast, we gathered again, and I explained the idea of the electromagnetic pulse bomb. "I had thought we might have to use one of those huge explosives that Auric tried to use before," I said. "I didn't have a good plan to get one to the temple. This makes it far easier." Bice, Kelly, and Chance knew my original plan involved Onyx, of course, but I didn't see the need to bring that up.

"And doesn't kill everyone," Bice said.

"I knew you'd approve."

"So how will you get back to the temple?" Kelly asked. "Won't they have the tunnel guarded even more now?"

"Probably. I may have to climb the mountains again."

"Do you…" Bice hesitated. "Do you think you could do that without Lainey?"

I looked down. I hadn't wanted to think about that. "I would not have made it the first time without her," I said. "But now that I've done it once, I think I can do it. I'll boost myself the entire way, if I have to. Whatever it takes."

"And what if the boosts stop working in the middle?" Don asked. Ouch. I shouldn't have admitted that to him.

"They won't. They can't."

No one said anything.

"Moving on to Viridia." I outlined what had happened, including the presence of Basil.

"You should have told me he was there," Don said.

"Why?" I couldn't remember any connection the two of them had.

"Because I would have killed him myself."

Oh.

"Let's think this through," Bice offered. "Viridia is planning something involving sources. We know he's done something in both Caesious and Auric."

"And the source in Viridia itself is destroyed," I said.

"Which leaves three more." Bice drew his finger on the table as if connecting dots. "What can he gain from connecting all five sources somehow?"

"You would know better than I."

He sighed. "I understood little of the magic even when I used it. We didn't have a name for it, then. Incarnadine's people called it resomancy."

"So… something to do with sound?" Jaden asked.

I forgot he'd worked in theater with Stacy. He knew a bit about sound.

"Yes. Which is why we were taught words to command it," Bice explained.

"They never sounded like words to me," I said.

"Yes, well, the words didn't really mean anything. It's about the formation of a specific set of sounds that brought the power out." Bice chuckled at a memory. "Some priests tried to claim the words were invocations to Viridia, but we knew better." He uttered something that sounded like "bo-ranadig."

"What?"

He shrugged. "That's one of the words. It means nothing. But those particular sounds could affect the wind movement. As long as I was in Viridia, near one of the outlets for the power." He held up his hand, palm upward with each finger extended. "Now we know the primary power is this 'source' location. All the smaller ones were outgrowths from it."

"Is it the same power in each city?" Kelly asked. "Would your special words work in Auric, for example?"

"No," Chance spoke up. "The power is different in each city. I know the ancient words that worked within the city of Onyx, but nothing of the others. I would have no power there."

"Then what good does it do Viridia to… do whatever he's doing?" I couldn't figure it out.

"I do not know." The young draconic shook his head. "Either the scientists were telling the truth, that these are monitoring devices… in which case, he's watching for anyone else using the power sources, or…"

"Or what?"

"Or he has something more sinister in mind."

I ran a hand through my hair, pausing when I hit the bald spot in the back where they'd cut into my head. "I vote for sinister. This is Viridia. Troilus Green. Monitoring is not his style."

"Agreed. Aside from Onyx, he was always the most cunning of the dragons."

And wasn't it wonderful that they were the two we had left to deal with? Ugh. I shook my head. "I don't know how we find more information. We may have to wait and see what his next move is."

"By then, it may be too late," Chance said.

"Everything is doom and gloom lately," Jaden complained.

Bice laughed. "It has been from the beginning, in some ways. But we hold on to hope." He smiled in the way I loved, the way that made me feel like it would all work out. "We have to believe that evil will fail in the end. Otherwise, why fight against it?"

With nothing else to report, and no other ideas to suggest, I dismissed the group. We couldn't do much of anything now except wait for Auric's people to build the device. I was already thinking about heading back to Caesious. I didn't want to wait for Caedan to return to find out what was happening with Lainey.

Wrapped in my thoughts, I hadn't noticed Chance remaining behind until I looked up from my chair and saw him staring at me. "Oh, Chance. Did you need something?"

He glanced toward the door before quietly whispering, "Onyx wants to see you."

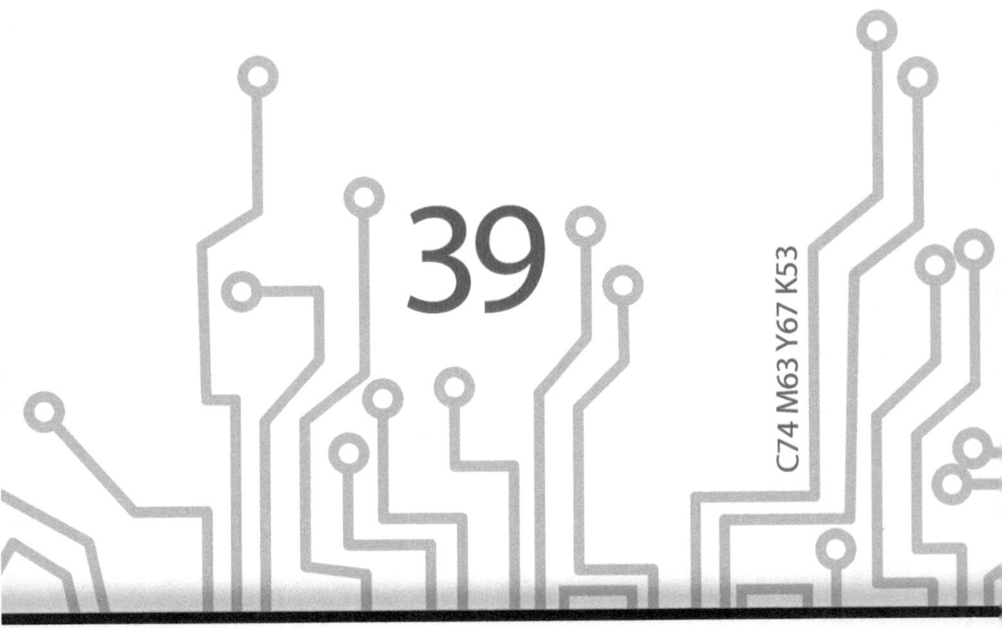

I frowned. "Why? I told him I'd contact him when I was ready."

"He is very insistent. In fact—"

"I don't care. I don't need him for the plan any more. I'm going to do it all myself."

Chance bowed his head. "He says… if you don't come, he may be forced to tear down a hospital in Caesious."

I froze. No. Already? Somehow, he knew about Lainey. I'd hoped to have at least a few more days before that information got to any of my enemies. And now it was too late to warn Caedan and the others.

"When and where does he want to meet?" I could think of no other way to protect them, at least for now.

"The Hub. Tomorrow at noon."

I would have to take the four-wheeler, but I could be there. This time, I would not just be out for a run. If he wanted to fight, I would be ready. My brain started to run through possibilities. And then I noticed Chance's head still bowed.

"Chance? Are you all right? He didn't… cause you any problems with this contact, did he?"

The young draconic lifted his head. "It is… harder each time. I did not allow him in, but he forced himself far enough to give me the message for you. It was unpleasant."

I nodded. "What… I'm sorry, but I have to ask. If he does manage to gain control of you, how much control will he have? Would he be able to force you to hurt Kelly?"

"I cannot say." Chance turned his head to the side, but his eye flicked back toward me. "In the past, such a thing rarely happened. To do our father's will was our purpose. He had no need to establish dominance. If he did, it was only to reinforce a command already given. We—I never felt actually controlled. It is more of a problem that he would be able to see through my eyes. He would be able to find this location."

I studied him for a moment. Amazing how I'd actually gotten used to the sight of a short, black-scaled creature walking around and talking with us. "I hope we can break that connection for good soon."

"You mean kill him."

"That's been the plan all along." I looked away, thinking. "Maybe even tomorrow."

"You can't hope to stand up to him all alone!"

"If he turns into human form and makes himself vulnerable, I may have to," I said, still thinking about how I might be able to do it. The sword was the most obvious, but he'd see me holding it. "To protect you, to protect Lainey… for all of us."

Chance nodded and started to leave the room. He paused at the door. "Do you wish me to come with you? It might throw him off his guard."

"No." I stood and shook my head. "I won't put you at risk that way." I smiled at the thought. "And Kelly would kill me."

He nodded with a serious look. "She would certainly try."

"Thanks, Chance." I chuckled. "Don't tell anyone else about this unless I don't come back tomorrow. I'll use some other excuse for why I'm leaving."

He agreed and left. I mused alone for a few minutes before I remembered another important task. I hurried down the hall and opened the door to the room where we'd left Glacier. The cat bounded out as soon as the door moved, pushing me against the wall. She growled, rubbed the top of her head against my chest, and dashed up the stairs outside. I guess she was feeling all right.

I found Bice and told him, "I can't just sit around for two weeks. I'm going back to Caesious to check on Lainey." I hated lying to him, but I told myself I would plan to go to Caesious after I met Onyx. That made it less of a lie.

"I understand." Bice smiled and put his hand on my shoulder. "I am praying for her. And you."

I swallowed. Where did this lump in my throat come from?

"Be careful. Caedan and the others can wander the city, but you're too recognizable."

"Yeah." I recovered my ability to speak. "I just have to know how she's doing."

"Of course." He glanced around. "Anything else need doing here while you're gone?"

"Not that I know of. Keep things normal, I guess." I snorted. "Whatever that means."

I turned to leave, but then stopped. I couldn't leave with that. "Bice…" I turned back. "If… if I don't come back from one of these trips, I need to know things will be all right here."

His smile didn't go away. "Do you know how many times Kelly, Caedan, and I have had that conversation?"

I guess I didn't, but it made sense. "That's good." I rubbed my face. "As long as there's a plan of some kind."

"Beryl. You will come back." He said it with such conviction. "This isn't over yet."

I wish I had his faith. I told him I'd be gone for three or four days at the most. I packed my bag and headed for the armory. I took my sword and debated over taking anything else. The shockspears and batons wouldn't be much good against Onyx. Besides, I had their capability built into my hand now. None of the other weapons Auric stocked here seemed appropriate. I toyed with a couple of larger bladed weapons, but I hadn't trained with them. Better to stick with what I knew.

I thought about taking Glacier along as back-up, but I didn't know where she'd gone. I searched around the immediate area of the base but saw no sign of her. Just as well, I suppose. She would've had to run all the way.

A few minutes later, I fired up the four-wheeler and set out. Lovat would be angry I didn't take him along, but Don would take care of him. I tried to imagine what would happen to each of them if I didn't return. Bice, Caedan, and Kelly would keep things going; I knew that much. Stacy would start up new ways of gathering information and spreading it too.

The rebellion would continue.

But for how long? They might be able to spark things with only Onyx to contend with. But not with the zealots. Eventually, they would find us. Secrets couldn't remain secrets forever. Just as Onyx had found out about Lainey.

Weeks ago, I'd been worrying about what would happen if I couldn't regain my boosts. Now I worried about dying and leaving everyone alone. Was that an improvement? I laughed at myself.

I had more than enough time to make the trip to the Hub before the deadline. I drove about three-quarters of the way there and found a place to stop for the night. I spent the entire evening sitting on a hill watching the sun set and thinking. I did this a lot lately. Did I have more time on my hands? Or was I becoming too introspective? I used to leave the thinking to others: Loden, Bice, even Rick. In some ways, I wished I could return to those days.

More than anything, I wanted to see Lainey. I wanted to survive this encounter with Onyx. And I wanted to win, to finish the tasks we'd set out to do, not just to free humanity from the tyranny of the dragons, but... to free myself and Lainey to live in peace together. Was that too much to ask?

In the morning, I prepared as well as I could. I spent some time practicing with my sword, reminding myself of the moves I'd rehearsed so many times before. Just in case, I told myself. Just in case.

I drove to the Hub, timing my arrival for shortly before noon. I was still at least a mile away when I saw the towering form of a black dragon waiting outside the train connections.

Onyx was ready for me.

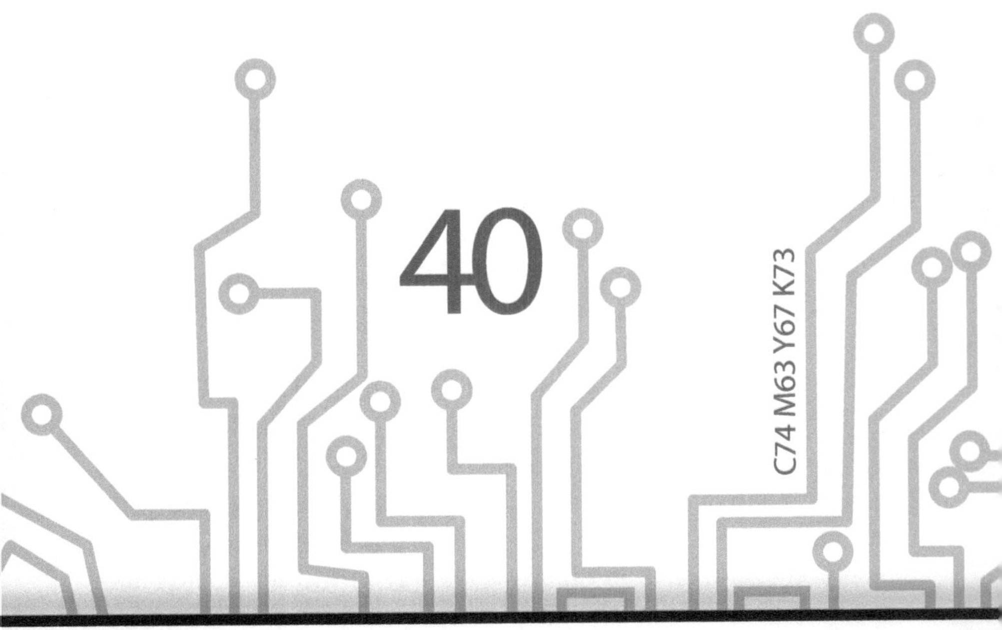

40

Onyx sat like a big cat—like I'd seen Glacier do many times—scratching at one of the scars on his foreleg. "Oh, there you are," he said as I drove up. "I was starting to wonder."

"As if you couldn't see me coming for miles."

He turned his head toward me in a lazy arc. "I don't have zooming bionic eyes like you."

"Are you sure? Switch to human form and try it," I taunted.

"Is that the same sword you thrust through my chest?"

Yeah, I didn't think he'd fall for that either. I got off the four-wheeler and faced him. "Why did you demand I come here, Onyx?"

His eyelids gave a slow blink. "I thought we were allies again. Shouldn't allies meet together?"

"Allies don't threaten each other's friends."

"Then perhaps 'allies' is the wrong word." Onyx shifted to face me more directly. "How about master and servant instead?"

"You want to be my servant?" I was quite proud of myself for thinking of that and actually saying it.

"Amusing." Onyx put one enormous foot down closer to me. His claws dug furrows into the ground. "When last we met, I had no leverage on you. Now I do. But come. We can still achieve a common goal. Tell me of your progress with the plan. Have you obtained the explosive yet?"

"Who said anything about explosives?"

Onyx gave an exaggerated sigh. "Beryl, why be difficult? We're fighting a common enemy now, one who seeks to control both of us."

I made a show of looking around. "And you think meeting out here in the most central place possible is the way to keep a secret from them?"

"I have other servants, you know. There are no zealots within three miles of this spot. I can guarantee it."

Three miles? Had I passed some of his servants earlier without realizing it? How comforting.

"We talked about Auric's explosives through my son," he went on. "We were both there when one of them exploded."

"And you could have stopped it and saved Peri."

He ignored me. "I assume you've been to the golden city now."

"I have. Are you aware that Viridia is planting devices of some kind on all the dragon sources?"

He made no obvious reaction. "I will instruct my people to remove them. Do you have any other distractions from our main topic?"

"It's not a distraction. They've rigged the devices to explode if anyone tampers with them. And we both know what happens when you explode something on a dragon's source. Auric's scientists haven't been able to figure out what they do yet. Are all of your people genuinely unaware of this?"

"Maybe that is all they do." Onyx turned to stare down the train line that led to Viridia. "Perhaps he is threatening me."

"How does that feel?"

"I should tear him apart."

I took a step closer. "Then you know how I feel."

"What?" He looked back at me. "Oh. Ha. You're comparing my threat against your girlfriend with his threat against every other city in The Circle."

"No, I'm comparing your threat against something I hold dear and his threat against something you hold dear."

"Very well. I always knew I'd have to eliminate that green draconic when the time was right." He pulled his foot back, leaving longer furrows. "It seems I've let him live too long already."

"You're going after him now?"

"No. He'll be prepared. I'll have to be more subtle about it."

I laughed. "Subtlety isn't exactly your strength."

"No? I thought I did quite well for the hundreds of years I spent among you people." He scowled. "Enough about Viridia. What about the plan for Chroma?"

"Chroma is dead."

Onyx lowered his head down to my level. "You never were very good at jokes, Beryl, so I have to assume this is some kind of ploy. Did Chroma convert you to her side?"

"She's been dead for hundreds of years. I saw her skeleton."

He stared at me for at least half a minute. I stared back. Onyx snorted smoke from his nostrils. I backed up, waving my hand in front of my face.

"Heh." The dragon chuckled, then burst into ear-splitting laughter. I backed further. He rolled on the ground and kept laughing. It's too bad I didn't have some other kind of enormous weapon: he was completely vulnerable in those moments.

At last he pulled himself back up and let his laughter fade. "Oh, Beryl. I should have sent you over there months ago. To think I've been afraid of her all this time. And she's not even there."

"How could she be?" I asked. "She didn't have a source like you did here."

"Well, yes, but…" He waved one claw in the air. "She's the immortal Chroma. Or was. Or wasn't, I suppose. Ha."

"So about our plan—" I began.

"You really shouldn't have told me," he interrupted. "This means there is no force strong enough to contend with me after all. I can squish those annoying zealots. I can fly over the mountain and lay waste to their temple. Then I can return and deal with Viridia. And you." His eyes locked back on mine. "Maybe I'll knock over that hospital on my way to the temple."

"Go to the temple," I said. "Go straight there. I want to see what happens." I smiled as big as I could.

The dragon's scaly eyebrows narrowed. "What do you mean?"

"Do you think they're unprepared for you?" I laughed. "Oh, they're ready. They have very specific plans if you show up." Maybe they did. Maybe this wasn't a complete bluff on my part. How would I know?

"Like what?"

"You just threatened to destroy the hospital again. Why should I tell you?" I shook my head. "One of these days, Onyx. One of these days, maybe you'll learn not to anger the people who can actually help you."

He growled.

"But look," I went on. "You've seen their tech. They have cyb stuff that makes our hands"—I waved mine in the air—"look positively quaint by comparison. I mean, it's in their very robes!"

"And yet…" Onyx settled down closer to me again. "They weren't prepared for you."

"Of course they weren't. Haven't you heard?" I spread my arms wide. "I was specifically built to fight them! It turns out that Auric and Loden were working together. Everything about me is designed to fight the zealots!" Maybe not everything, necessarily, but close enough.

"You have never been a good liar, Beryl… and yet I have difficulty believing you. Why should I?"

"Do you want me to let you listen to the recording Loden and Auric left for me explaining it?" I pointed in a vague way toward the north. "I can go get it. I'm not making this up. I really do want to see what happens when you encounter their tech."

"So the explosive solution you proposed… that was to take out the zealots, not Chroma?"

"Not just them. Their tech. They're all linked together in one spot there. If that place goes down, they all go down, even the ones here in The Circle. They'd lose all their special abilities." I took a few steps back toward the four-wheeler. "But if you think you can do it all on your own, that's your business. I mean, you just admitted you wouldn't go after Viridia yet, because he'd be prepared for you. But you think these guys, who've had centuries to think about it, haven't prepared." I waved. "Have fun with that."

"Fine. Where is the explosive from Auric?"

"They don't have any more."

This time, his growl made the ground vibrate. Black acid dripped from his mouth and burned holes in the dirt. "Then what is the point of all this?"

"The point is: I have a new plan." I pointed at him. "A plan that will take down the zealots. And I don't even need your help!"

"And yet you asked for it."

"That was before I knew the details myself." I crossed my arms and faced him. "Look, give me three weeks. If I haven't removed the zealots as a threat by then… well, I probably won't be alive. Then you can try."

"Three weeks?"

"These things take time. And have I failed yet? I killed Incarnadine for you. I killed Atramentous too, in case you hadn't figured that out."

"The zealots told me. Very well, Beryl. Three weeks. But should you fail, I will go after your friends first."

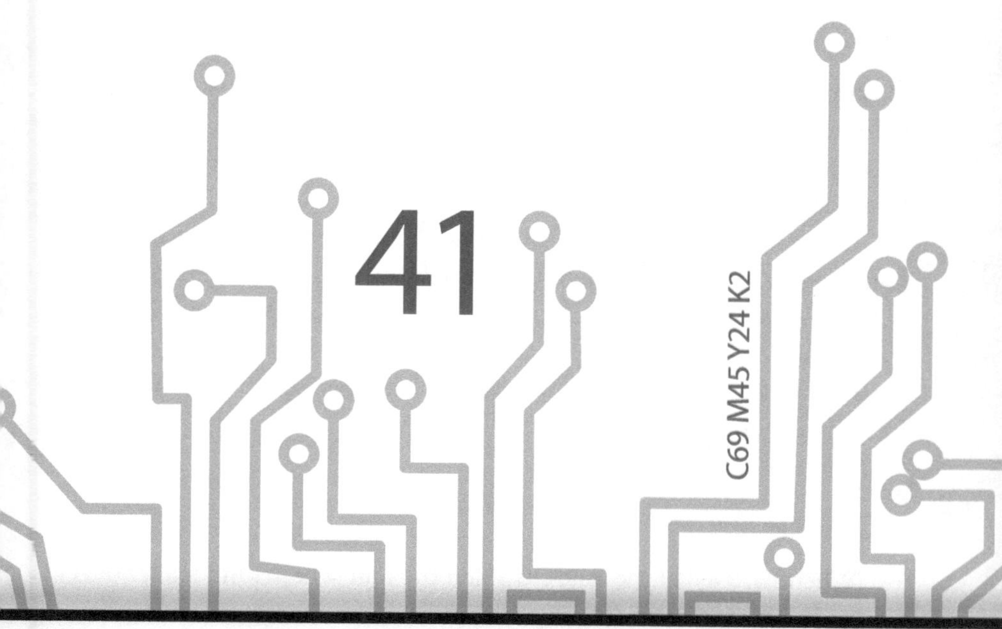

I shook my head. "You still aren't getting that 'stop threatening' thing down. Keep working on it."

"Amusing." He turned and hooked a bag off the ground with a single claw. He dropped it in front of me. "I have something for you."

"It's not my birthday. You should remember it, actually. It's the same as your brother Viridia's, and it's the day we met!" I paused before adding, "Worst birthday ever."

"Open it."

I gave an exaggerated sigh and opened the bag. I had no reason not to, other than to irritate him, which I found enjoyable. I pulled out a small device. "This looks somewhat familiar."

"It should. It's similar to the talkers your friend Loden designed. This one is more efficient. You can reach me anywhere in The Circle with that."

I frowned. "Why would I want to talk to you?"

"Because Enlil may not always be with you or available for our communication."

"Who?"

"My son."

"Oh. Chance. Right." I made a show of looking over the talker. "I'm not taking this back to my home only for you to follow me there."

"If I had that kind of tech, I would have found you long before now."

Onyx gathered himself up and spread his wings. "I just think you might need my help after all. If so, you know how to reach me now." He leaped into the air and swept away. The force of his take-off knocked me back several steps.

I examined the talker for a few more minutes, then tossed it into the four-wheeler's small storage bin. I'd have Cobalt look at it and make sure it didn't have another devious purpose. No matter what Onyx said, I didn't trust him.

I considered my options for only a minute before I turned the four-wheeler toward Caesious.

When I arrived at the blue city, I left the four-wheeler hidden far outside and walked the rest of the way. Apparently, someone saw me coming. Sapphire and Caedan both met me at the hospital doors.

"Didn't I tell you that you attract too much attention?" Sapphire greeted me.

"I know. But I couldn't stay away. How is she?"

Caedan gestured. "I'll take you. Come on."

"You didn't answer my question." I followed him through stark white halls.

"Yeah. Um." Caedan glanced at me. "I'll let Hunter answer you. I don't want to say anything stupid."

Part of me wanted to ask if he was really Caedan, but I wasn't in the mood to make jokes.

They'd moved Lainey and Carl to a different room from the last time I'd been here. I noticed some of Sapphire's guards posted at key points throughout the building. Caedan left me at the room's door to find Hunter. When I entered, I saw two beds, separated by a few feet. Both occupants lay still with eyes closed. I kept my movements as quiet as possible as I approached the bed on the right.

Lainey didn't look much different than when I'd left a few days earlier. Did she have more color to her skin? I couldn't tell for certain. Her left hand lay outside the sheets, so I placed mine on top of it. I bent down and whispered, "I love you. Please be all right."

"I should blame you." Carl's rough voice came as barely a whisper from the other bed.

I straightened up and looked toward him. He'd turned his head to face me. His left leg was encased in a huge cast, along with his right hand. Bruises covered at least half of his face. I winced and walked around Lainey's bed to be closer to him.

"I should blame you," he repeated. "You've always been far too reckless."

"I know," I managed to say.

He turned his head to face the ceiling. "But I can't. I went along with the plan, even though I knew the danger. And Lainey paid for it."

"I'm so sorry."

He didn't answer, and I didn't know what else to say. I stood around, feeling awkward and miserable, until the door opened and Hunter entered. I breathed a sigh of relief and met him in the middle. "Hunter. What can you tell me?"

"There is not a lot to tell," he said, his voice a little louder than I would have expected. "Lainey is in a coma. It is impossible to tell when she will come out of it, or what her condition will be when that happens."

I slumped. "So you weren't able to help?"

"I am assisting." He looked a little insulted. "But the doctors here are very competent. Their initial prognosis is likely correct."

"Is there anything else that can be done? Anyone else in all The Circle that could help?"

Hunter shook his head. "Believe me, if I knew of anyone or anything that would help, I would tell you."

"Could some kind of cybernetics help her?"

"No. I know this is not what you want to hear, but there is nothing we can do now except wait." He looked toward the bed. "Wait and see if she wakes up."

He was right: I didn't want to hear that. I was useless here. We were all useless.

"You can talk to her," Hunter suggested. "Some of us believe people in comas can still hear. Sometimes."

"All right." I moved back around to the other side of Lainey's bed. I considered kneeling, but Hunter pushed a chair over to me. I smiled and took it.

I talked to Lainey for about an hour, I suppose, until I had to leave in search of something to drink. I told her how much I loved her, how sorry I was for everything, and how much I missed her. When I ran out of things to say about the two of us, I told her everything I could remember about everyone else in our group. Carl never spoke again. I don't know if he could hear me or not.

In the hall, Sapphire and Caedan rejoined me. I drank a good bit of water before asking them how things were going in the city.

"Nothing much has changed since you left," Sapphire said. "We did discover an unknown device at the dragon's source. I'm assuming the Viridians left it there."

"They did the same in Auric," I replied. "And it's wired to explode if anyone messes with it."

"Our techs confirmed the same."

"Stacy is out making contacts," Caedan said. "She's hoping to get some word from inside Viridia. Maybe a hint as to what all this means."

I nodded. If anyone could find out, it would be Stacy. "You do have a leak somewhere," I told Sapphire. "Onyx knows about Lainey and Carl being here."

"You talked to Onyx?" Caedan exclaimed.

"More than I'd ever wanted. I just met with him at the Hub. He threatened to tear this place down if I didn't."

"What did he want this time?"

I explained about the idea of working together against Chroma, and how Onyx now thought he was unstoppable. "I convinced him the zealots were still a threat, so he's leaving them to me for now." I looked back toward Lainey's room. "I have three weeks before he takes matters into his own hands."

"And then what?" Sapphire asked. "If you succeed, what will he do?"

"I don't know. There's nothing good here. We'll have to plan to move Lainey and Carl before the time is up."

"They may not be able to move by then."

"If we don't, Onyx will kill them here. I don't want to risk them in any way, but if it comes down to letting him tear down the hospital with everyone in it, or moving them…"

"Yeah." Caedan looked at the floor and shook his head. "We need to take him down somehow."

"We'll keep trying to figure that out." The more I talked these issues over with them, the more confidence I gained. "For now, my focus is on Chroma. I want everyone else focused on protecting this place and figuring out Viridia's plans."

They agreed. "As for word getting out…" Sapphire shook her head. "I told you it would be difficult to keep everyone quiet." She gestured down the hall. "This place is full of doctors, nurses, patients, and even janitors. Word gets out."

"I know. But with that in mind…" I hesitated. "How long do you think I can stay?"

"If Onyx already knows about all this, then I don't see what the problem is," Caedan said.

"Except we have other enemies," I pointed out. "If Troilus Green finds out I'm here. Or the zealots…"

"You can't stay long," Sapphire said. "I'm sorry, Beryl. The longer you stay, the more dangerous it is for Lainey. And the rest of us."

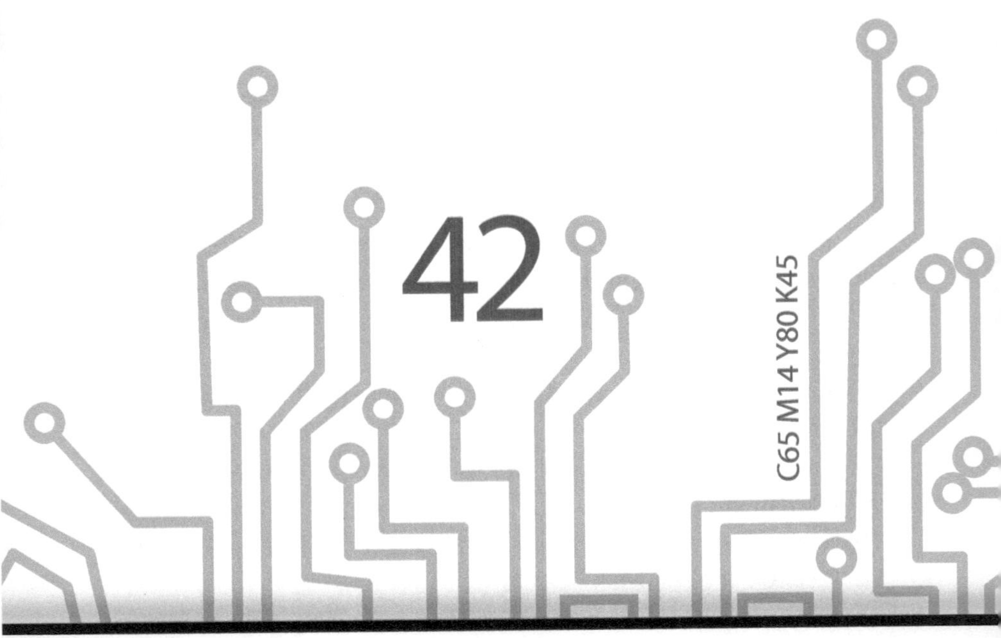

I spent another hour at Lainey's side. I don't know if I did any good for her or for me. I was in a place I'd never been before. Yes, I'd experienced the deaths of my parents and Loden and Peri, but this was different. Lainey wasn't dead. But she might die. A huge unknown loomed over the entire situation. I hated it and feared it.

Before I left, I sought out Hunter again. I found him in the hospital's dining hall. As long as I was there, I grabbed a few things to eat and joined him at the table. He glanced around to see if anyone else had noticed me, then leaned closer to speak: "I have no other news to tell you about Lainey."

"I know." I took a quick drink of some kind of fruit juice. It said apple on the outside, but it didn't taste much like apple. "I need to talk to you about me."

He raised his eyebrows. "Are you having further troubles?"

I stalled by taking another drink. It had some apple flavor to it, but it wasn't dominant. Something else. "I haven't told anyone this. My legs are… quitting on me."

Hunter tilted his head. "Describe this 'quitting.'"

"They stop working. I can't feel them. And then they come back." I hadn't wanted to tell anyone about this, but at least in this setting, Hunter couldn't tell Kelly or anyone else that would fret over me.

"Hmm. How often is this happening? How long is the duration of each event?"

"I don't know. Once every few days. It doesn't last long, though. Maybe a minute or two at most."

Hunter stirred some vegetables around on his tray. "It is troubling, but not altogether unexpected."

"What do you mean?" I took another sip. Maybe it was pear. That made more sense.

"We have had many discussions about your abilities and the process that created them." Hunter looked up at me. "I have tried to emphasize that all of this, every step of the process, was experimental. You are the first to ever possess an actual brain implant, not to mention all of the rest."

"Like my dragonish heart."

"Exactly. The results of all these experiments have been, to put it simply, astounding. You are extraordinary. Your boosts have done amazing things. You could power an entire dragon!" He pointed his fork at me. "But by the simple laws of technology and development, you should not exist."

"Huh?"

"So many of your capabilities were never tested before you possessed them." He waved the fork in the air. "The heart. The brain implant. The connections to various muscles. Every one of these things should have been extensively tested before you received them."

"In Loden's notes, he talks about testing some of it," I protested.

"Yes, yes. Some. But not to the extent any normal discovery would be tested. There should have been years of testing prior to any human experimentation. And that did not happen. So the fact that everything has worked so well for you is astronomically improbable."

"I don't understand."

He sighed and placed the fork back on the tray. "All I am saying is that, by simple mathematical odds, your implant should have failed long ago. At least part of it should have failed. It was to be expected."

"So… you think it's failing now? That it's going to quit on me entirely?"

"I am not saying that. But it is failing with your legs. And that…" He paused to think for a moment. "And that makes sense, after all."

"Because it's the first way I used the implant?"

He nodded. "For years, you thought the implant only helped with your legs."

"Loden said I couldn't walk without it."

"Yes. So you've been using that particular part of it longer and more extensively than the rest. Therefore, it makes sense that it would be the first to fail."

"The first. So do you think everything else will fail over time?"

He shrugged. "I cannot say. If Loden were alive, he might have an answer or a way to repair it. Or maybe those cyberneticists in Viridia. But it is all unknown territory. Perhaps you have only been experiencing glitches caused by the blow to the back of your head. Or perhaps it is more of a long-term failure. We can only wait and see."

"You're not very comforting." I looked down at the food on my tray. None of it looked very appetizing all of a sudden.

"I am sorry. This is outside my knowledge. Oh. How is the cat, by the way?"

"She seemed all right when I left. Ran outside and didn't come back."

"Good, good. At least one of our patients is on her feet."

"Yeah." I got to my feet. "I'll see you later, doctor."

He looked up with surprise. "You did not eat your food."

"I've decided I'm not hungry."

I found Caedan and told him I was leaving. I wanted to stay, of course, but what good could I do? Besides, if Hunter was right and my implant was failing, I might have a limited time in which to accomplish my goals.

"Send one of my boys back," Caedan suggested. "Saxe, maybe. He can use the trains. And then one of us will come find you if anything changes here."

"Good plan." After we parted, I slipped out of the hospital at twilight. By limiting my times outside to times when there wasn't much foot traffic, I hoped I kept my presence more of a secret. Once outside the city, I looked back at the lights of Caesious. Maybe one day, I could visit it in the open and walk its blue-lit streets in peace. Maybe.

I found the four-wheeler and started my trip home. At least all this travel back and forth ate up some of the days in the time for Captain Tawn's people to create the device I needed. The two weeks he'd suggested seemed like such a long time now.

What was I going to do for the remaining days? If I had to sit around our home and do nothing, I would drive everyone crazy. Kelly and Bice would talk to me about resting and being patient. I didn't want to hear that any more. I wanted to hit something. Or stab something with my sword.

With my night vision, I could drive the four-wheeler in the dark without turning the lights on. If not for that, I don't think I ever would have noticed I was being followed. My cybernetic eyes caught brief flashes off to either side as I drove along. The flashes showed up every few minutes, alternating sides, about twenty or thirty feet away from me. No sooner would I catch a glimpse of one then it would vanish, leaving behind a vague shadow.

It took me at least half an hour to figure out what I was seeing. I couldn't tell color in the dark, of course, but I knew: purple robes. The zealots were tracking me. If I allowed this to continue, I would lead them straight to our home. I could only hope they hadn't seen where I'd come from.

I drove the four-wheeler to the top of a hill and dismounted. I drew my sword and took a stand at the peak of the hill. I'd wanted a fight. Let's see if they were willing to give me one.

"I know you're following me!" I shouted into the night. "Are you brave enough to face me?"

Whispers and puffs of cold air swirled around me. I turned in a slow circle, sword at the ready, waiting for them to appear. "Beryl Godslayer," came the voice I'd heard so many times now. The first times I'd heard it, I'd pictured something far creepier than their actual appearance. Even so, the voice always gave me a bit of a chill. The cold air only added to it.

And then a different voice mingled in with that of the zealots', a darker and lower voice. It laughed at me, chuckling with a tone I felt I should know, distorted though it was by the strange tech.

"You are so predictable, human."

"Show yourself!" I shouted. "Face me."

"As you wish."

The familiar rustling and swirling air heralded the arrival of the purple robes. I shifted my sword grip and held my cyb hand out to the side, ready to grab hold of the purple as soon as I could. To my left and right, two of the zealots appeared, but my attention was drawn to the figure emerging directly in front of me.

He was far too large to be one of the zealots, but he wore one of their robes. Who?

The figure solidified into view. The hood of the robe fell back, revealing a dark draconic face with cyb reinforcements around its jaw.

"We meet again, Beryl," said Rimush Black.

43

I felt like giving thanks. I'd wanted a fight. Here stood the very draconic who'd hurt Lainey. I couldn't ask for anything more. I lunged forward and swiped with my sword as a distraction. At the same time, I reached for the robe with my other hand.

And Rimush Black caught it with his own. Powerful draconic claws wrapped themselves around my cybernetic fingers and held them.

"I'm prepared for your tricks." Purple tendrils from his robe lashed out and wrapped around my sword arm. I boosted both arms and strained against his strength. I couldn't see any sign of the two zealots without turning my head. They might be moving in as well.

"I see they repaired you pretty fast," I grunted.

"It was quite the revelation for me," the draconic admitted. His right hand pushed my left hand down while his robe pulled my right arm toward him. He bent his head down toward mine, and his horrible odor filled my nostrils. "Chroma's technology is quite amazing."

I tried triggering the electric charge in my hand, but if the draconic felt it, he showed no signs of it. Boosting both arms as hard as I could didn't seem to make a difference. How did this draconic get so strong?

I almost didn't hear when he leaned in even closer and whispered two syllables. He released my left hand in the same moment, but I had no time to react. The resonancy threw me back with a wall of air. The robe released my right arm only after the force dislocated my shoulder. I flew off the hill and tumbled down its side. I came to a stop at last, my head ringing. I pushed myself up from the dirt with my left hand. I'd lost my sword somewhere in the process. Couldn't use it with my right hand, anyway.

Two zealots warped in on either side of me. Either they weren't expecting me to recover fast enough, or they were just ignorant of my abilities. I grabbed a piece of the robe to my left and blew out his cybernetics with the electric charge.

"You are resilient!" Rimush Black called from the hilltop. While I struggled to my feet, he picked up the four-wheeler and threw it into the air. With another word, he threw a burst of magic after it. The four-wheeler exploded and rained fire and broken parts down toward me. I covered my head and waited for the rain to stop.

"No transportation. No weapon. No allies." The draconic recited my problems as he descended in slow steps.

I staggered a few paces, aching all over. How could he use resomancy way out here? We were miles from the cities and the power sources. Troilus Green had used it in our first train battle, but we hadn't been far from Viridia then. But maybe there was another similarity.

It clicked in my mind. Cybernetics. Troilus Green had them all over, and now Rimush Black possessed some, mainly in the form of that robe. Somehow, dragon technology (dragontek?) could use cybernetics to enhance the range on their resomancy. Or that was my theory, anyway.

"Just so I'm keeping this straight in my head," I said, backing up a few steps, "you're Rimush Purple, right?" Taunting him helped last time; might as well see if it triggered him again.

He growled at me.

"I know I fought a Rimush Black a few days ago, but he served Atramentous. You serve Chroma. Unless you change loyalties as fast as you change clothes. The purple does nothing for your black scales, by the way. Not enough contrast." I risked a quick glance to locate the zealots. The one I'd disrobed appeared to be searching through the debris of the four-wheeler. I didn't like that. I couldn't locate the other one. I didn't like that either.

The disrobed zealot held something up. "Dragon son! Look here!"

I squinted to see what he held. Onyx's talker? It survived the crash? Huh.

The draconic strode to meet him. I took the opportunity to scan the ground for my sword. It had to be here somewhere.

Rimush Black took the talker. "What is this? A way to contact your friends?"

I circled to the right, angling back up the hill a little. "It contacts my best friend. You should call him. I'd love to hear your conversation."

The missing zealot warped into view beside the draconic. "If it does connect to his friends, we might be able to locate them with it," he said.

"Do it." The draconic handed him the talker and turned back to face me.

Oh, this would be interesting.

The zealot extended some wires from his robe and attached them to the talker. He handed it back to Rimush Black. "If you can get them to speak with you for more than thirty seconds or so, I can find them."

"I don't think that's a good idea," I called. I took another step up the hill.

The draconic pushed the button. "Whoever you are, I have your friend Beryl at a disadvantage. Speak to me now, and he may yet live."

After a long moment, Onyx's voice came over the device. "Who is this?"

Even in the dark, I could almost see the draconic's eyes widen. He recognized the voice. I would have laughed, but I hurt too much.

The zealot didn't know what was going on, so he tried to answer: "You speak to—"

Rimush Black backhanded him and sent him flying across the grass. I guess the zealot hadn't been prepared for that attack; his robe hadn't protected him a bit. He hit the ground and lay still. The remaining zealot, with the ruined robe, backed further away.

"His name's Rimush," I called to the talker. "Black or Purple. I'm not sure which. We're about halfway between Caesious and the Hub right now. I think he wants to see you in person."

The draconic tossed the talker aside. "What is going on here?"

"You tell me. You recognized the voice on the other end." Without the other two zealots, I felt a little more comfortable about my odds. But not in a straight-up fight. I couldn't use my right arm, and there was still no sign of my sword.

"Ridiculous. You would not be in communication with him."

"Who are we talking about?" the last zealot demanded.

I glanced toward the sky. "You'll find out in about three minutes or less, depending on where he's flying from."

The draconic took a step in my direction with a growl. I stepped back and shook a finger at him. "Remember what happened the last time you charged at me in anger."

I really did want to see what happened now. Let's find out how Onyx liked being summoned.

No one moved or said anything for about a minute.

"This is preposterous," Rimush Black snarled and started toward me.

I backed up as he approached. "Do you hear wings?" I put my hand to my ear.

He responded with a low, guttural roar and lunged forward. I boosted my legs and darted out of his way with ease. The draconic whirled and extended a palm. This time, I knew what to expect. I sent a boost to my heart as he screamed his incantation. The resomancy wave swept over me with barely a tickle.

As hue as that trick was, I hoped I didn't have to use it very much. If continual usage caused my legs to stop working, maybe I shouldn't be boosting my heart very much...

"You cannot elude me forever!" the draconic said, trying to circle to my right.

"Actually, I pretty much can," I answered. "I could boost my legs and speed away right now, and you'd never be able to catch me." I definitely heard something now.

"Then why are you still here?"

"I was waiting for him." I pointed up and enjoyed the supreme satisfaction of seeing Rimush Black's disbelieving expression as Onyx slammed into the ground beside him.

"I didn't give you that talker so you could ask for rescue," Onyx rumbled.

I pointed at Rimush Black. "He's the one who called you. I just waited around to see what would happen."

The dragon's enormous head bent down to stare at Rimush Black. "Nephew Rimush. I never cared much for you in particular. Tell me: why are you wearing a robe of Chroma?"

"Mighty one." The draconic gave a short bow. "Do we not all serve the mother of us all? This human is wanted for acts of apostasy and treason both within and without The Circle!"

Onyx sighed. "Chroma is dead, you fool."

"No!" shouted the last zealot. "It's a lie!"

"Oh, one of you too?" Onyx turned and exhaled a massive burst of acid. I closed my eyes and winced. Thankfully, the clone's screams were short-lived. But it also reminded me how easily Onyx could end my life if this situation went the wrong way.

Rimush Black backed away. "Great one. I... I do not understand."

"No, you don't." Onyx glared at me. "Look what you've done now, Beryl! I can't let him go back and report to the zealots. But he's a Black! Not one of my own, of course, but still."

I started to shrug before I remembered my dislocated shoulder. Ouch.

"I didn't do any of this. They came after me."

Onyx let out another enormous sigh, this time dripping acid from his jaws. He turned back to the draconic. "You will listen to me and obey every word I tell you. Tell me you understand and agree."

Rimush Black knelt and nodded. "I understand and agree."

"You will speak of this to no one. I have recruited this human for a special task. With his aid, we will remove the outer influence of these so-called priests of Chroma."

The draconic shot a look toward me, but agreed again.

"Now…" Onyx scratched at one of his scars. "I can't have you going back to them. Therefore… Ah. I have it." He straightened. "Since this task is so very important, Rimush Black, I hereby assign you as perpetual body-guard to the human Beryl."

"What?" I think the draconic and I both exclaimed the same word.

"You will follow him everywhere he goes," Onyx continued. "Protect him from the priests of Chroma and anyone else who would do him harm."

"That's not a good idea!" I protested. "I can't take him with me where I'm going!" More importantly, I didn't want to be anywhere near this monster. I wanted him dead.

Onyx laughed. "I think this is a perfect solution. I only wish I could watch it unfold."

"Respectfully, mighty one—" the draconic began.

"No," Onyx cut him off. "If you do indeed respect me, you will obey me."

"I am not doing this!" I shouted. "After what he's done? He—" I stopped myself.

"What has he done?" Onyx settled into a crouch, as if waiting for a story.

I glared back at him.

The dragon laughed again. "This is better than I thought at first. You want him dead, don't you? Well, now's your chance to prove your ideals to me. Can you work with this draconic for the good of all? Or will you murder one who's assigned to help you?"

I gritted my teeth. Draconics weren't human. And this one was worse than most. He'd almost killed Lainey. I couldn't work with him. And I didn't need him.

"Let me put it this way," Onyx said. "If you kill him, then someone in that blue hospital dies. It's that simple. Finish the job you promised to do, and then you'll be rid of him. One way or another. I won't care after that."

"This… you…" The draconic stammered out what I probably would have.

Onyx brought his jaws down in front of Rimush. "Obey me in this, or I will end your existence here and now. There are so few of you left, I would hate to lose another one over something so simple."

The draconic bowed so low, his snout brushed the ground.

"Now." Onyx spread his wings. "I was in the middle of something more important than this." He shot a look at me that made me think of Rick's self-assured grins. "After all, should you succeed, I will need to be prepared for… the future."

The force of his wings' movement almost knocked me down as he took off. In moments, he'd disappeared from even my night vision. I hated to imagine what he could have possibly meant by those last words. I turned to look at my new companion.

"Have no doubts," the draconic said, straightening up. "I will obey him as though he were my own sire. However, once your current task is complete, we will be enemies once more."

"We're enemies now," I muttered.

"Where is our current destination?"

"I'm not going anywhere else tonight." I gestured to my useless arm. "I'm tired. My shoulder is out of joint. And my sword is hiding in the grass somewhere around here."

"Do you require assistance with the shoulder?"

I narrowed my eyes. "I don't trust you."

"As I said, you need fear nothing from me… for now. Onyx has commanded we work together, so that is what we will do."

My mind tumbled through the possibilities. I needed my shoulder back in place, but where could I go? I couldn't possibly take this draconic back to our base, or to Caesious. And anywhere else would take days.

"Fine. Do it."

The draconic approached, bent low, and examined my shoulder. "I am quite familiar with the workings of human bodies. I've spent many decades in the study."

"I don't want to hear about it."

"Nevertheless, that is why I understand what is needed here." Before

I could react, he caught hold of me with one hand and used the other in a quick palm strike against my shoulder. I screamed as it snapped back into place.

Rimush Black stepped back and nodded. "That should do it. Based on how easily it moved, I suspect this is not the first time you have suffered this injury."

"Yeah." I grimaced and flexed the shoulder. It hurt like anything, but it was back where it belonged. I would need to give it time to heal, like last time.

"Now. What is our destination?"

"I'm going to sleep," I told him. "In the morning, we can head toward Auric. There's something I need from there."

"You intend to walk that far?"

I pointed at the smoking debris. "You destroyed my vehicle, so… yeah. Not what I intended, either."

"Have you no other resources?"

"None that I'm willing to share with you." I sought out a soft spot where I could stretch out. My bedroll had been incinerated, of course, but I was tired enough to sleep on the ground. Once I'd gotten settled, I looked up and saw the draconic standing a few feet away, staring at me. "What are you doing?"

"Guarding you, as I was ordered. I do not require sleep at this time."

I rolled my eyes. "Then guard me from further away." I shifted to protect my shoulder and closed my eyes. Maybe he would go away while I slept.

No such luck. When I opened my eyes, I saw a black draconic face watching me. He held up my sword. "I located your weapon."

I groaned and got to my feet, brushing off my clothes. "Thanks, I guess."

He held out the hilt to me. "A fine blade. Did you take it from an Aurelian Sentinel?"

"Let's just say I had a relationship with their boss." I took the sword.

"You are a most perplexing individual." The draconic stepped back and crossed his arms. "Before this is over, I must understand. How is it you have had a relationship with Auric and Onyx, yet by all accounts, you have been the fiercest enemy of the dragons?"

"Yeah…" I walked away, and the draconic followed. "Uh, you'll need to wait here. I need to go, um, relieve myself."

"I have been ordered to protect you."

I looked around. "The biggest danger I see here is that tree over there. You keep a close eye on it while I'm gone, all right?"

A few minutes later, after I poked around in the debris left from the four-wheeler, I pointed in the general direction of Auric. "I guess we start walking."

"The Hub is nearer. One of the trains will stop for me. We can ride to Auric."

I shook my head. "Nah. Someone will recognize me. The train security guys will try to arrest me. I'll have to fight them. Not worth the trouble." I pointed again. "Let's walk, partner."

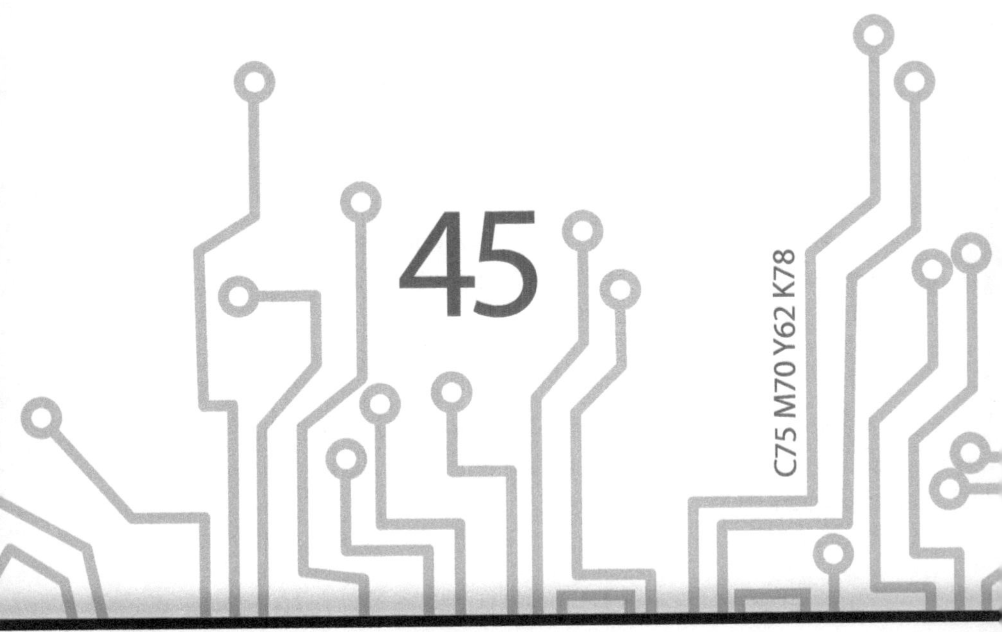

I tried not to look at Rimush Black while we walked. Every moment, I fought against the desire to spin around and put my sword through his head. I argued with myself over Onyx's taunt. He didn't care one way or another whether I killed this draconic. But he'd challenged my "ideals," or my "code" as Bice called it. I didn't kill other humans. But Rimush Black was a monster. I should kill it.

Except... I didn't know if I could. The pain in my shoulder kept me awake much of the night. I'd found part of a dead zealot's robe and ripped it up with my cyb hand. It made for a temporary sling to help hold the arm steady while we traveled.

The draconic appeared to have turned off the cyb abilities of his own robe. Without the waving and other motion, it looked like an ordinary piece of clothing. It reminded me of my first encounters with Troilus Green. He'd worn green robes with purple trim.

But even without the robe's capabilities, Rimush Black had proven a dangerous opponent. I'd defeated him the first time only by taunting him into a rage. He'd avoided that mistake last night. And I didn't know what other cyb enhancements the zealots had done to him besides fixing his jaw.

I had to admit it: he was in better shape for a fight than I was. Besides the shoulder, I was battered and bruised from the resomancy attack. I fought reacting to the pain with every step. We probably wouldn't travel far today.

Most important, of course, was Onyx's threat against Lainey. If I killed the draconic and then rushed back to Caesious, could I evacuate everyone before Onyx discovered it? Could we transport Lainey to our own base without hurting her?

"You are unusually quiet for a human." The draconic's words intruded on my thoughts.

"It's better for both of us," I muttered.

"Why? Do you fear what I may learn from your words, or do you fear what your words may inspire?"

"I'm… never mind." To be honest, I wasn't quite sure what he meant by that.

"So you are working with Onyx, the lost god who returned to us."

"Dragons aren't gods."

"And his first act on his return was to slay Viridia, the god of your home city, if I'm not mistaken."

I didn't answer.

"He then allies with my lord Atramentous and the priests of Chroma. Together, they slay Incarnadine and then Auric. Amaranth disappears, never to be seen again. And then Atramentous dies under mysterious circumstances."

"Is all that the official story?" I asked. "Because you've got some serious errors. And you left out Caesious."

"Ah, then perhaps you could shed some light on the series of events here. For rumor states you were present at some of these events."

"I was present for all of them."

He cocked his head. "As Onyx's agent among the humans, then?"

"You need a new information source, lizard. You can't get anything right."

"Enlighten me, then."

I laughed. "You wouldn't believe me if I told you the truth."

"And why is that?"

"Ask yourself why the zealots keep calling me Beryl Godslayer."

This time, the draconic laughed. "And exactly which god are you claiming to have slain?"

I opened my mouth to answer, but stopped myself. Should I tell him the truth? And if I did, was I doing it to antagonize him or to inflate my own ego? I settled on antagonizing.

"You're right that Onyx killed Viridia. But he couldn't have done it if I hadn't destroyed Viridia's source. And Atramentous killed Auric. I watched it happen." I looked at him and grinned. "The rest? All me."

"You claim to have killed four dragons?" He didn't appear very antagonized.

"Let's just say I was involved in two of them and two of them… were all me." I paused before emphasizing: "Atramentous? That one was all me."

"And do you have proof of these substantial claims?"

I reconsidered my words. And his twisting of the story bothered me the more I thought about it. If this was the story being circulated among the citizens of The Circle, then had all our work been useless? If the people believed that all the dragons' deaths had been a result of their own internal fighting, then…

"You offer no proof, I see."

"I have no reason to share anything further with you."

"I see," he repeated.

We walked on in silence for a while. My stomach growled, reminding me that all my food had blown up with the four-wheeler. I could survive a couple of days without food, and water was plentiful in streams criss-crossing the land out here. Maybe my new draconic pet could even catch something for us to eat. I considered bringing this up, when he broke the silence again:

"Tell me, did the girl live?"

I froze. Rimush Black took another couple of steps before stopping. He didn't look at me before continuing, "I know there were two others with you in the tunnel, but the Legionnaires were certain you cared mostly about the girl."

I clenched my fists, but didn't answer.

"I have not yet had the pleasure of interrogating the Legionnaires myself, of course. But I received their report. I sent word to have them both delivered to my lab. Since you were able to make them surrender so easily, I doubt they will last very long in my experiments, but I do so enjoy being surprised. Humans have amazing resiliency at times."

My hand touched the hilt of my sword before I could even think about it.

"Interesting. The fate of two of your enemies concerns you that much?"

I released the hilt. "They're humans," I answered.

"Ah. Species loyalty. I see. Still, you haven't answered my question about the girl."

"It's none of your business." I started walking again. Onyx said I couldn't kill him, but what if someone else did? A black draconic would not be very welcome in Auric, considering how Onyx and Atramentous had attacked the city. Maybe Taizong Gold or Captain Tawn would do this job for me. But would Onyx see it that way?

"In my experiments, I have found the female of the human species to be more fragile in most respects," the draconic went on. "Though they have also displayed surprising resiliency in ways the male does not. The differences between them are incredibly fascinating."

This time, I stopped and faced him. "Onyx warned me not to kill you," I said, glaring at the draconic. "But he didn't say anything about harm. If you continue to say things designed to upset me, I will break your jaw again, no matter what it's made of. One way or another, I will not hear your voice."

Rimush Black's robe emitted a rush of cold air. The strands fluttered in its self-generated wind. "You are welcome to try, little man."

"Onyx forced us together. Neither of us like it, and neither of us want it. Fine." I took a breath. "But maybe we should try to just… work together, like he said. For now. I won't say anything else to antagonize you, and you don't say anything else to antagonize me."

"Hm. I see but one problem with your suggestion."

"What's that?"

"A few days ago, you defeated me and left me for dead. I assumed my life had ended." The tendrils of the robe spread further out, some of them venturing closer to me. I took a step back. "But the priests of Chroma rescued me, repaired me, and enhanced me." He spread his arms out. "So you see, I have nothing to fear now. I have been on the very doorstep of death and come back."

With a sudden rush of air back toward him, the draconic's robe folded in around him, and he vanished. I drew my sword and spun in a circle. He could reappear anywhere.

"You see, Beryl, if I kill you, then I have revenge, despite what Onyx may say." His voice floated through the air, doing nothing to reveal his location. "But if you kill me, then Onyx will destroy that which you love."

With another rush of imploding air, Rimush Black materialized right next to me.

"I call that an acceptable outcome either way."

His claws struck at me from both sides.

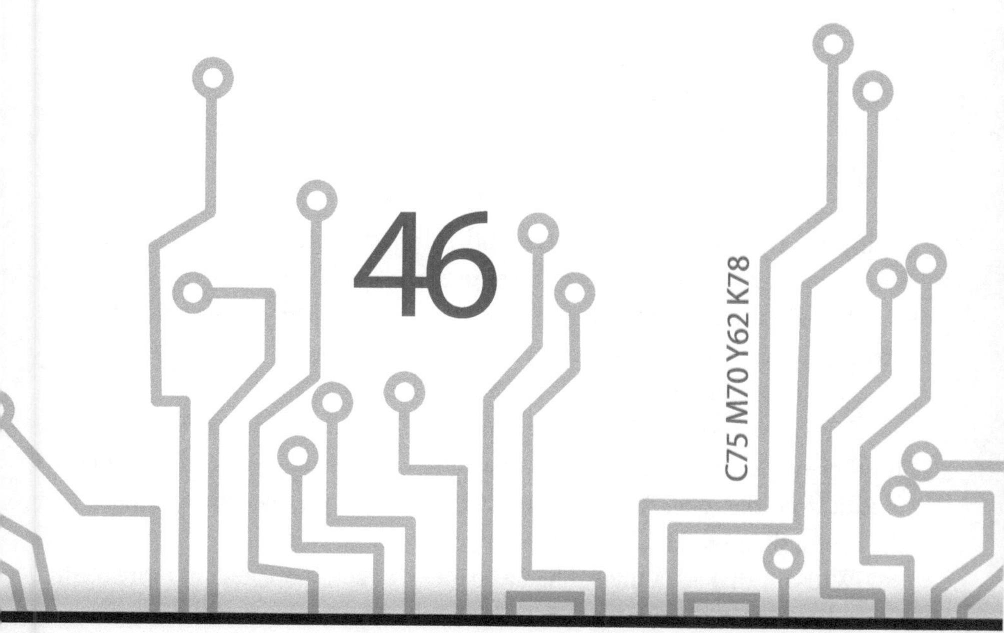

46

I eluded the draconic's grasp and ducked away. Now what could I do? Boost my legs and run?

"Should you run away," he said, anticipating my thoughts, "I will travel to this hospital in Caesious myself. If the girl yet lives, I will take her to my lab and see how… resilient she is."

Great. Just great. If I killed him, Onyx would kill Lainey. If I ran away, the draconic would kill Lainey. But if I let him kill me… what would stop him or Onyx from killing her, anyway? Not to mention everyone else?

My number one priority for the moment would be negating that robe. Actually, my number one priority was "don't die." And then the robe. I sent boosts into my hurting right arm and drew my sword.

"Why didn't you kill me in my sleep last night?" I tried to stall, but genuinely wanted to know.

Rimush Black swiped at me, narrowly missing my face. "When a god commands, you have no choice but to obey." My sword passed through some of his robe without connecting. "Once one has time to reflect, and once the dragon… aura has worn off, one is free to make his own decisions."

"So you needed to wait until you were sure he was far enough away before you disobeyed him?" Ugh. Even with the boosts, swinging the sword created waves of pain through my shoulder area. But I needed the left hand free to use against the robe.

"Onyx is not my god, nor my father. His orders weigh heavily on me, but given time, I can make up my own mind."

All right, I think I understood. All of the dragons had at least some ability to give commands that were difficult, if not impossible, to disobey. But once they were gone, their power over the mind diminished.

The draconic's claws caught my shirt and ripped shreds out of it. "You're choosing the purple zealots over the last dragon?" I demanded.

"I'm choosing myself."

"So you're just selfish." I waited until the last possible moment to duck another swipe of his claws, using that moment to reach out and snag one tendril from the robe. A quick burst of electricity from my cyb hand and… the robe collapsed. Finally!

Without that advantage, I had a chance. In fact, it opened up more options. I could beat him back to Caesious now. Maybe. I was still in no condition to travel very fast. But at least he couldn't warp to different places.

Rimush Black tore the useless robe apart himself. I switched the sword to my left hand. I wasn't as skilled with that hand, but at least it wouldn't hurt me so much.

Up until now, my boosts had been primarily for survival and dodging. I shifted to offense instead, using dodges to put me into position for quick sword strikes. How many times had I fought draconics now? I couldn't remember. But they were all the same, in some ways. They relied on their innate weaponry—claws and teeth—and their superior size and strength. Against a fast-moving target, they struggled.

Even as the momentum shifted in my favor, I didn't know what to do with it. Should I kill the draconic? If I did, what should I do next? I had to find a middle ground somehow.

A few breakneck moments later, I backed away, holding my sword pointed toward the draconic. He bled from multiple wounds while I remained untouched… except for my ripped-up shirt. "If I kill you…" I took a quick breath, struggling for the air to say what I wanted. Maybe my ribs were bruised from the earlier fight. "There's no coming back. Atramentous isn't around to father you again. You'd be dead forever."

"You think I am not aware of this?"

"Then why?" I stared at him in disbelief. "Why do you want to die in order to hurt me?"

"I do not expect you to understand."

"Try me. I've had long conversations with some of your, uh, relatives. Protogonus Blue. Taizong Gold."

I couldn't tell if my words were having an effect, or if the draconic was pausing to regain his breath. "You knew Protogonus Blue?"

"Yes!" I seized on the fact. "I talked with him a lot. I was with him when he died." I pointed off into the air. "He was killed by Onyx!"

"All the more reason to kill you then… since you now serve him!"

"No!" I dodged another rushing attack from him. I could do this for hours, as long as my boosts held out… and my legs didn't quit on me again. "It's a, a temporary alliance. I hate Onyx! He betrayed me and killed people I care about!" I put my sword away and held up my palm. "Can we… talk for a minute? I don't think you understand me, and I know for certain that I don't understand you. Shouldn't we resolve that before we try to kill each other?" I think Bice would have been proud of that speech.

He took a step toward me, and I took a step back. "What do you mean?"

"Let's lay out the facts," I said. "Right now, I really don't understand yours. You're attacking me because I work with Onyx, but you came with me because Onyx told you to. I think your impression of me might be just as confused."

"How many reasons do I need to kill you? You claim to be the one to have slain my father and god." The draconic held up fingers as he ticked them off. "You almost killed me. You work with Onyx, whom I despise in spite of his godhood. You've led other humans in rebellion against the gods. And finally… you're human. That is cause enough."

"All right, I can see your position." I licked my lips. "First, you're not wrong on a couple of those things. I did start the rebellion against the dragons. And I'm proud of that. I want humans to be free. That's my sole purpose. Along the way, I discovered the truth about Chroma and her zealots, so now I'm fighting them too. I have a plan. Onyx is, or was, a part of it, and that's all. Once I deal with them, I'm back to finding a way to get rid of him!" I waved my hand. "And if anything, I have far more cause to kill you, after what you've done!"

Rimush Black chuckled and spit something on the ground. "I fail to see how this has resolved our conflict."

"Fine! Maybe it hasn't. But I just wanted it stated out loud." I braced, preparing for another charge, but it didn't come.

"Is Chroma really dead, then?"

"Uh… yes. I saw her skeleton within the temple."

He snorted. But still didn't charge. "Onyx has always wanted to be the only god."

"Yes!" I seized on that. "Isn't that why the other dragons destroyed his city in the first place?"

"Mostly. Though I'm surprised you know that."

"I know a lot of things. Cerulean Books of Lore, you know. I've wanted Onyx dead more than any of the other dragons. But he's tough. And now that he's got the cyb enhancements, it's going to be even harder to kill him." I paused. "You said… you said you despise him. So there's one thing we have in common. Maybe we can work together based only on that?"

"On hatred of Onyx? But isn't this mission on his behalf?"

"No! Ugh. It's my idea. He's just trying to get in on it, because it's against the zealots." I wasn't going to mention how I agreed to work with him. Not important right now.

"Tell me the purpose of this mission."

I couldn't see any reason not to tell him. If it persuaded him, then we could move on. If it didn't, I'd have to kill him anyway. "Auric's people have a device that can destroy cybernetics. I'm going to set it off in the zealot temple and wipe out all of their tech."

"Hm. Could we not use such a device against Onyx, to remove his capabilities?"

I didn't think… I hadn't… oh. Auric had said the device would kill me, because of my brain implant. And if Onyx had the same thing now… "It would kill him," I said.

Rimush Black lowered his claws and stepped back. "Now that is a plan I could support."

"But the device is intended for the temple," I protested. "We have to stop them first, before their influence spreads too far."

"If the Aurelians can make one device for you, they can make two." He folded his arms. "I will work with you to use it against Onyx. Otherwise, we can resume our battle."

I sighed. "All right. You have a deal."

Wonderful. Dangerous alliances everywhere I looked. I would not be able to sleep again until this was all over.

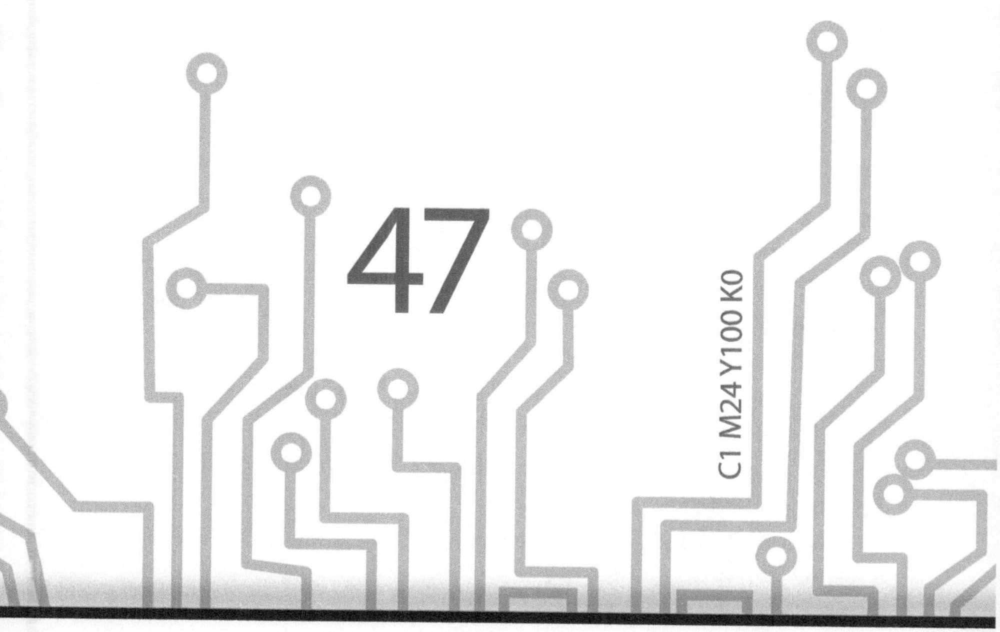

Now that Rimush Black and I were both banged up, we agreed that walking all the way to Auric wasn't feasible any more. Time for a new plan.

"I've jumped on a moving train a few times," I said. "Think you can do the same?"

He snorted. "If you can do it, I should be able to handle it with ease."

"Right, right." Sounded like something annoying kids said back in the Learning Years. And he was supposed to have centuries of experience?

After a rest, we hiked a few more miles to reach some tracks. By my estimation, this was still the track from Caesious to the Hub. We sought out a place along the rails where they took a sharper turn. The train would, of necessity, slow down, giving us an opportunity to board.

To my surprise, this particular maneuver went off without any difficulty. Rimush Black and I both made it on board a flat car and found a place to rest while we waited out the trip. Unfortunately, once it passed the Hub, the train turned southeast toward Viridia. We were forced to jump off and hike back toward the north to find a train going toward Auric. This time, we had to wait for five or six hours until one came.

Our arrival in Auric stayed quiet for all of about three minutes. We'd walked maybe two blocks from the train when we were surrounded by Sentinels. After hearing our identities, they took us into the city and to the underground areas I'd been before.

No one expressed any shock or dismay at the presence of a black draconic. Taizong Gold insisted on taking him to have his wounds seen to. Rimush Black protested at first, but eventually gave in. This gave me time alone with Captain Tawn.

"I'm quite curious to know the story behind your current companion," he observed.

I put my head in my hands and rested it on the table in his office. "It's ridiculously complicated. Can you give me a safe place to sleep tonight? He'll insist on being near, but I need to be safe from him too."

"Do you need us to remove him?"

"No," I groaned. "If he dies, someone I care about dies too. I'm stuck with him for now."

"Hm. Well, despite your early return, the device you requested should be ready by tomorrow morning."

I lifted my head. "That's the best news I've heard in days." I closed my eyes and let out a sigh. "But you're going to hate my next question."

"You have another request? Why am I not surprised?"

"Two, actually. One should be easy. Can you… deliver a message to my people for me? Maybe in one of those tube-things like the one you used when you first contacted me?"

Tawn's face didn't move. "It's not impossible."

"I can't go back there right now, not while I have this… follower."

Tawn glanced toward the door. "I… see. And the other request?"

"I need a second device."

Tawn barked a short laugh. "Ridiculous. Why would you need a second one?"

"To use against Onyx."

That got his attention. The captain folded his hands and placed them on the table. "Why do you think the electromagnetic pulse would be effective against a dragon?"

"Because Onyx is not just a dragon. He's like me." I straightened up and tapped my cyb fingers together. "He has a cybernetic implant copied from the one in my head. Auric himself told me that if the pulse went off near me, it would destroy my implant and kill me."

"I was there." He frowned and thought for a few moments. "Let us assume, for the sake of theorizing, that we were able to provide you with such a thing. Since his arrival, Onyx has rarely stayed in one place for very long.

His movements are erratic. How would you go about getting to him?"

I pulled the talker out of my pocket and held it up. "I would call him on this and say I needed to meet with him. He'll come."

"And then what?"

"I'd set it off in his face. That's what."

"Knowing that you would die also."

"If that's what it takes, I'm ready." I swallowed. "You and I have rarely seen eye-to-eye. But my entire purpose in life has been to rid the world of the dragons and set humanity free. If my death is what it takes to get rid of the last one… then my purpose will be fulfilled."

He stared at me, face unmoving, for several more moments. At last he sighed with a slight eye roll and looked away. "I mostly believe you, to my own surprise."

"Mostly?"

"Like most who claim to be ready to die, I don't believe you've thought through the full ramifications of such an act. That being said… I see no downside to your plan." His fingers tapped the table. "While I would never have supported your original goal, now that Onyx is the only dragon left, I find myself on your side."

Captain Tawn stood up. He moved to the door, opened it, and took a quick look. He closed the door and returned, but didn't sit down. "I cannot provide a second device at this time, but… I will speak to the technicians. Perhaps a second one can be built in a shorter time period than the last."

I put my head back in my hands. "Thank you. Now I just need that sleep."

"Do you also require medical attention?"

"No, it's just bruises this time. I'll be all right."

"Very well." He summoned a Sentinel and gave him instructions. A few minutes later, after walking much further than I'd have liked, he took me up an elevator to a room similar to the one I'd used on my first trip to this city. It might have even been the same one.

"Should you need anything, there will be guards outside the door," the Sentinel informed me. "Your… companion will be in the room next door." He pointed to a side door. "Through there. It is locked, however, and cannot be opened from either side without the other unlocking it."

"That's perfect. Thanks."

Once he left, I went to the bedroom and stripped off what remained of my clothes. I should have asked for a new shirt while I was making all those requests. I stretched out on the bed and closed my eyes. If this was the same room as the first time, I'd slept on the couch that time. Lainey slept on this bed.

At the thought of her, a pain gripped my chest. I touched the pillow beside me, imagining her head lying there, her face smiling at me… It hurt so much more than my shoulder, all the bruises, and other physical pains combined. You would think having a genetically-engineered dragon heart would be immune to this kind of pain. But maybe that made it worse.

It took far longer than I would have liked to fall asleep, and before I did, I had to switch pillows. The first one grew too wet from tears.

In the morning, I wrote a letter to Bice and Kelly, a second one for them to send to Caedan, and a third one for Captain Tawn. I sealed them up a moment before a Sentinel brought me a nice breakfast. I enjoyed every bite before I finally got around to unlocking the side door and letting Rimush Black enter.

"If you had been in danger during the night, I would have had to break down this door," he pointed out.

"I figured you could handle it."

The draconic looked ready to complain some more, but a knock at the main door brought new guests. A full squad of Aurelian Sentinels arrived to take us to the edge of the city. Were they putting on a show for Rimush Black, or did they genuinely fear him that much? And not me? Maybe I should have been insulted.

Taizong Gold and Captain Tawn met us at the edge of the city. The golden draconic held a large package almost as big as me. "This is what you came for," he announced. "Use it wisely." He set it on the ground and opened it. I looked down at a confusing piece of metal and wires. It did look somewhat like the smaller version I'd used on Atramentous, though.

Taizong Gold pointed to a switch. "Here is the activation. This dial can also set the time for detonation, giving you more of chance to escape before it happens."

"I appreciate that." It was a significant improvement on the last one.

I turned and handed the letters I'd written to Captain Tawn. "Thank you for everything." He gave a crisp nod.

"Are you going directly to… your target now?" Taizong Gold asked.

I glanced at my draconic companion. "I don't see any reason not to." I took a deep breath. "Let's end this. All of it."

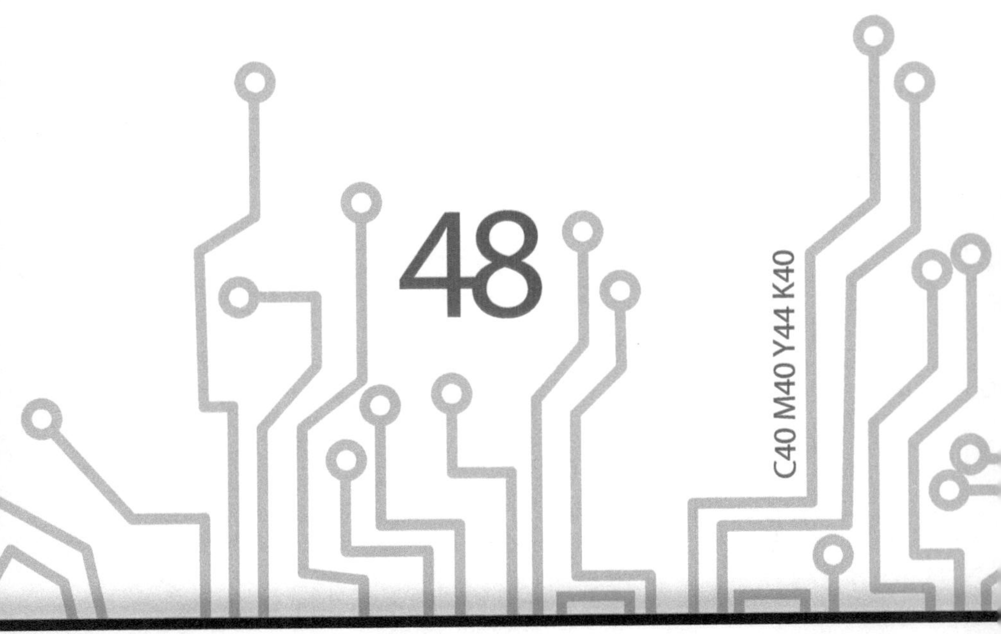

Fortunately, Taizong Gold had arranged train passage to Caesious. "That is the nearest spot to your destination, is it not?"

"Sure, that'll work." Now that it came to it, I was no longer sure about my path to Chroma's temple. At least I would have time to think it over on the train.

As we walked to the train, Captain Tawn stepped next to me. "We have been unable to remove the Viridian device from Auric's source. In addition, we have confirmed the presence of the devices in both Amaranth and Incarnadine."

"Sounds like it's all the cities."

"We suspect it is part of a plan to exert control over the entire Circle."

"You mean like Auric did with his rolling explosives? Threaten to blow up the source and half the city with it if people don't do as he says?"

"Something like that."

"My note to you has some suggestions related to it."

"I look forward to reading it." Tawn nodded and stepped away.

Rimush Black and I had a passenger car to ourselves. I couldn't help laughing at how many times that had happened now. And to think I'd never even been allowed to ride the trains before I started the rebellion.

"What is the plan now?" the draconic wanted to know.

"That depends. Do you think we can get through the tunnel?"

The draconic toyed with the latch on the device's box. "The zealots have greatly increased their security. It would be... difficult, but not impossible for ones such as us."

I snorted. "I appreciate that. I think." I paused. "Well, then I guess we have to climb the mountains."

"That... would be a difficult feat."

"I've done it once already. It wasn't fun." I clenched my fist, remembering Lainey's presence on that climb. I tried to push my anger aside and consider the practical: I would need warm clothes and...

"If you hadn't ruined my robe, it would be a different matter," Rimush Black mused.

"What do you mean?" I realized the answer before he could answer. "Wait, you could warp us there?"

"No, no." He shook a claw at me. "The spatial movement is very limited. However, with its capabilities, I could utilize my resomancy abilities to get us through the tunnel."

"So you just need a working purple robe." I smiled. "I think we can do that."

I settled in to rest and preserve my strength for the job ahead. I watched the hills and plains of The Circle pass by through the windows. The beauty outside had been one thing, but the beauty of the land here was equal, if not better. I suppose I loved it. If I could look out at it for the rest of my life, I would be happy... if Lainey were beside me.

I rubbed my face and ran my hands back through my hair. Thinking like that would only depress me or incite my rage. Neither one would be beneficial to the current mission. I needed to focus.

The goal to deliver the pulse device to Chroma's temple was in sight. Assuming all went to plan, I could return to The Circle with my eyes toward the remaining problems: Onyx and... whatever was going on with Viridia. I had a plan now for dealing with Onyx. I could summon him with the talker and set off another pulse device as soon as he arrived. Unless I could figure out a way to deceive him, it would kill me as well. I could accept that... except I wouldn't want to leave everyone else in the grips of Troilus Green's plan, whatever it might be. We might have to deal with that first... or convince Onyx to deal with it.

I almost started to doze off, hypnotized by the hum of the train and the motion of the scenery outside. I jerked and glanced toward Rimush

Black. I still didn't trust him enough to fall asleep in his presence. I needed to be careful.

Hours later, the train slowed for a brief stop at the new junction with the track leading into the tunnel. Some kind of cargo exchange took place. Rimush Black and I left the train and followed the tracks at a safe distance, keeping an eye out for zealots.

It worked even better than I'd hoped. We spotted a single zealot not far from the tunnel entrance. Rimush Black engaged him in conversation while I slipped around behind. I seized hold of his robe and yanked the hood from his face. A draconic punch knocked him out, and we had an intact robe. It wouldn't fit the draconic, but he didn't need it for a covering. He tied portions of the robe around his neck, hanging it on his back like a cape.

Armed with what we needed, we boldly entered the rail workers' camp next to the tunnel entrance. We found a rail rider similar to the one I'd used before, loaded up the pulse device, and entered the tunnel. While I drove, Rimush Black crouched behind me, muttering words I couldn't understand. I felt a few brushes of a breeze, but nothing more. I couldn't see it, but the draconic surrounded us with a bubble of solid air as a shield.

As we rushed through the darkness, I tried not to think about the last time I'd done this. Lainey's unmoving body lying beside the tracks filled my mind. I could pinpoint the exact location where she'd been.

I caught glimpses of zealots warping in and out around us. Two tried to penetrate the resomancy bubble but were thrown against the tunnel walls. After that, they seemed content to monitor our passage.

"They'll be waiting when we emerge," I told my companion. He kept muttering his incantations. I activated a few small boosts to prepare myself. Even so, I don't think I was prepared for what awaited us.

The instant we exited the tunnel, gunfire rang out all around us. I saw flashes of light here and there as the bullets were thrown off by Rimush Black's power. We might have been able to barrel our way straight through for miles... except that they'd built a barricade across the tracks using multiple boxcars.

I managed to bring the rail rider to a halt inches away from the barricade. For a brief moment, I considered trying to smash through it, hoping the resomancy bubble would work as a battering ram. But I realized the rail rider would come off the tracks no matter how well the ram worked.

Gunshots continued around us. Rimush Black continued to mutter. I couldn't ask him for ideas without interrupting the shield. From what I could tell, the shooters were stationed at high points around the tunnel entrance. I caught glimpses of purple robes flitting in and out in the same areas.

"The path of least resistance seems to be ahead," I said, loud enough for Rimush Black to hear me over his own incantations. "Probably best to go to one side of the barricade, letting it shield us from the other. Do you think you can switch your power from a bubble to shoving out to one side as we run?"

He gave a short nod and gestured to the right as his choice for our escape. My eyes darted around, checking all the possibilities I could imagine. I thought it would work. The draconic pointed at the pulse device. Right. If he were busy concentrating on the resomancy stuff, I would have to carry it. Time for some serious boosts.

My shoulder protested in agony as I lifted the device, even with the strongest boosts I could give it. "I'll count down," I shouted. "Go on three… two… one!"

A rush of wind swept past me as I leaped off the rail rider. Rimush Black screamed his words of power now, throwing up his arms in sweeping gestures. Together, we charged to the right of the pile of boxcars. A blast of power spun the first boxcar to the left, providing us further cover. Even so, a few bullets smacked into the ground near us. I saw one strike the back of the draconic's right calf, but he kept moving.

We raced past the barricade and into the open. I pointed further to the right where trees could provide more shelter. A zealot warped in directly in front of me. I barreled into him with the box holding the pulse device. Falling down with it may have saved my life.

From the trees ahead, four soldiers suddenly stepped into view and leveled their guns. "Look out!" I shouted. Rimush Black had been looking back to his right, and jerked around to see, but it was too late. His incantations ceased as multiple bullets slammed into his body. Two of them passed right over my head.

As he started to fall, the draconic shouted and threw his hand forward. The four soldiers flew backward, slamming into trees and tumbling over and over. I pulled the box with me and scrambled over next to Rimush Black. He looked up long enough to growl one word: "Run!"

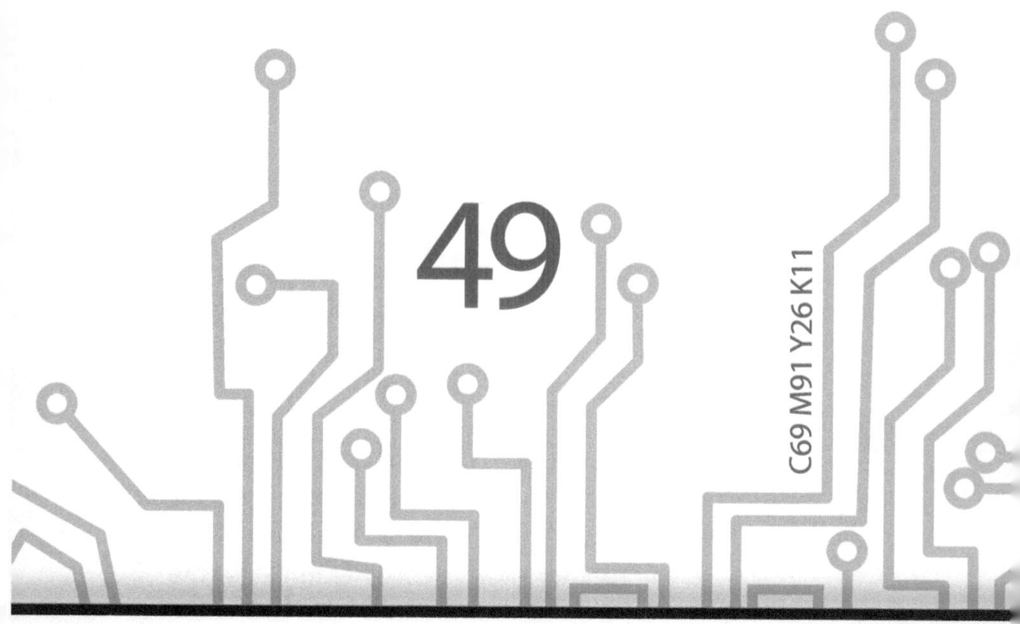

Ten minutes later, I had to concede that this wasn't an ideal situation.

When I raced in amongst the trees, a few more gunshots followed me. Thankfully, none of them struck home. But I soon learned the pursuers hadn't given up. I caught glimpses of purple every so often, whispering through the forest.

My own movements were even more erratic. I carried a box almost as big as me while pushing my way through underbrush and between more trees than I'd ever known existed. And thanks to the mountains behind me, all of the terrain led downhill. I tripped at least five or six times in the first few minutes. It took constant boosts to my arms just to be able to hold the device, and constant boosts to my legs to keep from pitching over even more. And my shoulder hurt so much, I knew it had to be dislocated again.

Yep. Not ideal.

"Beryl…" The whisper came from off to my left. I whirled and saw a single purple tendril slither around a tree trunk before vanishing. "Beryl…" the voice repeated from the opposite direction. Ugh. Stupid zealots. I could outrun the men with guns, but the warping purple robes could keep up with me. How could I possibly lose them?

More importantly, how could I get this device to the temple? If they were staying close with me, they would see me try to drop the device off next to it. And then they'd remove it, unless I stayed with it and sacrificed myself. But, before I could even consider any of that… I had to find the stupid temple! I knew I was on the wrong side of the tracks and still miles away.

I could think of only one solution, and I hated it so much. The next time I stumbled, I rested the box against the ground and pulled out the talker. I took a deep breath and pushed the button. "Onyx? I need help."

I didn't hear anything for several moments. I glanced around, wary of the purple robes. I didn't want them listening, if I could help it. And was this thing even working this far away? Outside The Circle?

An exasperated sigh came through the static of the talker. "Beryl. You try my patience."

"Sorry. I just thought you'd want to destroy the zealots. I'll find someone else."

"Fine. Tell me."

I summed up the situation as fast as I could. "The zealots just killed Rimush Black. I'm sorry, but he got me this far. All I need is a quick lift, if you know what I mean."

"Where are you?"

I gave him an approximation of my location and shoved the talker back into my pocket. I hefted the box and set out again, pushing my way through some annoying scrub bushes.

"Beryl…"

"Oh, shut up," I mumbled.

Ten minutes later, my legs gave out.

After spitting dirt and moss out of my mouth, I pushed myself up off the ground. I sat next to the box and waited. How long did it take a dragon to cross the mountains, anyway? Especially if he hadn't done it in centuries? This should be interesting.

It didn't take long for the zealots to grow curious. I saw them flitting about at first. Finally, one of them stepped into my view about a dozen feet away.

"Beryl…"

I waved.

"What do you think you are doing?"

"Just waiting for my friend to catch up."

The zealot paused before answering: "The traitorous draconic is dead."

I gave a dismissive wave. "Not him. The other one."

My answer must have confused him, because the zealot stepped back and disappeared from my view for a few minutes. Maybe he was talking it over with his friends. I tried to move my legs without success. Oof. If Onyx found me like this, it would be embarrassing.

The zealot reappeared. "You did not come here with any other companions."

I shook my finger. "You're good. Nice work. Nothing gets past you, does it?"

"Your behavior is illogical."

"Yep. That sounds about right."

Another zealot warped into view off to my left. I gave him a casual glance, then returned my gaze to the first one.

"Who is this companion? The draconic is dead." The usual creepy voice actually sounded perplexed. If I weren't hurting and unable to move, I would think this hilarious.

I made a show of looking around. "He should be here any minute now." Still no feeling in my legs.

"There is no one coming," said the zealot to my left.

I put a hand to my ear and cocked it upward. "You might be able to hear him coming if you listen carefully."

"This is a bluff," the left one said. "He is injured and pretending."

I pointed at him with my cyb hand. "You are welcome to test that theory."

Neither of them moved or spoke again for at least a full minute. "Come on, you big stupid black lizard," I muttered.

I pretended to look around again and included the sky in my gaze this time. I didn't see anything. Ugh.

"What is in the box?" one of the zealots asked.

I patted it. "This is my lunch. Fighting you guys makes me hungry."

They didn't answer.

I gave an exaggerated sigh. "You also have no senses of humor at all. Do you lose that when you get cloned or whatever it is?"

My toe twitched. Oh good. I stretched my arms up over my head and yawned. "Well, I guess I've waited on him long enough. Might as well get moving again."

"You are surrounded. You will not be going anywhere."

"Oh, I think I will. You haven't been able to stop me yet." I could definitely feel my legs now. I gave them a gentle boost. There it was.

I glanced up and saw a black dot in the sky. Was that him? It grew bigger. I took a closer look with my zoom vision. "I spoke too soon. Here he comes now."

The zealots looked up. I laughed and got to my feet. They backed away, vanishing from view.

A few moments later, Onyx smashed into the ground, knocking a couple of trees over. His head swung around, slinging ice and snow. The dragon glared down at me. "Do you have any idea how difficult it is to get over those mountains? There's a reason why I haven't done it in centuries!"

"But you could have." I picked up the box, wincing from the shoulder pain. "It raises all sorts of questions."

Onyx looked over his shoulder. "There was a group of soldiers approaching you, but they fled when I descended." He looked back at me. "Did you decide to take a break while you waited for me?"

"Something like that." I looked him over and set the box back down. "All right. I'm going to climb onto your back, and then you can hand me this box."

He snorted smoke from his nostrils. "Don't be ridiculous. I'm not going to let you ride me."

I massaged my shoulder. "Do you have a better idea? The device requires human hands to activate it and set the timer. I figure you can fly us over the temple, and I'll drop it. They won't be able to stop us."

"I thought you said they would have defenses ready for me."

"Yeah, yeah." I pulled on one of his scales to see if it moved. With a few extra boosts, I leaped up high and climbed aboard. "But I think if we stay high enough, we should be all right." I found a spot on his spinal ridge. I could hang on up here easily. "The box?"

He snorted again but picked up the box. He twisted his arm around to get it high enough. The angle wasn't quite right, but I managed to get hold and yank it back toward myself. I fell against his scales, but caught hold of one of the spines to keep from sliding off.

"What are you doing?"

"Hang on." I pulled myself and the box back up. Now that I thought about it, I didn't need to keep the device inside the box any more. I opened it and pulled the device out. The empty box slid down Onyx's side, bounced off his knee, and hit the ground.

"Are you quite ready?"

I pulled in between two of the larger spines and settled in. "Ready. Let's go zap some zealots."

The black dragon crouched and leaped into the air. And I rode with him.

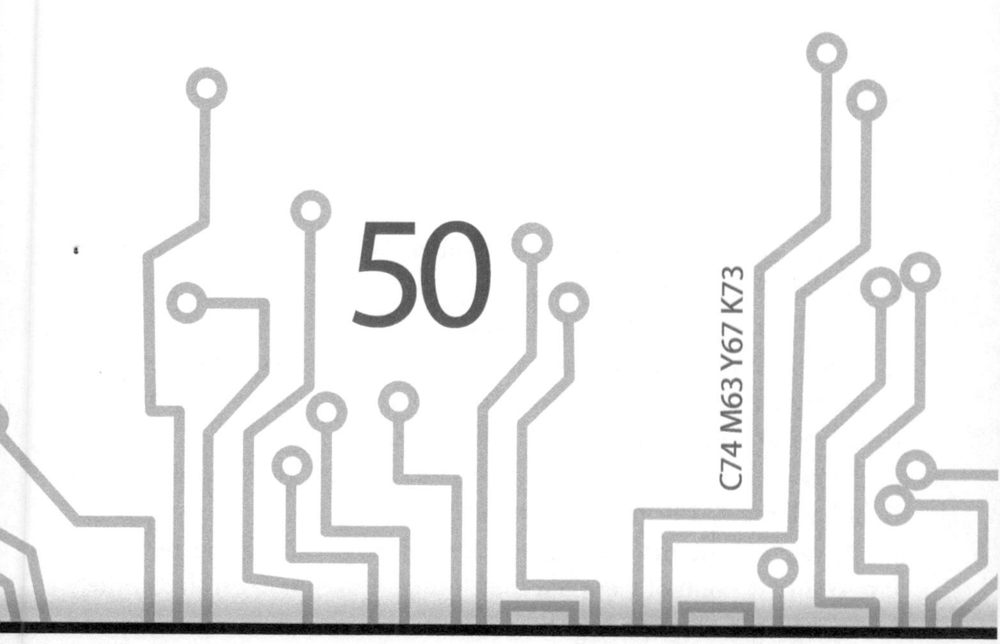

50

"This is ridiculous," Onyx complained again. "Who ever heard of riding a dragon?"

I didn't answer. To my own surprise, I found myself enjoying the flight. In some ways, it was more enjoyable than the times I flew the Sky Claimer. I didn't have to worry about the controls or about the direction or anything, really, other than hanging on. With all the spines and spiky scales on Onyx's back, I didn't have much trouble with that, even though I had to keep a tight grip on the pulse device too.

"When we reach the temple, I should just drop you with it," the dragon went on.

"And then I'd never activate it and leave you to deal with the zealots by yourself," I said. "Plus, they'd gain access to Loden's technology from my dead body. How would that go?"

He snorted in response.

"Look, we made a deal. It was your idea. We work together until Chroma is defeated, right? Or are you going back on your word?"

"That was before I knew Chroma was dead."

"How did that change anything? The zealots are still an enormous threat you couldn't face alone. I'm literally holding the solution to dealing with them. Once it's done, and we're back in The Circle, we split into our two sides and see what happens next." I waited, and when he didn't answer, I added: "Right?"

"For now. But we have to deal with Viridia also."

"We can talk about that. Um… what's that?"

"What's what?"

Oh, right. He couldn't see if I pointed. "There are two specks in the sky ahead of us and to the right."

"You're the one with zoom vision."

I felt like an idiot. I zoomed in on the area of the sky, wobbling a bit to get my view straight. "That can't be good. They're some kind of flying machines, and they're heading straight toward us very fast!"

"I can tell their speed myself," Onyx observed. "You'd better hold on tight back there. This might get tricky."

I watched the machines draw closer. Onyx was moving incredibly fast, from my point of view, but these things looked faster still, definitely faster than the Sky Claimer. Bigger, too. The machines were sleek and pointed with wide wings. The pilots were inside an enclosed space with plenty of glass to let them look around. I had just noticed some smaller pointed devices mounted underneath the wings when two of them shot forward away from the machines at an even more unbelievable speed.

"They've launched some things at us!" I shouted.

"I see. Hang on."

I wish he'd told me what to expect. My stomach wasn't prepared when Onyx folded his wings and dropped like a rock. My head jerked back. I watched the slender devices pass above us. If we'd been there, they would have both struck the dragon. I had no doubt they were weapons of some kind, probably explosive.

Onyx's wings snapped back out. With quick and powerful flaps, he changed direction back upward almost as fast as we had dropped.

The flying machines shot past us. If I could have spared my hands, I would have covered my ears from the tremendous roar of their engines. Onyx swerved up behind them and sprayed his acid breath. A few drops struck the back side of one of them, but didn't seem to be enough to do any real damage. The two machines split up, rocketing in opposite directions.

"Annoying," Onyx grumbled. He spun in pursuit of the one that banked right.

I sent boost after boost to maintain my grip on both the dragon and the pulse device. Without my enhancements, I would have tumbled off his back during that first dive.

The machine outdistanced Onyx, but not as quickly as I would have expected. "Keep an eye out for the other one!" he shouted back at me. I swiveled my head to look behind us. I couldn't see it anywhere.

I heard it before I saw it. I jerked my head up, but still couldn't find it. "Somewhere above!" And then an absolute spray of bullets struck us. Most of them ricocheted harmlessly off Onyx's scales, but a few tore small holes in his left wing. I risked one more quick look before crouching to make myself a smaller target. "He's diving out of the sun!" Bad enough they had those explosive weapons, but they had guns too? At the same time, I couldn't help thinking: given enough technology, humans actually could defeat dragons, couldn't they?

But maybe not today. Onyx twisted with a roar and shot almost straight up to meet the descending attacker. It banked to the right, trying to elude him, but it was too late. The dragon ripped the left wing completely off the zealots' machine. It fell into a smoking spiral toward the ground far below.

I heard the distant explosion of its impact even as Onyx spun back around, looking for the other enemy. "Where did it—?"

One of the pointed weapons slammed into Onyx's side beneath his right wing and exploded. The dragon roared in pain. His wings faltered. For one terrifying moment, I thought we were going down. The thoughts that cascaded through my head raced from how completely helpless I was in the moment to how much I wanted to see Lainey again before I died.

Onyx strained and leveled out. I couldn't see the severity of his injury from my perch, but I caught glimpses of blood spattering against his back leg, and his wing didn't seem to beat with the same strength as before.

Freed from the terror of the fall for the moment, I scanned the skies for the second enemy. The weapon came from the right, but at the speed these things moved… "Below us to the left!" I shouted.

Onyx spun and spewed acid breath in a torrential flow. He caught the back end of the vehicle as it sped away. I couldn't tell exactly what happened, but black smoke poured out behind the machine. It turned and shot off toward the north, leaving a dark trail in the sky.

"Where's that temple?" Onyx snarled. "Let's get this over with before they send more of those things!"

I agreed, but I had no idea which way to direct him. I could see the mountains, so I knew it couldn't be far. As Onyx rotated in a slow circle, I scanned the ground. "There! I see the city. The temple is next to it!"

"I see it too." Onyx gathered himself and swept toward it. "You might want to calculate the timing for the bomb."

"The what? Oh." I looked down at the pulse device and the timer. "Um. Huh. I don't know how much time to give it. If it hits the ground before the timer runs out, it would probably be too damaged to work, but I don't want it to go off too soon…"

"It's a simple math problem," Onyx answered. "Calculate it from 5,000 feet."

I glanced over the side. "I… have no idea how to calculate that. Didn't it have something to do with square roots or something?"

"Did you ever learn anything whatsoever in that education system of yours?"

"Why do you think I worked in a bike shop, Onyx?"

After a brief pause, the dragon announced, "It will be just under eighteen seconds."

"That's all?" I adjusted the dial. "Um, maybe we should go higher and give ourselves more time to get away. If we're too close when it goes off, it'll kill us both."

His head swiveled enough for one eye to look back at me. "What do you mean?"

"It takes out cybernetics, remember? And we've both got them in our brains, smart guy."

"Fine. I'll ascend to 10,000 feet."

"So… thirty-six seconds?"

"No, you idiot. It accelerates the longer it falls. Think… twenty-four."

"Right, all right. I'll get it."

From somewhere below us, I heard a distant boom. A few seconds later, something exploded in the sky off to our right. "What was that?"

"They're shooting at us with some sort of large guns," Onyx said. "Another good reason to go higher." He aimed himself almost straight up as we ascended. With every beat of his wings, we rose. I shivered, wishing I had warmer clothes. What remained of my shirt didn't offer much protection from the frigid air the higher we climbed.

Two more of the explosions went off. One hit close enough that a few shards of metal bounced off Onyx's scales.

I looked back over my shoulder, straight down thousands of feet below to the temple of Chroma.

"Drop it!" Onyx cried.

I flipped the switch on the pulse weapon and released it.

51

Onyx turned and sped back toward the mountains. I tried to count in my head to twenty-four seconds. I didn't quite get there when I heard a dull thump behind and below us. I guess that was it.

"How will we know if it worked?" I asked aloud.

Before Onyx could answer, an enormous explosion erupted from the same place. I whirled around and stared back to see a gigantic fireball rise out of the temple. Smoke cascaded up even higher. "That wasn't supposed to happen!"

Onyx laughed. "When they lost all their power, it appears to have set something else off. Maybe they were using some kind of energy that needed containment, and they lost that." He chuckled again. "Either way, it doesn't matter. The zealots are defeated. We've won this particular battle."

I suppose he was right. But I didn't feel good about it. The entire point of the pulse weapon had been to take them down without loss of life. With this result, we may as well have dropped one of the larger explosives on them. But that would have created its own set of problems just getting here, I guess.

"I need a moment to rest," Onyx announced, descending slowly.

"Shouldn't we get over the mountains first?"

"That's why I need a rest."

Oh. I didn't pretend to understand dragon physiology. Maybe being this far from his source made him tire faster. Then again, he had crossed the mountains once already and then done all this aerial fighting. I guess he deserved a little break.

The dragon came to a stop beside a stream flowing down from the mountains. He drank from the water while I waited. I stretched a little, but didn't get down.

"Afraid I'll leave you behind?" Onyx asked.

"The thought had crossed my mind."

"You needn't worry. I'll stick to the agreement. That devastation was pretty spectacular." He gestured back toward the temple. I looked and almost gasped. The tower of smoke from the explosion was not only still visible, but looked higher than the mountains even. What had we done?

Onyx gargled some of the spring water and spat it out. I considered sliding down to get some myself, but even with his assurances, I had doubts. I kept reminding myself never to trust this monster. My legs were a little sore from this position, but at least here I could warm up. Without the bitter cold high in the sky, the warmth of the dragon beneath me radiated through my body.

He twisted his head around and lifted his right wing to get a good look at his wound. "Hmph. Not too bad. It should heal in time."

"Makes you wonder how bad it could have gotten," I said. "What if they'd had a dozen of those machines?"

"They caught me by surprise," he countered. "If I knew what was coming, I could take on that many." A strange look swept over his face, and he turned toward the mountains.

"What was that?" I asked.

"I don't know. I felt… something wrong. Like a sudden loss of energy, but it came from in there."

I didn't like the sound of that.

"Maybe we should get back, after all. Hang on."

Before I could respond, Onyx swept into the air again. How could something so big get up into the air so fast? He took a sharp angle up, following the general ascent of the mountains. The air grew colder and colder again. I huddled as close to the dragon's skin as I could.

"Not… good…" Onyx said about two-thirds of the way up.

"What? What's not good?"

The dragon's wings stopped beating. We coasted, closer and closer to the mountain itself. "Onyx? What's going on?"

He didn't answer. I boosted both hands to strengthen my grip. A moment later, the dragon plowed into the side of the mountain, sending rocks and dust cascading all around us.

I waited until the dust cleared before lifting my head. "Onyx? Are you all right?"

He lifted his head from the rock with obvious difficulty. "The source is being drained. It's affecting me."

"What source? I thought you were using all of them?"

"Atramentous. It's become my primary. But… this might be all of them."

Viridia. The devices. It had to be.

Snow drifted around us. My teeth chattered together, and my shivering grew by the second. "Can you find enough strength to get us over the top? We'll freeze to death up here. Use your boosts!"

"I'm trying. I'm… not as efficient at it as you are."

My throat and mouth were shaking so hard, I didn't think I could say anything else. I tried to embrace the warm dragon scales closer, sending my own boosts throughout in an attempt at warming myself.

"Don't… let Viridia win," I whispered.

With an extremely long grunt-growl, Onyx pulled himself to his feet. He spread his wings, lifted his head, and launched into the air again. At that point, I may have blacked out for a few moments. All I know is that a few minutes later, Onyx grabbed hold of one of the mountain peaks and used it to push himself over and downward.

Heading down into The Circle was much faster, of course, and easier on the dragon. With his wings spread wide enough, he could glide much of the way. It didn't take long to break through the haze and clouds and see The Circle spread out below us. I'd seen it from the Sky Claimer, but it hadn't been this high, and my view from the mountains with Lainey had been restricted by other difficulties. But here and now, I could see almost everything. I zoomed in on one city after another, amazed at how they looked from so far above. The screens in Onyx's tower hadn't done them justice at all.

When I zoomed in on Viridia, I saw flashes of light, but we were still far too distant for me to discern their source. I could make an educated guess, though. "Something's happening in Viridia," I called. "I think it's at the Emerald Ascendancy!"

"Makes sense," Onyx growled. "I killed him once, but it wasn't enough. Let's do it again."

I glanced toward Caesious, where I really wanted to be. But… this was the moment. This was my purpose. If we could take Troilus Green down now, it would be two threats removed in one day. I couldn't pass that up.

"I'm with you," I said. "Take us in."

Onyx swooped and soared, changing direction to find the best wind or whatever it is flying creatures did. His wings only moved when he shifted direction, beating once or twice to stabilize the new pattern. I finally stopped shivering, but I still didn't feel warm. At least the sun was shining.

In less time than I expected, we soared down over the city where I'd grown up. Acres of dull concrete passed beneath us. But there, in the center, lay the Emerald Ascendancy, home of the green dragon Viridia. How many times had I been inside it now? Too many. I wanted to burn the place down.

A crackle of light burst out of the Ascendancy. Or did it burst in? Like lightning, it appeared for a moment and vanished.

Onyx banked and swept up and over one of the outer arches. We came down into what once had been the lair of Viridia. But how it had changed! The mounds of debris had been cleared, the entrance to the caverns sealed over. A massive oval platform had been erected in the center. Five massive pillars rose around it, ending in globes of radiant crystal: black, blue, red, rust-red, and gold. Light flashed from one to another and sometimes down toward the center of the platform.

And there stood Troilus Green, the draconic I thought I'd killed, now claiming to actually be Viridia, the dragon Onyx thought he'd killed. But he'd changed even more than the Ascendancy.

"Brother!" he cried on seeing Onyx. "Welcome! Welcome to the restoration of my glory and the final victory!"

Staring at what he'd become… in that moment… I believed him.

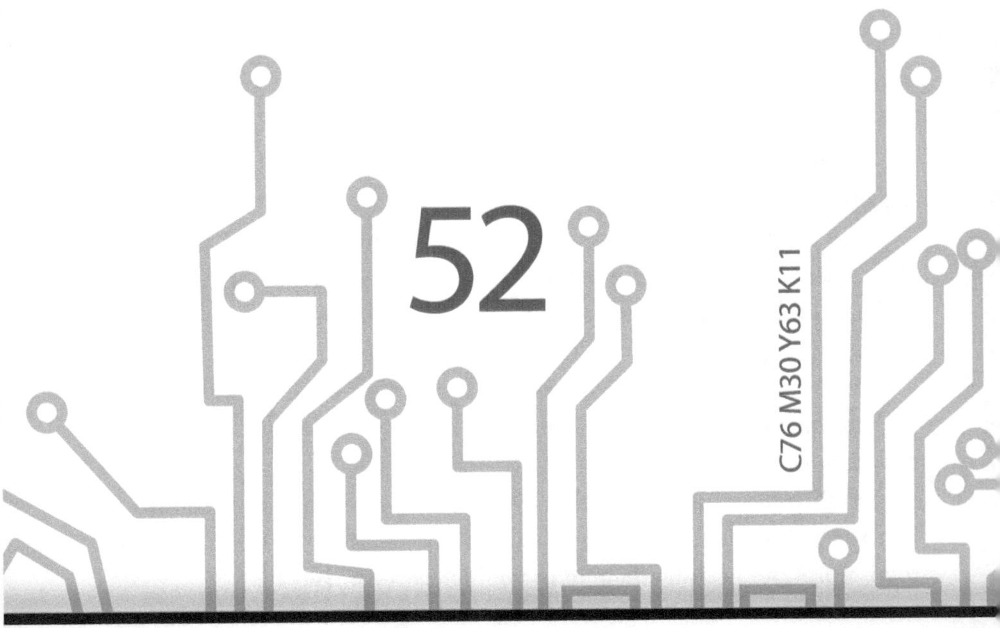

Troilus Green lifted his draconic arms and light erupted from two of the pillars. Bursts like lightning flowed down to his arms and as they did, he grew.

Already, he'd grown three times the size he'd been. And as he grew, he changed. His neck and tail grew longer. Two protrusions erupted from his back, the beginnings of wings. He was becoming a dragon again!

"What are you doing?" Onyx shouted.

With no one paying attention to me, I slid off the black dragon's back and dashed to the shadows near the inner walls. I glanced up at all of the windows surrounding the Ascendancy's core, wondering how many of Viridia's followers were watching right now.

"Becoming what I was always meant to be!" the green creature cried. "I am Viridia, the one true dragon god of this world!"

I don't pretend to understand how this worked. Why would siphoning power from the five dragon sources transform Troilus Green into an actual dragon? Did all draconics have this potentiality built into them? My brain imagined a whole new flock of dragons recreated and terrorizing humanity all over again. Yeah, this was bad.

"Stop this at once!" Onyx rumbled toward the platform.

Troilus Green—Viridia—laughed. "Are you feeling weaker, brother? Not quite up to your full abilities?"

"I'm strong enough to tear your head off again."

At that moment, I saw human figures pouring out of a door off to my right and spreading in both directions around the inner wall. Priests of Viridia and their elite white-robed guards. As if things weren't crazy enough already.

Viridia brought his hands together as if holding an invisible ball. More of the lightning shot into him with enormous crackling sounds. I could see his mouth moving, but couldn't make out anything over the electrical noise. He swept his hands toward Onyx. I recognized that motion.

The black dragon staggered back, struck by a wave of resomancy. He didn't fall, but neither did he continue his advance on the platform.

"For decades, we have sought cybernetic enhancement to extend our lives!" Viridia shouted. "When all along, the true solution was right here, below our feet. Nothing can stand against this power!"

I drew my sword and started forward. I didn't know what I was going to do yet, but if I stayed next to the wall, the white -robed guards would come after me. I would much rather fight a dragon than one of them again. I heard the priests muttering behind me. They'd seen me, but weren't coming out.

Viridia spotted me then. "Beryl! So both of my great enemies are here!"

"You're betraying Auric's memory, Troilus Green" I called. "Why are you doing this?"

"I am Viridia! And I am reclaiming my power and position. You are nothing." He gestured toward me, but I was prepared. A short boost to my heart, and I ignored his resomancy wave.

"Then why am I still here?" While I spoke, Onyx gathered himself and started forward again. "You've tried to kill me over and over. And the last time, Auric ordered you to do what I asked."

"Auric was a fool," he growled. "And his orders were only for that time. He's gone now. They're all gone. Except this one!" He battered Onyx again with a rush of solidified air. The black dragon snarled in defiance, but even I could tell he was weakened.

Around us, the priests began some kind of chant. They were repeating Viridia's name endlessly, along with some other words of praise I didn't care about. It made me think of their services and temples and all of the horrors that went along with it. My anger grew. But so did my confidence. I knew something he didn't know.

I kept walking toward the platform. "Everyone will be against you now, Troilus Green! We could have made some kind of agreement to work together! But you're making yourself the enemy of all!"

More energy poured into him from all five crystals in almost a continuous flow now. He was over half the size of Onyx already. His wings were almost fully-formed. But he didn't drop down on all fours like the dragons. He remained upright, his posture draconic. His cybernetic parts—the claws, face plate, and chest shield—grew with him.

Onyx launched himself at the nearest one of the pillars. White energy exploded out of it, throwing him across the Ascendancy floor. Priests scattered as the black dragon smashed into the side of the building. Steel and glass shattered and crumbled.

"Your arrogance will destroy you, Troilus Green!" I shouted as I reached the edge of the platform. It was four feet up. I boosted my legs and jumped onto it.

"You couldn't defeat me in our last fight," he pointed out. "What makes you think you can now?"

I spread my arms out. "Because I'm not the one who's going to defeat you! I'm not alone. I've never been alone."

The half-dragon pretended to look around. "Other than my worthless brother, you appear to be alone to me."

Despite the pain in my shoulder, I lifted my sword and pointed it at him. "Humans, Viridia! Humans will tear you down. You think we're sheep. That we're here to amuse you or worship you. I say we're here to defy you!"

I might have imagined it, but I think the gold crystal blinked off and on. The flow of energy continued, though.

"Since the first day you and I met, it's been building." I pointed off to my left. "Do you remember the police station, Troilus Green? When you sat across from me, asking about a stranger in our city?"

"It was him!" He pointed at Onyx, who'd managed to gather himself back up and advanced a few steps.

"Yeah, but that's not the point. Since that day, I've been meeting people. Humans like me." I glanced up at the crystals. Come on. Come on. "People who hated you dragons. Or maybe they didn't hate. Maybe they were just tired of living under your control. Either way, they joined me. Joined us." I shook my head. "I'm not alone, Viridia. I have an army.

And we're taking you down."

"I see no army." Viridia, now getting close to full dragon size, gestured at his own followers. "I see only my worshippers, celebrating my return. Where is this army of yours?"

I closed my eyes for a moment. I wasn't praying exactly. Or maybe I was. I had faith in my friends, but some divine intervention, if it existed, would sure help right now.

"They're everywhere." I opened my eyes and looked up. The gold crystal blinked again… and went out, taking its energy flow with it. Captain Tawn had succeeded. "They're in Auric!" I pointed at it with my sword.

Viridia snarled. A spray of poison erupted from his mouth at me. Boosted legs helped me race out of the way. I ran to the right so he couldn't watch Onyx and me at the same time.

The blue crystal blinked and went out. Way to go, Caedan and Sapphire! "And in Caesious!" I shouted.

Viridia took a step toward me, and the platform shook. Only three crystals continued to pour energy toward him, but he'd grown as large as he'd ever been before… and he kept on growing.

Onyx crept forward ever so slightly, like a cat stalking its prey.

The rust-red crystal faded next. "They're in Amaranth!" The other red crystal swiftly followed it. "And Incarnadine!" Thank you, Bice and Kelly and whoever else they'd involved. "I told you! We're everywhere! And your time… is over."

The final crystal, the black one linked to Atramentous, exploded, scattering shards in every direction. I hadn't expected that. I didn't even know who could have done it.

"You can't stop us all, Viridia. The Circle is home to a million humans. And no matter how powerful you are…" I shook my head. "You're just one."

"A million is nothing," he rumbled. "And I'll start by devouring you!" He lunged in my direction.

In that instant, Onyx leaped between the pillars and slammed into him. The black dragon threw the green dragon back against one of the pillars.

The final battle, the rematch of their previous fight, had begun.

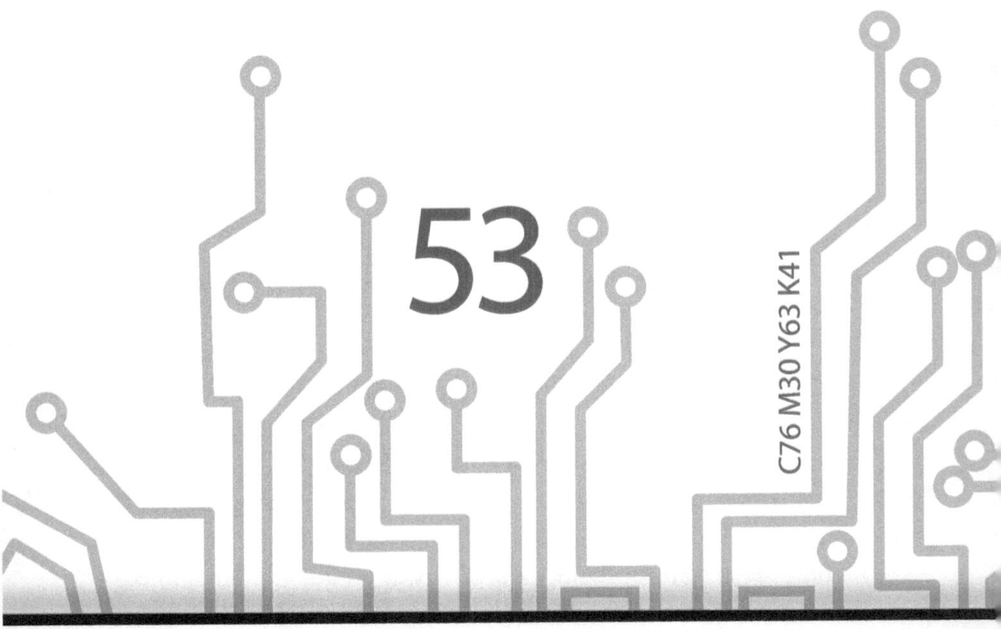

53

My letters had reached everyone. And minds much smarter than mine had figured out what to do. I'd told Bice, Kelly, and Caedan to get people to each of the dragon sources and try to discover a safe way to disconnect Viridia's devices. And if the devices started doing something, which they'd obviously done, to disconnect or destroy them, whatever it took. I'd told the same to Captain Tawn. And they'd done it. Viridia's plan had failed.

Except, of course, that he'd become a dragon again… and looked like he might be the most powerful dragon ever.

The platform shook from the impact of the two monsters. I struggled to keep my footing.

Onyx tore at Viridia with his cyb hand. Viridia responded with his own cyb claws. Dragon blood spattered everywhere. Viridia attempted to take to the air, but Onyx caught hold of his leg and yanked him back down. The green dragon spat poison at the black, who responded with his own acid. The smell of burning scales and cybernetics filled the air.

Though he'd been weakened by the source-draining, Onyx still had his implant, giving him greater strength in his upper arms. He'd already shown a dependence on them for this fight. But Viridia was now larger and more powerful. I didn't see how Onyx could beat him. I fingered my sword handle, thinking hard. How could I possibly help in this fight? Assuming Viridia won, he'd be hurt and weakened, but I couldn't handle him on my own. Ideally, they'd kill each other, but that didn't seem likely.

In watching the titanic struggle, I almost missed the two priestly guards climbing onto the platform to come after me. Fewmets. I didn't want to fight them!

"Get out of here!" I tried to wave them away. "This is the last place anyone should be!" As if to illustrate my point, a spurt of burning acid struck the platform between us, sizzling and burning a hole through it.

"Betrayer and heretic!" one of the guards shouted, raising his hooked sword. "You will face Viridia's justice today!"

"Oh, please." I boosted my legs and charged. I leaped the still-sizzling hole, deflected a sword-swipe with my own weapon, and threw my good shoulder into his chest. The impact knocked him back where he staggered, wavered, and fell over the edge. The short fall wouldn't hurt him, but it would take him out of the fight for a couple of minutes.

I spun around just in time to dodge a swing of the second guard's sword. I didn't have time for this!

Onyx slammed Viridia into the Incarnadine pillar almost right above us. It exploded with the impact, raining dust and concrete chunks. The guard and I ducked and ran in opposite directions. The platform tilted in the other direction; I fell and started sliding back. I slammed my cyb fingers into the platform's surface and stopped myself. Viridia seized the fallen red crystal and shattered it against Onyx's head. The black dragon roared and stumbled back. Shards of red remained embedded in his face.

Viridia kicked off the Amaranth tower and tackled Onyx. They landed on the other side of the platform. Instead of tilting, it snapped in half from the sudden impact. My section crashed back to the ground. I slid off onto my feet and crouched to shield myself from more debris.

I took a quick look around. I couldn't see as many priests around the edges, but the dust and smoke may have hidden some of them. About thirty feet away, I saw the two guards that came after me. One lay on the ground, unmoving. His companion knelt next to him. It didn't look like they would be bothering me for the moment. The platform lay in shambles, one pillar destroyed and one leaning. Pools of acid and poison dotted the debris-strewn landscape inside the Emerald Ascendancy.

My shoulder ached. I shifted the sword back to my cyb hand. What good would it do me? If another guard came after me, it would be helpful, but against the dragons? The only reason I'd hurt Incarnadine with a sword was because I crawled up inside his head through his eye socket…

Huh. Maybe they did have a vulnerability, but getting to it would be insane. I put my sword back in its sheath and jogged in the direction of the battling dragons. "Insane" defined my life, after all. Might as well try it.

Onyx swiped at Viridia again, but when the green dragon dodged, Onyx continued the momentum and whipped his tail around to knock Viridia off his feet. He roared, tearing scales from the tail as he fell. His wings hit the building wall, shattering more windows. The handful of remaining priests in the area raced for cover.

I picked up speed. Getting started would be the most difficult part. Except the last part: that would be the most difficult part. All right, everything would be the most difficult. As Viridia got back to his feet, I ran behind him. A thousand voices in my head screamed at me not to try it. I ignored them.

Viridia's tail swept in my direction. I boosted my legs and leaped as high as I could. I landed near the top of the tail and seized hold of the edge of a scale. The tail whipped back in the other direction. Boosts into my cyb hand kept me in place, but it was a near thing.

In Viridia's original form, he didn't have as much of a spinal ridge as Onyx. But this new form, grown from the draconic body of Troilus Green, sported far more spines and rough edges to his scales. Even in constant motion, it provided an excellent climbing surface.

I think I made it between his wings before he noticed me. "You're an annoying insect, Beryl," he growled. He caught Onyx's arm and yanked him off his feet. I fought back the urge to respond with some kind of wisecrack, especially since I probably would have to scream it to be heard.

Onyx used his wings to bludgeon Viridia. I stopped climbing and held in place while the dragons fought. As soon as they broke apart again, I resumed my upward scramble. Once I passed the shoulders, the climb grew more difficult. I had more spines to grasp, but Viridia's neck was in constant motion. More than once, my legs slipped free and I hung out over a long fall, held only by my cyb hand's grip.

From this height, I got a different perspective on the fight. Both Onyx and Viridia had suffered huge wounds with dozens of scales ripped from their bodies and scattered across the ground. Blood poured from gashes and openings all over their massive bodies. And yet they showed no signs of slowing down at all. Their endurance matched their destructive power.

"What do you think you're doing, Beryl?" Viridia took a moment to swat at me. I had to let go of my grip and drop further down his neck to dodge the claws. I caught hold again even as Onyx tore into Viridia's right wing with teeth and claws. Viridia screamed and grabbed at Onyx, flipping him onto his left side and sending him sliding into the side of the building again.

I took advantage of the distraction to scramble back up Viridia's neck. The spines grew huge as I approached the head, some of them as big as me. But my target was in sight. Clinging to the back of the dragon's head, I drew my sword. I gave my arm extra boosts to endure the pain in my shoulder. I hoped all this usage wouldn't make it harder to heal, but I needed the other hand to hold on. It would all be over soon, one way or another.

The left side of Viridia's head wouldn't work, protected as it was by the cybernetic plate. Troilus Green gained that after Rick stabbed him in one of our first encounters. I had to go for the right. I waited until his head stopped moving for a brief moment to make my move. I scrambled over the base of Viridia's right horn, caught hold of a spine with my cyb hand, and stabbed my sword down at his eye.

The sword snapped. My shoulder dislocated again. I lost my footing and swung loose. How? What was the eye made of?

"Fool." Viridia snapped his head upward. My fingers couldn't hold the sudden change and lost their grip. I flew up into the air.

And came down toward the dragon's open mouth.

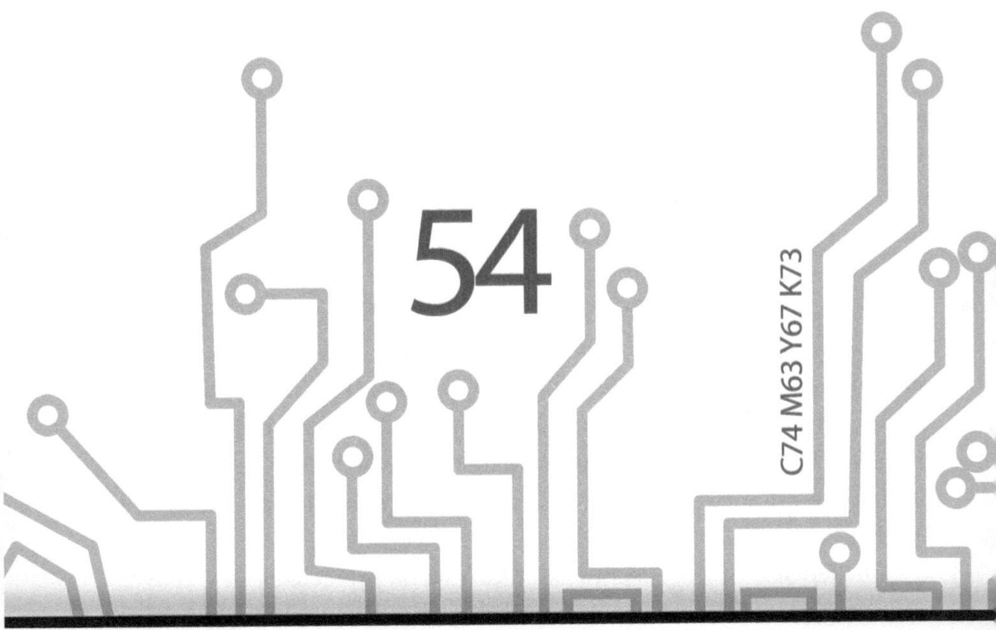

It might be my worst nightmare: falling into the open maw of an enormous creature. I had no control, no options, no way out.

Time seemed to slow, or maybe it only appeared that way because I boosted everything I could imagine, including my brain. I broke things down into two immediate problems: don't get cut in half by the dragon's teeth, and don't go down the throat. I could think of one thing that might solve both problems.

In my heightened speed, I reached forward with my cyb hand. I seized one of the teeth and yanked forward, accelerating my descent. I launched past the teeth as they came down, flipping over onto the tongue. My cyb hand still held the tooth.

The jaws slammed shut. My cyb hand tore and ripped apart as it was caught between the teeth. All light vanished.

In that moment, I realized my next peril: poison. Viridia's mouth was full of it. It coated his tongue. Saliva-poison dripped from the roof of his mouth. I had seconds before I succumbed to the sheer toxicity around me.

I blessed Loden and Cobalt's brilliance as I unleashed a burst of electricity through my ravaged hand. The tongue buckled. I did it again, focusing on sending it through the hand jammed down at the base of the dragon's teeth. Viridia's mouth burst open, ejecting me into the air.

I gasped for the clean air as I plunged toward the ground. No boosts could fully protect me from a fall this high, but I boosted everything anyway and rolled into a ball. The impact knocked me unconscious for a few moments. I couldn't... I couldn't push myself up. My right arm hung useless, and my left hand was a mangle of cybernetic pieces. Green slime coated most of my body. In addition to my shirt, I'd now lost both shoes. Strange how that bothered me so much.

I managed to turn my head before I vomited. I hadn't eaten much of anything in the last twenty-four hours, but it all came out. I hacked and gagged, trying to get it all out so I could breathe.

The dragons continued their battle, but I couldn't focus on their movements. Shadows fell over me, and then disappeared. The sun's warmth felt oppressive in their absence.

I rolled onto my back. Everything hurt. Everything. Some other things might be broken. I couldn't tell. I coughed more gunk out of my mouth. I tried to wipe my face off with my left forearm. A green haze filled the edges of my vision.

My eyes caught the motion of another pillar crashing to the ground not far away. The roars of the dragons filled my ears. The earth shook beneath me. I think I lost consciousness again for a few seconds.

I stared up at the green-tinged sky. A cloud of dust drifted into my view. Only then did I notice the silence. I leaned on my left elbow and used it to roll up onto my knees. I lifted my head and scanned the Ascendancy. All of the other humans had fled, though I caught glimpses of faces staring from the building windows. The two dragons sat facing one another across the utter devastation, catching their breath, I assumed.

Gaping wounds bled freely on both monsters, even more than I'd seen before. Massive patches of scales torn off exposed the softer skin beneath. Of their four wings, three were shredded. Only Viridia's left wing remained mostly intact, though it sported a couple of gaping holes as well.

Onyx looked worse. Shards of crystal remained embedded in his face. The wound under his right wing where the explosive had hit him looked worse than ever. Claw marks around it showed where Viridia targeted the injury, tearing even more flesh and muscle from the black dragon.

"For all your vaunted cybernetics, you can't win, you know." Viridia's voice remained strong, echoing across the desolate battlefield.

Onyx said nothing.

"I know how it all works," Viridia went on. "The brain implant. The boosts. My scientists studied the human's discoveries as well. We recently were able to observe a similar operation on a young human child."

He meant Lovat. I wavered, almost falling. I closed my eyes and took steadying breaths. I had plenty of boost energy available still, but I couldn't think of how to use it.

"I even had the help of one of your followers. A girl, I think. She didn't want to help, but it's amazing how pliable humans can be when you start removing parts of their bodies."

Oh. Dusk. Troilus Green told me he'd returned her to Onyx. He'd lied. Poor girl. She'd betrayed us, but even she didn't deserve that.

Viridia took a step toward Onyx. "Do you know what we finally concluded? The process doesn't work. Not in the way we wanted it to. You may have succeeded in giving yourself a temporary enhancement in your arms, but it would never be enough." He gestured. "By now, you've already discovered that you have no more boosts left. Your heart cannot generate any more."

Really? And yet it worked for me, and I had a dragon heart. No… not a dragon heart, exactly. Cerise said Loden grew my heart, using dragon genetic material. We'd called it a dragon heart, but it was more of a human-dragon hybrid. And it worked together with all of my cyb parts, implant and everything, to channel huge amounts of boost energy, not limited by my small body. Though Onyx had an immensely larger heart than mine, his enormous body consumed too much energy just to keep itself moving. At least, I think that's what Viridia meant. "You could boost a dragon!" Hunter had said.

I pulled one foot up and slowly stood, wavering and struggling for balance. I had a ridiculous idea, but I had to move. I sent boosts to my legs to steady them and start walking. I took a few steps and stumbled. I fell against a large chunk of one of the pillars. I pushed off it to keep myself upright. My left ankle didn't want to work. I looked down to see burnt flesh. I'd been hit by acid there at some point. I gritted my teeth, sent more boosts, and walked on.

"Beryl was right," Onyx rumbled. I looked up in surprise at his voice. It sounded weaker than I'd ever heard it. "The humans will rise up and defeat you."

Viridia laughed. "How? With Beryl dead and you out of the way, I can rebuild this place and absorb as much power as I'll ever need. I can rule them all for eternity!"

I stumbled again, taking three fast steps to the right before recovering my balance. Had to keep moving. Neither dragon had seen me yet.

"But they know now," Onyx said. "They've seen Beryl's example. They know the dragons... they know we are not gods. That we can be defeated."

"It doesn't matter. My priests will spread the word. It will take time, but I have all I need now. I will establish dominance over all six cities... and then who knows? With Chroma and the zealots gone, I can look beyond The Circle at last. I can be the true god of this entire world!"

"You underestimate them." Onyx's eye flickered in my direction for an instant. He'd seen me. "As I did for so long. But they're capable of so much more than we ever believed."

I staggered within a few yards of the black dragon. Not far now...

"Your dying thoughts are about humans?" Viridia threw back his head and roared with laughter. "How far you have fallen, son of Chroma. Humans are nothing. Humans can do nothing. We—I—am everything."

I made it beneath the shadow of Onyx's wing. I lifted my devastated left hand and looked at the exposed wires and circuits. I took a deep breath, plunged it into Onyx's open wound, closed my eyes, and channeled every bit of boost energy I could into my left hand.

And I boosted a dragon.

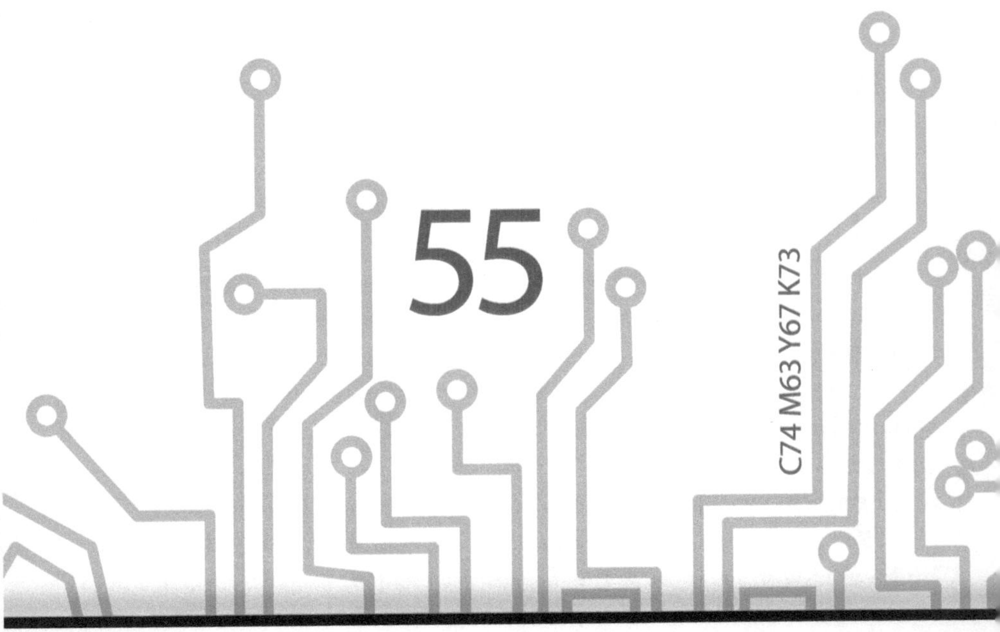

Onyx roared louder than I'd ever heard him. He lunged across the Ascendancy toward Viridia. The abrupt motion threw me off my feet, and I tumbled to the ground, completely spent. I pushed up on my left elbow just enough to watch what happened.

The black dragon slammed into the green, lifting him and throwing him back against the building. He seized Viridia's head with his left hand and smashed it against one of the Ascendancy's huge arches. Weakened, the arch broke. Without stability, it bent inwards and collapsed, throwing up another dust cloud and hiding the dragons from my view.

When I could see again, Onyx had his cyb hand's claws grasping the edge of one of Viridia's chest plates. The green dragon shoved him back, but he tore the metallic plate away, exposing Viridia's scaleless skin beneath.

"This… is not possible!" Viridia shouted. "You can't do this!"

Onyx barreled back into him, wrapping his arms around Viridia and pulling him back toward the center of the Ascendancy. "One human, Viridia!" he screamed. "One human caused your downfall!" He caught Viridia's head and turned it to look directly at me. "From the moment you two met, he's been destroying you!"

"No!" Viridia jerked his head free and brought his jaws down on Onyx's shoulder. He bit deep, tearing through scales, flesh, and muscle.

Onyx roared again and lifted Viridia off the ground. I could see the scars on Onyx's arms pulsing with energy. My energy. He hoisted Viridia higher and then brought him down on top of the blue pillar. The crystal of Caesious pierced through the exposed part of Viridia's chest and burst through his back. Onyx staggered back, leaving the green dragon impaled.

"Not… possible…" Viridia gasped. His body slid down the rest of the pillar. "I… am… a god."

The green dragon stopped moving. Viridia, Troilus Green, whatever else he'd been… was finally dead.

And when I looked at Onyx, he looked dead as well. The black dragon lay unmoving, eyes closed.

I pulled myself up onto my elbow and knees and crawled across the debris toward the black dragon. The eye facing me opened halfway and watched my approach, but he made no other move.

About ten yards from the dragon, my legs stopped responding. I collapsed onto my stomach. Summoning what little determination I could, I dragged myself forward with my one working arm. "Onyx!" I called.

"Viridia was right, Beryl," he rumbled, his mouth barely moving. "A dragon's heart couldn't handle that power."

I lifted myself up on my elbow. "Are you saying I killed you?"

He snorted. Acid and blood together flowed from his jaw, burning into the ground. "You killed all the dragons, Beryl. I'm just… the last to go."

I didn't know how to react, how to respond to that. What was I supposed to say? It's what I'd wanted. What I'd set out to do. And yet…

Onyx trembled. His entire body shook. And then he started to shrink. His mangled wings folded in against his body and fused with it as the tail shrank away. All of his black scales faded. His snout pulled in, the horns vanished, the claws shrank into fingers and toes.

And my friend Rick lay there in the midst of the devastation. In human form, his injuries looked far worse. But now they bled human blood. He looked to me and reached out a hand.

I tried to swallow, but too much dust clogged my mouth. I gagged again, feeling the poison still working its way down my throat. I concentrated as hard as I could, trying to access a boost, even a trickle. At last, a brief flow of warmth cascaded through both legs. Before it could fade again, I scrambled over to Rick. My right arm might still be dislocated, but I could at least put my hand in his. He gave it a weak squeeze.

"I'm… sorry, Beryl. For everything."

"I—"

"Don't talk," he interrupted. A coughing choke shook his body. He spit something green onto the ground. "Let me say this." He took a shuddering breath. "You… almost made me change. I almost decided to stay… human."

Oh.

"But… the power was too much. It called to me. I could be a god again."

"Rick…"

"I'm not a god, Beryl." His eyes rolled back, and his grip on my hand slackened. I thought he was dead, but he jerked suddenly, taking in a short breath. "I don't know what happens next. I'm… scared, Beryl. Tell Bice to find out. The truth."

"I will."

He took in a couple more shuddering gasps of air. His skin grew pale. A faint breeze swept across the battleground, stirring dust around us.

I closed my eyes. In some ways, I didn't want to say it, but I knew I should. "I forgive you, Onyx. Rick."

He gasped. His body shook one more time. His chest stopped moving, and his hand fell away from mine.

"Goodbye, my friend," I whispered. I rolled onto my back and looked up at the sky. In addition to my many injuries, Viridia's poison pulsed through my body. I thought of Bice and Kelly and Lovat and Don and Stacy and Loden and Rick with us, running through the streets of Viridia, fighting Troilus Green. And I thought of Caedan and Protogonus Blue and Peri and the others from Caesious. And most of all, I thought of Lainey. Would she ever know what had happened here? Would we meet together somewhere beyond this world?

I coughed. My eyes closed.

The fever woke me some time later. My body shook with shivering, even though the sun's heat radiated down at me. The poison was hard at work. When I survived the last time this happened, Loden thought my boosts had something to do with it, that I'd somehow boosted my own immune system. That wouldn't happen this time. I had no boost energy left. I'd given it all to Onyx. My eyes fell shut again.

Rapid footsteps. Too rapid. Made no sense.
"I found him!"
The voice. So young, but not as young as it had been.
Lovat.

56

"…hoping this is the end of this particular habit."

I knew the voice. Just hearing it brought a lump to my throat. I pushed it down and croaked out, "Bice?"

"Hey, hey. You're awake. Don't try to speak any more until I get you some water."

I opened my eyes and saw a white ceiling. It didn't look familiar. Then Bice's face appeared. He slid a hand under my head and helped me lift up enough to swallow some water. The coolness of the liquid emphasized the warmth of the rest of my body, followed by the pains. My shoulder ached, but appeared to be back where it belonged. I shifted it a little. Painful, but working. My left ankle was heavily wrapped in bandages. And everything else just….hurt in general. What skin I could see outside the bedsheets was black and blue everywhere. Nausea overcame me for a moment before Bice let my head back down. My stomach rumbled.

"Where?" I managed to ask. My voice sounded strange to my ears.

"Hospital in Viridia." Bice waved at the rest of the room. "The same hospital, believe it or not, where you recuperated the first time we met."

"The… priests. They're letting us… be here?" My throat hurt with each rasping word. A relic of the poison, I suppose.

Bice chuckled and pulled a chair back up next to my bed before sitting. "A lot has happened in the last few days."

"Days?"

"It's been four—no, five—days since the death of the dragons. For a long time, we didn't think you were going to make it, either. Viridia's poison had a deep hold on you."

"Lainey?"

"Ah. I'm sorry. There's nothing new to report there. She's—"

The door to the room flew open and Lovat darted in. "Beryl! You're awake!"

I tried to smile. "Hey man."

He rushed over beside my bed. "Did Bice tell you I ran all the way from Amaranth to Incarnadine? And I was fast too!"

"Slow down!" Bice laughed. "I haven't told him much of anything yet. He just woke up."

"I want to hear it all," I whispered.

"We can do that." Bice sat back and started telling. Lovat interrupted multiple times with his point of view.

Upon receiving my letter, they'd rushed into action. I had a hard time grasping how fast they'd all moved: Bice, Kelly, and Jaden to Incarnadine; Don, Lovat, and Cobalt to Amaranth; and Turq, Saxe and Royal to Caesious, with plans to send others on to Atramentous if possible.

Three different science teams discovered how to deactivate Viridia's devices. Auric's people had been at work the longest, followed by the ones in Caesious. My letters suggested shutting them down if they started doing anything, which, of course, they had. Both of those cities turned them off without trouble. Cobalt assisted Amaranth's scientists in figuring out a solution at the last minute, prompting Lovat's city-length dash to Incarnadine to let them know how to do it.

"Atramentous?" I wondered. I don't think any of us had expected that one.

"It's hard to say," Bice said. "Caedan had contacted someone there, a woman named Raven, I believe. We don't know much about her... or what happened. It didn't go as well. The source detonated."

Oh.

"But Atramentous's source was actually far enough from the city borders that no one was killed," he hastened to add, "except, we assume, those who were trying to stop it."

Lovat bounced on his feet, apparently anxious for Bice to finish. "And now the dragons are all dead! Did you kill them both, Beryl?"

"The stories have spread from Viridians who watched the battle," Bice said. "But of course we'd like to hear it from you."

"They killed each other," I whispered. "I'll… tell more later. How… how are we here?" I tried to gesture at the room, but it hurt too much.

"Everything's changing," Bice answered. "Viridia's body is still impaled on that tower in the Ascendancy. Everyone knows it. The draconics are in hiding. Most of the priests have, uh, quit their jobs. And everyone's trying to figure out what to do. Officials are talking about forming a new government."

I almost whimpered. So good. Exactly what I'd always wanted.

"The same thing is happening in the other cities. No one's seen a glimpse of the purple robes. All the oppressors are gone. The draconics in Auric are the only ones working with humans. All the others are hiding or being hunted down." Bice's smile had never been bigger. "The reign of the dragons is over, Beryl. You did it."

"We did it."

Sleep pulled me down. Lovat chattered away some more, but I couldn't concentrate on his words. My consciousness slipped away, and I let myself fall after it.

Three days later, I got back to my feet, and Bice agreed I could leave the hospital. With the help of some sympathetic nurses, Bice and Lovat smuggled me to the train station. Apparently, my face was so well known now that I might cause a riot just by being seen. I wasn't sure if they meant a riot of people cheering for me, or a riot of people wanting to kill me… or both.

I insisted on going to Caesious. Bice suggested going to our base and waiting until some of the turmoil died down, but I refused. I had to see Lainey.

We timed our arrival for after dark. Once there, they snuck me into this hospital in the same way we'd snuck out of the other one. I expected Sapphire and Caedan to meet us, but Bice took me directly to Lainey's room without encountering anyone I knew.

Some of Lainey's bandages had been removed and some of the bruising had cleared up, but otherwise, she looked the same as when I'd left her. Lovat pushed a chair up for me. I thanked him and took my seat beside her.

"Hey, Lainey." My voice still sounded strange to me, with a low rasp and much quieter than I kept thinking I should be. "I, um…" I paused and swallowed. "We won. The dragons are gone. The zealots are gone. I'm… I'm done. I have nothing left. To do, that is. So, as long as you don't mind…" I took a deep breath. Talking took such an effort. "I'll stay here with you. Until you wake up."

I didn't notice when Bice and Lovat left. I talked for a while, telling Lainey little details about everything and musing on what we might do after she recovered. I told her about the changes happening in The Circle. "It's everything I wanted, Lainey. But if you're not here… I can't… I can't be truly happy about it." I waited a long minute before whispering, "Please wake up. I love you."

I'd like to say my presence and my words snapped her out of the coma in that very moment. Wouldn't that be a great ending to the story? But it didn't happen.

Bice came for me some time later, maybe an hour. I don't know. "There are some people who want to see you," he explained. "I think you can spare them a few minutes."

I agreed and got to my feet. My legs wobbled, and I caught hold of the chair to keep from falling.

"Do you need help?" Bice asked.

"I can make it." I added a boost to both legs and followed him out. He took me down an elevator to another floor, where we made our way along a way-too-long hallway to some kind of dining room. Bice opened the door and gestured for me to go first.

I limped inside and saw… everyone.

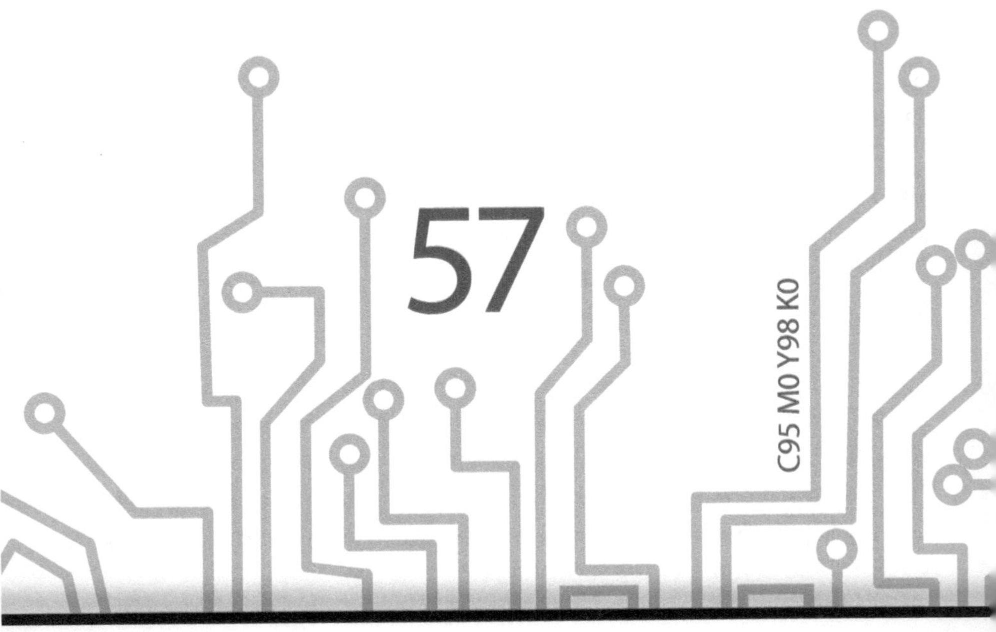

57

Caedan was the first one to reach me. Despite my injuries and Bice's cry of alarm, he grabbed me and lifted me off my feet in a ferocious hug. It hurt, but I found I didn't care.

Kelly came next. Her embrace was gentler, and she gave me a quick kiss on the cheek. "It's finally over," she whispered.

I glanced around the assembled group. "Chance?" I asked.

"He stayed behind. It… wouldn't be safe for him in the cities."

Right. We would have to deal with that somehow.

They crowded around me then. All of them. Stacy, Jaden, Sapphire, Royal, Saxe, Cobalt, Turq, Hunter, Fern, Don: everyone who'd been living with us in the wilderness. And there were others. I saw Marcus and Cerise with a tiny baby! Had it really been that long? Stacy introduced me to some of her other friends from around The Circle, people who'd been part of her network, doing their part in the fight against the dragon. Cobalt showed me off to some scientists from Amaranth. Some looked at me in awe. Some tried to hide it, but I could tell they were confused, expecting someone more impressive.

Fern and some others were setting up a table with food, including an enormous cake for some reason. People broke off into various groups, chatting and laughing. Fatigued, I took a seat and motioned Bice to come closer.

"Where's Carl?" I asked.

Bice shook his head. "He's here somewhere. He made one short trip back through the tunnel, but came right back to be near his daughter. I invited him to this."

"But he didn't want to come." He probably still blamed himself for her condition. I hoped he would be all right.

I looked around at the celebration. At all these people I cared about so much. And I thought of those who weren't with us now, like Loden and Peri.

"What happens now, Bice?"

"Now?" He chuckled. "It's a new world, Beryl. Everything's changing. Fast. Everyone here will be needed in helping people transition to... whatever comes next." He patted my good shoulder. "But you get to rest and do whatever you want. You've earned that."

"What about you?"

He took a deep breath. "The tunnel is waiting for me. I've said all along what I would do if we won."

"You're leaving then."

Bice looked down at me. "I have to. Somewhere out there, someone knows the truth. I spent too much of my life serving false gods. I'll spend the rest of it, if I have to, searching for the real thing."

I nodded. "Onyx said you should do that."

"You didn't tell me that part."

Before I could answer, Lovat pushed in with a tray full of drinks. "Take one! Both of you!"

Over near the cake, I saw Caedan jump up on one of the tables. "Can I have everyone's attention?" he called, holding his drink high.

Everyone quieted and turned to face him. I got to my feet to join them.

"You all know why we're here," Caedan said. "I'm guessing this is only one of dozens—maybe hundreds!—of celebrations around The Circle over the past few days. The dragons are dead!"

Everyone cheered and lifted their drinks. "The dragons are dead! The dragons are dead!"

Caedan pointed at me. "And none of it would have happened without this guy! He, he, uh..." Was Caedan choking up? Caedan?

Stacy climbed on to a chair next to the table and put her hand out toward him. "You're not the one for giving speeches, love!" He laughed, took her hand, and pulled her up onto the table. She gave him a kiss to hoots and cheers from the others. I laughed with them all. It felt so good.

Stacy pointed her drink at me. "A wise man I once knew told me something one day. He told me the dragons were going to be defeated. 'We're going to meet some people,' he said."

I almost choked on my drink. She did an amazing impersonation of Loden's voice.

"'There's one in particular you need to pay attention to. He's going to change everything.'" Stacy grinned. "And you have, Beryl. You've changed everything. You fought and you fought and you bled and almost died, over and over."

"Everyone here was part of it too!" I protested as loud as I could.

"Yes, we were," Stacy agreed. "But not like you. You did it all, Beryl. And every man, woman, and child in The Circle owes you a debt they can never repay."

"Let's hear it for Beryl the dragonslayer!" Caedan shouted.

The entire room erupted in cheers. I saw several drinks fly into the air. Caedan kissed Stacy again. Lovat jumped onto another table and did a somersault. Any second now, the hospital staff would be charging in to tell us to keep it down.

I fell back in my chair, not only because I was touched by their outpouring, but because my legs chose that moment to quit working.

They never worked again.

Epilogue

"You actually finished?" Chance asks.

I look at what I just wrote and take a breath. "For now. Got all the way to the end. Sort of." I glance through my office door to the next room. "Is she…?"

"She's outside somewhere. Gardening, I think. Are you ready to go out?"

I nod. I could write more, and maybe I will sometime. But that's it for the high adventures. The rest isn't so exciting. All the politics and stuff. Where people went next. What they did. Caedan became mayor of Caesious. I still laugh at that. He blames his wife, Stacy. Says it was all her idea.

Kelly took a major role in transforming Viridia. With her mom's help, she led efforts to tear up a lot of the unnecessary concrete and beautify the one ugly city. She'd hated to leave Chance, but he encouraged her to do what she loved. And she visits us almost every week. She's the one who insisted I needed to write my story down. Stacy was threatening to make it into a play, or one of those new movie things.

Everyone else mostly returned to the city they'd come from, except Don and Lovat. They couldn't seem to stay in one place. Last I heard, they'd headed out into the wider world to go exploring. Before that, they did have a bit of a crisis when a Viridian cyberneticist tried to take control of Lovat. Like I'd worried, the implant did have one or two little additions.

Don sought out Cobalt, who'd gone back to his own tech studies in Caesious. Together, they rescued Lovat and defeated the cyberneticist. I missed the whole thing. Turns out people can have adventures without me.

Chance moves behind me and takes the wheelchair handles. He pushes me out into the living room and then to the front door. As we pass through, I pat the doorframe. I should write about the day they all showed up to build this cabin. I never expected that.

We roll out into the open air of the hilltop. It's a beautiful day, like so many others here. This was exactly where I wanted to be, exactly where I wanted to spend the rest of my life.

And I'm with exactly who I want to spend it with. She comes around the corner of the cabin now and smiles to see us. Her hands are dirty from planting some flowers or something around the backside. I'll go see them later. But for now, seeing her is all I need.

"Lainey," I call, her name still the greatest word I can utter. One of Glacier's cubs bounces around at her feet. She named this one Gerald, I think.

The three months it took for her to wake up from the coma were the longest days of my life. And the recovery process hadn't been easy either. But she was here. Now. And nothing else matters.

"Hello, husband." She leans in and kisses me. "Done with the writing?"

"For now." I take her hand.

"I see him," Chance says. "He's almost here."

I turn to look at the path. My friends built it with the cabin. It spirals down the hill, past the entrance to our old headquarters, all the way to the base, where a dirt road leads off toward the nearest train station. The road doesn't get used much. And the figure walking up the path toward us probably hiked instead of driving.

Bice's face split into a huge grin when he saw my family waiting for him. I knew in that moment he'd found the answers he'd been looking for. And that he'd tell us all about it tonight while we celebrated his visit.

Together. And free.

The End

For more information on the Dragontek Lore series,
and other upcoming books,
visit timfrankovich.com

Joining the mailing list is the best way to stay informed,
plus you get free stories!
(including Rick's story before he arrived in Viridia!)

If you enjoyed this book, please post a review
on Amazon, B&N, Goodreads, etc.
There's no better way to spread the word.

<h1 style="text-align:center">Author's Notes</h1>

Well, here we are. The journey took longer than I anticipated, but only here at the end. In case you weren't following along in the newsletter or blog, this final book got a serious delay. My cover artist who handled all six previous books suddenly became unavailable. I'm still not entirely sure what happened. But the fantastic Tremani Sutcliffe stepped in and provided the excellent illustration on the front cover! I cannot possibly thank her enough. Check out more of her amazing artwork at decisivearts.com.

As I've said many times, I started this series with the idea of writing something I wanted to read when I was 13 years old, riding my bike to the library. I intended it to be over-the-top, fast-paced, and full of outrageous action. But at the same time, some serious concepts and themes slowly worked their way into the stories. In the end, I'm quite proud of Beryl's story. He grew a lot over the course of these seven books.

Speaking of the end… I've had that final scene in my head since early in the *Viridia* writing process. It was incredibly satisfying to finally write it out. I hope it was just as satisfying for you.

Thanks to my prime beta readers who've been there from the beginning, Allen Perkins and Stephen Tallman. Thanks also to my wonderful wife Denise and daughter Lily who were the first to read *Chroma* and let me know what they thought about it.

So what's next? This is the end of my existing young adult content, at least for now. I have a couple of other series ideas in vague sketch form. Someday, I'll get to them. In the meantime, I'm continuing on with epic fantasy and an upcoming genre blend. If you thought cybernetics and dragons was crazy, wait until you see… Oh, wait. That would be telling.

If you want to keep track of my progress on all my writing, you can connect on timfrankovich.com, my Facebook author page, X-Twitter, etc. But the best way, which keeps you informed and gives you exclusive previews, is to join the mailing list. Sign up on the website. (You'll get free stories too!)

Tim Frankovich has been exploring fantastic worlds since third grade, when he cut up a grocery sack and drew a Godzilla-meets-superheroes story. Since then, he's gotten a little bit better at the writing part (not so much with the drawing).

His goal as a writer is to transport readers to another world, make them care deeply about characters in dire situations, and guide them deeply into life itself.

At the moment, he is probably suitably conscious somewhere in Texas with his beloved wife, awesome four kids, and a fool of a pup named Pippin.